Other books by

Daniel J. Darrouzet

Stories From the Tin Box
Volume I

featuring

STORIES FROM THE TIN BOX

UNTOLD ADVENTURES OF

SHERLOCK HOLMES™

VOLUME II

by

Daniel James Darrouzet

To Andrew
all the best
God bless
Boompa

SHERLOCK HOLMES, and are trademarks of the Conan Doyle Estate Ltd.® Sherlock Holmes is protected by copyright and trademark law and is used by permission of Conan Doyle Estate Ltd.®

Cover by: Diana Craft/Melody Jahn

Volume II - Second Edition, January 2020

To my Grandchildren

Special thanks to my wife

Ingrid Julia
for her encouragement, reviews
and her expertise in the recovery of lost computer files

Joe Guida
For his advice and counsel,

Lorraine Whatley and Gary Price
of Salisbury Cathedral
for their information and time

and

Mary Frances Leahy Darrouzet
for her reviews, thoughts and prayers

<u>CONTENTS</u>

From the pen of
Dr. John H. Watson

I, *Dr. John H. Watson, bequeath this and other stories, to which I have delayed writing about or have held from publication, to my great-grandson, I hope, yet to be sired. Should by God's good grace I have such issue, I hope these stories will be published and that my notes will be sufficient to allow my thoughts on these adventures to be transcribed into more full stories. Some have been sworn to secrecy in my lifetime. But there are others that I have yet to complete the entire adventure so that my readers shall be satisfied. With this aspiration on my part, I recall and set to writing the events of some of the as yet untold adventures on which I assisted Mr. Sherlock Holmes.*

My last name is not Watson, but Dr. John H. Watson, was my great-grandfather. And neither am I his great-grandson, but his great-grand-daughter.

When my mother passed, I was bequeathed a rather large tin box. Within it, I was told, were stories and notes about my great-grandfather and his famous friend that had never been made public. I have done my utmost to fill in gaps to complete the stories based on my great-grandfather's notes. I apologize, but the stories are in no particular order.

I am proud of my great-grandfather and his accomplishments. To have lived with the famous detective, about whose cases he recorded for all of us to enjoy, must have been extraordinary. I still wonder at the solutions by such a talented man. I believe from what I've learned about my great-grandfather from my family and his writings, he will be pleased at this additional publication.

As I stated emphatically in Volume I, I accept my great-grandfather's and my family's belief, that there has never been nor will there ever be another one of the likes of Mr. Sherlock Holmes.

THE ADVENTURE OF THE NOTTINGHAMSHIRE SALE

During that late autumn storm, when the winds rose strongly from the southwest and the whole sky was weeping, there came a knock upon our door. In our doorway, Mrs. Hudson was standing next to a well-dressed lady of, I judged, roughly two score in age.

"Mrs. Hudson, good evening," greeted I.

"I tried to call up to you, Doctor. I guess with that wind a howling as it is, you did not hear me. This lady here is in need of help. I informed her that usually an appointment is necessary, but with this storm raging, I thought it might be best to not turn her away and force her to find her way back through it. A mighty one is upon us!" said Mrs. Hudson.

"That is quite hospitable of you, Mrs. Hudson. Please, Madam, come in and rest yourself. Thank you, Mrs. Hudson, I shall see to her."

"Goodnight, Doctor. Please make sure to put that bucket out again if that dripping reappears. I paid Mr. Smart good money to fix that leak in the roof. I cannot afford further damage if he did not do it correctly," she cautioned me.

"I am prepared, Mrs. Hudson. I will let you know immediately if the leak reappears. Goodnight, mum."

"Yes, well, goodnight again," she mumbled as she began her slow descent down the stairs.

I looked at our guest's hand as I shook it and observed her wedding ring.

"Well, Madam. What can I do for you?"

"You are Dr. Holmes? No one told me you were a doctor."

"No, no, I mean, yes, Madam. I am a physician. My name is Dr. John Watson."

"I came to speak with a Mr. Holmes. Is he a doctor also?"

"No, Madam, he is not, in the legal sense of the word.

But as to his abilities, he is as intelligent and clever as any doctor you would ever wish to consult."

"Is he here?"

"No, Madam, he is not."

"I have travelled all the way from Truro, in Cornwall, to speak with him."

"Madam, I am sorry to disappoint you. No doubt your journey has been an exhausting one?"

"Yes, quite so. It is so disappointing. I was told this Mr. Holmes could help me. Now, I know not what I shall do."

"I can offer you my services for the present. I have assisted Mr. Holmes on many of his cases. I would be honoured to help you."

"Oh, Doctor, I do not know. I am quite confused about it all." Her voice had a tone of helplessness to it.

"Well then, perhaps you should sit down and, here, I can offer you a sherry, if that is not too presumptuous of me?"

"No thank you, Doctor. We Methodists do not drink."

"My apologies, of course not. Let me then get my notebook and if you will let me know what is troubling you, we can begin together to perhaps solve your problem. Will that suit you, Madam?"

"Perhaps, Doctor. I am quite tired. Do you expect Mr. Holmes soon?"

"I am afraid I do not know my friend's plans. You see, he often keeps to himself. In fact, I have not seen him myself for several days. Should you not wish to start now, I advise you, Madam, to seek some shelter here in London for the night. I can recommend the Hotel Great Central. It is a fine new establishment not far from here. All the cabbies will know the way. It's just south on Baker Street, turn right and you will find it a few blocks down on Marylebone Road. I believe you will find it most accommodating to all your needs. If Mr. Holmes returns tomorrow or the day after, I can then send a note and alert you to his presence. Can you wait for him?"

"Another day? Oh! I suppose I have no choice. I will follow your advice, Dr. Watson. I shall leave you now and I am sorry to have interrupted your evening, sir."

"Not at all, Madam, not at all."

And, with that, she left.

That was my introduction to her. In my haste to accommodate her, I failed to get even her name. After I could no longer hear her footsteps on the stairs, I realized that Holmes would be most unimpressed at my failure to ask this most fundamental of all questions. No doubt, he would blame it on my failings when it came to being in the presence of handsome women, a fault for which he had criticized me often enough. But this woman was not a '*basket of oranges*' as they say. She was average in appearance. I do not know why I was not able to get such a simple thing as her name, but I did not. I retired that evening chastising myself for failing in this basic duty I should have provided to my friend in his absence. I slept fitfully.

When I awoke, from what little sleep I was able to acquire, I found Holmes present but in a somewhat beleaguered state. I suspected he had gone to Chinatown. He had the demeanour of one who had been under a cloud of that coca plant from South America. Or perhaps it was that hideous scourge of Asian poison, opium, which I also knew he indulged in on occasion. I had more than once cautioned him as to the negative effects of these drugs on the human body, but he had rejected my concerns and said he was merely 'experimenting'.

While I had served in Her Majesty's service in Afghanistan, I had seen more than a few fellows fall into the powerful clutches of either opium's, or its more refined brother's, heroin, deadly grasp. Some became addicted after receiving injections of morphine to help with the pain of their wounds. Once dependent on morphine to deal with their pain, they then could not do without its more basic form. Others simply experimented and had fallen under its influence while trying to escape from the tortuous nightmares of the battlefield.

Watching a friend die or be maimed for life drove some poor souls to seek the false hope that the drug would somehow relieve them of their misery and allow them to escape from their memories of the horrors of war. It was a sad thing to see how a man wasted away once he was unable to free himself from its grasp.

I was certain the same fate would befall my friend. In my professional opinion, it was only a matter of time until he would no longer be the incredible sleuth I had come to know and admire. This one filthy habit of his, dabbling in such dangerous drugs, I could not bring myself to reconcile. I had, though, given up pleading with him.

The oddity of it was, that each time I was convinced one of them almost had him in its death grip, he somehow, always managed to surprise me, and was able to shake it from controlling him completely. This was in stark contrast to those lost souls, even here in London, who risked the insidious seductions of these drugs, all while attempting to escape the torturous pressures of life in such a large modern city, but could not escape its grip that could only end in a piteous death.

"Watson, I know you are upset with me. I can see it in your face," stated he.

"Holmes, you know my thinking on the subject. I respect you enough to not deliver a lengthy lecture to you again. It will kill you some day. There really is no more to say."

"You are a good friend, Watson. I thank you for your concern. I hope our new case will be a worthy one and distract me from it. My dabbling with these natural chemicals is not as satisfying to me as I think you believe they are."

"How did you know we had a visitor last night?"

"Your ash tray is empty and I see that two sherry glasses were set out but not used. I concluded it was a woman who does not drink. But then again, I must confess, Mrs. Hudson mentioned her to me upon my arrival this morning before you arose. A Mrs. Whitehead, correct?"

"Yes, ah hum, she seemed quite concerned and had travelled all the way from Cornwall to see you."

"And shall we see her again today?"

"If you believe you are fit to see her, I can send for her now."

"Please, Doctor. That would be most kind of you. I am in need of a challenge. I shall retire to my room for the present. Please awake me when she arrives."

With that, he left to sleep off the remainder of his induced stupor and its resulting slothfulness. I found it difficult to watch him when he was in such a state. My hope was that he would be sober enough to speak to her, as he needed to be, when she did come. I sat down and wrote a brief note to Mrs. Whitehead and had it sent over to the Hotel Great Central. I recommended she call at ten o'clock. I decided to keep to myself my failure to get her name. No doubt Holmes had gotten her name from Mrs. Hudson. I was not up to having Holmes chastise me for my failure and simply accepted the stroke of luck that had befallen me.

It was perhaps thirty minutes later that I received a short reply stating she would be here at the suggested hour.

On time as I expected, Mrs. Whitehead appeared more relaxed and had an air of confidence lacking from our previous encounter. Her dress was certainly a recent purchase I concluded from the brightness of the fabric, but the style seemed not quite up to date with the latest in fashion that I had seen on the ladies in London. Having gathered her wits after the long journey from the day before and during such a drenching storm, I could now see she was a determined client and not as helpless as I had concluded the night before.

"Good morning, Dr. Watson. I wish to speak to Mr. Holmes as soon as I can. I must catch the noon train back to Truro."

"Yes, Madam. Please come in and I will fetch Mr. Holmes."

I assisted her with her outer coat and bonnet. She took a seat on our couch. She sat just on the edge.

"Ah, Mrs. Whitehead, how are we this morning," said Holmes, as he entered with his hands in the pockets of his dressing-gown.

I could see by her expression that Holmes' attire was not what she was expecting.

"Sir," said she, as she looked away from him, "perhaps if I came back, you would have time to dress more properly."

"But Mrs. Whitehead, what has the style of my dressing have to do with your problem?"

"I am not used to talking to men I have just met while they remain in their night clothes. It makes me feel quite uncomfortable, sir."

"I see. Well, if you do not approve of my attire, I suggest your little problem could perhaps be solved by going to see a certain Inspector Lestrade at Scotland Yard. I am sure he is dressed properly and will be happy to solve whatever quaint problem you have. Good day, Madam," said he. He turned and was heading back to his room.

"Holmes, just a moment."

"What is it, Watson?"

"Madam, please allow me a moment in private with Mr. Holmes, yes?"

She, already in shock at Holmes' rude remarks, merely nodded her head hesitantly in agreement, still avoiding eye contact with Holmes.

I grabbed Holmes' elbow and ushered him into his room. I had to salvage this case. My fear was that should this woman leave, he might be drawn back to Chinatown.

"Holmes that was no way to speak to her. She is a lady and I dare say she was correct in her assessment of your clothing. Please change into something more acceptable and come back out."

"Watson, I am not impressed with her."

"You've hardly spoken to her. We don't even know what her problem is yet. It could be one you have never experienced before. How could you pass up an unknown puzzle?"

"Hmm, perhaps you are right. It might be an intriguing case, but also it may not."

"You will not know unless you listen to her, correct?"

"I will follow your prescription, Doctor. Please apologise on my behalf and let her know I will be available in a few more minutes. Thank you, Doctor."

Having the battle half won, I now had to convince our new client to stay. When I returned, she had already retrieved her outercoat and bonnet. She had the former on and was starting to put on the latter, as I spoke.

"Mrs. Whitehead, I apologise. Mr. Holmes sends his apologies. He is changing to more suitable attire, as we speak. He has had a rather difficult last few days and sometimes his manners and dress elude him. I believe those that suggested you contact him likely warned you of his eccentricities. Am I correct?"

"Well, yes, Doctor. They did."

"Ah, well you see, they have not been disingenuous then. I can tell you, while his habits may from time to time seem a bit queer, he is a brilliant detective. I have never known him to fail in solving his clients' problems. If you will but give him a chance to help you, I am sure it will all turn out as it should."

"All right, Doctor. Your words are more soothing than his and I will attempt to converse with him one more time."

She placed her bonnet again on the rack. Then I assisted her in removing her outercoat and hung it up for her.

It was a few minutes more when Holmes finally appeared. He was dressed in his best suit of clothes and had combed his hair this time.

He had not had time to shave, so his several days of beard was still visible even from where I sat. I admired his effort with regards to his clothing and hair. I simply decided to let the interaction occur as it perhaps was meant to proceed. I grabbed my notebook and began taking notes as they discussed the case.

"It is Mrs. Whitehead, correct?"

She answered with a nod as Sherlock shook her hand in the most gentlemanly fashion that I had seen from him in quite some time.

"Please, accept my apology for my earlier rudeness. How is it that I may assist you?"

"Thank you, Mr. Holmes. I have never spoken to a private detective before."

"Consulting detective," he corrected.

"Yes, all right, *consulting* detective, if you wish."

"You see, we live in Truro, in Cornwall. We do not have much need for such men as yourself. Nothing much happens in our village that is not easily understood or explained," said she and then continued.

"But I cannot speak to anyone in Truro about it."

"And why is that, Madam?"

"It involves my suspicions about my husband and…"

"I understand, Madam. You are concerned about his relationship with another woman, I take it?"

"Yes, how did you know?"

"Madam, when a married woman comes all the way

from western England and asks for help involving her husband and does so discreetly by seeking the help of a detective, be they private or consulting, there is likely only one cause. You are not the first to request I investigate such matters."

She blushed with embarrassment at Holmes' statement. Then the lack confidence of the night before returned as tears began to well up in her eyes. She produced a small lace edged handkerchief and dabbed away her tears.

"Mr. Holmes, what shall I do?"

"Mrs. Whitehead, the question is what shall I do? If I investigate this matter, in all likelihood you will find out things perhaps you had wished you had not learned, as is often the case. But my experience though, is that knowing is better than imagining. What are the facts that have led you to believe of your husband is guilty of some sort of indiscretion?"

"That's just it, Mr. Holmes. I have none."

"That will not do, Madam. Please tell me why you have sought my counsel?"

"It is my suspicion. My husband is a successful businessman, well respected in Truro and all of Cornwall for that matter. His advice is sought, accepted and acted upon by most people in Cornwall. He is a confident man but not boastful."

"How is this then suspicious, Madam?"

"He has become almost overnight, a man in hiding. He will not leave his study. He simply answers now 'I don't know', whenever I ask him even the simplest question. This is so unlike him."

"You say this occurred 'overnight'? Is that a fact or just an expression to embellish your problem?"

"Well, it is an expression, my expression. But it has occurred in perhaps just the last two weeks."

"Have you queried him with regards to his sudden change in behaviour? What does he say?"

"He repeats, 'I don't know what to do' and then says to 'leave him alone' in a harsh tone."

"Hmm. Perhaps a meeting with Mr. Whitehead is in order. How does that sound to you, Mrs. Whitehead?"

"No. You mustn't let him know I have consulted you, but I do not know what I shall do."

"I believe it would be best that I should observe your husband. Perhaps I shall call on him with regards to a business matter. I could arrive seeking his counsel. He would not have to know of my real reason, would that do?"

"Yes, Mr. Holmes, I suppose that would allow you to see for yourself."

"Then I will pursue this path. What type of business does your husband conduct, Mrs. Whitehead?"

"He mines granite, sir."

"Well, then I shall come to speak to him about that igneous rock. Give me a few days, and I shall present myself to him. After that I shall let you know what I think. Good day to you, Madam."

And with that, he had arisen, marched back to his room and abruptly closed his door.

"Dr. Watson?"

"Do not worry yourself, Madam. His behaviour is odd at times, but I assure you, you may count on Mr. Holmes to find out what is troubling your husband. I recommend you return to your home in Truro and Mr. Holmes will contact you soon."

"All right, Doctor. I will do as you say. We did not discuss payment. How am I to know what this will cost me? What are Mr. Holmes' fees?"

"I would not concern myself with that at this time, Madam. I have seen him accept fine jewels from clients of royal blood, only several pounds from some and then nothing from others who have nothing to offer. All I can say is that you will be treated fairly in that regard should you choose to continue consulting him."

"Very unusual, sir, I must say. I shall return as he suggests. Thank you very much, Doctor. Good day to you."

"And to you, Madam. Please have a safe journey home."

She left and I was now again concerned about my friend. While I tried to explain away his rudeness in front of Mrs. Whitehead, I was sure we had witnessed a sublime performance as he overcame the lingering effects from the drugs, that were no doubt, still pulsing through his body. I concluded he had exhausted himself and was not able to converse further, so I left him alone. I was rewarded later that evening when he arose and began to engage in conversation that was more normal than that which I had heard earlier that morning.

"Watson, did I pass?"

"Holmes?"

"I said, did I pass?"

"Pass what, dear friend?"

"The test with Mrs. Whitehead."

"Oh, Holmes, you were magnificent! I was sure that you would object to my reprimand. But you exceeded my expectations. I am quite sure you were still under some poison's influence, but you held together without question. You amaze me!"

"I told you that it does not have the draw on me that you believe it does. A case is always the preferred stimulant to any of those drugs. When my mind has something to work on there is no better distraction."

"When shall you go to Truro, then?"

"I need to prepare. A man does not seek counsel and receive it when the counsellor does not believe the one seeking such advice. I need to learn some things about *granite* before proceeding. I shall visit the Geological Museum today and make some inquiries. Hopefully I will present myself knowledgeable enough to not raise his suspicion of my true reasons for talking to him."

"Please let me know if I can assist you."

"You can be certain, Doctor, I will."

That ended the beginning of our adventure and I have to admit, my dear readers, that my involvement in it had to become a lower priority since the number of patients at my surgery had increased at about this same time. Looking back, it was a fever of some unknown origin that had passed through London with no known lasting serious effects, but the intensity of its symptoms brought many to my doorstep.

By the end of that week I had perhaps seen as many as

eighty or so patients with varying degrees of the same symptoms, fever, nausea and occasional bowel problems.

I am sure the local apothecaries were delighted in my brother physicians' and my own issuance of so many prescriptions to treat these symptoms.

While tired from the constant visit to my surgery from my patients, I was not as exhausted as I had been on other similar occasions. I felt sure that a few days rest would return me to a more balanced routine.

"Watson, I am to Cornwall," declared Holmes.

"How long will you be gone?" queried I.

"I think but a day or two. I suspect this is a rather simple case, Watson. I believe it will not provide me with the challenge I am in need of, but as you suggested, it is perhaps better than that which is to be found in Chinatown."

I wished to blurt out 'Holmes, I am proud of you' but I thought better of saying it aloud. I believed staying silent was the better reinforcement of his decision, but I cannot explain why I thought so at this moment. It just seemed the correct response.

"Let me know if I can do anything here for you."

"Of course, of course."

With that he was gone. I expected him to return in a day or two and to have already solved the case. No doubt, Mr. Whitehead was involved with another woman. Holmes would track her down, let Mrs. Whitehead know and enquire if she would want him to continue or not.

These type cases were common and Holmes rarely took them on. In general, I have chosen not to bore you, dear readers, with these types of tales as they rarely are of the level of the other of our adventures I have written about before. But this adventure proved to be different and thus I share it with you now.

I did not hear from him for either of those two days, but then on the third day, received a telegram which stated:

"IN NEED OF ASSISTANCE - COME AT ONCE"

I found this unimaginable, but most intriguing. This was but a simple case. What had happened to cause Holmes to call on me to follow him west to Truro in Cornwall?

I saw my last patient and quickly consulted my Bradshaw's and found a late train from Paddington that would send me first to Plymouth and then on to Truro on the Great Western line.

When I arrived, Holmes was there to greet me.

"Holmes, what has happened?" queried I.

"It does not appear to be the simple case we presumed it to be," Holmes answered.

"What is it you need me to do?"

"Our situation requires observations at the Whitehead home. I cannot visit there without suspicion since I have communicated to Mr. Whitehead in person on business matters, thus I need your assistance. I appreciate your accommodating me on such short notice."

"Holmes, it is of no concern. You know I am always at your service. Besides, it will be good to be out of London while that fever comes to an end. I believe I have done my part to ease my patients' pain. I am lucky to have avoided its invasion of me so far. If I had stayed, I believe my luck would have run out."

"Let us then get you settled in and I will explain all."

I checked in the small inn where Holmes had requested the inn-keeper hold his last room for me. We then set out to find a meal as I had not had time to eat and catch the train.

After we ordered our meal, Holmes began describing his inquiries to me.

"Watson, it is strange case. I was able to obtain a meeting with our Mr. Whitehead in the guise of wishing to acquire some of his granite for, as I told him, a new building in London. As much as I had learned from Mr. Foster over at the Geological Museum about granite, I believe I failed to properly educate myself about the builders in London."

"I introduced myself as John Kelly. His first question was not about granite, but for which masonry and stone contractor did I work?

"I had no immediate response to this and he quite quickly concluded something was not correct. My eventual answer was that I was representing myself as a new company. He was suspicious of this answer and queried me again as to where I had learned my trade. For whom had I worked so as to be able to start my own business.

"I was off my guard, Watson. He was getting the better of me.

"I retorted that if he did not want my business, then I would no longer waste his time. I rose to leave and he responded as I hoped he would.

"He said, 'Now, now. Please sit down, sir. I meant no harm. It is that I know all of the major masonry and stone firms in London and have done business with all of them for many years. I've not heard of you or your company before.'

"He continued further, 'Once one is not paid for shipping one's granite to a site, well, you understand, it is quite the bother to deal with folks who don't pay you. I have had this happen once or twice and it is not a pleasant experience. I have learned to only do business with people who pay their bills on time. Certainly, you can understand that?'

"He continued, 'I will, though, be up front with you. Since you and your company are unknown to me, I would require a deposit of fifty percent of the price of the granite and the remaining fifty percent upon delivery at your site. Those are my terms, take them or leave them.'

"I was relieved to have dodged his assault on my pretence. I stated I understood and that his terms were a reasonable precaution. I volunteered that I had experienced similar difficulties with other persons that did not pay in full when it was due to me.

"Thus, Watson, whatever was troubling him and affected his behaviour in the presence of his wife was not affecting his business acumen."

"Have you been so far able to identify this other woman?" queried I.

"No, and it is strange. Normally in cases such as these the straying dog manages to find a way to disappear to accomplish such meetings. So far, I have not seen him do anything but leave his abode and go straight to his office. He eats his lunch in his office and then goes straight home, not varying off his path, and remains there until the next morning.

"I suppose it is possible that I have not observed him long enough and that he has his dalliances at longer intervals, but my experiences in these cases lead me to conclude they usually occur within more frequent intervals."

"Have you spoken to Mrs. Whitehead?" asked I.

"No, I think my presence would be noticed and this would complicate things enormously. That is where I need your help, Doctor.

"Mrs. Whitehead knows who you are and knows you are a medical man. I would like you to visit her on the pretext of some desire on her part to seek your counsel for some sort of ailment."

"I suppose that would work, Holmes. But what do you wish me to do?"

"I want to know if we are simply victims of, perhaps, Mrs. Whitehead's imagination. I would like you to see her when she is with her husband and determine if she is imagining his behaviour or if it is as she stated to us when he is at home."

"Please contact her and inform her that you will arrive at her request. I must expect that she will provide a reasonable story to convince her husband that you are acceptable and not arouse his suspicions by her not seeking counsel with some local doctor."

"Hopefully that will suffice, Holmes. He seems to be a quite observant gentleman."

"You are correct. But this is our only move forward now."

The next day I informed Holmes that I was to meet with Mrs. Whitehead at 10 o'clock in Truro at a local Tea shop, called *Ruth's*. At the appointed hour, I met Mrs. Whitehead.

She informed me that her husband seemed more agitated last night since he had received a letter in the evening post. She was convinced it was from the woman.

"I know it was from her. The handwriting on the envelope was definitely a woman's script. I left it on the tray where Fredrick, our butler, leaves all the posts.

"After dinner, he went to check the mail as is his normal

habit. As soon as I saw him pick it up from the tray, his face went pale. He did not see me watching. He stuffed it in his coat pocket and walked off."

"You looked at it long enough to determine the handwriting, but did you notice the return address?"

"There was none."

"And the post mark, was that legible?"

"Nottinghamshire."

"I see. Well, each little piece of information helps. Mr. Holmes wishes that I be able to observe your husband here at your home. How might that be possible do you suggest?"

"I have a woman friend in London whom I used as my excuse to come see Mr. Holmes. I have been complaining to Gerald, my husband, that I have been having trouble with my eye.

"Yes, I did notice your eye when you first came to us in London, but it was not for that ailment you sought help."

"Is it serious, Doctor?"

"No, I believe a simple ointment should take care of it."

We've discussed my seeing someone. I could simply say that Julia, my friend, referred you to me."

"How do we account for my coming here rather than you coming, say, to London?"

"Do you not travel for leisure, Doctor?"

"I do."

"Then perhaps you were on a trip to visit Plymouth and its rich history. Perhaps you wished to see where Sir Francis Drake lived in nearby Tavistock. My husband enjoys naval history, you see."

"I am not so acquainted, having been an army surgeon myself, but if it can alleviate your husband's suspicions, I will attempt it."

"Good, I will expect you tomorrow. Perhaps after teatime? I will insist to Gerald that you stay for dinner."

"I shall be there then," confirmed I.

"Good day, Doctor."

"Good day, Mrs. Whitehead."

I informed Holmes of my progress and especially the letter and its point of origin.

"How very odd, that a letter all the way from

Nottinghamshire would cause such disharmony. Do try, Watson, to get hold of that letter. I think that piece of datum would move us forward immeasurably."

"I will do what I can, Holmes, but I am doubtful as to my ability to acquire it."

"Doctor, I have faith in you. You will find a way; I am sure."

I arrived as agreed. The reception by both the Whiteheads was at first, most cordial. Mr. Whitehead apparently had been told of my impending presence and was as polite as one would wish a host to be.

Mrs. Whitehead explained again how lucky she thought she was that I would be in the area and that her friend Julia knew of my practice.

Gerald, while acknowledging the serendipity of the situation, seemed pre-occupied shorty after my introduction and for the remainder of the evening for that matter.

Due to the stately appearance of the house, I would have thought it would have led to a more formal dinner setting and accompanying meal. But, to my surprise, we ate a simple country dinner, despite being surrounded by, what I judged to be, rather expensive furnishings and accoutrements dispersed about the Georgian style mansion.

After the meal, I requested the opportunity to examine Mrs. Whitehead's eye. Permission was granted and we retired to the parlour where there was more adequate lighting. Mr. Whitehead, retired across the entry hall into his study and closed the doors.

"Mrs. Whitehead," said I, "I have not seen any behaviour in your husband as you have described to Mr. Holmes and me. Your husband's behaviour appears quite normal from my observations."

"I agree with you, Doctor, but I tell you, he is not his normal self."

Just then a loud voice shouted, "Fredrick! Fredrick! Come here this instant!"

I stood up and walked closer to the open door leading into the entrance hall across from the study. Fredrick, who came quickly, slid open the doors of the study that had been left slightly ajar and enquired, "Yes, sir?"

"Who has been through my things?"

"Sir, I am sure I do not know what you mean."

"I don't know what to do. Someone has been in my desk I tell you!"

"Dr. Watson, perhaps I should go assist in this matter."

I bowed to her suggestion.

"Gerald, what is the matter?" queried she, as she strode across the entry hall and into the study. "We have a guest, Gerald, please!"

"I do not care! Someone has been in my desk!"

"Gerald, you know that cannot be true. Who could that be?"

"Oh, I don't know. But I am missing a letter."

"What letter?"

"Never mind. I don't want to discuss it further."

"Then please, Gerald, can you not wait until our guest has left before you continue with such outbursts?"

"Yes, yes. Leave me alone, now!"

"Alright, Gerald."

With that she slid the door back together completely, turned and walked back into the parlour.

"You see, Doctor. This is what I have been trying to tell you and Mr. Holmes. These outbursts are not like him. Do you think he suffers from some fever of the brain?"

"No, Madam. I do, though, believe something from outside this house is troubling him greatly. Is there any way I could see the letter about which you told us?"

"Oh, I don't know, Doctor. Perhaps he has just misplaced it. But I am afraid if he found me with it, he might go into a rage."

"Alright. I will leave it to you. But obtaining that letter could help resolve this entire mystery. Please see what you can do."

"I shall return tomorrow and will have had the chemist concoct a little remedy for your eye. From what I see it is but a mild infection that can be easily cured with a tincture of a medicine I ran across while in India during my service to Her Majesty. After a few treatments, it shall bother you no more. Shall we say again about teatime?"

"Yes, that would be fine"

"Good evening to you, Mrs. Whitehead and give my thanks and best to your husband."

After returning to the inn, I was able to describe to Holmes what had transpired while visiting the Whiteheads.

"What chance, Watson, do you think she will be able to produce the letter for our review of it?"

"I am not optimistic, Holmes, but I should know this evening. She does not seem to be afraid of him, but I do believe she wishes to avoid a confrontation should her intuition about all this be incorrect."

"Yes, that does make sense. She was frank with us and said she had no proof. I hope you will be successful in retrieving the letter or at least a handwritten copy."

We went to our separate rooms as it was getting late. The air being quite cleaner than that of London, I left open my windows and enjoyed a cool breeze that afforded me a pleasant sleep.

Holmes was anxious for teatime to come as that was then his only hope in receiving more data. I visited the local apothecary and had him make up an ointment I had seen prescribed for my patients from time and time.

The day seemed endless as I waited with Holmes for teatime to approach. About half-past three o'clock, I headed off to my appointment with Mrs. Whitehead. Arriving just before four o'clock, I was again shown into the parlour of the grand house, by Fredrick.

While Fredrick was still there and Mrs. Whitehead had arrived, I opened the chemist's jar and began telling her what to do with it.

"I will want you to close you eye and apply this on your eyelid. Please repeat this, four times each day."

"Will there be anything else for you or your guest, Madam?" enquired Fredrick.

"No. Thank you, Fredrick. That will be all."

"Yes, Madam." After which he bowed and left the room sliding the parlour doors behind him.

"Oh, Doctor!" exclaimed Mrs. Whitehead. "I've got it!"

"Got what Madam?" queried I.

"The letter!" said she with a pleasant smile on her face.

"Yes, yes of course. May I read it?"

"Yes, and it ...it's not a love letter! I was sure it was going to be a love letter." said she, quite excited to be wrong.

"You say?"

"Read it yourself."

I took the letter and read it. It was but a few lines.

Gerald,

Reggie has died. I need your help. Can you not spare something for me, please?

Kat

"So, you see, I am relieved. I do not know exactly who this 'Kat' is or why she is asking for Gerald's help, but it is not a love letter!"

"How did you find it?"

"He has a bad habit of putting letters in his pocket and forgetting to take them out. I found three others but they were all about business matters. Then I found this one."

"This is helpful Mrs. Whitehead, but I would like to advise you to be patient. I have seen in some of our cases that sometimes the road we think we are on takes an unexpected turn and leads to an unexpected place.

"Until Mr. Holmes is satisfied that the case is over, I can only caution you to be careful and remain observant."

"Yes, Doctor, but because it is not a love letter. I am relieved and for me that is enough!"

I returned and told Holmes about the letter and its brief contents. He acquired a most puzzling look on his face.

"Watson, this is indeed a strange case. On the face of it there does not appear to be anything to it. A woman suspects her husband of certain infidelity, a letter arrives, presumably from the other woman who is located three hundred miles away and which does nothing more than ask for help because of a death?" Who is this 'Kat'? What attachment is there to our Mr. Whitehead that he would react so intensely? Who is Reginald? Did he simply die, or perhaps, did she kill him?

"I believe there is more to this and I shan't feel comfortable walking away from this request of Mrs. Whitehead until I know for sure she is in no danger."

"But Holmes, there was no threat in the letter. It was a simple request for help."

"That may be, but simple requests have a way of escalating into demands. Only time will tell, Watson."

I briefly spoke to Mrs. Whitehead and she seemed quite satisfied, that since the letter did not express an amorous attitude, she did not think she needed Sherlock's or my help any longer. I cautioned her one last time and that was the last I spoke with her. Holmes and I returned to Baker Street. I hoped that another case would soon present itself so that I'd not have to again be overly concerned about Holmes' needing to revisit the darker side of London.

It was several weeks later, when who should suddenly be knocking on our door, but none other than Mrs. Whitehead.

"Doctor Watson! Oh, Doctor Watson!" said she as she burst into tears passing over our threshold.

"My dear Mrs. Whitehead, what on earth is the matter?'

Through her tears and moaning that she had obviously kept in check throughout her journey to London but were now released like a ruptured dam, I could barely hear her tale.

"He's gone to Nottinghamshire."

"Madam, um…"

"He's gone to see her…."

"I am so sorry Madam. How do you know this?"

"He said he had business in London a few days ago. He was gone for three days. I thought nothing of it until I turned out the pockets of his coat. I found a punched ticket to London but also another used ticket for further on to Nottinghamshire. He's gone to see her!" she wailed as she finished her sentence.

"Mrs. Whitehead, please, calm yourself if you can. I know these type revelations can and do overwhelm one. But I have observed you to be a strong woman. Mr. Holmes shall be returning shortly. I know that he will be willing to help you, but please understand he will need you to be as clearheaded as you can possibly muster."

"Yes, yes, Doctor, I understand. It is so embarrassing. Please forgive me for my outbreak." At this she seemed to regain her composure.

We waited in silence for about another half hour. Holmes let himself in and quickly surmised the situation.

"Mrs. Whitehead, I am sorry things have not gone well for you. How can I help you?"

"Oh, Mr. Holmes, can you please find out who this woman is? I want to know what is happening."

"I will do my best Mrs. Whitehead. I recommend you return home. I will contact you shortly."

She rose in silence. All the passion had drained out of her. She nodded to both of us, then head down, she left as if attending a funeral.

"I'm heading to Nottinghamshire, shall you come too?"

"Yes, this is strange business and I must know what it is all about. The man must be quite mad to treat his wife in such a manner."

We acquired passage on the next Great Central train heading north to Nottinghamshire. We then arrived and settled in for the evening.

The next morning, I found Holmes dragging me with him to the local constabulary.

"How may I help you gentlemen?" asked the clerk.

"We are looking for reports concerning the recent death of a man called Reginald…"

"Reginald Greene? Katherine Greene's husband? Aye he died; oh, it's been nearly three months ago now. What business with the family Greene might you be having?"

"We represent a life insurance company from London and wish to contact Mrs. Greene. Unfortunately, our records were damaged when a water pipe burst and we could not make out the exact address here in

Nottinghamshire. It would be quite helpful to us if you could let us know where we could find her."

"Oh, I sees, well, she works down at the Bird & Hare. Can't miss it. It's on the corner two blocks to your left and one block to your right."

"Thank you, sir," said Holmes as he slipped a shilling across the counter.

"Oh well, thank you, sir! If there's anything else you need to know, me name's 'Jim' and I'll be happy to answer any other question you might have.

"I think that's all for now, Jim, thanks again," said Holmes, as we walked out the door.

"Shall we not catch our meal at the Bird & Hare today? What say you, Watson?"

"It appears we shall," answered I.

"A shant of bivvy for ya gentlemen?" queried the bar maid.

"Only your best local shall do. Have you anything to eat?"

"We got some biscuits but that's abou' tall ov it. If you're after a full meal, go next door. Oliver 'ill be glad to fill you up."

"Thanks, we'll try your local and then perhaps go there," said Holmes.

"I's appreciate that, don't care people eatin' a full meal, mind ya, but don't need to be scaring new customers away neither. You gents from London by the sound of ya?"

"You've got a good ear, Madam."

"Well, I's spent some time there meself, so I's guess I's can calls it out when I's hears it.

"What business brings you to Nottinghamshire?"

"We are looking for a person."

"Aye, and who might you be alooking for?"

"Her name is Katherine Greene."

At the sound of her name, she froze.

"What do you want with her?"

"We just want to speak to her."

"About what?"

"Well, now that's between her and us. Do you know her?"

"Aye. I's she."

"Mrs. Greene, our condolences on your most recent loss."

"Ah, thank…ya. But how'd ya know…what do ya need to speak me about?"

"We are here on behalf of Mrs. Florence Whitehead, do you know her?"

"I's do not. But the last name sounds familiar."

"Come now, Mrs. Greene, we know all about it."

"Gerald didn't send you?"

"No mum. You see his current wife is concerned about your continuing relationship with Mr. Whitehead."

"Is she now?"

"Yes, and I must warn you that any further contact with Mr. Whitehead will not go well for you."

"You be threatening me?"

"No mum, just explaining that while you may be a tough circumstance at present, having just lost your husband, resorting to blackmail will not go well for you."

"Who said anything about blackmail?" queried she.

"I am confident that Mr. Whitehead would be quite willing to confess publicly his former marriage to you. And while the law we know has changed on the subject, I have inquired and have been able to confirm your separation from him would be looked on as acceptable seeing as how you wilfully left and married Mr. Greene."

"All I's was asking for was a little help. When my Reginald died, he left me with nothing."

"We understand, that is of course unfortunate, but we want to make it clear to you that you should not contact Mr. Whitehead again."

"I's see, gentlemen. He'll not hear from me again."

"Good day to you, mum."

She said nothing in return.

We then returned to Baker Street and awaited Mr. and Mrs. Whitehead's arrival. Holmes had written a private note to Mrs. Whitehead and ask that she and her husband come to London. He would explain all then.

The look on Whitehead's face when he saw Holmes was one of confusion.

"Florence, why are we here with both Dr. Wa…"

"Watson," I reminded him.

"Yes, um, Dr. Watson and this Mr. Kelly, isn't it?"

"Yes, yes, please come in, both of you, won't you. Please sit down and we shall sort this out shortly," said Holmes as he raised his hand asking for their coats.

Silence followed until we were all settled.

"Gerald," said Mrs. Whitehead, "This man you called Mr. Kelly, is Mr. Sherlock Holmes. I employed him to find out what on earth has been the matter with you. Mr. Holmes, what have you to say?"

"Mrs. Whitehead, we believe we have gotten to the bottom of your little mystery. But I first have a few questions for you and your husband.

"How old was your husband when you married him?"

"He told me he was but a score and ten."

"Where had he come from?"

"London, is what he told me, is that not true?"

"Both would appear not to be correct, Mr. Whitehead?"

Mr. Whitehead sat silently and just gently nodded his head.

"Mrs. Whitehead your husband was born in 1856. That makes him 43 years old. You were married five years ago which means he was thirty-eight when you got married."

"Well, truth be known, I've been known to take a few years off my age as well. Is that what this is all about? You must know I've no worries about that, Gerald, don't you?"

"Did you know he was married before?" said Holmes.

"What? I don't believe you!"

"Yes, it's true, to a woman in Nottinghamshire. Her name's Katherine," said Gerald.

"Gerald, you never told me this. So, this is what it is all about. How dare you?!" she raged at her husband.

"Florence…"

"I want proof of this marriage!" demanded she.

Holmes handed her a photograph of the Marriage License which clearly showed Gerald Timothy Whitehead and Katherine Anne Housley being married on 5 June, 1876.

After it had sunk in, she composed herself.

"So, what you are saying is that I am not his legal wife and this woman is?"

"No, I am not saying that, exactly," said Holmes.

"Well then, what are you saying?"

"Ultimately, it will be for a court to decide and I am not counsellor in matters such as this."

"It should be plain and simple. He either is still married to this woman and I am married to a bigamist or he divorced her and she has no claim on him now."

"Gerald, where are your divorce papers?!"

He finally spoke up.

"There are none."

"What! So, you are a filthy bigamist!" At that she began to cry and buried her face in a handkerchief.

"Florence, please, it is not like that at all! Have I ever, but for last week, travelled to Nottinghamshire? Have I ever shown you anything but my love and affection? Have I ever even placed my eyes on any other woman but you?"

Her rage was a bit calmed by the tone of these endearing questions. But she still was furious as her breathing was intense, her eyes watery and the flush of her face spoke of all the emotions swirling inside her.

"I suppose not, but what is happening here?"

"Please explain it to her, I've not the courage nor the heart to do so."

"Your husband, and I believe he is your husband, did not divorce his first wife in such a way that is quite acceptable by the law of today."

"What do you mean?" she queried.

"He sold her," said Holmes, in a matter of fact manner.

"He what?!!!"

"He sold her. Despite the law allowing for divorce, you must know it is a painful, lengthy and expensive process. It is more likely to be made use of by the upper class who have the means to avail themselves of what our good King Henry VIII allowed for himself. Most country folks cannot afford such expenses. So, for many a century, under the common law of England, men have 'sold' their wives, their property, to break the marriage contract. In smaller towns and villages, the locals know when these happen and nobody seems to care."

Then Gerald spoke up.

"I did it and I was glad to be through with her. She'd

been unfaithful with a man called Greene. I decided it would better that they be together than me miserable for a life time. I was drunk one night and the local boys were giving me a difficult time about it saying I should kill him for breaking up my marriage.

"I'd always heard about selling wives and thought it repulsive when I first thought about it. Then it hit me that it'd solve my problems and I could get a fresh start. I set a price, more than she was worth to me anyways, and Greene paid it. It was best for both of us, I thought.

"I didn't hear from her again until a month ago. Reggie Greene died all of the sudden and Katherine had nowhere to turn. She reached out to me.

"I'd actually thought it was all behind me. Forgotten all about it, really. Then when she wrote it all came rushing back at me. I didn't know what to do. I was so confused. I guess with all my business dealings I learned how the law gets enforced when things don't go right, so when her letter came, I panicked.

"She and I thought we were through. Reggie thought we were through and the folks in Nottinghamshire that knew about it, they knew we were through, but would the law think we were through?

"I'm so sorry, Florence. I didn't mean to hurt you. I just didn't know how this would all turn out."

"Mr. Holmes, oh, what should we do now?" asked she.

"Mrs. Whitehead, I suggest with Mr. Whitehead's contacts that he shall be able to find adequate counsel from a solicitor on the matter. I recommend to both of you, that you seek such advice and put this matter to rest once and for all. I believe there was no offspring between you and Katherine, correct, Mr. Whitehead?"

"This is true, how did you know?"

"A quick check at the GRO was all that was needed."

"Ah, yes."

"That I believe is the end of this little adventure, Watson. I shall take bath now," said Holmes. He headed towards his room and I observed him beginning to loosen his dressing gown. No doubt his mastery over his desire to avoid what proper English society required of him was beginning to wane since the problem was now solved. It was clear I needed to spare his clients any embarrassment.

"Yes, well, Mr. And Mrs. Whitehead, please so kind to be on your way now," said I.

I quickly urged them to the door and assisted them with their hats and coats.

"I'm afraid Mr. Holmes has already excused himself from obeying any more social formalities for the rest day.

"But what about the fee?"

"Please believe me, working out the problem itself, was payment enough. Should Mr. Holmes desire any further compensation for his efforts, he knows how to contact you.

"Have a safe trip back to Truro and good luck to both of you."

THE ADVENTURE OF
THE MISSING SOMMELIER

"**W**here is he, Mr. Tomes?" I heard the woman ask, as she entered the wine shop. "Good morning, Mrs. Everette. How are we today?" replied Tomes.

"I said, where is he? Where is Xavier?" she repeated.

"I'm sorry. I do not know what you mean?" said Tomes.

"Xavier did not come home last night!" said Mrs. Everette, with a voice desperate for answers.

"Oh! That is unusual," answered Tomes.

"He had told me yesterday in the morning that he was planning to stop here on his way home. Did he not come by?" queried she.

"Indeed, he did. I had sent him a note yesterday that the four bottles of wine he had ordered from Colombia two months ago, had finally arrived. He came by just before closing last night and collected them."

"Columbia? From the capital of America?" queried she.

"No, mum. Colombia, the country in South America."

"Oh, yes..."

"In any event, I fear something awful must have happened to him as he never came home," said she, as she gripped her mouth with her white gloved hand, closed her eyes and began a most restrained cry. She tried unsuccessfully to hide her panic at the thought, of which she feared the most, now being confirmed by Mr. Tomes.

Her emotions overwhelmed her, and she soon lost even the strength to stand erect. Seeing that she was likely to faint, I quickly offered my assistance.

"Mr. Tomes, please, a chair for the lady?" said I. "Eddington! A chair please!" called out Tomes. His assistant came from the back with a questioning look at his master. Tomes then motioned his finger back and forth showing his concern of the fainting lady to his assistant. He then quickly went and returned and positioned a chair to accommodate the lady's descent as I held her hand and elbow, thus helping her maintain her stability until the chair was in position.

"There, there, Madam. All can be made right, but first we shall get you settled here.

"My name is Dr. John Watson, I am a physician. If you would allow me to help you, I would like to offer to you my services now."

"Oh, Doctor, I …I…am so scared!"

"It is all right, Madam. You are likely in shock and we will see you through it.

"Tomes, might you have a brandy available?"

"Yes, yes of course, Doctor."

Tomes soon returned with a small fine crystal cordial glass of brandy which my newest patient sipped slowly and after several minutes, consumed the last of it.

"Now, Madam, please tell me all you can about this unfortunate incident."

"I do not know what to tell you, except that Xavier, he's … he's my husband. He did not return home last night. I do not know where he is or what to do!"

"If I may suggest, we should notify Scotland Yard immediately. Tomes, can you please contact the Yard and request Detective Inspector Lestrade come to your shop at once. Tell him Dr. John Watson is requesting his presence."

"Yes, yes, I shall do so."

"What has happened to him, Doctor? What has happened to my Xavier?" said she, repeating her query.

"Madam, I do not know, but we shall find out. Please do try to relax."

Having dealt with her low blood pressure and its resulting near fainting spell, I was now concerned it would swing in the opposite direction.

"It is best that one stay as calm as is possible in such situations. Rest assured, we are here to help you through this," said I, speaking and repeating those words again slowly, in hopes they and my cadence would help her relax and that her confidence perhaps would return.

I was concerned that the lady, being consumed by her fears, could easily harm herself by raising the pressure of her blood above a safe level. Unfortunately, I had not my medical kit nor were we near my surgery, where I could employ the new sphygmomanometer I had obtained only a few months back. With it I could discern the pressure of her blood with reasonable accuracy.

"Please, Madam, rest. We have contacted the Yard and Inspector Lestrade shall be u here soon. Try to rest and stay calm," I repeated. Luckily, she began to calm down. I managed to keep her that way talking piffle about London.

It was nearly an hour before Lestrade arrived. I was most disappointed in his tardiness and his lack of sympathy for the situation once he arrived, but perhaps I should have known better. Undoubtedly his many years of constant dealings with the tragedies of human existence had numbed him.

"Ah, Dr. Watson, they said you called for me. So, what have we got here, Doctor?"

"This is Mrs. Everette, Inspector. Mrs. Everette, this is Detective Inspector Lestrade of Scotland Yard." Lestrade turned to Mrs. Everette and tipped his hat, but without saying any more than mumbling "mum" to her.

"It appears Mr. Everette, her husband, did not return home last night and was perhaps last seen here at Mr. Tomes' wine shop, where he picked up some wine."

"All right, well … don't seem like any foul play in that so far. Perhaps he tried some of his wine on the way home and it'll likely be we'lls find him in an alley somewhere between this shop and his home" said he with a smart little grin to say he'd seen this play out many times before.

"Where do you live, Madam?"

This statement pertaining to Inspector Lestrade's speculation as to the likely event and whereabouts of her husband, put Mrs. Everette into an unbelievable state. Her emotions of fear and anger appeared to battle each other. Anger evidently won out as the insulting comment likely charged her with emotion and her previously wan face became flush. I was then even more desperate with concern for the pressure of her blood.

"My husband is no such man!" said she, bursting out and attempting to stand up to Lestrade's insult and attack on her husband's character.

"Sorry, Madam, but from my experience all these years, that what these folks do."

"Lestrade, can you not see this lady's situation? You dishonour the Yard with such attitudes and comments."

"All right, all right. My apologies, mum. If you'll come down to the Yard, we'lls takes a full report on your husband's supposed... his disappearance."

As he turned to leave, Lestrade pulled me aside and whispering, said to me, "Doctor, I've seen these types before. They cannot believe their spouse loves the drink more than them. He'll show up in a few days as being picked up for drunkenness. You mark my words. I only came here due to them telling me you'd requested I come. I should have just sent a constable, but as it was you Doctor, I came.

"I do thank you, Inspector, but..." said I.

"Perhaps Mr. Holmes would care to take on this one. I've not got time for cases like these. I've got real crimes to solve, you know."

"Again, I do appreciate your coming, Inspector. I will encourage Mrs. Everette to file the report as you suggested. There is, though, something about this case that does not seem as you describe. In talking to Mr. Tomes while awaiting your arrival, he indicated that this Mr. Everette is quite a well-known master sommelier here in London and not the drunk you believe he is."

"A what?"

"A master sommelier."

"What's a master somm...somm...? The head of some sort of secret society, eh?" said he again, with that little smile as if he'd made quite an insightful joke that would somehow cover for his ignorance of the word.

"No, no. A sommelier is a person who is a master of wines. They know about each wine in detail, or they can discern when and where a wine was grown just by smell and taste. Mr. Everette teaches all of the 'wine butlers' in London's finest restaurants. They seek him out to learn from him. He is no drunk as you have suggested."

"I donna know, Doctor. Even if he is this, somm…"

"Sommelier."

"Right, a somm-a-leer, he's like as not, drunk a bit too much of his wine and we'lls pick him up, and then we'll get him home. You mark my words."

"He is not a drunk. Mr. Tomes vouches for him. He is a gentleman. The wines he imbibes are of extraordinary value and these wines are not the type some drunk would procure. These are wines for a sophisticated pallet."

"Well, it all tastes the same to me, that's why's I's prefers a good ol' pint of ale to any of that fancy stuff. 'A pint's a pound, the world around!'[1] as they say. Have her come down to the Yard. Give my regards to Mr. Holmes. Goodbye, Doctor, Mrs. Everette," said he, with a hat tip again and a slight bow.

"Goodbye, Inspector," said I.

"Well, I never…" huffed Mrs. Everette.

"I apologise for the Inspector's behaviour, Madam. I truly do not know what to say about it. He did though suggest that this may be a case for my colleague, Mr. Sherlock Holmes. You have perhaps heard of him and his numerous cases?"

"Indeed, I have. I've read stories about him, written by someone who waits on him. I believe the writer is his valet, butler or some such servant."

"No, Madam. His colleague is a physician. I am he."

---

[1] Editor's note: – While likely the science behind Lestrade's expression is unknown to him the saying is based on the facts and reasonable assumptions as follows, where: cf = cubic feet; ci = cubic inches; & δ = specific gravity (density) of a substance as compared to the same volume of H_2O.

$$\frac{1 \text{ cf}}{62.4 \text{ lbs of } H_2O} \times \frac{1728 \text{ ci}}{1 \text{ cf}} \times \frac{1 \text{gal}}{231 \text{ ci}} \times \frac{128 \text{ oz}}{1 \text{ gal}} \times \frac{\delta \text{ Ale } 1.04}{\delta \, H_2O \, 1.0} = \frac{15.96 \text{ oz of Ale}}{1 \text{ lbs}}; \text{ or}$$

15.96 oz* of Ale $\approx$ 1lbs   and since 16 oz = 1 pint;   ∴ **1 pint of Ale $\approx$ 1 lbs**

NOTE: 1) * In this equation, the <u>weight</u> of a '*volume* in ounces' is being calculated.
2) the density (δ) of Ale > density of H_2O by a factor of 1.04

"Oh, pardon, me, Dr. Wat…"

"Watson."

"Pardon, me, Dr. Watson. I do believe I am in a terrible state this morning."

"It is quite all right, Madam. You've had quite a shock. I do believe Mr. Holmes and I would be able to assist you with your predicament.

"Here is my card. I will be returning to 221B Baker Street forthwith. I believe Mr. Holmes is in today. I encourage you to come by at your earliest opportunity after you have gone to Scotland Yard, should you wish that Mr. Holmes consider your case. Should you decide otherwise, I wish you good luck in finding your husband. Good day, Madam."

"Thank you. Doctor. I believe I will contact Mr. Holmes. And thank you for assisting me earlier."

"It is not a problem, mum."

"Mr. Tomes, should you hear from Xavier, please have him come home as soon as possible!"

"Yes, Madam, of course."

I opened the door for her and Mrs. Everette exited. She quickly hailed a cab. I assisted her in and heard her instruct the cabbie to take her quickly to Scotland Yard. The cabbie whipped up his horse and they were off.

I headed back home pondering the strange encounter I had experienced this morning. I hoped Mrs. Everette would soon be reunited with her husband and that her world would return to the normal rhythm to which it likely had previously been accustomed.

Something about the whole encounter drove me to the conclusion I would not see her again. I do not know why, but I somehow doubted she'd accept my offer of Holmes' and my help.

Upon arrival at 221B, I found Holmes in a somewhat jovial mood. That my dear and faithful readers will know can be an infrequent event. I explained the encounter I'd had at the wine shop. He showed neither excitement nor disinterest.

"I do think, Watson, shall she have another meeting with Lestrade, he will likely again refer her to me. My thinking on the subject says she shall be here by 11 o'clock at the latest. Lestrade will brush her off quickly."

I left Holmes' comment alone. His statements of these type, when made with such certainty, annoyed me at times. While I had known for some time his abilities in understanding and predicting human behaviour allowed him to easily forecast other's move like a grandmaster at chess, it upset me that he was one or two steps ahead of even me in a case he'd not even participated in as yet. It can be unsettling at times knowing that someone can predict or deduce your very thoughts, as it would seem Holmes could do.

I checked my watch and saw that it was three minutes past 11 o'clock and there had not been a knock at 221B yet. I confess, dear readers, my annoyance was replaced by a certain amount of satisfaction in my friend's seeming failure, this time, to predict the future.

"Well, Holmes, your soothsaying regarding Mrs. Everette has been inaccurate. It is after 11 o'clock, my good fellow."

"Are you sure, Watson?"

Just then there was a knock on the clapper. Mrs. Hudson answered and soon there was the sound of footstep ascending to our rooms.

"She is past your time."

"I object to your conclusion, Watson. Have you heard the 11 o'clock bells from London University ring yet?"

Just then the bells began their toll announcing the eleventh hour.

"I believe your watch is running fast, Watson. I conclude you have not set it recently, eh?"

"Holmes!" exclaimed I, at his confounded supremacy upon the argument and his victory, again.

With our guest, Holmes' new client, at our door, there was no more opportunity to rebut my roommate's comment and I was forced to withdraw my defence. It took me some time to calm myself down.

Holmes answered the door and I remained in a state of mind that argued my points in my head, and I must confess I was not focused on Mrs. Everette as well as perhaps I should have been. I implore my dear readers to be patient with me and please grant me dispensation should my notes be confusing upon this meeting.

I retreated into silence and forced myself to let go of my confrontation with Holmes. I finally found myself following the conversation at hand.

It did though, remind me of a time when I was arguing with one of my fellow surgeons in Afghanistan out in the field, but had to quickly let go of our intense discussion as the wounded were being brought in for immediate care. I can remember the distinct feeling of *letting it go*, but, strangely, I do not remember what it was that the other surgeon and I were so vehemently discussing. The wounded came first.

"Oh, Doctor. I am so glad you are here."

"Not at all, Mrs. Everette. Pleased to assist you."

"Now that you have met Mr. Holmes, perhaps you could tell him again about your missing husband. Xavier is his name, correct?"

"Yes, yes. Xavier is my husband."

"Please have a seat over here, Mrs. Everette," said Holmes as he waved his arm in the direction of our small cushioned but somewhat tattered lounge.

"Where should I begin, Mr. Holmes?" queried she, somewhat sheepishly.

"Wherever you think best," replied Holmes.

"My husband, Xavier, is a gentleman. That insulting inspector or detective or whatever he calls himself, believes him to be a common drunk. He is not, I tell you!"

"Please madam, no doubt your husband is such a gentleman, but it will be best if you can give us facts and do your best to push out of your mind the emotions that, no doubt, are overwhelming you at the moment," instructed Holmes.

"Well, yes, I understand, I think," replied she. "It's just that that Inspector…"

"Mrs. Everette, let us forget the Inspector. No doubt he told you to come see me after your visit to the Yard."

"Yes. Yes, he did. He said if there was anyone who

could find my husband, it was you, Mr. Holmes. And he said I should come over right away so as to make sure you did not engage another client before me."

"Wasn't that kind of Inspector Lestrade? If, I am to help you, madam, I will need you to stick to the facts of what you know. Shall we not start again?"

"All right. My husband is a gentleman. That, sir, is a fact!

"When was the last time you saw him?"

"It was just yesterday, Tuesday morning. He had his breakfast and left for his office. I walked him to the door. Handed him his hat and cane after he put on his coat. Then he left for his office."

"His office?"

"Yes, he is an actuary for the Greater East London Insurance Company."

"But, Dr. Watson has told me you husband is a master sommelier. Is that not correct? What is this about him being an actuary?"

"Yes, well. My husband's father owns, I should say, owned a winery in France when Xavier was a child. Xavier grew up around wine. Though the vineyard was in his blood, you might say, his mind was meant for more challenging things.

"He went to school and did very well. His teachers convinced his father he should go to college in Paris. He was one of several boys and he was told early on he would not inherit the vineyard, and so it was arranged.

"He excelled in mathematics and soon found his skills especially in statistics. Upon graduation he was offered a position in one of France's best insurance companies.

"After a few years and having written several papers on statistical methods for use by actuaries in the insurance profession, he was offered a job here in London.

"That was very fortunate for me, as I met Xavier soon after he had come to London. He was so charming and I was so enthralled with his continental ways.

"We fell in love and were soon married. He has been a loving and faithful husband. I am a lucky woman. We have never had any trouble like this before. But now!" she looked as if she might shed a tear, but after a brief pause seemed to regain her composure.

"Though he worked diligently as an actuary, he never gave up his interest, study and knowledge of wines. One evening, several years ago, we were at a dinner for some of the insurance company's clients and the gentlemen in attendance were discussing wines.

"It was not unlike the men to brag a bit about wines, and once Xavier began explaining to several of them about the character of wines that he made the statement, that he could tell what type of wine it was, where a wine was from and even the year of its harvest. The others did not believe him, and a wager was made.

"Three unknown wines were ordered, and they were dispensed without Xavier seeing the bottles from whence they came.

"He was asked to identify them. The wager was £20. He tasted each and made notes on each. Clearing his palate, between each tasting, he finished and presented his results to the group.

"The first was an 1879 Riesling from Germany. The second was an 1881 Merlot from Bordeaux. And the third was an 1865 Tempranillo from Spain.

"The wine butler was called over and was then questioned. Xavier was correct on all three accounts. The other gentlemen were flabbergasted and practically accused him of some sort of chicanery. He quickly pushed back on this accusation and said that persons with a knack for the favour and smells of wine could do the same. It was a matter of experience, exposure and training. He collected his bet and we thought that was the end of it.

"Within the next week, the wine butler who had been in attendance that night of the bet, had tracked Xavier down and implored him to teach him more about wines.

"At first Xavier felt he had not the time to meddle in such things. But I had noticed that his time at home was, shall I say, dull, in that I could tell he was looking for some other outlet from the pressure of his office work. I said out loud that I thought perhaps he should begin teaching about wines. He enjoyed wines so much and certainly sharing his joy of them with others would be a good change from the ubiquitous numbers of his daily work.

"It was not too long after he started a small group that met first just once a month, but now meets every two weeks, and they discuss a different wine and experience the wine together.

"I believe this wine he had ordered, this *Colombian* wine, would be tasted at their next meeting. They'd been waiting for it for quite some time. This outlandish story that Inspector put forth makes no sense whatsoever!"

The renewed thought of Lestrade's cavalier attitude and the insinuation that her husband was a drunk, brought a new flush to her face and I sought to calm her down.

"Xavier seems quite the gentleman to me," said I. "You must be a very proud wife."

"Yes, I am very proud of my Xavier. But I fear something awful has happened to him. I need your help, Doctor, Mr. Holmes!"

"I am happy to have your information that you have just given us, Mrs. Everette. But let us return to yesterday," redirecting our guest.

"As I said, he left after breakfast and we had no discussion out of the ordinary. He mentioned he planned to stop by Mr. Tomes' shop on the way home as Tomes had indicated the wine would be ready for him to pick up that afternoon. It would be very much like Xavier to go by the shop, as it is on the route he takes to and from work.

"Dr. Watson witnessed what transpired at the wine shop. Has he not told you that story?"

"He most certainly has, but I would prefer I hear your version on the off chance the good Doctor has not fully relayed the story to me."

She began her version that, in the end, covered the same points that I had given to Holmes earlier. Nothing new was reported by her except her account of her actions arriving just prior to my presence. These points added nothing that impressed Holmes, or me, as providing any important additional data.

After concluding her story, she pleadingly said, "Please, Mr. Holmes, won't you help me find my Xavier?" Then she closed her eyes and began to cry softly as the lack of her ability to solve the problem and regain her husband's presence on her own, apparently overwhelmed her.

"Mrs. Everette, I appreciate your faith in me that I might help you. Rest assured, I find your case interesting and quite the challenge. I accept your request and I shall begin its resolution forthwith."

"Oh, Mr. Holmes, please do find him."

"Mr. Holmes shall do so, madam," interjected I, hoping to help her regain her confidence that her nightmare she was living in, would come to a happy ending.

"Please, tell me, when would the next meeting of Xavier's group be?"

"Short of a fortnight, that is Monday the 17th."

"And where would the meeting be held?"

"That I am not sure. You see it changes and is held at the hotel or restaurant where the wine butlers who are in the group work. It rotates between them and I do not keep up with where the meetings are held. I can find out, if you think it is important?"

"Yes, please do. Send word to me and perhaps the name of the host would be helpful. Lastly, might you have a picture, or better yet, two pictures of your husband?"

"Pictures?"

"Your husband has disappeared. As we make inquiries it will be most helpful to show people a picture of your husband. If he was seen, then it will help in tracking where he might have been seen."

"Oh, I see. Yes, yes of course. I will do so right away."

These assignments seemed to give her a spark in her attitude, as she now had something she could do to help find her husband, however seemingly unimportant it was. It was a task about which she could provide help and an answer.

She rose and I escorted her to our door. She thanked us both again and we bowed at her departure. The door was shut. Holmes immediately grabbed his hat, coat and cane.

"Watson, I've work to do to catch up on this case."

With that he quickly exited, and I found myself alone. Since he had not requested my accompanying him, I decided to settle down into my chair and read the news of the day which so far had eluded me.

For some reason that day, I found myself drifting a bit as I read. I would suddenly sense I had dozed off and felt myself jerking slightly as if to wake myself up and continue to read. I must admit that on more than one occasion, I believe I found myself dreaming I was a character in the story I had just been reading. This phenomenon surely happened several times that afternoon and I eventually concluded a more intentional nap was in order.

I went to my room and disrobed to a comfortable level, lay down and fell asleep.

Awaking several hours later, I quickly recalled my dream of tasting wines and asserting which was the better, much to the chagrin of the others present in the dream. I tried with great earnest to convince the others that my opinion was based on sound reasoning. My clear declarations regarding the wine I had proclaimed the better of the lot, however, were falling on deaf ears. I awoke frustrated that I wasn't convincing enough.

As my head cleared and reality flooded into me, I smiled at my dream and felt glad to be free of the false frustrations which it had imposed on me.

It was shortly thereafter that Holmes returned.

"What luck have you had, Holmes?"

"Watson, you know better than to ask such a question of me! *Luck* has nothing to do with it. 1st class detective work solves cases such as these," exclaimed he.

"Then what progress have you made?"

"An iota of evidence here and there is all so far. But I've the Baker Street irregulars on the job now. If our actuary is still in London, it won't be long now before they find him."

"I have them searching the path between Mr. Tomes' wine shop and his residence. I walked it once myself and then instructed them to scour three blocks either side for anything that might help our case. I've given Wiggins instructions to alert me as soon as possible if anything is found."

"But, Holmes, can you count on them to be as diligent as you and I would be? Shan't we go and look?"

"I have offered such a reward as to make sure they turn over everything they encounter. I am confident if there is anything to be found, they will find it."

Holmes went to his room and rested for a short while. He emerged ready for diner. Agreeing on a meal at Simpson's-in-the-Strand, we soon found ourselves sitting down to a satisfying meal. Holmes wished to play chess, as other games were in progress around us, but I declined.

We settled for mere chitchat about the events of the day and were having a pleasant time. Dessert arrived and I then requested a cup of Arabic coffee to top off meal. Holmes joined me with a cup and we then both lit up our pipes. It was a most relaxing time.

The fullness and satisfaction of the evening was short lived.

The interruption began near the entrance with the maître d' shouting "Wait!" The outburst was quickly followed by "You can't come in here!"

We sat up a bit from our slouched posture in our chairs to see what was the trouble.

Soon the maître d' was dancing back and forth between the tables and chairs, slowing to avoid hitting any of his prized customers. "Stop. Stop!" he repeated.

Several patrons began rising from their chairs so as to avoid being run over by whatever had gained unauthorized entry into the restaurant. Surprise and laughter could begin to be heard. Whatever the maître d' was chasing seemed to be headed towards us. Each of the patrons that stood up, however, blocked our view of what it was that was to disrupt the end of our evening meal.

All of the sudden, the maître d' was before us, having seemingly trapped his quarry between himself and our table.

"Mr. Holmes! Mr. Holmes!" cried a bedraggled street urchin about eight years of age.

"I'z finds it first!"

"No, you didn't, I'z did!" cried the other one about the same age and equally dirty. Suddenly a third, older looking boy squeezed in from behind the maître d'.

"Both of youz gets outta here, right now!" yelled Wiggins. He grabbed both of them by their ears, one in each of his hands and they began squealing in a high pitch, like little girls.

"Wiggins! what's the meaning of all this commotion?"

"Sorry, Mr. Holmes. I told 'ems to wait outside fer youz but theyz wouldn't hearz me."

"Take them outside immediately," commanded Holmes. Then quickly reconsidering, he commanded, "No, I want you to take them to Baker Street and wait for us. We shall be there shortly," added he, as Wiggins pulled hard on the tiny lobes. "Ooo's" and "ouches" accompanied their exit.

"C 'mon youz two," Wiggins pronounced.

The maître d' gave Holmes and me a very satisfied look and followed Wiggins and his captives along to the front door. As things began to settle down one of the boys got loose from Wiggins' grasp and turned around. He kicked the maître d' in the shin and then stuck his tongue out at him and then ran out.

The maître d' exuded the sound of restrained pain trying not to upset his customers any more than they all ready had been. His attempt to restrain a vocal release from the pain resulted in him hopping around like a frightened bunny on one leg. This was an astonishing scene! The hopping maître d' became the focus of the entire restaurant, laughing at his misery, as one did at a theatre featuring Karno's slap-stick comics assaulting one another.

Holmes and I quickly finished our coffee. Paid our bill and meekly headed for the door. We avoided direct confrontation with the maître d' but tipped our hats to him as we exited. His earlier satisfied look turned to a stern stare.

We arrived a Baker Street and found Wiggins and his two young protégées waiting on the steps. Several of the other Baker Street irregulars were standing around as well.

"Mr. Holmes! Mr. Holmes!" cried the two young boys we encountered earlier at the restaurant.

"Quiet, youz two!" countered Wiggins.

"I'z found it first!" blurted out one of them.

"Jonesy? What did we'z talk 'bout?"

"Uh, we'z found it, sir" he said this time in a much less enthusiastic voice.

"And just what did you find?" queried Holmes as he crouched down to look the boy who had spoken, square in the eyes.

"Uh, uh…"

"We'z findz the bottlez, zir," spoke up the other of the two.

"Yes, sir. That'z right, we found the bottles," spoke the befuddled one.

"Wiggins?"

"Mr. Holmes, theze two stumbled across some broken bottles in an alley way 'bout 3 blocks from where youz told uz to look. They looked like wine bottles to me. But they hadz funny writing I'z never seen before.

"Here's one of them." Wiggins reach into a pouch he had slung around his shoulder. Out came a dark green wine bottle. The top had been broken off and there was no wine to be found except sticky dregs of the former occupant.

The stained and somewhat torn label read as follows:

Vino Tinto

1889

de la viña de

Carlos Gonzales
Blanco del Valle Augardiente
Colombia

"You say there were more?"

"Yez sir, three more just like this one. Top broken off and nothing inside."

"I need you to show me where you found these. Watson fetch our torches and let's be off as soon as possible. I'll hail a cab."

I immediately ran upstairs and grabbed the torches. By the time I returned, Holmes was all ready in the cab. Inside with us were Wiggins and the two youngsters. The remaining irregulars were hanging on the outside of the cab.

Wiggins' two were smiling from ear to ear. One or two hitching a ride on the back of a cab was one thing. Rarely did they get caught as they weighed so little, the cabbies couldn't tell they were carrying such light stowaways and the cabbies rarely saw them. They'd done that on many occasions. But riding *in* the cab was truly a treat neither of these boys ever imagined. The rest were hanging on all about the outside yelling and screaming aloud with excitement as Holmes had paid the cabbie extra for these legitimate leeches. Two were battling each other with sticks as if they were knights of old riding upon chariots or steeds.

We soon found ourselves at the end of a dark alley way. We disembarked and the other boys jumped off with hoots and hollers.

"You lads stay here while Dr. Watson and I search. How far down was it, Wiggins?" queried Holmes.

"T'waz about three doors down on the right, sir."

Holmes and I proceeded down the unlit alley. It was strewn with all sorts of trash from the day, especially the lighter materials with which the wind could bat around whichever way it desired. There were opened crates and discarded food. The smell was unpleasant, and the neighbourhood rats scurried as we approached their feeding ground outside a café, or so it seemed from the alley side. After passing the third door we found our sought-after treasure.

On the ground lay three more bottles just like the one Wiggins had shown to us.

"We have an odd case, Watson. Why open wine bottles in this fashion? Why allow the wine to fall to the ground?"

"Holmes?"

"Look, Watson. The contents are all over the ground. The wine has stained the stones and there remain puddles of it trapped in between them."

He moved his torch from side to side and the reflection of the reddish liquid sparkled in the darkness. The slight slope of the alley had allowed the wine to run farther away ahead of us. It would take a fresh rain to wash the remaining traces of it away.

I was looking in detail at the wine that had returned to the earth when Holmes turned and headed back to the cab. I quickly followed and soon caught up.

"Wiggins, is this all you found?"

"Well, sir, not exactly. You said furs uz toz looks for wine bottles, and wez did. We findz 'em."

"Yes, you did, and your reward is forthcoming." Holmes reached into his pocket and picked out two half crowns and flipped one to each of the younger boys who'd been arguing since we saw them at dinner.

"Thankz yuz sir!" they both said almost simultaneously.

"Now, what else did you find?"

"Jonesy, come here," commanded Wiggins.

"What?"

"I sez, come here!"

Reluctantly the young lad strode ever so slowly over to them carrying with him the stick he'd been sword fighting with his friend.

"Showz Mr. Holmes what you finded."

"I finded it and itz mine!" shouted Jonesy as he tried to hide the stick behind his back. It was taller than he, so its top stood out behind the back of his head. The crown of it appeared to be gold.

"May I see your stick, young sir," asked Holmes.

The lad said nothing and hesitated. Wiggins looked at him, nodded and mouthed to him "*go on, give it to him!*"

The youngster slowly brought it from around his back and handed it to Holmes.

He held in his hand a cane of a gentleman.

He brought the head of the cane up close to his eyes then handed it to me. I shone my torch upon it and read from it:

To XE from ÆE

Where did you find this, Jonesy?"

"By the wine bottles, sir. I was too late finding the bottles, but whilez theyz wuz looking for all ov 'dem, I'z findz this. And it'z mine!"

"I know it's yours," said Holmes.

"Would you like to sell it to me? I'll give you half a crown like the other lads?"

"Two crowns!"

"Jonesy, this is Mr. Holmes, not some mark out on the streetz. Don't playz gamez wid 'im."

"How about one crown, eh?"

"Tha'd be finz sir!"

Holmes reached in his pocket again and delivered a crown into the young boy's hand.

"Thank you all, lads. Here's a shilling each for the rest of you for trying to help me out."

He handed several more coins to Wiggins.

"Make sure they get something good to eat. Night lads."

"Thankz youz zir," was the chorus we heard from them all. We then headed back to Baker Street.

"Finally, we have clues and facts that we can use!" said Holmes excitedly. "I believe we have found our missing Sommelier's cane, eh, Watson?"

"Holmes, I agree with you," said I. "But, Holmes what does this mean?"

"Watson, at this point I believe our Mr. Everette was attacked, by a person or persons unknown. As to why, we have yet to find out. We must answer the questions of why were all the bottles broken? Where is Mr. Everette? Had he been murdered we'd have surely found his body. It is a queer case indeed."

Disembarking, we began the journey up the stairs to our rooms. As we got to the landing, there awaiting us was our landlady, Mrs. Hudson.

"Oh, Good day Mrs. Hudson," said I.

"Good day Doctor. A lady dropped this for you, Mr. Holmes. She said you would know what it was about."

She presented us with a package with a note attached.

"Thank you, Mrs. Hudson," said he without much fanfare. He took the package and continued upstairs. No further discourse with Mrs. Hudson was in Holmes' offering.

"We are on a case, Mrs. Hudson. You know how he gets when the chase is in progress."

"It's all right, Doctor. Yes, I know how he gets. Good luck on this one, whatever it's about."

By the time I entered, Holmes had already read the note and was opening the package. I picked up the note. It was on the stationary of a lady.

Mr. Holmes,

I have made enquiries and the meeting next Monday is to be held at the Café Royal on Regent Street. I have enclosed two pictures, as you requested, of my dearest Xavier. I do hope you find them useful. I am ever so grateful, Mr. Holmes, for your help find my husband.

Sincerely,
Alice Everette

"Watson, I believe our next enquiries are to the local hospitals and gaols. It will save time if we split up. I shall enquire at the local gaols, and I would ask that you check the hospitals. I am as familiar with the local lockups as you are with the hospitals.

"But, Holmes, I cannot wander around trying to see if each patient looks like our man."

"No, Watson, that is not what I would expect of you. I would, though, with your authority as a physician, ask that you simply inquire if any man has been treated or admitted showing signs of a struggle. Once you are able to find such persons, you can then compare him to the picture."

"Yes, yes of course. I believe that would work."

"If my thinking is correct, we should start with the closest sites to where the lads found his bottles and his cane. I would hope that he managed to get himself to hospital nearby, if he was in fact able to do so. Or perhaps some good person took pity on him after seeing he was in great difficulty."

"It would be to his great luck should the latter have happened," answered I.

"I will check the gaols in case perhaps he was picked up by a local constable much to the delight of our Inspector Lestrade. We will not hear the end of it from Lestrade if indeed he's been picked up for drunkenness. While that will no doubt be the charge, because he will likely have spilt wine on his person and attire, I doubt he will have drunk a drop. If beaten by his assailants, then his movements would likely be perceived as drunkenness by an inexperienced constable."

"I shall begin at St. Mary's, as I believe it was closest to the location at which we found his cane."

"Good, and I will visit the constables closest as well. Shall we say, return by half-past four o'clock?"

"Yes, I believe I can make it at least by then," said I.

"Let us begin then, Watson."

"I shall leave right away," replied I.

"Watson, don't forget the picture. Take it with you," admonished Holmes. I was so anxious to get started that I'd begun to leave before grasping the photograph out of his hand. I returned and took it. I hailed a cab and was off to hospital.

It had not been but a short while ago that I'd been to St. Mary's, having attended there a lecture on von Basch's invention[2] and some of the other newest advancements in my profession just a few months ago.

I made my way to the ward where the indigents were admitted and cared for. After introducing myself to the head nurse on duty, I explained I was looking for any gentleman admitted as recent as last Tuesday. Rather than adhering to Holmes' advice, I simple showed her the picture of Mr. Everette.

Unfortunately, she said she was quite sure there was no one in her care who matched his appearance or likeness. She offered me to stroll the ward if I cared to do so. I accepted her offer, but my venture produced no success.

I next went to Wellington and proceeded in the same manner. The head nurse there was less helpful than the one

---

[2] Editor's note: the 'invention' is the one Dr. Watson mentioned at the beginning of this tale, i.e. a *sphygmomanometer,* which is used by physicians to measure the relative pressure of the patient's circulating blood.

at St. Mary's. I was interrupting her scheduled duties and she saw no reason for her to change that schedule to help me find a lost man. I finally persuaded her to allow me to look for myself, as she had no time to even ponder the photograph.

I carefully strolled through the ward. Unsuccessful again, I bid her good day and left to find my way back to Baker Street. It was not reasonable to visit other hospitals, as they were too far away from where we found the cane and broken bottles.

Whence I returned, I found Holmes all ready smoking his clay pipe, with eyes closed, lounging on our sofa, no doubt in contemplation of our latest adventure. I chose not to disturb him and thus said nothing.

"What have you to report, Watson?"

"Ah, nothing, Holmes. No luck at all."

"I keep reminding you, Watson, it is not luck. It is like a hound dog who keeps sniffing and searching until it locates and corners its prey. Alas, I was not successful either."

"Tell me, where did you go after St. Mary's?"

"Wellington of course but had no lu… it was empty also."

"And what about Nightingale?"

"But, Holmes, Nightingale is a woman's hospital," retorted I.

"Watson, you do yourself injustice. Were you injured would you avoid help simply because the closest establishment is for women? I think not. You would be as practicable as possible and know that the necessary items for your care would be at the closest facility having them. You would ignore the protocols and seek help immediately."

"I suppose you are correct Holmes."

"Well, then shall we not return and see for ourselves if our lost man is hidden amongst a hospital full of women?!"

My investigations had seemed in such vain, I could not but agree to this off chance of Holmes' idea. I was somewhat desperate to find something of consequence for Holmes. I fought off my intuitive conclusion I had earlier arrived at, that he could not be there, but instead forced my reason that yes, Holmes could be correct, and that in such a state a man might enter the Nightingale Hospital to seek help.

We arrived and when asked about our presence at the establishment were sent to the head administrator's office.

"Gentlemen, I am Mrs. Harris, how may I help you?'

Holmes nodded in my direction and so I took the lead.

"I am Dr. John Watson. This is Mr. Sherlock Holmes."

Expecting a reaction at introducing Holmes, I paused. There was no response or inquiry from Mrs. Harris. It was as if she had never heard of Holmes.

"Uhm, we are looking for a gentleman, who was accosted nearby a few nights ago. He was likely severely beaten and if mobile, would have sought medical attention. Here is a photograph of him provided to us by his wife who has employed Mr. Holmes and me to find him. He has been missing for two days."

Mrs. Harris took the photograph from me with one hand while she lifted her glasses and put them on with her other hand.

"Yes, well we were wondering when someone might come calling for him. He has been in quite a state, mostly delirious or unconscious.

"Please, follow me."

We walked behind her as she led us down to the basement. In a small, damp, ill-lit, windowless room, we found Mr. Everette. He lay quietly as if asleep. He was heavily bandaged about his head and one eye was shut with swelling. His belongings were on a side table. A billfold, a gold pocket watch and gold key chain lay there undisturbed.

"How did he arrive here, Mrs. Harris?" queried Holmes.

"One of our nurses was reporting in for her night shift and found him stumbling out of an alleyway. She knew he needed immediate attention and helped him here. We attended to him as best we could that night. The next morning our doctor said, he'd likely survive but needed rest and care. Since there was no indication as to who he was, nor did he converse with us in any way, we felt it best we quarter him down here due to our normal patients not expecting there to be any men here. The staff talked it over and it was agreed that tomorrow we would arrange to have him transferred to St. Mary's, unless of course, he awoke and was able to leave on his own.

"It had occurred to us that by his dress, he had the appearance of a gentleman and it was likely someone would come looking for him."

As she spoke, I took his pulse and observed that the bandages had been placed in quite a professional manner.

"You and your staff have done well, Mrs Harris," said I.

"Thank you, Doctor."

"Now that we have found him, we shall arrange for his return to his home," said I.

We thanked Mrs. Harris and returned to Baker Street. Holmes wrote a quick note, and had it delivered to Mrs. Everette. She arrived shortly thereafter.

"Where is he?!" said she in a most excited voice.

"He is in hospital at the moment."

"Hospital!? Is he injured?"

I held out my hand and took hers. Guiding her to a chair, my other hand implored her to sit.

We then explained that we'd found him at Nightingales and that he was being cared for, but we must arrange for his transfer to St. Mary's. I did my best to reassure her that they had taken as good a care as was possible under the circumstances. She began to calm down knowing that her dear Xavier had been found and was alive but worried he was not conscious.

"Thank you, gentlemen, thank you, thank you!"

"It is not a problem, Mrs. Everette. Not a problem at all. It was our pleasure to help find your dear husband.

"I will come by tomorrow to hospital and check in on him if that is acceptable to you?" queried I.

"Yes, Dr. Watson. I insist!" And with that, she was off.

"Well, Holmes, another little adventure solved. Quite an easy one as it were."

"Hmm, perhaps it is as you say, Doctor. But I believe we've not seen the end of this one yet."

"What can you mean, Holmes? The man is found!"

"Yes, but there is one rather queer question that I haven't been able to answer yet?

"How can there be, we've done our job and found the missing man. What else is there?'

"Watson, if you accost a man, leave him for dead, break all his wine bottles open and leave a valuable cane, billfold, gold watch and key chain behind, what was the point of the attack?"

"Maybe they were interrupted?" offered I.

"I'll grant you that is possible, but I counter it is unlikely, not probable.

"No, there is something wrong with our little case. Much too easy, much too easy…"

Holmes muttered that phrase several more times as he sauntered to his room.

"Good night, Holmes," said I with a raised voice, attempting to gain a response, but he was all ready thinking of what he had postulated. There was something missing in this case.

The next few days were of no consequence with regards to our *solved* case. I must admit, dear readers, I began other endeavours and had thought that Holmes was too stuck on this case. While I agreed his question was difficult to answer, I was quite convinced my explanation was satisfactory.

We received a note from Mrs. Everette on Wednesday which stated that Mr. Everette had regained consciousness and was improving. She thanked us again and hoped that soon we would be available to meet her husband.

It was the next day that Holmes' concern about the case began to show up. There was a visitor at the door asking for me. I looked down the stairwell and saw that it was Mr. Tomes from the wine shop.

"Mr. Tomes, what brings you here sir?"

"Dr. Watson, I am confused and in need advice," replied he.

"Please come up and speak to both Mr. Holmes and me."

While he ascended, I went and awakened Holmes to our visitors' presence and that perhaps new information was to be given to us.

Holmes was not quite awake and had not coffee nor tea to spur him into a more focused attitude.

"I am quite sorry to intrude on you gentlemen so early this morning, but I am greatly confused," he began his story.

"Today a very unusual event occurred. I received another shipment of wine from Colombia."

"What is it that is so unusual about that fact, Mr. Tomes?" queried Holmes.

"I did not order it," answered Tomes.

"What's that you say?"

"Yes, I did not make but one order for Colombian wine."

"And the shipment you had received two weeks ago?"

"I checked my records and the order for Mr. Everette was correct, but I had not ordered any other shipments of that wine, nor any other from Colombia."

"I see…," pondered Holmes.

"Was this shipment the same wine or was it a different type or from a different vineyard?"

"Exactly the same, as far as I can tell."

"Do you have the bottles still?"

"Yes, my assistant was late this morning, has not arrived yet, so I received them myself and they are at my shop."

"Then what are we waiting for? We must go see them at once. Give Dr. Watson and me a moment to dress and we shall go back with you post haste."

We both dressed and were down to the curb in as fast a time as I can recall. Tomes had a carriage waiting and we tumbled in and making a quick trip back to his shop.

The shop was still locked and empty. There was nothing amiss, thankfully. Tomes took us to his back room and showed us the unopened crate. After a few moment's discussion, Holmes took the crowbar used for un-crating and opened the mysterious shipment.

There we found four bottles of Colombian wine. The labels confirmed that they were from the same vineyard and winery as the previous ones. Holmes retrieved one of the bottles and walked out the back door of the shop.

"Yes!" cried he loudly.

"What is it Holmes?"

"The answer to the whole mystery, Doctor."

"What answer?"

"All shall be made clear soon, Watson.

"Mr. Tomes, I would like to purchase this wine from you."

"But sir, it's not mine and as I have already paid the invoice for the original shipment, there was no invoice for this one."

"How long has your assistant, Eddington isn't it, been with you, Mr. Tomes?"

"Eddington? He started six months ago."

"What do you know of him?"

"He is quite valuable to me. He was born to English parents while his father was a High Commissioner in British Guiana. His experiences afford him the ability to speak, read and write several languages. This has proved invaluable to me as my customers have for the last few years been interested in what they believe to be *exotic* wines from other parts of the world, not unlike Mr. Everette's order."

"What do you mean, '*believed to be exotic*'?" queried I.

"Oh, Doctor, I do not wish to be disingenuous. Most of my customers do not know that the grapes of the Americas are, in reality, originally from Europe. There are a few that are natural to the new world, but most were simply transported there by emigrants out of Europe. The soils in which they now thrive are different, but in many ways, similar to those here and on the continent, but differences do occasionally produce flavours somewhat unique than those grown on this side of the Atlantic. But having said all that, they are still the same grapes as are grown in Europe."

"And the wine, Mr. Everette ordered?" queried Holmes.

"Ah, originally from South America. He, being a sommelier, knew that most new world wines originated in Europe, but in this case, he told me he wished to educate his wine butlers on something not from Europe."

"Where is Eddington, now?" asked Holmes.

"I do not know. He is usually quite prompt, and on the occasions when he has been ill, he has sent word by now."

"Do you attend these gatherings that Mr. Everette has with the wine butlers?" enquired Holmes.

"Yes, on occasion. I planned to attend this upcoming one since Xavier was to expound on the Colombian wine.

"Was that not planned for this coming Monday night?" asserted Holmes.

"Yes, you are correct. But with Xavier in such a state, I would think it would be postponed. I have not yet been able to speak to him about it."

"I think a visit to the Everette residence is in order, would you accompany us, Mr. Tomes?"

"What am I to do with the shop? Without Eddington to attend to it I must decline."

"All right, I see. And the wine?"

"Help yourself, Mr. Holmes."

Holmes gathered up the small crate and we left the shop. We returned to Baker Street where Holmes relocated the wine.

"Watson, I am off to visit the Everettes. I would ask that you will keep watch on our newest acquisition. I am fairly confident we have absconded with it without being observed. Your life is more valuable than our treasure, so defend it not with your life should such an event manifest itself while I am gone, but I implore you not to let it out of your sight, if possible. Understood?"

"Yes, Holmes, but what is this all about?"

"Monday night shall reveal all, if my plan should work as I would wish. Don't wait for me. But do not leave for dinner. The crate must not be abandoned between now and Monday night. I will, in fact, leave word and extra coin for Mrs. Hudson to cook you something special tonight.

"I must be off." And with that Holmes had left our rooms and me with a strange crate full of Colombian wine, or so I thought.

The night passed uneventfully, and Holmes returned about eight o'clock.

"How did you find Mr. Everette?" queried I.

"Conscious, but quite worse for the wear. His memory is like a sponge of the events that took place. There are holes in all that happened that evening. He claims the last he remembers is walking home. Being accosted by someone. Yelling for help and then awaking at Nightingale's. He is sore and in pain. Time is all that will help him at this point."

"Can he not identify his assailants?"

"He claims not. It was twilight and he said his eyes are not quite what they used to be. No doubt from closely looking at numbers all day long.

"He intends to go to the meeting on Monday and while I recommended that he not, I cannot prevent him.

"We must, though, be present. I expect a final solution to our case, Watson. You will come, will you not?"

"Of course, Holmes," confirmed I.

"Yes, well then, I've had these flyers printed and have gotten the Irregulars to place them around. It should hopefully bait our prey into turning up as well."

WINE TASTING
MONDAY NIGHT — 7.30 PM

COME TASTE WINE FROM
COLOMBIA!

£ 1 ENTRY FEE

CAFÉ ROYAL ON REGENT STREET

"I do not understand, Holmes. Why are you advertising the existence of the wine? It can only cause more trouble, shall it not? And a pound?"

"We are laying a trap, Watson. I am confident it will be sprung. We do not want anyone, but only those would be willing to spend a whole pound to retrieve what they believe to be theirs."

No more came from his mouth on the subject. The next few days were unsettling to me as I awaited the outcome of Monday evening's events.

Finally, the time came, and we arrived at the restaurant with the wine in tote. We entered the salon off the main lobby and were soon joined by others who no doubt knew each other and had been members of this elite little club for some time. There were a few strangers who asked to whom should they pay their pound. No one seemed to know, so they placed their money back in their pockets for safe keeping.

Soon, Mr. and Mrs. Everette arrived. Mr. Everette was in a rolling chair being pushed by Eddington, who I recognized from my experience at the wine shop.

The wine butlers immediately gathered around Mr. Everette. They were all excited in their comments of joy and relief at hearing he had survived his misadventure of a fortnight ago.

Holmes remained aloof and stood close to the crate of wines. I was sure he was not going to allow his bait to disappear while distractions abounded around us.

No other guests arrived by 7.30. It was decided amongst all to perhaps wait a few more minutes before beginning. But by 7.45 still no one else had joined the event.

"Shall we not begin, Mr. Holmes?" Xavier said pleadingly looking at Holmes.

"Yes, please do," answered Holmes.

"All, I thank you for your care and concern for my wellbeing. You are true friends.

"Tonight, we embark on a new adventure by exploring wines not of European origin. We have a red wine from Colombia. I want each of you to experience it, write down your impressions and we will then share our thoughts together. Please, Eddington, will you open the bottles, decanter them and let them air for a few moments."

Eddington looked concerned about this request. He hesitated. He then approached the bottles and retrieved one from the crate. He removed the wax and inserted a corkscrew into the cork. He twisted and then uncorked the bottle. He looked nervous the entire time.

Finally, he began to slowly pour the wine into the decanter at a rate as perhaps a child would who did not understand how to pour such liquid between containers. The longer it took the more anxious he looked. When the contents had been fully evacuated from the bottle he was exasperated.

"What!" yelled he. He took the bottle and held it up to the lights of the chandelier. A surprised look came over him and he reached for the remaining bottles, holding each up to the light.

"*Maldición!*" he cried out.

"Perhaps this is what you are looking for?" queried Holmes as he reached into his vest pocket and pulled out four long, thin, reddish, stick-like objects. They were no thicker than my thumb and perhaps eight to ten inches in length.

"You! Give me those! Those are mine!" yelled Eddington as he lunged towards Holmes.

Suddenly two of the larger wine butlers caught him and restrained him.

"I shall not give it to you, for I bought that wine from Mr. Tomes just the other day."

"Inspector!" cried out Holmes. "Glad you could join us."

I turned to look behind me and there indeed was Lestrade. His countenance was frustrated as he realized once again Sherlock had done his job for him. He came up to the two oversized wine butlers and spoke to them with familiarity.

"Make sure that one doesn't get loose from you now."

"Yes, sir, Inspector," said they together, confirming my just realized suspicion that Holmes had convinced Lestrade to offer the assistance of having two of his burlier constables play the roles of wine butlers at the event.

Holmes then went over to a table and sat down. All followed him over and surrounded the table to see what it was he was about to reveal.

He took a cardinal red napkin and unfurled it. He laid it out square and flat upon the table. He then laid out the four sticks upon the napkin.

He next took out a pocketknife and cut one of them in the middle. It was then I could see they were tubes made of a reddish wax not unlike that used to seal the bottles. Inside they were white.

Holmes took his *minimus manus*[3] and with its slightly extended nail, scooped out a small amount of a white powder from inside the tube. He then lifted it to his mouth and licked it slightly.

"Just as I thought," commented Holmes.

"Cocaine!" blurted out the Inspector.

"Yes, Inspector. Quite good quality if I may say."

"Eddington Marshall, I am arresting you on the charge of smuggling illegal substances into Her Majesty's Kingdom. Take him away."

"And if you don't mind, Mr. Holmes, I'll be taking the evidence as well."

"Certainly, Inspector." Holmes grabbed the four corners

---

[3] Editor's note: Dr. Watson's use of the medical term, *minimus manus* (sometimes *mi'nimus ma'nus)* is a physician's terminology for one's 'little' or '*pinky*' finger.

of the napkin and handed the entire lot to Lestrade. Lestrade turned and was walking out when Holmes said to him in a low voice, "You're welcome, Inspector."

Lestrade turned and looked over his shoulder.

"I am not deaf, Mr. Holmes." He then turned and walked out.

I looked a Holmes. I was doing my best to restrain from chuckling out loud, but Holmes smirked as perhaps only I could observe having known him as long as I have.

"Well, that certainly seems to have solved your adventure, now," said I.

"I believe you are correct Watson."

"Oh, Mr. Holmes what is to happen to poor Eddington?" said Mrs. Everette.

"I would not waste much empathy on him, Mrs Everette. I believe the truth, when all is known, will reveal it was 'poor Eddington' who attacked your husband."

"What? Why on earth would such a nice young man do such a thing?"

"Mrs. Everette, that nice young man is a dealer in cocaine. This small shipment was likely only a sample. But never-the-less, he would have killed to get that substance. There is money to be made trading in this illegal substance. He practically did kill your husband save for the luck that he was found in time by a good soul. Once he gets his buyers addicted, it is a very difficult drug to refrain from using."

"Oh, Mr. Holmes, I didn't understand."

"I recommend you now take Xavier home and tend to him as I am confident you will. I am sure he will recover with your nursing him back to good health."

"Thank you, Mr. Holmes, again thank you too, Dr. Watson. Good night."

"Holmes, you said it was luck he survived.?"

"Yes, that was luck, Watson."

"How did you know that it was Eddington?"

"I wasn't sure, except that he was a possible suspect as it had to be someone who knew what the bottles contained. It could have been Tomes just as well. As you know Doctor, I have dabbled with the substance and it is quite alluring. But for my mental powers that advise me when enough is enough, I should likely be in the same trouble as the customers of that young man.

"I made inquiries about how the substance I obtain for my own use, only on occasion, as you know, is secreted into the country and from whence it originates. Once that was known and I'd seen the sticks in the bottles when we inspected them, it was clear that whoever accosted Mr. Everette was, in fact, looking for the cocaine. That's why the bottles were broken open on the spot, but no robbery of personal items took place. All that was wanted was the drug.

"The mix up about shipments and then that young Eddington had lived in the part of the world where the plants that produce such drugs are grown and thus so readily available, I concluded he'd been exposed when growing up there and once back here could not resist importing it. He became the prime suspect, but it could have been any addict in the area. All that was needed was to force him to expose himself for the crime.

"Lestrade might be upset with my remark, but now that he's collared a drug importer, he'll receive praise at the Yard. I think in the end, he'll let bygone be bygones and come asking for assistance from me sooner than later."

"Holmes, I believe you are correct, sir. Shall we now retire, eh? This evening has been quite exhausting."

THE ADVENTURE AT OSBORNE HOUSE

May seemed to come early that year. If asked, I would have sworn March had just begun. The year was racing forward.

I had been quite occupied during the late winter and early spring months as a virulent illness had infected half the city. The bad news was that nearly everyone had either been afflicted with it or at least had been nursing someone who had it.

I saw many a patient with the disease and was surprised that I did not contract it myself. My constant exposure to such ailments likely has kept me safe, as my body has been exposed to so much over the years. Having accepted Koch's postulates regarding the causes of such outbursts of disease as being the result of microscopic bacterial attacks upon the body and their transmission to others around them, I was sure this was yet another of these type infections, but the actual microscopic culprit was as yet unidentified. While I knew several of my contemporary practitioners had yet to be convinced of Koch's claims, I myself had seen enough to convince me he was on the correct path of defining these diseases for what they really are.

They were not the result of '*miasma*'[4], no! Our bodies were being invaded by unwelcome creatures too small to be seen without a microscope! These 'bacteria' had been making people ill since the beginning of time and now, finally, we saw them for what they were! Invaders! Parasites! Wanting nothing more than to infest and feast on our bodies so that they might live at our expense!

---

[4] Editor's note: Dr. Watson is referring to the commonly held belief, at this time, that disease was caused by 'bad air' (*miasma*). His acceptance of Robert Koch's postulates of bacterial infection, published in 1890, places him in the category of modern physicians, accepting of the new discoveries in the advancing field of medical science in the late nineteenth century.

There were not many deaths, though, which was the good news. Only some of the very old, who had not retained their strength, and a few of the very youngest, with underdeveloped capacity or so I speculated, were unable to fight off these attacks, and thus succumbed to it. In the end, I accepted these unpleasant outcomes as the way nature had always dealt with this unending battle between these single-celled organisms and our multi-celled bodies. I thanked heaven I'd not had any of my patients lose either an elder or infant. The emotional pain of losing a person to such selfish little creatures has never been acceptable to me. London was now beginning to return to normal, as the last of those who succumbed to it were laid to rest.

After seeing my final patient for the week, I decided to visit Holmes, as my wife had left the city a few weeks back to avoid the illness. She was to return on Monday. I sent her a telegram of my visit to Baker Street should she change her mind and come home, only to find me missing.

When I arrived again at 221B Baker Street, it was if I had never left. I experienced a hearty greeting by Mrs. Hudson. She had aged a bit more and her hearing had become a bit worse. We chatted as she prepared a cuppa and we ate a few biscuits. She reminisced about the many times she had called up to tell Holmes, and me, of a visitor.

She said she had even done so just this morning, but she got no answer from him. The lady requesting him said she would return, and try to reach him once more before she left London tomorrow.

I felt sure Holmes was out and about town now, as he usually was when on a case. But Mrs. Hudson confounded me by saying he rarely left his rooms these days. On the other hand, it was possible he was out obtaining a few necessities that he could not obtain otherwise. Since he had not left word with Mrs. Hudson, there was indeed no telling when he might return. It could be at any minute, or more worrisome to me, it might be several days from now.

After we finished our tea, biscuits and catching up, I asked would she mind letting me wait for Holmes upstairs.

She readily agreed and thought that the jolt that Mr.

Holmes would get, when entering and finding me there, was one with which she wished to surprise him and wished she could witness his reaction.

She offered to let me in, but I confessed to her that I still had my old key and that if it didn't trouble her, I would let myself in, saving her the effort of climbing the stairs.

Her agreement was immediate. She told me her knees were not what they once were. They were "worn down by life" she said.

No doubt she was correct, as I had discovered in my practice, that many of my older patients seemed to constantly be complaining of a plethora of aches and pains all brought on by the joints and muscles worn out over a lifetime. It was if our bodies were like carriages. They start off new, freshly springing down the roads and providing a jolly good ride. But after years of use and traveling on too many unsound roads, the bumpy journeys shake the parts and pieces so that they become loose and then slowly, they start creaking and groaning when put to use, making even short trips most uncomfortable.

Upon entering, I had the impression that Holmes had not bothered with my desk and easy-chair since my departure. My deduction by observation from the door was confirmed when I walked over and placed my hand on my desk. I brushed it swiftly and found on my fingers a thick layer of dust.

I went and ensconced myself in my old chair. Lying next to it was the morning edition of today's Times. By this, I concluded that Holmes had been here earlier in the day, but had left before his lady visitor had arrived. Knowing Holmes' habits, I then thought it likely that he would soon return.

Feeling quite at home, I returned to reading the paper. In a few moments I felt as though I had travelled back in time. The feel of the room, the easy-chair with the paper in my hands brought back the most wonderful memories.

After indulging in these feeling from the past, I began reading and soon was engulfed in the stories. The burden of my patients' visits had left little time for reading the papers. For the last few weeks I had returned home but was too tired to partake of my favourite pastime.

So, while I read, I dozed off. For it was not until morning that I awoke.

"Doctor! It is a joy to see you," said Holmes.

"Holmes! You are back. Oh, my good friend, the joy is all mine! Oh, my! It seems I've slept the night away, I'm afraid. It's been quite tiresome these last few weeks with all this illness about. How are you?"

Holmes shrugged, smiled and retrieved his pipe.

"What have you been working on lately? Oh, I do miss our adventures together!"

"Nothing of late, unfortunately. A fortnight ago, I was brought in to solve the theft of several gems down Hatton Garden way, but it was an easy case. I'd have sent word for you to join me, but it was over before you'd have been able to do so.

"Working on a new monograph. This one is on haptic communication. I feel it will help in situations where the spoken word is not sufficient when dealing with another party, be they client, victim or perpetrator."

"Will you again allow me to be the first to read it, as you have done before?"

"Certainly, Doctor, I would much appreciate your comments. No doubt, it is an important method used in your practice, and thus you are a perfect reviewer of my exploration of this form of communication."

"Will it be ready soon?"

"In a week perhaps, if I do not become engaged otherwise."

"Excellent, then. I look forward to reading it, Holmes."

It was just then that we heard the bell at the front door and Mrs. Hudson answering it.

To say that Sherlock was anxious for a new case, might be too extreme, but he did appear to me to be more than excited at the prospect of an adventure which would challenge his mind.

He opened our door out to the stairwell and shouted down to Mrs. Hudson, "Please send them up, Mrs. Hudson."

"Right away, sir," she replied. We heard her instruct the person to ascend the stairs and that Mr. Holmes would see them.

"Good morning, Madame…?" greeted Holmes, as she

alit from the last step. "Please come in, sit down and let me understand your problem."

She moved towards our door but had not said a word yet. After passing over the threshold, she looked about the ill-kempt room and soon decided to move over to the couch, that is, once she saw that I had cleared away the discarded newspapers of the morning that had laid claim to the only spot in the whole room that she could sit down in a lady-like manner.

As she looked at me and then back to Holmes, Holmes immediately spoke as if on cue.

"Please let me introduce my associate, Dr. Watson."

"How do you do, Miss…?" said I.

It was the second attempt of both of us to have her explain to us who she was. But again, there was no reply. No helpful statement of her name came forth, following our inquiring and hesitating 'Madame and Miss…?'.

She sat and continued to take in the room's surroundings. Perhaps she was debating in her own mind if this decision to seek out Holmes' help was such a good idea after all. No doubt, what she expected to encounter and what she was now experiencing were apparently two different things. In any case, she appeared to be truly observing the room, not just looking around it.

This, I am sure, caught Holmes' attention. He sat down in his chair opposite her and studied her as she studied the room. When she finished absorbing the room, she began to stare at Holmes in the most peculiar fashion.

"You are indeed a most fascinating visitor, Madame. I am afraid that we are not communicating well enough yet for me to help you. I can tell you are approximately one score and ten, are married, and most likely paint watercolours on a regular basis.

"Without further communication, verbally that is, I am not sure that I can help solve the very troubling situation in which you find yourself and for which you have sought out my advice."

"How do you know dese dings about me?" queried the woman in English with a heavy German accent.

"And you are from, perhaps, either Munich or Vienna, is that not correct?" continued Holmes.

"*Mein Gott*, you are a mind reader! How is dis done?"

"I, as you, observe the world around me, just like what you have been doing. So, in the same way you have learned about me, by observing my abode and studying my face and features. Only someone who truly observes the world around them does what you have done.

"I also looked at your hands, Madame, and I see the darkened cuticles of your fingernails that betray your use of water colours. I determine you do so frequently, as there are not too many women in London who would allow themselves to be in public with such stains upon their fingers. I conclude your passion for the art is such that you have accepted it as a price you must pay to perform it. The discolouration has become habit to you and your passion to paint has overcome any idea on your part to cover or spend time cleaning them more than you have today. Vanity is not your vice."

"You are quite obserwant. I dink you are de man to help me."

"I think it wise, at this point, Madame, that we should know your name, eh?"

"Certainly, *Herr* Holmes. My name is Josefine Swoboda *und, ja,* I am vrom Austria."

"I see. It is a pleasure to meet you, Mdm. Swoboda. This is my colleague, Dr. Watson. He has accompanied me on many of my cases and is known for his discretion."

"*Ja,* I mean, yes, I have read of his adwentures vith you, so I know he vill be ov help.

"Vell, I cannot find my brooder, Rudolf. I sent him a note vor us to meet, but it could not be deliwered. I vent to my brooder's house but could not raise him. His door vas locked. De curtains vere drawn. He is no vhere to be vound. Dat is not like him at all. I did not know vhat to do. I vent to de poleez *und* dey vrote a report. But dat does not help me. I must vait, dey say.

"Dey suggest you can help sooner, and I dink I must see *Herr* Holmes."

"Might you have a picture of Rudolf?" queried Holmes

"*Ja.*"

She opened her bag and pulled out a small sepia of her brother. He was a handsome man, apparently close in age, maybe older, to Holmes' newest client.

"May I keep this?"

"*Ja, Herr* Holmes."

"Vhat do you adwise me to do next?" asked she.

"Please write down your brother's address. Also please provide me with an address at which I can contact you. I will do so as soon as I can. Is there anything else you think I should know? For example, does your brother have any enemies? In what business is your bother, by the way?"

"*Herr* Holmes, ve are bod artists - painters. He has no enemies dat I know about. You must vind him, *Herr* Holmes, please, ja, yes?"

"I will do all I can, Mdm. Swoboda."

With that assurance Holmes' newest client rose, bowed slightly to both of us and headed for the door. I proceeded her there and opened it for her.

"Until we meet again, Madame."

"Dank you, Doctor Vatson. Gootbye."

"Holmes, this would seem a simple case. What have you planned all ready?"

"I intend to visit the brother's abode and see what there is to know about him. Has he left on his own? Was there a struggle? There shall be clues abundant, if we but observe them. That is my first move. Shall you accompany me?

"I take it you will make entry without permission, if necessary. Am I correct?"

"Watson, I know you disapprove of these technicalities concerning the law. You have accompanied me before, have you not?"

"Yes, Holmes, but that was years ago. I'm much more established now. I cannot afford to be caught breaking the law! What would my patients think? And Mary, why Holmes, I would never hear the end of it! It would embarrass her to no end, should I be hauled off to gaol by some constable for 'breaking and entering' tonight.

"While the fondness of my memories of our past

adventures says to me, 'go', I must refrain and tell you, that, 'no', I cannot."

"Watson, it is of no mind. I understand your situation. This of course is only one reason I have chosen to remain in the unmarried state. A wife would never do. How could I perform my services at all hours of the day or night? Certainly, I could not but concern myself with her safety while out on such cases, especially should the adversary with whom I was challenging at any given time, knew a wife of mine to be home, sitting vulnerable to their wishes. It is as the Chinese say, 'man who chases two rabbits, catches neither'. One cannot profess to be the world first and best consulting detective and simultaneously be the full partner as one should be to one's spouse, which I know you are to Mary.

"Besides, the things of which women spend their time on, are of no interest to me, unless it somehow pertains to a case. I would bore a woman to death, I suppose. And to be quite honest, unless they are in some trouble, as my new client is, I find them quite boring, in general."

I then thought to myself 'What about, Irene? Would you speak of her this way?'

There was only silence. I should not have thought these thoughts, but his short pontification regarding remaining a bachelor, his belittling of the fairer sex, and the backhanded attack at least as I took it though he might not've meant it, upon my dear Mary, provoked me no doubt.

"Sorry, Holmes. I will have to decline your offer. But I will assist you as best I can. Perhaps I could stand guard and alert you should you suddenly need to take cover? Will that not be of any help?"

"Yes, that will do fine. Let us catch some lunch. We can then retire back to Baker Street and rest up for the night's adventure. What say you to that?"

"That sounds good, Holmes."

Our discussion turned to the latest cases Holmes had been involved with, but to which I was not privy. Were I now to digress into describing those solitary adventures that Holmes conveyed to me, I fear I would not do them justice, my dear readers, having not participated directly in them. I shall attempt, at a later date, to memorialize the tales he told me. It will take my further quizzing him for some time to extract all the details to satisfy your curiosity.

We waited until midnight before we left Baker Street. Each of us grabbed a torch and Holmes his set of *locksmith's* keys.[5]

The night was cool and the breeze while on our ride, invigorating. Our carriage took us several blocks from our ultimate destination per Holmes' request. The streetlamps were lit, and we had little trouble finding our way to her brother's residence.

He apparently was a successful artist, as his house, while small, was in a pleasant part of London. The entrance faced east and was a half story up from the street level. All the other houses only had windows facing east, and in the rear, windows facing to the west. The modest style was similar to those up and down the lane, except that his house was on a corner. This allowed there to be a whole additional side to the home with windows facing northward, no doubt chosen to provide excellent light for performing his art as a painter. Walking around further, we gained a glimpse of the house from the alleyway on the west side. It was only the south side that was windowless as it shared a common wall with the adjoining house.

We went to the alleyway and found a gate into the rear garden of the house. We looked each way and saw no one. I stood guard there as Holmes, ever so gently and nearly silently, lifted the unlocked latch. The old rusty hinges creaked loudly in the dead silence of the night. I decided staying here would not do as a sufficient lookout post, since I could not see the front or side of the house. I thought that a position across the street would be a better spot, so that I could observe both the east and north sides simultaneously.

"Holmes," whispered I, "if I flash my torch into the north bay window, that will be our signal to conceal yourself."

---

[5] Note: I have chosen this description, should this particular tome ever be published. To describe them otherwise would perhaps implicate Holmes in possessing illegal instruments. These were, in fact, those 'tools' which he had acquired over his lengthy career, having encountered, and in some cases, befriending, some of the more unsavoury elements of London's citizenry - *JHW*

"That should do fine, I shall keep my eye out for it."

With that he was gone from my sight. Closing the gate, I hoped no alarm would come from its aching cries.

I walked over and soon took my position, finding a less than well-lit spot to station myself.

Our luck was not with us at that moment, as no sooner had I secreted myself in the dark shadows of a large tree, than a constable, upon his beat, could be heard coming my way. The neighbourhood was silent but for the crisp clack of the constable's boots as he approached me.

Rather than have him discover me in the shadows at this ungodly hour, and have him become overly curious at my behaviour, I decided on a more assertive move to make my presence a bit more reasonable. Going on the offence seemed like the right course of action to me.

"Thank God you are here, Constable!"

"Why sir, I did not see you. What is it?"

"I am a doctor and I have been called to attend someone, but I appear to have gotten myself lost. Would you happen to know where this address is?" queried I.

I showed him the slip of paper we had received from Mdm. Swoboda with the address on it.

"Why certainly, sir. You're practically there all right. The house is just across the street."

"That is wonderful," said I.

"Let's go get you in there."

Before I could stop him, he had crossed the street and was walking up to the short steps leading to the front door.

"I say, Constable, you may wish to stay back. I cannot guarantee this is not a case of that illness that has been visiting the city."

"Yes. Well, sir. I hope there is nothing so serious as that in there. But you think it might be more of it?"

"It may be. You've helped me find the house, I am grateful for your assistance, but I would be unkind to not warn you, should it be such a case."

"Yes, sir. I'll be back to my rounds then, sir, if you don't mind," said he, in a grateful tone that I had saved him from possible exposure.

"Not at all, Constable. Again, thank you for your help."

"My pleasure, sir," said he, as he quickly came back down the steps and was on his way again.

I had no choice but to make use of the brass lion's head knocker on the door, as I would have done so, had my visit been a real one.

Holmes must have been a bit startled at first, but he was able to see it was me when he looked through a side lite to the door. He opened the door enough for me to enter and I was in.

"You have changed your mind, Doctor?"

"I had no choice, having been spotted by one of London's finest."

"Well, you are in now. We shall make this quick. My study of Constables and their routes tells me in general we have roughly thirty minutes before he will pass this way again. My watch says it is 12.38. Let us be done by 1.00, 1.05 at the latest and we shall be gone before he returns."

"That is fine with me, Holmes. I do not wish to be brought before a magistrate this morning."

That being settled, I pursued helping Holmes as I had on our many previous adventures. We turned our torches on to reveal what lay hidden in the darkened house. As best we could tell, so far, it was without occupants.

Being at the foyer, we studied it quickly, but with no results. All appeared in order. Next, we turned our backs to the front door and climbed the staircase to the second floor. Here there were two sleeping chambers. Between was a newly apportioned toilet room with a commode, a lavatory and a silver clawfoot bathtub. There was nothing amiss in there.

One bedroom appeared to have been recently used as we found a poorly made up bed and some night clothes draped over the foot of it. The door of the dark wooded armoire was ajar. When Holmes opened it fully, we saw a reasonable amount of clothing for man such as Mdm. Swoboda's brother.

The second room was apparently for guests, as it was in pristine condition with nothing appearing out of place.

Next, we returned to the first floor and visited the kitchen. Again, nothing appeared disturbed but for a cup, saucer and dinner plate, with a fork and spoon upon it, that appeared to have been set down on the sideboard next to the sink without violence. Holmes inspected the leftover crumbs and merely said softly, "Breakfast".

Our next stop was to the studio which was in the parlour. The strong odour of the linseed from the oil paints used there, which I had noticed upon entering the house, was much stronger now but pleasant to my olfactory nerve.

"Watson, the clues present themselves like a thunderstorm shouting out its coming towards one. Look and we see that he was clearly interrupted and likely has been kidnapped."

"How so, Holmes?"

"Observe, Watson, the painting first. A fine landscape in the making. But better yet, the paint brushes."

"I smell the fresh paint and see their colours match that which is on the canvas. But, Holmes, that is to be expected," countered I. "There is no mystery about that."

"Watson, any painter uses his or her tools as an extension of his or her body. They care for their tools as one does one's own hands. Do you not give such great care to your instruments in your surgery? Look at these brushes again. What do you see?"

"Ah, yes. They are filled with paint."

"Yes! Had Herr Swoboda left of his own accord, he'd have cleaned them thoroughly so as to not ruin the bristles. You can tell these are the finest brushes, as their handles bear the *Bechhofen* name. They are German made and I believe, considered by most artists, to be the best in the world today.

"This clue alone tells me he did not leave here willingly."

We flashed our torches about the room and quickly saw two more paint-clogged brushes several feet away on the floor, further establishing Holmes' conclusion.

I checked my watch and found we had exhausted our time and had failed to leave as we'd agreed. It was 1.12 and our departure without witness was in jeopardy.

"Holmes, shall we not check the basement?"

"I have seen enough to convince me he left unwillingly. But you are correct, I shall check it myself. I'll meet you at the back door."

Holmes departed downstairs, and in a few moments had returned. He shook his head and said to me, "Nothing."

We exited. Holmes relocked the door with his 'tools'. We departed through the rear garden gate as we had come.

Next, we rounded the corner of the alley and were heading east along the northside of the house. In the dead of the night, I again heard the clacking of the approaching Constable's boots upon the pavement.

In a moment, he was in view and Holmes, ever cognizant of our predicament, suddenly grabbed my shoulder and feigned weakness. I immediately grabbed him as one would a weakened soul, assisting his every step.

"Doctor, do you need help?" queried the constable.

"No, but, thank you, sir. I recommend you keep your distance, as my patient here is in need of hospital. I am quite sure he has the scourge.

"I intend to get to the main road and there, hail a cab."

"At least let me go ahead and do so for you," offered he.

"Quite grateful, if you would please?" answered I.

He began to trot to help us more quickly with our journey. He no doubt encountered the cab that Holmes had paid to remain for us and persuaded them to 'assist a doctor and his patient'.

We embarked and thanked the constable profusely. Holmes kept his head down and obscured his face as best he could. For by now, his interaction with Scotland Yard and many of the local constabularies had occurred often enough, that many of London's finest knew him by sight. The enthusiasm and youthful appearance of the constable led me to the conclusion that he was rather new to the force and perhaps not as familiar with the great detective as others might have been, but I knew that in no time at all, he would be. Our behaviour sought to delay his acquaintance of Holmes at least until their next encounter.

We finally escaped, and before long, were back in our warm and familiar rooms at 221B Baker Street.

The next morning, Holmes immediately sent word to Mdm. Swoboda. As we waited for her reply, we enjoyed a hearty breakfast prepared by Mrs. Hudson.

While at first, I felt my presence was a burden to her and told her so, she assured me that it was not. In fact, she said preparing such a breakfast for the two of us brought back good memories of when I resided there with Holmes.

We finished and were reading the morning editions when there was a ring of the bell below. Soon we heard footstep coming up the stairs.

I grabbed the papers and our finished meal and placed them in my old room so as to make all a bit more presentable to our visitor.

The knock on the door was light, but firm. I opened our door to find our latest client. There was an anxiousness to her face.

"Please come in, Mdm. Swoboda."

"I receive your note *und* came right avay. I vas coming myself, because I received dis note late yesterday' night. I could not sleep."

She handed the note to Holmes. It took him longer to read than I would have expected. It wasn't 'til he handed it to me that I understood why he took so long.

Befolgen Sie diese Anweisungen genauestens! Sonst stirbt dein Bruder - das ist ein Versprechen!

Wenden Sie sich nicht an die Polizei oder Scotland Yard - wir haben dort Augen und Ohren und werden wissen, ob Sie es tun.

Sagen Sie uns Bescheid, wenn Sie das nächste Mal nach Osborne House fahren. Sie tun dies, indem Sie eine persönliche Nachricht in die Times eintragen, in der Sie angeben, dass Sie Mr. Jones am Tower treffen und das Datum angeben möchten. Wir werden dann wissen, wann Sie ankommen

Sobald Sie dort sind, werden Sie kontaktiert.

WIEDER KEINE POLIZEI!

I could not translate it fast enough. My German was a bit rusty from my days back at Barts, as many of the newest medical journals, I frequently read nowadays, had begun being translated into English, especially the German articles.

All I could quickly discern was the obvious warning of 'No Police'. I placed the note aside and continued to listen to this woman's fascinating tale.

"As you can see, it varns me not to contact de poleez.

I den remembered one of your stories, Doctor. I dink you and *Herr* Holmes helped find a kidnapped man. Vell, is dat my problem, *Herr* Doctor?

"You are correct, Mdm. Swoboda. We visited your brother's house last night. Thankfully, there were no signs of violence, but certainly we think he left unwillingly," Holmes reported to her.

"So, dey have kidnapped my brooder *und* have dreatened to kill him should I not cooperate. Ja?"

"Yes, that is the gist of it."

"Oh *Herr* Holmes, vhat must I do now?"

"Before I answer that, I am in need of some more information. Could you please tell me why the note mentions your next visit to Osborne House? What business have you there?"

"Dat is vhere I paint quite often."

"And just what is it that you paint there?"

"I paint portraits of Her Majesty and dose of her vamily."

"Now the pieces of this, what do they call them now, eh Watson…?"

"Jigsaw puzzles?"

"Yes, now the jigsaw puzzle pieces fit together!

"Mdm. Swoboda perhaps had you revealed this fact earlier we'd have gotten here much sooner. But it is of no concern now. We have quite a case, hey, Watson?"

"You vill still help me den, *Herr* Holmes?"

"*Ja, ich werde dir helfen, Madame*," said Holmes.

"*Oh, danke, vielen danke!*"

If one were observant, one could see that the weight the woman had been carrying on her shoulders had been lifted quite a bit, even if for a short while. Her posture became more erect and I even saw a small smile appear for an instant on her face. Holmes had finally given her hope and at this point, that was enough to sustain her, I concluded.

"I shall keep the note," stated Holmes.

"*Ja*, please. Please help me vind my brooder. I am so concerned vor his savety. But, vhat do I do now, *Herr* Holmes?"

"I know it will be difficult, but you must wait. The people who have contacted you may have followed you here, but maybe not. Return home. I shall contact you."

"But, my brooder?"

"I know you must be very concerned. But, again, our best plan is to wait until you have heard from them. Do you know when you will be going back to Osborne House? Next week perhaps?"

"*Nein*, I do not. I have yust vinished a portrait ov one ov Her Majesty's grandchildren. It may be some vhile bevore I am called again. I cannot yust show up dere."

"Yes, of course not. That is my point. It will be important that you do not let anyone know about this. Should someone at Osborne House be as observant as you or I, they could likely press you as to why you appear so distressed.

"Tell me, have you ever recommended a painting and then the Queen has ordered it to be painted?"

"*Ja*, I have done so."

"Then I suggest you do so again. Our villains will not necessarily understand that you cannot return there at your whim or desire. They may get impatient. To try to solve this before harm comes to your brother, we must get you back to Osborne House sooner than later. Do you understand?"

"*Ja, Herr* Holmes. I shall do my best."

"I shall contact you if I need you. In the meantime, you must let us know if you receive an invitation to return to Osborne House. Do not place the notice in the paper. I shall take care of doing that. Is that clear?"

"*Ja, Herr* Holmes. I vill avait your directions. *Danke*."

Again, I escorted her to our door and bid her '*Auf Wiedersehen*.' It was as she was descending that Mrs. Hudson stepped out and informed me of a telegram that had arrived. I went down and retrieved it. It was from Mary indicating she was delaying her return for another week. She no doubt remembered in my last communique with her, that I intended to come and visit with Holmes.

I climbed back upstairs and retrieved the note to our client. After a few short minutes and with the help of Holmes' English-Duetsch dictionary, I was able to translate the entire message:

> Follow these instructions to the letter! Otherwise your brother dies - that is a promise!
>
> Do not contact the police or Scotland Yard - we have eyes and ears there and will know if you do.
>
> Let us know the next time you go to Osborne House. You shall do so by placing a personal in the Times stating you wish to meet Mr. Jones at the Tower and give the date. We will then know when you are to arrive at Osborne House.
>
> Once you are there, you will be contacted. Again - NO POLICE!

Holmes went to the mantle. He grabbed the slipper and filled a briar bowled churchwarden with tobacco. Lit it, then came back over to the sofa, laid down and began his silent thoughts, or so I thought.

With his eyes closed, he blew a large cloud of bluish smoke up into the air. The pleasant aroma delighted me, and again fond memories flooded back into my mind. I decided then and there, that I would join Holmes. I too filled my pipe and was soon again reclined in my old chair, relaxing and remembering the many times we had performed this ritual of sorts in the past.

I expected Holmes to sequester himself in his own mind,

travelling down the many paths that he could imagine based on what little we had learned today. But I was mistaken!

"Watson, what do you think of this case?" said he, with his eyes still closed and his pipe stem only out of his mouth long enough to ask me his question.

"I think it shall be an exciting one, Holmes. I dare say, it does concern me that she has associations with Her Majesty. What I mean is, I would gather from all I have learned from you, that she is perhaps merely a pawn in a larger game, eh?"

"My thoughts exactly. We cannot be cavalier about this adventure, Watson. It is so fortunate you are here to assist me, since the ultimate target may be our dear Lady herself, or Her Family. Anything else?"

"More data?"

"You've not forgotten a thing, Watson. I am most proud of you. Tell me anything else that you have thought of."

"I think the key will be the message telling our villains she is returning to Osborne House. Then it is all a matter of timing, yes?"

"I agree, but I believe we shall find that we perhaps are in need of alerting Mycroft to potential danger. I have sent him a note requesting we share our evening meal with him at the Diogenes Club. You can come as well, correct? We shall convey what we know so far and hopefully that will allow him to provide sufficient protection.

"We must, however, not presume this alone will protect the Family. I suggest a quick day, or perhaps overnight, trip to East Cowes. Perhaps we leave tonight after dinner and come back tomorrow. What say you?"

"I am with you Holmes. Mary has delayed her return for a week, so, I am free to join you. Let me check the timetables.

"Ah, yes, Bradshaw's indicates it is less than six hours each way and there is a train leaving at 18.20 tonight. We are scheduled to arrive by ferry at 23.56."

"Excellent!" and with that he fell back into the routine with which I was accustomed. The room fell silent and billows of bluish pipe smoke continued to fill the room.

My exhaustion from the last several weeks was perhaps

worse than I imagined. I soon found myself in a drowsy state attempting to read the same article over and over, realizing each time I started, I had drifted off before getting to the end. I finally succumbed and put down the paper.

It was later that I was awakened by Holmes' voice.

"Watson, are you fully rested now?"

"Oh, why yes, Holmes," said I, startled at his voice. I then realized I had been fully asleep.

"I am sure my body has prescribed such rest for me. The last weeks have been extraordinary and quite exhausting."

"We've but a few minutes to meet with Mycroft and have dinner. I have a cab waiting, if you are up to it?"

"Yes. Let me splash some water on my face, then let us be off."

I went to the bowl and did as I had said. The sensation of the cool water on my face finally awakened me. I wiped my face with a cloth and now felt refreshed. My mind instantly told me the adventure was truly real. I had not dreamed it. I was on a case with Holmes again! We were to engage our wits against an unknown adversary as in the past. The thrill of the case had suddenly raised my excitement beyond anything I had encountered during the previous weeks. While helping the ill has its own rewards, joining Holmes in an adventure, I must admit, exceeds the routine of my daily practice, even responding to help those against the recent illness.

Our dinner with Mycroft was short. While he appreciated the description of our case, he seemed to be preoccupied about some other, undisclosed issue. We knew better than to pry. He reassured us that the security at Osborne House was sufficient, he felt, to deal with any such events that might transpire. He did, though, do two things which were of assistance to us. He promised to alert those in charge of the Family's security of the possible danger. He then wrote a short note which, he said, should help us get past the outer boundary of security at Osborne House. He then excused himself and we were left alone.

Sherlock was, of course, not overly impressed with his brother's apparent lack of concern, at least to the degree which Sherlock believed Mycroft should have possessed. He soon dispensed with his displeasure saying he had done his duty to pass on the information. We had our note and that was enough. We left for Waterloo immediately to catch the evening train.

The trip was as expected. The train took us to Southampton West station that had recently opened. It was quite a splendid structure. From there, we went by carriage to the Town Quay. I realized I'd been there many years before when I embarked to my overseas deployment, initially with the Fusiliers. Our last leg was by ferry across the Solent, then up the mouth of the River Medina to East Cowes itself. We arrived late at just past midnight.

We lodging in a small inn on Link Road, which was a short walking distance from the docks. Holmes and I settled in for the night.

The next morning, we arose early, grabbed a quick breakfast and were off. Unlike London, where there were hansoms at our beck and call, here there were none to be found, let alone hired. We headed out to the main road to see if we'd have better luck. It only took us a few minutes to realize it was but a mile or so to the outer boundaries of Osborne House. Holmes and I decided that a walk there would do us good, having sat so long on our journey from the night before.

We headed out southeast upon York Avenue which soon turned almost due south. There were open fields to our right, but the road was heavily tree-lined to our left, which blocked our view of Osborne House which lay farther to the east. Suddenly, the road turned to the east and we found ourselves save but a few yards from the main entrance to Osborne House. Holmes whispered to me to keep walking past the gate.

There did not appear to be any difference of protocol at this location from that which we were familiar with back in London concerning Her Majesty's guard. There were several guards at the closed gated entrance who watched as Holmes and I strode by showing their alertness to our presence.

Holmes, wanting to get the full picture of this country home of the Queen and her family, continued on down York Avenue until we reached what appeared to be another gated entrance. Again, we encountered guards, although fewer in number, and they paid less attention to us than the first. The gate, again, was closed.

We continued our journey until reaching Whippingham Road. It was farther down this road, I estimated to be at least one hundred yards, that we saw a third entrance. The engraved stone near the entrance announced this as the "Barton Estate".

As we approached, we witnessed several lorries approach only to be waved on through the gate without so much as stopping. These lorries appeared to be carrying building supplies of different types. One was full of heavy timbers while another appeared to be struggling to regain its speed to move forward, after having slowed down to make the turn. It was burdened with a heavy load of bricks.

"Follow me here, Watson. I think I read several months back, that Prince Albert is having more renovations constructed at Osborne House. It would appear this is true. We can thus conclude there shall be more than normal access to Osborne House by persons unknown to the Royal Family."

"It would appear so, Holmes. Why these guards simply wave these people through, not stopping them whatsoever!"

"It may be likely that they have made many such deliveries and the guards have gotten to know them by sight. I suspect that should we approach now, we would be stopped and inquires made as to our purpose and presence."

"I believe you are correct, Holmes. But you have the note from Mycroft, do you not?"

"Yes, but now is not the time to make use of that. Since we now have this data, we must contemplate what advantages this allows our adversaries. I recommend we continue our investigation of the grounds without arousing any interest into who we are or why we are here."

With that he continued our journey to circumnavigate the entirety of Osborne House grounds.

We continued south-easterly, having now to also go around the old Barton Estate, which, we later learned, had been acquired by Her Majesty many years before.

This added to our proposed goal and made it more of a challenge. Once we were able to eventually turn north eastward, it was not long before we had reached the sea.

This forced us to make a decision. Were we to retrace our monotonous steps, or follow the shoreline and risk detection by guards who no doubt kept an eye on this littoral approach to the Royal grounds?

Holmes was determined to keep our presence unknown until absolutely necessary, and so we retraced our steps ending the morning back at our starting point at the inn on Link Road. We found a small tea shop nearby and proceeded to have lunch, being somewhat famished after our morning excursion around the southern portion of Osborne House. Holmes suggested that after a short rest after lunch, we should conclude our survey of the estate by checking the northern boundaries although he had concluded that the tradesman entrance to the compound was the most likely advantageous entry to be used by our villain.

Our journey after lunch produced no further data of consequence and to describe it now would be trivial to the solution of the case that was before us.

We had planned this to be just a one-day excursion, but the data we acquired regarding the building being performed, required at least one of us to stay longer. Holmes asked me to make discreet inquiries in the village as to how long the construction had been in progress and to obtain any other information that I found relevant. He, on the other hand, had chosen to make other inquiries regarding the specifics as to who were in fact the builders gaining access to Osborne House.

"Watson, I must return to London, but I shall be back on the morrow. Continue your casual inquiries making sure you arouse no suspicions as to our goal. I have spoken to the innkeeper and have arranged a rate for the week. I believe our adventure demands such, as the data so far indicates we have a more complex case to solve. I will be in touch soon."

"Yes, of course, Holmes. You can count on me."

Holmes, after delivering what I knew by now were his last instructions to me, whilst he disappeared to make further inquiries on his own, abruptly left. My first encounter with this behaviour of his, had left me quite befuddled. But as I grew to know the master detective's habits over all these years, I accepted his directions and told myself that they were as important to him in this case as any I had performed previously in our prior cases.

I spent the next several days appearing to be a visitor to East Cowes puttering about the Isle. To avoid exposing Holmes' and my adventure, I took upon a character as, I believe, Holmes would have done and I would hope to have made Holmes proud, had he witnessed it. I took on the personage of a traveller having never been to the Isle before, calling on this shop and that one.

Talking to apothecaries and inquiring about such medicines that I knew had just been made available in London, but not likely available here yet. This, of course, allowed me to strike up conversations by which I gained some, what I considered, important data, but, if I was truthful, perhaps Holmes would find unimportant.

It wasn't until my visit, to what I had decided was to be my last shop to make inquiries for that day, that I gained some valuable information at a small apothecary called "Drewberry's" which seemed to be a bit more fashionable than the others I had visited.

It was here that I believe I discovered the shop that provided for the necessary medicinal needs of the Royal Family when in residence at Osborne House. There was no seal, no sign, but the posture of the chemist and his attitude to my inquiries quickly led me to conclude he was the guardian of his patients' privacy to an extent I had not encountered in the previous shops I had visited. But his ability to keep such information private, I eventually found lacking.

I was, however, able to, in a roundabout way, conclude that the Royal Family had been able to avoid the most recent outbreak that had struck London. I concluded this as the particular bismuth salts we had been prescribing in London for our patients and which, due to so many prescriptions being dispersed, had quickly exhausted the London apothecaries' supplies, were here, readily available. In fact, they could not recall the last time they had to fill more than an occasional order.

"I say, as a visitor to the Isle, I have heard others I have met say that this current building by Prince Albert is putting quite the strain on the village. Is that so?" I had directed my question to the chemist, but I noticed an attractive woman behind the shop's sweets counter who seemed interested in my comment. I had a vague feeling I'd seen her before somewhere, but paid it no mind. I smiled politely to her, and she to me, as I continued my talk with the chemist.

"No. sir. Not in the least. I am not sure who it is that would say such a thing. Her Majesty, and Prince Albert of course, would never impose on her subjects any more than was absolutely necessary!" said the chemist.

"Didn't mean to offend. You do appear quite aggressive in your defence of the Family," said Watson.

"They are a most welcome part of our village, sir. I take it, you are from London, by your accent. While those in London may find it easy to diminish the Family's grandeur with sarcasm and jokes when they make decisions for the betterment of the Empire but that perhaps impose some burden on their subjects, but we here on the Isle appreciate them and honour their presence."

"Right, but I've seen them often in London on all the special occasions. They of course seem so remote and act so distant from us. I guess it just confounds me at times."

"Oh, sir, I think you are mistaken. They are most pleasant and are quite cordial and appreciative of those who serve them."

"You talk as though you know them personally."

"Well, sir…"

"Yes?"

"You must keep this to yourself," whispered the chemist.

"Of course, man, I am no spy of the *Boer*. Go on…!"

"Well, you see… we do call on Osborne House when they are in need of our services. So, yes, we do know them personally, but only in a professional capacity, you understand."

"Oh, I see. You provide them their apothecary needs. Well that certainly explains your admiration, yes indeed it does. That must be quite fascinating."

"It is, but of course, I can say no more."

"Understandable, quite understandable," retorted I.

Having gathered this final piece of information for the days' work, I returned to the inn. After a modest meal of the catch of the day, I retired and entertained myself reading the papers that had come over on the last ferry.

I was expecting to hear from Holmes, but there was no telegram awaiting me when I arrived earlier, and still none by the time I decided to get to sleep. I went to sleep confident I would see or at least hear from him in the morning.

The new day started out much as the day before. There again was no message for me from Holmes, so I caught a quick bite and began my inquiries about town.

It was not until late that evening that I finally heard from Holmes. I received a telegram which read:

WILL ARRIVE THURS – AM
MEET AT INN

I checked the ferry timetables and saw it would arrive, if on schedule, at 10.24. This sudden contact by Holmes assured me he had made his plan of attack. All I need do now was meet him and make sure I was ready to assist him.

When he arrived, he explained he wished to change and would be going to the tradesman's entrance that afternoon. He did so and when he re-joined me was dressed as a tradesman. Since I'd not seen him for the few days he'd left, he'd not shaven and looked the part of a scruff and hardened workman. He had brought both his revolver and my service revolver with him. He handed me mine and also handed me my passport.

"Here is yours. I fear we are in for a rough time of it, Watson. If my information is correct, we'll be against one whom we have battled before, and he plays for keeps."

"I understand, but why did you bring my passport?"

"Watson, this is a delicate game as we get so close to the Royal Family. While I have Mycroft's note, I fear our identity may be questioned. Anyone could have stolen Mycroft's note and pretend to be us. How would a guard know any difference? So, I bring them as insurance."

This, I again understood. I was now focused on who it was we were up against.

"Please tell me, Holmes. Who is it?"

"Not yet, until I am sure. So that you know, Mdm.

Swoboda has been requested to Osborne House, she tells me by note. I have placed the requested text in the Times, and she soon returns here."

"What have you learned while I was away?"

I relayed my encounter with the chemist at Drewberry's and he wished to visit the shop on the way to Osborne House. I showed him the way and soon we both entered.

I promptly engaged the chemist again, but when I turned around, I found that Holmes was in a conversation with the attractive sweets clerk. Knowing his disinterest in the female of the species, I quickly concluded he was on some mission unbeknownst to me.

He paid the clerk, took a bag from her and walked out. I apologised, excused myself to the chemist and followed Holmes outside. He hastily motioned me to get out of site of the shop window. Having done so, I queried him.

"Holmes, what is it? I wanted you to meet and talk to the chemist. You completely ignored both him and me!"

"It was out of dire necessity, least we spoil the whole trap!"

"What do you mean?"

"My suspicion and my theory were likely just proven accurate. Did you not recognize her, Doctor?"

"Recognize who, the sweets clerk?"

"Yes, the sweets clerk."

"No, I paid no attention to her. I am happily married, Holmes. I do not spend my time looking at women anymore, be they attractive or not. While I do not deny she is attractive, I made her of no concern to me."

"I am fairly certain she did not recognize me in my disguise, but I am less certain she did not recognise you, Watson."

"Recognise me! What are you talking about Holmes? I have never met that woman before in my life!"

"Ah, but you would lose a bet should we make one. She has either become a cool one or seeing you did not trigger her memory. I do not remember her as being in quite such good control of her emotions the last time we met, but people can change. I think though that she did not recognise you and so hopefully our trap remains hidden."

"Who is this woman, then Holmes?"

"I will help you remember when we have finished here. Do not return to the shop. She must not remember you or my trap may be in jeopardy. I must get on to the trade entrance immediately. Please be ready to receive Mdm. Swoboda here at East Cowes tomorrow. We must speak to her before she reports to Osborne House."

"Yes, Holmes, I shall avoid the shop and wait for Mdm. Swoboda's arrival as you have directed."

Holmes then left me, heading towards Osborne House.

I did not see him again until evening. He returned to the inn and used the back entrance so as to not arouse curiosity in his tradesman's attire by coming through the front way.

"Holmes, how did it go?" queried I.

"I have an idea to catch our villains."

"Is it Moriarty? Surely, this scheme is likely his work."

"I cannot fault you for concluding that, as it is to the level of plots which he conjures up, but no, it is not Moriarty this time."

"Who, then? Ever since you implored me to not return to Drewberry's, I have tried to recall that woman. I know I have seen her before, but cannot remember when or where. Now that your trap is set, please tell me who she is."

"I will let you think about her a while longer. I take it Mdm. Swoboda has not arrived yet?"

"No."

"Well then, we must make sure we meet Mdm. Swoboda when she arrives. I must impress on her, that for this trap to work, she must do exactly as I say."

After that, I could get no more from him. We then waited for Mdm. Swoboda to disembark. She arrived with the next scheduled ferry. This time, the train, coach and ferry had the unusual occurrence of being each on schedule. She came to the inn and we three went next door for tea and to discuss our path forward.

Mdm. Swoboda relayed to Holmes that she received a note and was told by the kidnapper to 'paint a picture of one of the Queen's young granddaughters while she played at the note seashore'.

With this data we can finish setting the trap, Watson. We've only to wait for it to spring. "Mdm. Swoboda, I am happy to tell you we know who has your brother."

"*Ja,* dis is *sehr gut*!"

"But now I must ask that you please follow my instructions exactly. While we believe he is in London, he is still in danger. We think if we attempt to grab him away from his kidnappers, he will be harmed.

"It is likely, though, if we capture the mastermind of this escapade, those who hold your brother will release him since they will not be paid as this villain has likely promised them.

"To capture the mastermind, we need your help."

"I am here to help, *Herr* Holmes! Vhat do I need to do?"

"We are asking that you go to Osborne House and pretend to do as you are told by these villains. We shall have men ready every step of the way to protect you and make sure no harm comes to you or your charge."

"I shall do so, *Herr* Holmes."

She rose, and left the tea shop.

"Holmes, what shall we do now?"

"It is time to go to Osborne House and make use of our note from Mycroft. Make sure your revolver is at the ready. I do not trust that our villain will give up easily. He is a desperate man."

With that warning he said no more, nor could I convince him yet, to tell me with whom we were battling.

By now he had changed and we both were presentable to the guards at Osborne House. We approached and of course were challenged as to our person and purpose. Holmes presented both of our passports and then the note from Mycroft. We were then taken into a separate room of the guard's lodge on the side of Osborne House proper. Here we met Colonel Stitchins, the head of security for the Royal Family while in residence at Osborne House.

My dear readers, I cannot reveal to you all that was said, agreed to or planned in this meeting as I, as well as Holmes, were sworn to secrecy. I will, though, continue on now with the remainder of this tale. What I am permitted to reveal may provide you with enough information to reconstruct our meeting for yourself.

A young girl of about eight was handed into Mdm.

Swoboda's care. With her painting accoutrements under her right arm, she held the young girls' hand in her left hand as they walked from the House eastward towards the beach.

Between the House and the shoreline was a thick grove of trees. Holmes, the Colonel, several of the Colonel's men and I had taken up various positions along the route.

It was just after having left the cover of the trees, the site being obscured from any windows of Osborne House, that our villain struck.

He seemed to come from nowhere, grabbing the young girl away from Mdm. Swoboda. They both screamed and a flurry of action then took place.

The Colonel was the first one there.

"Pappa!" screamed the young girl, reaching her outstretched arms towards the Colonel.

He was like a lion taking down a gazelle. The ferocity with which the Colonel attacked the man was none like I had ever seen, even in Afghanistan. He separated the young girl from the man, pushing her out of harms' way. Mdm. Swoboda dropped her painting paraphernalia, grabbed the girl and whisked her back towards the trees. Holmes and I were next to the scene. It was we that had to separate the man from the Colonel. The Colonel was beating the man to a bloody pulp.

Once separated, we need not worry about the man escaping as the Colonel had rendered him unconscious.

As the violence subsided, the Colonel began to regain his composure and ordered his men to take the man back to the guard's lodge. The young girl left Mdm. Swoboda's care and ran to her father, who picked her up and carried her along. As we approached the guard house a woman came out and the young girl let go the Colonel's grasp and ran to the woman.

"Mamma, mamma."

The woman grabbed the young girl in her arms, and they disappeared from our sight.

"We've caught the bastard, Mr. Holmes," said the Colonel practically shouting, still struggling to regain his composure as we all entered the guards' lodge.

"Colonel, he is more than that. We have known of this

man's evil for many years."

"Holmes, this is not Burnwell, is it?" queried I.

"One and the same, Watson. George Burnwell. *Sir* George Burnwell, as he was once known. We met him when he had briefly stolen the *Beryl Coronet*."

"Then clearly, that woman was Mary Holder?"

"Good, Watson. Very good!"

"Oh my!"

"We have met this man before, as I told you Colonel, but he has escaped justice for many crimes. And now we have caught him, or perhaps I should say you caught him. While I was willing to allow him to get close so as to capture him, I was not keen on allowing your daughter to pose as one of Her Majesty's granddaughters. Is she all right? Perhaps Watson, you could look in on her?"

"My wife is with her now. She's a strong lass and her duty and loyalty to her Queen was proven today."

Just then Burnwell was coming to.

"What is happening here? Let me go!" he yelled.

"Burnwell, you will not be going anywhere except to gaol. Attempted kidnapping should put you away for a while," said the Colonel.

"I doubt it," came his insolent reply.

"I have an ace in the hole, you see. Holmes, isn't it? And his foolish assistant, Doctor Watson?" he said, staring at Holmes and then glancing my way.

"And just what would be this ace? As I see it, your hand is empty and worth nothing. You should fold," replied Holmes.

"We have the painter's brother, you see. If I'm not let go immediately and do not return with the young girl, well, he will be killed."

"So, you admit to kidnapping another, and threatening to murder the captive?"

"Yes, I always have alternate plans."

"As do I Burnwell. Bring her in."

One of the Colonel's men went out for just a moment and returned with Mary Holder.

Burnwell's posture and face fell as if struck again by the Colonel, although he hadn't laid another hand on him.

"We picked up your accomplice and she was kind enough to trade the information of the exact whereabouts of Mdm. Swoboda's brother for the court to consider leniency at the trial that she knows awaits her.

"She has stated you have forced her into to this whole scheme and she would never want to bring harm upon a child. Isn't that correct, Miss Holder?"

"Yes, yes!"

"So, now who has an ace in the hole?"

Burnwell lowered his head into his hands and then both into his lap. All we could hear was a muffled grumbled-like scream coming from Burnwell.

"Take them away," ordered Stitchins.

The guards came and began to escort Burnwell out of the room. Suddenly there was a scuffle. Burnwell had managed to get behind Mary Holder and put one arm around her. Up against her thin neck of ivory white flesh he placed a large shining knife which he produced from some unknown place on his person.

"I'll kill her if you make a move against me!" he raged.

He began backing towards the door. Step by step he came close and closer to making his escape.

Then a quick step forward by the Colonel and he had relieved me of my revolver that I'd had stuck in the front of my trousers. In an instant he had cocked the hammer and had the barrel pushing into the flesh of Burnwell's temple.

"Drop the knife!" he commanded.

Burnwell slashed upward and ducked at the same time. But the Colonel held firm and maintained the barrel to his quarry's head when he pulled the trigger. Burnwell was dead before he hit the ground.

Mary screamed, breaking lose from his arm-hold as he fell. Our ears hurt from the report of the guns' discharge in such closed quarters.

Others ran into the room. Mary was bleeding from a deep gash under her chin. I attended to her immediately. We stopped the bleeding with compression, and I called for more bandages.

"She needs hospital, Holmes, Colonel!" shouted I.

The Colonel shouted orders to his men to arrange her passage by coach to Frank James immediately. I accompanied her there. Once out of danger, I returned to find out the rest of the story.

"She will very likely survive, Holmes. She may be disfigured, but he did not cut the jugular, which spared her life.

"She'll stand trial?" asked I.

"I think she will have to. I believe her story to be one of survival, once she was caught."

"Holmes, how did you know it was Burnwell?"

"I did some checking when I returned to London. I wished to see who each of the material suppliers and contractors were for the new addition. The entrance for the construction was a weak link, as we had observed.

"Most were old names. The heavy timber supplier, though, had recently been acquired by an 'SGB, Ltd.' Not that that, in and of itself, caught my attention. It did however cause me to look further into who owned this SGB, Ltd. It was then that I saw Burnwell's name. This led me to plan a trap, even though I was not certain he himself would be here.

"When we went in Drewberry's, I recognized Mary Holder immediately. Luckily for me, I was all ready in costume, or likely she would have recognized me and the whole trap would have been tripped too early.

"Seeing Mary here in East Cowew, I was more confident Burnwell himself would show up.

"Once the Colonel insisted his daughter do her duty and become the bait, well I knew we had to capture him. I would have preferred his trial, showing to the Empire that this man was brought to justice and his downfall be a public humiliation to him. But that was not to be. Justice was served although it was violently administered. I suppose in the end, with the other crimes I am aware of that he was accused of doing, perhaps the outcome would have been the same.

"Thank you, Colonel. Your quick actions on both occasions, won the day."

"My duty to my Queen and the Family, sir."

"I'd say more than duty, today."

"Perhaps you are correct. While when I suggested my

daughter to participate, it was like a planning an action from when I was in the 1ˢᵗ Boer War. Saw it as a tactical event.

"But suddenly, when it all was actually happening… well, something came over me. It was different than any emotion I have ever felt before, even on the battlefield. It is one thing, I guess, to feel the desire to fight for Queen and country, to save one's blokes, but when it was my own flesh and blood I was protecting, and my own darling little girl, I felt I had the strength of ten men. Nothing was going to prevent me from saving my daughter from that bastard!"

"I think I understand, sir. Please give our thanks to your daughter. She is one very brave little girl," said I.

"I will," said the Colonel.

We found Mdm. Swoboda and escorted her to the dock. We intended to return to the Town Quay and back to London before days' end. The three of us stood watching as the ferry landed and the crew cast their lines to secure the boat.

As we waited for those aboard her to disembark, there suddenly came a voice from on board, "Josefine! Josefine!"

"Rudolf!" yelled back Mdm. Swoboda.

Rudolf broke free from the crowd as he came to the end of the gangway.

"Oh, Rudolf, you are safe!"

"Ja, danks to *Herr* Holmes. Vhere is he?"

"Dis is *Herr* Holmes, Rudolf, and his associate, Dr. Vatson."

"Danke you *Herr* Holmes, Doctor," said Rudolf as he thrust his hand out to each of us. Holmes and I shook his hand.

"Herr Holmes is a genius! He has swaed you and protected Her Majesty and her family vrom dat ewil man. I am so glad you are safe," said she, hugging her brother."

"How can ve pay you vor all you have done vor us? queried Rudolf.

"I seem to recall a landscape at your studio. Is it a commission or for sale?"

Rudolf had a confused look on his face. Perhaps Holmes had omitted telling him of our midnight visit to his studio.

"Neider. I was trying out some new ideas, vhy?"

"I admire it very much. I think that when it is finished, it would look quite proper on my wall. What say you, Watson?"

"I agree, Holmes."

"That will be payment enough," said Holmes.

"Den it will be yours, *Herr* Holmes."

"Watson, Mdm. and Mr. Swoboda, they are boarding now. Shall we not all catch this last ferry back tonight and be home by morning? Let's be on our way."

THE ADVENTURE OF
THE MOORFIELDS NURSE

Although Portugal's choice to move its capital from Europe to South America had been rare for a colonizing power, it had chosen to do so in 1808. Napoleon had helped make the choice easy for Queen Maria I once he invaded Spain. She had made Brazil the court of her Kingdom in 1815 transferring it from Lisbon. The courts of Europe were incensed that a European court would do such a thing, that is, move to a colony. But moving her court was survival, as the Queen saw it.

Brazil was tremendously larger than the somewhat isolated country of Portugal which sometimes felt it could easily be pushed into the Atlantic by Spain. Brazil allowed the Portuguese to stretch out their arms.

Unfortunately, despite its desperate attempt to hold on to its new-world empire that had been established three hundred or so years earlier in 1500, Portugal failed. The inhabitants of Brazil had just recently chosen independence over continuing to be subjects of a monarch. The Treaty of Peace gave Brazil its independence from the Kingdoms of Portugal and Algarve.

Along with Brazilians' new-found freedom, there came a lawlessness which the new-born country had not yet been able to completely learn how to control.

Although gold had been found in Brazil as early 1690 and a later discovery in 1745, which gave opportunists a chance at imagined fortunes, there had not been much exploitation until recently. But just a few years before, in 1825, just one year after Brazil's independence from Portugal, in the State of Minas Gerias, the Gongo Soco mine had commenced operation and was steadily producing copious amounts of gold. Just prior to its opening, the land that held the mine had been sold to the Brazilian Mining Company, based in Torbay, Devon, England, for £80,000. William Cochran worked for the BMC.

Juan Cerqueira, a Portuguese native, was ill that morning. The mine captain, Cochran, was concerned Juan could not make it to the dock in time for the departure of the ship. Cochran, from Cornwall, England, was determined to fulfil his duty to the company. He would make sure the transport of two large boxes of gold would be placed safely on the ship. Juan wanted to go, as it meant a bonus to him. But Cochran was not willing to trust such a valuable cargo to a man who could not even climb out of bed, let alone defend himself and the precious cargo from would-be thieves. In the back of Cochran's mind was still a lingering doubt about Juan's loyalty to the company instead of his newly-formed independent country of *Brazil*.

On 17 February, the two boxes of gold were first taken by Cochran south to the small village of Betim. After a brief stay, Cochran made his way, with the boxes, to Rio de Janeiro. Once there, he saw that they were loaded onto a clipper ship, *The Orangeman*, bound for Plymouth, Devon, in the south west of England.

Relieved, with a receipt in hand, Cochran returned to the Gongo Soco and began his mining duties again. By this time, Juan Cerqueira had recovered. Cochran had not appreciated the pressure that Juan Cerqueira had experienced on a monthly basis, transporting the gold and knowing that around any corner there could be a villain waiting to rob him of his precious cargo. Cochran now understood that Juan Cerqueira had performed his duties with much loyalty in the past without question, since never was there any difference between the amount of gold leaving Gongo Soco and the amount received at the Rio docks.

Cochran thought to himself that perhaps he should increase Juan Cerqueira's bonus. Worrying about cave-ins and flooding was enough for him. Dealing with robbers and thieves, was not what he'd signed up for. To have someone he could trust to deliver the gold safely was worth more than he had previously realized.

The Orangeman departed Rio on 18 February 1840. Captain Lawrence Redstone was a trustworthy man with plenty of experience. His two score years of seamanship had earned him his captaincy many years before and his determination to meet the schedule for arrival made him a trusted and reliable employee of the line.

But on this journey, due to some seasonal weather in route, the voyage took twenty-nine days, rather than the normal twenty-one, with *The Orangeman* reaching Plymouth on 19 March 1840. Captain Redstone was not pleased at the duration of the journey, but after having the cargo unloaded, he felt a certain satisfaction in knowing that he had brought the gold to England, safely. Once he received the paperwork transferring the gold to Messrs. Kearney and Co. he rewarded himself at the nearest pub with three fingers of the finest Scotch they offered.

But Plymouth was not the final destination of the cargo. It was loaded aboard a small ship owned by the Belfast Ship Company, named the *City of Belfast* which carried it to London's docks on the Thames, just east of the Tower Bridge. The gold was off-loaded at the company's dock. This journey to London took an additional four days, with the gold arriving there on 22 March.

The agents for the Belfast Ship Company, that is Messrs. Harvey and Co., received a document from Messrs. Kearney and Co. of Plymouth directing Messrs. Harvey and Co. to release the gold to the person arriving at their offices from Carlisle and Co and presenting the correct documents for its retrieval.

The clerk at the Belfast Ship Company, a Mr. Robert Gabbart, received such a person and upon such person's presentation of such documents, released the shipment as he had been instructed to do.

Gabbart, was not in any way suspicious of the recipient as he presented himself in a collected and authoritative manner. He paid the wharf charges as required without any objection.

The boxes containing the gold were placed in a cab and the collector of the gold was gone, but not before tipping the dockhands a double florin each for loading the boxes, as he alighted into a cab.

Much to Mr. Gabbart's despair, it was but several hours later that another agent presented similar papers to him from agents of Messrs. Carlisle and Co. requesting transference of the gold.

Mr. Gabbart, with much confusion in his response, explained that it had already been handed over to its rightful claimant and required proof of this second requestor's *bona fides*. After a short while, and with much protestation, it was discovered that this second agent was in fact the authorized agent sent by Messrs. Carlisle and Co. A great theft had been accomplished! With the value of the gold estimated at nearly £8000, the police were soon involved.

The Belfast Ship Company, now at fault, was desperate to retrieve the gold. Failure to do so would undoubtedly cause the collapse of the company.

An investigation was commenced immediately. Detective Inspector John Foster was assigned the case and quickly tracked down the cabbie who frequently worked the docks and had transported the gold and its dubious claimant.

The cabbie reported that he had taken the fare north to Cambridge Heath. There, the passenger, and his cargo, were set upon a lorry. One queer observation of his, was that, when he picked up his fare at the docks, the fare appeared with an elegant moustache and was dressed as a gentleman, complete with top hat and cane. This description matched that given by Robert Gabbart. But upon arriving at Cambridge Heath, the 'gentleman', was said by the cabbie, to now be in the apparel of common dress, was clean shaven and wore a simple grey applejack cap.

The cabbie, like the dock men before him, was tipped a double florin and that is the last he saw of the 'gentleman'.

Further investigation by DI Foster revealed that the lorry had been a hired one. The lorry company's records showed the load had been delivered to an address of a house on Bethnal Green Road, to a Mr. C. Babcock.

DI Foster arrived at the residence and shortly began his questioning of Mr. Babcock. Babcock claimed he knew nothing of the shipment delivered, claims he did not sign for it and had no idea what all of this was about.

Upon further questioning of Babcock's servants, it was discovered that the cook had seen the butler talking to a lorry driver a few hours before. Foster's further inquiries with the cook produced a clue which would eventually lead to apprehensions of at least some of the villains.

The butler had resigned from his service to Babcock this very morning and had immediately left, they said. Babcock's valet thought he heard him mention he was headed to Charring Cross. When asked about his final destination, the valet could only conclude it was for points unknown, as the butler kept that to himself.

The butler, a Mr. Christopher Gabbart, was soon discovered to be the uncle of Robert Gabbart, the clerk at the dock at Plymouth. Foster had obtained a fair description of the butler and with only that as his guide, left for Charring Cross as fast as a hansom could carry him.

As fate would have it, Foster found his suspect waiting on the station platform, albeit nervously, which was to Foster's advantage, for Gabbart's train's departure had been delayed.

DI Foster, with two constables at his side, approached Mr. Gabbart and introduced himself to Gabbart.

DI Foster expressed how amazing it was, that by some miraculous coincidence he just happened to be the uncle of the desk clerk that witnessed the theft of gold this very morning. He further stated to Christopher Gabbart that it also seemed a very strange coincidence that the stolen gold was apparently delivered to his former employer's residence, but that the master of the house had no knowledge of receiving it, but that the cook had seen him talking to a lorry-man and had received something.

Mr. Christopher Gabbart, who under the stress of the situation, confessed that, there had indeed been a conspiracy between his nephew and him to abscond with the gold shipment that his nephew had told him was coming.

Christopher Gabbart, though, was no longer in possession of the gold as he had sold it to parties unknown at a value far less than what the current market would bring.

His only knowledge of the buyers, a man and a woman,

was that they spoke with an accent and had paid him £1000 on Bank of England notes. Upon the transfer he left as soon as possible. He had no idea where the gold was now. DI Foster relieved him of the twenty £50 notes he had with him and ordered him taken away.

It was his later confrontation with Robert Gabbart that further helped resolve the case, but only to a degree.

After hearing of his uncle's confession and realizing, the game was up, he also confessed and offered up information that sent DI Foster, again with much haste, to track down a Mr. and Mrs. Jehan.

Once found, he was able to apprehend these two fences but was only able to retrieve approximately £2000, also in £50 notes.

The Jehan's story was similar in that they had received the gold and sold it to unknown parties for £2000. They too no longer possessed or knew where the gold was.

The trail was at a dead end at that point. No statements provided by the Jehan's led to any more reliable information and the actual disposition of the stolen gold was never found.

DI Foster speculated that after a week or so it would be impossible to track down the stolen gold and that it had likely been melted down, made into jewellery or into simple bullion to be traded amongst thieves.

While DI Foster had wished to pursue its retrieval, his superiors eventually required him to move on to other cases.

Belfast Shipping survived, just barely. With the return of the £3000 that DI Foster had recovered and Belfast Shipping's insurance on their business, they survived for several more years until the day of the clipper-ships, in which they were dependent on for their business, gave way to the steamers. Between the onslaught of the steamers which they could not afford to purchase and the opening of the Suez Canal in 1869, their business dried up and was finished.

Daily Telegraph, 17 October 1890
MOORFIELDS NURSE MISSING!

Miss Helen Talberg, 24, was seen on Wednesday last, 15 October, leaving Moorfields Hospital after her shift ended at 11 o'clock p.m. that night. Her friend and fellow nurse, Miss Ruth Threlfall, told Inspector Lestrade of Scotland Yard that they had left together and had progressed down City Road in the direction of Old Street Tube station.

Here the two had parted ways with Miss Threlfall continuing on down Banner Street as she normally did, headed for the Barbican Station.

When Miss Talberg did not report in the next afternoon, her supervisor had been concerned. Shortly thereafter, a Mr. Harry Browner had arrived at the hospital and inquired about Miss Talberg's presence. Miss Threlfall validated that Mr. Browner was known to her and, in fact, confirmed to her supervisor that Mr. Browner was indeed Miss Talberg's betrothed.

At that point the supervisor made the decision to contact Scotland Yard, due to the concern all the parties had for Miss Talberg's safety.

Inspector Lestrade arrived at hospital and quickly took charge of the investigation into the whereabouts of the missing nurse.

To date no information has been discovered as to the location of Miss Talberg.

If anyone has knowledge of the current location of Miss Talberg, please contact Detective Inspector Lestrade at Scotland Yard.

Holmes was writing, no doubt, on his new monograph he had mentioned to me the day before, which was on the subject of fingernails.

He had been contemplating the evidence he had observed over the years in his peculiar occupation that fingernails fell into two categories.

His observations were that for some people their fingernails were quite thin and to some degree rather flexible, whereas others were quite hard, durable and thick.

The flatter the thin ones were, the more likely to break easily. If, however the thin nails were more rounded, the curvature tended to make them sturdier.

The thicker ones were certainly more durable, with rounded thick nails the most durable of all.

His reasoning was that this difference was important to take into consideration when tracking down an assailant, for example, he argued.

Those with thin and flexible fingernails would, in most cases, keep them short as breakage was a likely outcome in most circumstances especially when grasping at a resisting victim. Whereas those with more 'primitive' nails as he called them, thicker and more durable, like the claws of a savage animal, would not bother to clip them and were thus more likely to leave scratch marks on their victims. Curved thick hard nails were the epitome of the 'primitive' type.

He was certain these differences were an example of Darwin's theory in his masterpiece, *The Origins of Species*, which Holmes had read several times over.

Perhaps these thicker nails were simply leftover inherited traits from more primitive peoples?

His interest in Darwin, and continued reading of Darwin's tomes had, though, caused some doubt in his thinking on several subjects. It was Darwin's later book, *The Descent of Man*, that concerned him the most. He found it disturbing in some ways and yet ironic in other respects.

The natural world constantly eliminated the unfit of a species. One would wish the human race to continue its upward trajectory, getting better in each generation. But it was Darwin's point that the human race would act in the opposite of the natural world. That humans did not eliminate the unfit of its species, troubled him.

It occurred to me, that I, myself partook of this process when referring my patients to an ophthalmologist, for instance. Indeed, obtaining glasses allowed those with poor eyesight to continue to live, perhaps even prosper, but also to breed and pass down their poor eyesight to their progeny. If left to nature's ways, however, they would soon be culled and not able to pass on to their offspring this undesirable trait.

Quite a dilemma, thought I. I was helping those in need to live healthier lives, but was I polluting the race? But then I reminded myself, that when I look into a microscope, I am seeing living creatures not able to be seen by me with my God-given eyesight or even by those with 'perfect' eyes. What Hooke and Leeuwenhoek discovered opened up an entire new world for medicine![6] Glasses, microscopes, telescopes are but extensions of our senses, (are they not?) I asked myself. Perhaps if all eyes were perfect, would we have not had a need to invent such instruments? But then, so much of the world and the universe we now know about would remain undiscovered! Diseases would then be left unconquered?

As I contemplated these musings and finished the remainder of the column in the Telegraph about the disappearance of the young Moorfields Nurse, Holmes and I received a knock on the door.

Knowing Holmes was consumed in his monograph and did not hear the knock, or more likely and correctly, ignored it, I arose and answered the door myself.

"Ah! Inspector Lestrade, what brings you here today," queried I.

"Good day, Dr. Watson, I came to see Mr. Holmes," as he strode into our lodgings without any invitation.

"Inspector, Holmes is busy. I don't think you should ..."

---

[6] Editor's note: Dr. Watson is referring to Englishman Robert Hooke who, in 1665, peered into microscope at a piece of cork. The plant structure he saw, he named 'cells', as they reminded him of the uniform rooms in monasteries in which monks slept (*cella* in Latin, means 'small room'). Dutchman Antonie van Leeuwenhoek, "Father of Microbiology", on 9 October 1676 reports the discovery of living single celled creatures and calls them, '*animalcules*', or 'tiny animals' in Latin.

"What is it, Lestrade? The missing nurse?" queried Holmes without looking up or interrupting his writing.

"Why yes, yes, it is," said he.

"I shall be with you shortly, please have seat while I finish writing down my thoughts."

It was perhaps ten minutes later, when Lestrade stood up in his impatience and announced, "I shall return later."

Holmes, smiled ever so slightly, and put down his pen.

"There." said Holmes, now standing up and addressing Lestrade face to face. "How can I assist you, Inspector?"

Realizing, that he now had Holmes' attention, Lestrade returned to the sofa upon which he had been impatiently waiting as Holmes then came over and sat in his chair. Holmes laid his head against the back of the chair. He then closed his eyes and placed the thumb and each finger of his long hands against one another in a posture I had become accustomed to seeing him in, when he desired to concentrate on the oral information he was about to receive.

"I am at a loss on this one, Mr. Holmes. This young woman has disappeared, and we have nothing to go on."

"I disagree, Lestrade. You have much to go on."

"How do you know that, sir?"

"Why the Telegraph article has more data than you do."

"What do you mean?"

"Watson, please, if you will, read the article again aloud for the Inspector."

"Yes, of course, Holmes."

I began reading the article as Holmes had requested.

> "Miss Helen Talberg was seen on Wednesday last, 15 October, leaving Moorfields Hospital after her shift ended at 11 o'clock p.m. that night."

"Stop. You know who is missing, when she went missing, both the time and date. Pray continue, Watson."

> "Her friend and fellow nurse, Miss Ruth Threlfall, told

> Inspector Lestrade of Scotland Yard that they had left together and had progressed down City Road in the direction of Old Street Tube station."
>
> "Here the two had parted ways with Miss Threlfall continuing on down Banner street as she normally did, headed for the Barbican Station."

"Stop. We now know who saw her last and where she was headed. Continue, Watson."

> "When Miss Talberg did not report in the next afternoon, her supervisor had been concerned."

"Stop. We now know her disappearance started sometime between 11.10 pm and 3.00 pm the following day, 16 October."

"Why 11.10?"

"Because that is how long it takes to gather one's belonging and walk from Moorfields Hospital to Banner Street. Continue."

> "Shortly thereafter, a Mr. Harry Browner had arrived at the hospital and inquired about Miss Talberg's presence. Miss Threlfall validated that Mr. Browner was known to her and, in fact, confirmed to her supervisor that Mr. Browner was indeed Miss Talberg's betrothed."

"So, we know she is not married, but is soon to be. Her betrothed is named a Mr. Browner and he is no stranger to Miss Talberg's friends, as Miss Threlfall knows him. Watson?"

"At that point the supervisor made the decision to contact Scotland Yard, due to the concern all the parties had for Miss Talberg's safety.

Inspector Lestrade arrived at hospital and quickly took charge of the investigation into the whereabouts of the missing nurse.

To date no information has been discovered as to the whereabouts of Miss Talberg.

If anyone has knowledge of the location of Miss Talberg, please contact Detective Inspector Lestrade at Scotland Yard.

"This is where you come in and ask for help from the public. Have you questioned this Browner fellow yet?"

"No, we've not been able to locate him."

"Have you checked Miss Talberg's flat?"

"No, why would we do that? Why would he be there?"

"Lestrade, you are impossible! Shall we not go and find this Mr. Browner," said Holmes.

Sherlock opened his eyes and arose from his chair. He mumbled something about his monograph having to wait and grabbed his coat and hat.

There was a brisk wind that day and the sky was clearer and seemed bluer than normal. The sun shone but the sky was quickly to fall dark as the autumn days had already commenced getting shorter and shorter.

Lestrade did have the address of the missing nurse and we soon found ourselves knocking at the door to her flat.

A young man opened the door with alacrity, but upon seeing our faces, suddenly his face gave way to a despondent expression. He turned away and we were then greeted by a young woman.

"Yes, gentlemen, what do you want?"

Lestrade took charge.

"I am inspector Lestrade of Scotland Yard. This is Mr.

Sherlock Holmes and Dr. John Watson. Is this the residence of Miss Helen Talberg?"

"Yes, yes, it is. How can I help you, Inspector?"

"May we come in, Miss....?"

"My name is Jane, Jane Browner," she replied.

She opened the door wider and we all entered.

She assisted us with our coats, hats and canes and then walked us into a small living area.

The young man who had opened the door, sat over in the corner of the lightly furnished room, with both his hands covering his face.

"Harry, this is Inspector Le..."

"Lestrade," said Lestrade, with some frustration.

"This is Dr. Watson and, I am sorry, I'm not very good with names... Mister..."

"My name is Sherlock Holmes."

At the sound of his name, Harry turned and looked Holmes in the eyes. His face and eyes were red as he had obviously shed a tear or two, not unexpected for a man whose fiancée has suddenly disappeared.

"You are Sherlock Holmes!?"

"I am."

"Oh, sir, it is so wonderful to meet you. I have read about you and your cases. Can you please find Helen? Please, sir, you must!"

"That remains to be seen. I think you should first speak to Inspector Lestrade, then perhaps we shall talk afterwards, eh?"

"I will leave you gentlemen alone," after that, the young women retired to a bedroom and closed the door.

"Thank you, Mr. Holmes," interrupted Lestrade.

"Now, Mr. Browner, why did you disappear?"

"What do you mean, disappear?"

"We were called to Hospital and when we got there you were nowhere to be found. We went to your address and you were not there. Why did you leave Moorsfields?"

"I went to look for Helen, of course. Why would I stay there and not go look for her?"

"I'll be asking the questions, here," rebuked Lestrade.

"When is the last time you saw Miss Talberg?"

"I walked her to Moorfields right before her shift began. We said our goodbyes and she went in. I returned to my flat."

"When did you know she was missing?"

"Not until the next day. We were to meet for lunch and do some shopping together before her afternoon shift began. We were going to meet at the pub and then she didn't show up. She's been late before, but not more than thirty minutes. After an hour I became concerned. I went to Moorfields and waited. About two forty-five Miss Threlfall showed up, and was startled to see me. She asked 'where was Helen', and I said something like 'isn't she here?'. Ruth said 'no' or 'I don't know', or something like that, my mind's a bit hazy on that, and then I began to feel ill to my stomach. I asked Ruth had she left the hospital with Helen last night. She said she had and that they parted ways at their usual spot on Banner Street.

"Ruth then suggested we check with the supervisor and we did. Mrs. Jackson, Ruth and Helen's supervisor, was wondering the same thing and just hadn't checked yet to see why she wasn't there. Mrs. Jackson then suggested we call the police. We did call and they said they would arrange for someone to come from Scotland Yard."

"And you didn't think it would be wise to be there when I arrived?" Lestrade asked, as if Browner had meant to insult him personally.

"No, not at all. My only concern was for Helen and I went to try to find her."

"Where did you go?"

"I went to where Ruth said she'd last seen Helen. I saw nothing and became quite upset. Then I came here."

"Why did you come here?"

"Why shouldn't I?"

"Are you married, Mr. Browner?" queried Lestrade.

"Why, no. What do you mean by asking me that question?" Browner said, suddenly standing and tightening his muscles in his arms and hands as if preparing to take a punch at Lestrade.

"There, there, gentlemen. No need for a dust up. Mr.

Browner, it will do you no good to strike an officer of the law, however his words may have insulted you," said Holmes.

"I didn't insult anyone," Lestrade said.

"Ah, but perhaps it was unintentional, Inspector," Holmes said.

"Was that not your wife that answered the door just now?" scowled Lestrade. "Jane Browner!"

"I dare say Lestrade, you must pay more attention to details. Mr. Browner, would you please invite your *sister* in here to join us?"

"Sister?" asked Lestrade incredulously.

Harry retrieved his sister and sat down again.

"Miss Browner, would you mind showing the Inspector Lestrade your left hand?"

Miss Browner acquiesced to Sherlock's request with a gesture reminiscent of earlier days when a lady offered her hand to be gently kissed by a gentleman upon introduction or greeting.

"You will observe, Lestrade, there is no ring on the ring finger of her left hand. There are but a few married women who today would not display our societal symbol of their status. Looking closer you shall see that while she has other rings on other fingers, none appears on that finger.

"Now I call your attention to the jaw structure of both Mr. and Miss Browner. You can easily see the squareness of the jaw and thus the sharing of the same parental feature.

"We see the despondence of Mr. Browner amply displayed in front of Miss Browner. Were he her husband, should he display such emotion in front of her?

"I would venture to say, that perhaps it was Miss Browner who knew Miss Talberg first, as they appear to be roommates. Miss Browner no doubt introduced her brother to Miss Talberg and thus we conclude it is only natural that Mr. Browner here would retreat to both his fiancée's abode but that also of the comfort of his familial connection."

"You are correct, Mr. Homes…"

"Holmes," I corrected her.

"Yes, *Holmes*, so sorry," said Miss Browner. "Helen and I met here in London and both needed lodgings that we could afford. It has worked well, and we have become close friends. When Harry came to visit me a year or so, he met Helen. He moved to London and their courtship has been slow and steady. I believe they are a wonderful match.

"Please, Mr. Holmes, can you find Helen?" said she.

"Scotland Yard will find her, *Miss* Browner. I have simply brought Mr. Holmes along as he sometimes enjoys such little puzzles as these and occasionally helps the Yard out. We get a bit busy at times and can use an extra hand now and then."

"But I have heard of you, Mr. Holmes, through the articles written by, you, Dr. Watson, correct?" said Harry.

"Well, yes, I have on occasion written a story or two about Mr. Holmes' adventures, it is true," admitted I, but wanting to avoid that fact, knowing Holmes' thoughts about it.

"Can you and Dr. Watson find her, sir?" asked he again.

"I shall, with the Inspector's permission, be happy to assist in any way I can. What say you, Lestrade?"

"Well, I suppose you cannot hurt the investigation. But please make sure you do not delay my investigation in any way, Mr. Holmes."

"Certainly not, Inspector."

Holmes then produced a card from his vest pocket and handed it to Mr. Browner.

"I am available tomorrow, Mr. Browner. Please feel free to come by Baker Street and we shall discuss several points I wish to cover with you. Watson, we should leave now."

"Do not concern yourselves. With Mr. Holmes on your case he is sure to produce satisfactory results. It was a pleasure to meet you, despite the unpleasantness which has caused our meeting to take place," said I.

Miss Browner retrieved our coats and hats and we soon found ourselves hailing a hansom to return to Baker Street.

"A strange case, is it not Holmes?"

"It is either a kidnapping or a runaway, I cannot tell which yet, Watson."

"A runaway?" queried I.

"Certainly, you have not thought that perhaps the fiancée has had doubts? It does happen, you know."

"Why yes, but there appears to be no set time for the wedding, and I have always heard such desperate acts occur close to the wedding date itself, yes?" queried I.

"I intend to keep all possible motives open for her disappearance at this time. We have acquired very little more data to analyse right now. I hope we will learn more tomorrow when Harry Browner appears. I know I could have interviewed him there, but I think I am quite certain Lestrade would have taken offence. Since he brings me cases, he himself cannot solve, I wish to maintain a certain level of decorum so as to not have him restrain himself from coming to me."

"Yes, of course, I see, Holmes."

"There may come a day when my relationship with Lestrade will be such that any offence I send his way will not be a blow to his sense of authority. But for now, I am not willing to risk it. We've only worked a few cases together, you see."

It was earlier than I had expected when Harry Browner showed up. I had just arisen, but Holmes was still asleep, or so I thought.

I had offered Browner some tea when suddenly Holmes opened his door, "Ah, Mr. Browner, glad to see you so early and ready to solve this adventure. I hope you slept well?"

"Not really, sir. I am very worried about Helen. Who could do such a thing?"

"That is for us to find out, shall we get started?"

I provided all of us a cuppa and then sat to hear upon which direction Holmes was to go in solving this latest mystery. I was concerned that Mr. Browner was not quite at ease with Holmes' attitude, seeing as he was showing less empathy than I thought he should towards his new client.

Pulling him aside for a moment I spoke to him.

"Holmes, you are enjoying this too much in front of our client. He does not understand how it is that you find this stimulating. His glances when you turn away from him tell me he is not sure that your manner is sincere enough. Please less enjoyment and show more concern at the seriousness of the event, please, will you?"

Rather than acknowledging my admonishment and suggestion to me privately, he quickly turned to Mr. Browner and spoke again to him.

"Mr. Browner, please accept my apology if I have appeared to you as unconcerned or, in fact, seemed cavalier about your problem. I have rather a bad habit of not seeing these problems as anything but a puzzle to be solved. The logic of it all is my interest and sometimes it is easy for me to forget that my clients are not capable of getting past the emotional tidal wave that hits them when such event as these are happening to their loved ones. I cannot indulge in the emotion of the puzzle as it would distract me from the solution that my logical approach requires. The emotions will not solve the problem. It is a primitive part of our psyche which does nothing to get us closer to a solution.

"Please do not believe for a moment that I do not share in your concern, but I tell you that I must simply repress these feelings to be successful at solving these type mysteries."

"I…I understand, Mr. Holmes. I wish that I were able to do so, to…to limit myself to a logical approach, but… but I cannot. The bond with Helen, is not just an intellectual one. Our emotional bond is very strong, you see."

"I understand. You mind the emotions and I shall mind the logic and together we will find your Helen, safe and sound."

"Can you think of any reason why someone would want to abscond with her?"

"No, that's just it. Everyone whom I have met that knows Helen, well, they all are good people. I mean, she does not have friends or acquaintances that are in any way of an unsavoury character."

"What about others with whom she comes into contact? Where she eats her dinner, or with whom she does not have a full relationship with? Has she complained about anyone? Has she had any issues with any of them? Has she ever mentioned a patient with whom she has had a bad experience?"

"No…I don't recall… but, wait a minute! She did have an unusual patient a few months back."

"What was unusual about this patient?"

"It was a woman. The woman was admitted to hospital, but the doctors could not find anything actually wrong with her despite all the symptoms she claimed she had. After a week or so they discharged her. She became quite angry about that. Helen was one of her three nurses."

"Sounds like a case of hypochondria. I prefer Kant's definition over others," said I. "She's likely a bit unstable mentally, those patients tend to be that way."

"I guess you're right, Doctor, but Helen said she did not seem that way. In fact, when not complaining about her ailment, she had a way of turning each conversation around to where they would end up talking about Helen's family. At first, Helen said she didn't think of it as unusual as some patients do form relationships with their nurses. But after a while it was different from what Helen had experienced with other patients. It was a bit odd as she began asking Helen where her family was from, what were their names. Her parents, her paternal grandmother especially, even Helen's great-grandparents. Helen was willing to discuss it with her since that was the only time she wasn't complaining. Helen thought it would cheer her up a bit. She seemed genuinely interested in Helen's family history. But Helen took it in stride, thinking this was helping the woman through whatever she was experiencing. No harm, you know, just chit chatting with a patient to get them to calm down."

"Do you remember the patient's name?"

"No, I'm afraid not."

"I will call at hospital and find out," boasted I. "Surely it will be in the records. Do you happen to recall the day or week this took place?"

"I am fairly sure it was the last week in August. I remember Helen meeting me after her first shift in September. She said the lady had been turned out before the end of the month. They needed the bed and since there was nothing wrong with her, they forced her to leave."

"That will do. I know Collins over there. He's in charge of admission, dismissals too. I'll check the records and we'll see who that lady was," said I.

"Were there any others, Mr. Browner? We must be a thorough as we can be. Can't hang all our hopes on this one patient, right?"

"I agree, sir, but I cannot think of any others at this time. I'll try my best to remember any others that Helen might have mentioned."

"Good. Watson, suggest you check with your friend Collins today, if possible. The quicker we pull on this thread, the better."

"I'll leave now, Holmes. I should have some answers in just a few hours, that is, if Collins is available. Which hopefully he will be. Good day Mr. Browner."

I left and decided to walk to Moorfields. The excitement of the case had infused me with that jolt that often overwhelms one's body when excited, and I was sure a brisk walk would help me wear it off.

By the time I had reached the administrative wing where Collins' office was located, I had worked off most of the stimulant my body had previously produced.

To our luck, Collins was in. I chatted with him about old times for a short while before diving into our little problem of identifying his former patient. After a quarter of an hour his secretary came, knocked on his door, and handed him a file concerning the patient in question. Her name was Mrs. Nancy Gilcrest.

I returned and informed Holmes of the patient's name. To each of us and Mr. Browner, the name meant nothing. I had also obtained the street and number of her domicile.

Holmes thanked me for the information. When Holmes later spoke to Mr. Browner, he indicated that the patient's name meant nothing to him.

"This is a most disorienting case, Watson. All we know so far is that a Moorfields nurse appears to have been abducted on her way home. She had a patient that inquired about her lineage. Her fiancé seems sincere enough and does not appear to be involved in her disappearance. There has been no ransom note nor has, thankfully, been a body reported.

"I must retire and work with the facts we have. Lestrade may have been closer to the truth as we do lack better data.

You have heard me say there is not enough data, but sometimes it does not lack for volume, but does lack for quality. But to continue, I must this time resort to some speculation if for no other reason than to consider what might have happened to establish our most probable next steps."

With that he helped himself to a large quantity of tobacco from the slipper upon the mantel and reclined on the sofa. After alighting his pipe, he closed his eyes. I knew then that until he spoke to me again, there was no use disturbing him with any issue related to our new case or not.

I had thought to myself that a walk would do for me what Sherlock's reclining would do for him. I retrieved my hat and cane and left Holmes to his self-imposed isolation. My only hope was that I might happen upon a thought or two that might progress our case at least one step further.

Lestrade was correct despite Holmes' earlier injection of hope. There was not sufficient data with which to work. Miss Talberg was gone. No ransom note, no body but only inquiries about her family. Thinking of the perhaps helpless young woman, I soon found myself adrift in my thoughts and began daydreaming about a young lady I had met several weeks before, at a dinner party of one of my colleagues. As I completed my walk, I realized I had not remained focused on our pending case. The whimsical interlude of my imagination of how I might spend some new time with this young woman I had met, was now challenged by the reality of having to pay attention while crossing the busy street, having finished my walk in the gardens without such concern.

I had failed both Holmes and our client by letting myself succumb to the soothing effect of my daydream and thus alleviating the anxiety that overcame me while thinking about our case at hand. I quickly reminded myself of performing my duty, not unlike when in the Army, attending to the wounded, where personal cares mattered not.

When I arrived, Holmes was sitting at his desk and drawing a sketch of some sort.

"What's that you've got there, Holmes," queried I.

"It's the only fact of any merit that we have to work with so far, Watson."

"Oh, and what is that?"

"Having no other data to work with, I have conjured up a possible scene that until we get more valuable data, I intend to pursue.

"Why did our Mrs. Gilcrest not stop after asking Miss Talberg about her mother, why her grandmother and her great grandparents? Most people have never met their great-grandparents, some, not even all their grandparents. It would have seemed to perhaps have been some casual conversation had she asked about all her ancestry, after her father only on the distaff side of her paternal relative? And lastly, with such interest only on the maternal, why stop at her great-grandmother? Why not further back?

"I have drawn this little chart to help align my thinking with these generational questions."

I viewed his drawing and there were lines connected to names and dates.

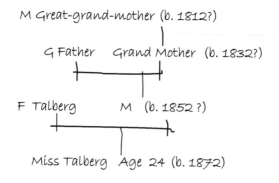

M Great-grand-mother (b. 1812?)

G Father   Grand Mother (b. 1832?)

F Talberg   M (b. 1852 ?)

Miss Talberg Age 24 (b. 1872)

"As of yet I do not have the actual dates of her ancestors' birthdates, but using a nominal twenty years per generation, we can project backward that the inquires pertain to some event that perhaps occurred when the great-grandmother was over the age of majority? Say twenty-one? I think our case really began sometime around 1832 or perhaps a few years either side. I will know more once I obtain actual birth years. But as I said earlier Watson, this is all speculation. Without further data, I will follow this trail until more is available."

"Is there anything I can help with now, Holmes?"

"I think not, Doctor, but should your walk have produced any ideas, I would like to know."

"Sherlock, but you were pondering the case. I saw you light up you pipe and withdraw?!"

"Your habits proceed you Doctor. I have on more than one occasion witnessed you leaving for a walk whence I have been 'pondering' as you call it. Such a creature of habit as you are, Doctor, it is but a simple deduction, for the likes of me."

"I will be going to a play, tonight, should you care to join me. It is a revival of Dionysius' 1841 masterpiece, *London Assurance*. Until I am able to request all the certificates of birth necessary to assemble the pieces of the puzzle together, there is no need to speculate endlessly. A night watching others perform their art is suitable for clearing the mind, as does sorbet between courses."

"I am willing to go with you, Holmes. As I am unfamiliar with this masterpiece, as you call it, I hope it is not one of these *new dramas* I have heard about. The old ones are good enough for me."

"My dear Doctor, do not fear, this will be, then, to your liking with the condition you have just attached to it. Shall we go now and regenerate ourselves beforehand with a hearty meal?"

With that encouragement we grabbed hats and canes and left our case and abode behind us.

*   *   *   *   *   *

"Where is it?"

"Where is what?" replied Helen.

"Do not play coy with us, missy."

"I have no idea what you are talking about."

"We know who you are."

"Who am I, that you believe I know something of importance? So important that you have kidnapped me off the streets?!!", yelled Helen in confused frustration at the situation in which she found herself.

"You are Helen Talberg. Your father, Johan Talberg, was the son of Francis Talberg and Mary Jehan. Mary

Jehan, your grandmother, was the daughter of Michelina Jehan, correct?"

Helen stared at them in amazement after hearing the litany of her ancestry which no one but her was likely to care about.

"I do not understand. What do my parents and grandparents have to do with me and you?" said Helen with a more than befuddled tone to her voice.

"You are Michelina Jehan's great-grand-daughter. Yes?"

"You are correct. But what has that to do with me?" said Helen again, with more than enough worry in her voice spoken to strangers, who knew of her family in such detail. She hoped by confirming her lineage they would reveal more about why they had abducted her.

"So, you see, Oscar, we have the right one after all. Didn't I tell you?" The silent Oscar nodded his head reluctantly, mumbling that he wasn't still sure, but acknowledged his accomplice's apparent success.

"What do you want with me?" cried out Helen, frustrated at the ropes that tied her to the chair into which she had been placed against her will.

"Where are your parents and grandparents?"

"All, but my mother, are dead," answering again so as to hopefully gain her freedom by cooperation.

"Do not lie to us!"

"I am not." said Helen, in a somewhat defiant tone that was beginning to show more fight than fear.

"Where is she, then?"

"Unless you untie me right now, I shall not answer any more of your questions."

The man turned away from her, but then, revolved swiftly and violently slapped her across her face with the back of his hand.

"You do not bargain with us!" yelled he.

Helen dropped her head and was crying after the startling attack that had just occurred.

"Where is the gold?"

"What gold?! I have no gold," said Helen.

"Your family must have the gold!"

"I do not know what you are talking about!"

"You are the great-grand-daughter of Michelina Jehan! Where is the gold!?"

"I told you, I don't…"

But an additional strike delivered such a blow that she now fell unconscious.

"It's time to go," said Oscar. "If she doesn't know, I now know who must know. We must find her. Bring her with us."

*   *   *   *   *   *

"Watson, have you a moment?"

"Of course, Holmes. What have you?"

"I have been to the Registry Office and have obtained more accurate data concerning the family tree:

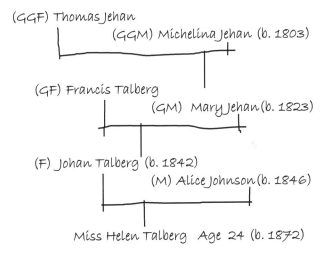

(GGF) Thomas Jehan
(GGM) Michelina Jehan (b. 1803)

(GF) Francis Talberg
(GM) Mary Jehan (b. 1823)

(F) Johan Talberg (b. 1842)
(M) Alice Johnson (b. 1846)

Miss Helen Talberg   Age 24 (b. 1872)

"You see, we were accurate enough with our twenty-year estimate. There is something queer about this lineage, though, it seems familiar, but as yet, I cannot place it."

"No doubt it will come to you, Holmes. I have faith you will solve it."

"I am also confident I will," said he. "Perhaps I shall return to my monograph and clear this present problem from my mind. I will return before dinner."

And with that he had grabbed his coat, hat and cane and was off with his manuscript, on the subject of fingernails, under his arm. This was the first time I'd seen him seek solitude elsewhere whilst writing, but then it would not be the last time I would be surprised by his decisions. I thought surely, he would continue work here, but I was amiss in my judgement of his choice of actions.

I picked up the afternoon paper and began to read latest of the day's news. There was nothing more with regards to our little case, as yesterday's paper had quoted Lestrade as implying it was a run-away, much to the paper's chagrin. No more to the story was there.

It was before dinner that he returned. His lack of interest and disrespect for his monograph, that he had flung onto his desk, alerted me that not all was as it should be.

"Holmes, a successful outing?" I confess I baited him.

"Watson, you know better!"

"What is wrong, Holmes?"

"This case absorbs me. I know there is a link in the past but I have not found it."

"What, then, do you have in mind?

"If, we are correct that the case's solution lies in the past, then to the past we must go to find the solution.

"I shall not trouble you, though, with such a tedious task. I intend tomorrow to use the time machine, as it were, that we have at our disposal and find the solution to this puzzle."

"Holmes, what on earth are you talking about?" queried I.

"A *Time Machine*, Watson. That is all we need."

"Wells' machine is pure fiction!"

"Ah, but I have found one good enough for our purposes. Good night, Doctor!"

I could get no more response out of him. His fanciful thought of transporting through time, as had just been proposed by a twenty-nine-year-old fiction writer about what the science of the future foretold, astonished me. Had he been dabbling again with those unconscionable drugs?

I knew I would no longer get an answer from him, so I too retired for the evening.

The next morning, Holmes was nowhere to be found. I had made a fitful attempt to sleep through the night and was most unsuccessful as a result. I believe I awoke more exhausted than before I retired. After a quarter hour or so, I realized I had not seen the note he had left for me on the mantle. It read simply:

> Do not worry my friend. I shall
> send word when the time is right.
>
> - Holmes

What is one to do when left with such directions, or as was this case, virtually, no directions at all? I spent all of the next several days with Holmes maintaining his incommunicado status.

It is not that I had not experienced this behaviour from him before. As my dear readers know, the first time or two this happened, it completely bewildered me. But even now, not hearing his words explaining his thoughts, not having some idea of where he was or what he was doing bore on me like carrying a heavy sack of sand and not knowing how far I was to carry it.

It was several days later when a runner delivered a note:

> Watson,
>
> Be so kind as to make yourself ready to accompany me once I have located our victim. You shall need your pistol and, (as I would not have been permitted entry with mine), could you please have mine loaded and ready to go as well? Also please prepare six lengths of rope, 3 feet each shall do. We will be challenged no doubt, but I am confident we shall win the day with both surprise and being armed on our side.
>
> Holmes

P.S. I am anticipating my return to
Baker Street at 3 o'clock this very day.
S

As Holmes had committed, it was three o'clock when the door opened, Holmes entered and simply stated, "We must leave at once, have you our pistols ready?"

"Yes, Holmes. Here is yours, freshly cleaned and loaded. But where are we going?"

"No time for that now, our cab waits for us. Be quick now!"

I followed Holmes as fast as I could, barely keeping up with him as he practically slid down the toe of each step. I nearly tripped trying to keep up.

We rushed into the cab but Holmes had tapped the ceiling of the hansom with his cane before both my feet had entered. No doubt Holmes had informed the cabbie there was a large tip for him should he get us to our destination as quickly as possible. The crack of the cabbie's whip instructed the massive beast powering our cab into its sole purpose of transporting us. It lurched us forward and I was thrown into my seat. It eventually gained top speed that neither of us could have maintained for much time on our own.

Holmes sat in silence. I reminded him he was to explain our quest once we were on our way.

"Holmes, where are we going?" quired I.

"To rescue Miss Talberg, of course," replied Holmes.

"You have found her?"

"I am quite certain where we will find her. It is the only logical place."

"So, you are guessing?"

"Not guessing, Watson. It is the only place that makes sense."

"But our pistols and the ropes? What awaits us?"

"The villains we are dealing with would appear to be playing a rough game, Watson. I believe they have killed before and I do not want to take any chances that we would put ourselves in more danger than we could handle. Our pistols shall level the pitch a bit. The ropes will be obvious when the time comes. Three for each of us should do just fine."

Within a few more minutes, Holmes rapped the ceiling hard this time to overcome the sounds of the speeding coach. It came to as abrupt a stop as could be expected after the cabbie had had his steed as full out as possible. We lurched forward suddenly in our seats and I fell on the floorboard.

Holmes leapt out and handed the cabbie his fare and tip. He motioned me to the wall alongside the street and waited 'til the cabbie had disappeared before saying anything.

"We've a block to go on foot, Watson. I cannot have a fast cab arriving and causing attention."

We began a casual walk eastward. We had travelled the block and I found us across the street from a modest house with a very small but ill kept front garden path leading up to a withered front door in need of a fresh coat of green paint.

"Watson, we must take advantage of the element of surprise. It is very likely they will not be expecting our arrival. I intend you to play the part of a visitor, but knocking on the wrong door. I ask that you distract them as long as possible. I shall secret myself around to the back entrance and enter either with ease or otherwise. You must distract them long enough. Can you do so? There are two women's lives at stake, Watson, and we mustn't let them down."

"Two?" queried I in confusion. "I shall do as you say, Holmes. You let me know when to start."

"Have you your watch?"

"Yes, of course."

"Approach the door in two minutes."

Before I could confirm I would do so, he was off. I watched as he went back to the side of the adjacent house. I kept my eye on my watch. As the two minutes were completed, I began walking towards the house but feigned a confused appearance as to exactly where I was headed on the oft chance someone inside might have caught sight of me.

I stopped as if making up my mind on my next action and pretended that I had decided to make an inquiry as to where a 'Mr. Rutherford' might live nearby.

I walked up the path and once at the door I used the faded brass door knocker somewhat vigorously to arouse the occupants and notify them of my presence.

Daniel J. Darrouzet

At first there was no response. My immediate thought was that perhaps Holmes had the wrong abode. I wondered if perhaps they would just ignore me, and Sherlock's plan would suddenly collapse. Maybe they had not even heard the knock?

I decided to try again. This time I heard footsteps approaching the door. The door did not open.

"Go away!"

"Pardon me, I'm not selling anything. Is this where Mr. Rutherford lives?" asked I. "Mr. James Rutherford?"

"I said, go away"

"But I am sure this is the address at which Mr. Rutherford told me to meet him."

"No one here by that name, now go away!" shouted he, this time more angrily.

"Excuse me then, but is there then a neighbour nearby perhaps, by the name of Mr. James Rutherford?"

At that moment I heard the metal latch being unlocked. I braced myself as to what I would next encounter. My hand slipped into the pocket of my overcoat and I gripped the handle of my trusted service revolver.

The door opened but a few inches and one eye of my host looked through to see me standing there with as pleasant a face as I could muster under the circumstances. The face below the eye was rough and hadn't been shaved in some time, I observed. It wasn't a neatly trimmed beard, just scruff.

The door then opened a little wider and the whole face of my host was exposed for my viewing.

As I tried my best to take in the features of the man of about equal height to me, I took a step back as next the barrel of a pistol came through the gap between the jamb and the door and was levelled at me.

"I said 'go away'!" he screamed at me.

"Yes sir. Meant no harm. Must be the wrong house, you see."

"I don't care who or what you are, I said 'go away'. If you don't, I'll make you wish you never …"

"Oscar! Help!" came a yell from the back of the house. It was a woman's voice.

My host turned towards the shout and I saw my chance.

I charged the door putting my shoulder against it while at the same time drawing my weapon out of my pocket.

My sudden aggression caught my host off guard and he stumbled backward as the door hit his head hard. I heard his cry of the sudden pain I had inflicted. His pistol discharged, but the angle was up and away from me as he fell backwards. I rushed in and pointed my pistol at his head while he lay flat on his back on the floor. The gash to his forehead, produced copious amounts of blood as most head wounds do.

"Let go your weapon," instructed I.

"Holmes!" cried I. "Holmes?"

"It is fine Watson, excellent work. I have his partners back here. Tie yours up and bring him here."

Still dazed by the assault I bore on him; he obeyed my command and I was able to remove the pistol from his hand. Next, I turned him over and tied his hands firmly behind his back.

I found a small tablecloth on a table near the door which I used to stem his bleeding head.

I helped him to his feet and with my pistol digging into his back, prodded him into the back room.

There I found Holmes, who was finishing tying up my host's partners. A young man and an older woman.

Next to them were two women, gagged and tied in two separate chairs. One was a young woman and the other appeared older.

Holmes, having finished, turned to the older woman first and removed her gag. I went to the younger one and removed the gag tied so tightly about her mouth.

"Oh, thank you gentlemen!" shouted the younger.

"Yes, thank you!" said the older one with quite an exasperated voice.

"Who are you?" queried the younger one.

"I am Dr. John Watson and he is Mr. Sherlock Holmes."

"You would be Miss Talberg," said Holmes to the younger, "and you would be Miss Alice Johnson, no doubt."

"Yes, but how did you know and how did you know to find us here?'

"All in good time. Watson please go and find the

constable two block over. Have him contact the Yard and give him this address so he can tell Lestrade where to find us. I've already sent word to Browner to join us. I will untie the ladies and keep watch over our little family."

It seemed longer but it was only twenty minutes before Lestrade arrived. He was accompanied by several constables. Mr. Browner and his sister arrived a few minutes later.

"Good afternoon, Lestrade," said Holmes upon the Inspector's arrival.

"What have you for me today, Mr. Holmes?"

"I present to you, the recently abducted Miss Helen Talberg and Miss Alice Johnson."

"Helen!" shouted Mr. Browner, as he pushed past one of the constables and embraced her tightly in his arms.

"I see you've found our missing nurse, eh, Mr. Holmes?

"Yes. Yes, indeed. Also, let me introduce you to Miss Talberg's mother, Miss Alice Johnson."

"Mum."

"Who are these three you have tied up?"

"They are our kidnappers, and likely thieves and perhaps murderers, should you take time to delve into their past."

"But how'd you find them, Mr. Holmes?" queried Lestrade.

"As you know Inspector, our little adventure began this time with the queer patient that had made inquiries about Miss Talberg's grandparents and great-grandparents."

"I thought it all began when Miss Browner disappeared," responded Lestrade.

"Is this not the patient you attended Miss Talberg while she was in hospital?"

"Yes, it is she, but her hair is quite different. I thought she looked familiar."

"So, you see, Inspector, her asking such detailed questions immediately indicated there was something not quite right about it at all. But obviously, it was connected to the past. Thus, I needed a time machine, and I found one."

"A what?"

"Like that Mr. Wells' story, is what he means, Inspector. Holmes is joking with you," said I.

"Not entirely Watson. We do possess such a device, but perhaps not in the form or as an exquisite one as Mr. Wells' device is described to be."

"Holmes?" queried I.

"Watson, I have spent the last several days absent from you in the only time machine available to us, that is the *Times'* repository and I have reviewed many of their pertinent archives regarding the facts of our case. I experienced the nature of our fair London, some sixty odd years ago by reading about it.

"It was quite the struggle to read so many articles from so long ago and then make sense of all that has been laid out in front of us."

"Yes, our adventure, if truth be known, actually began some fifty or sixty years ago.

"It would seem that a shipment of gold from Brazil to be delivered here, was stolen once it arrived.

"The story is long, but in the end a Mr. Thomas Jehan and his wife Michelina Jehan were involved in the theft. The gold was never found. It was presumed to have been sold. But I now believe it was not.

"These three are a family set, you see. I believe their name is Gabbart, or at least descendants of the Gabbarts."

"How do you know that?!" Oscar asked angrily.

"Who are these…these Gabbarts?" asked a very confused looking Inspector Lestrade.

"They were the original conspirators who stole the gold. Not these three, but a young man and his uncle. These are their descendants.

"As I said, the gold was never found. Thomas and Michelina were the last known possessors. They claimed they sold it off, and that was the end of the trail. I believe that perhaps they only told the police that they had sold it. These descendants of the Gabbarts, no doubt, have heard the story of the stolen gold over and over. Why not contact the only living relatives of the Jehan's and see where the gold, if there is any left, might be?"

"Any truth to what he just said?" Lestrade turned to the three tied up villains. He got no response.

"I would suggest the one person here who would know the answer would be Miss Johnson. What say you, madam?"

"You are correct, Mr. Holmes. My husband's grandmother, on his maternal side, was Michelina Jehan. I too heard the stories about his grandparents and their involvement in the crime.

"I understood that, once they were released from prison, they moved to the country and lived a quiet life. My husband said they lived modestly, but the odd thing was they never worked.

"He was quite certain that the idea they'd hidden the gold for themselves was true. When his mother passed, his father had died first, he inherited a chest. The letter his mother had written to him explained that it was the stolen gold. She and her husband had decided to just disappear from London and live a less conspicuous life once they got out of prison.

"The amount of gold had been depleted quite a bit by the time my husband received it. At first, he would not touch it or use it. But he could not give it away either, as he wished the whole affair to remain forgotten.

"As we got older, we fell on some hard times ourselves and we both agreed we'd take only a little of it to bide us over the rough times.

"Life is long, sir, and before we knew it, we'd used up most of the gold left to us."

"So, there is some left?" enquired Lestrade.

"I gave the last of it to those three, two days ago, begging them to let me go. Then they brought Helen in and I knew we were in trouble since there was no more to give them."

Lestrade went over and instructed the constables to search the pockets of the three. In a moment or two the larger of the two constables came over to Lestrade and handed him two small ingots of gold. I would estimate only several ounces each at best. While not a small amount, and it could keep a person comfortable for a year or so, they certainly did not add up to the great fortune our three villains where seeking.

"And what do you know about this, Miss... Miss Talberg," queried Lestrade.

"I know nothing of it."

"She's telling you the truth, sir" said her mother. "I never told her of the gold."

"She's lying!" yelled the older Gabbart's woman.

"She's got more! She has to have more!"

"You are mistaken. I gave you all that was left," said Alice.

"It was we Gabbarts that did the stealing! We thought it up and we took the risks and you Jehan's got all the gold! It isn't fair, I tell you. It isn't fair!" she yelled out in a desperate voice, as if the all the pain it had brought her somehow justified her family getting a reward.

"Constable Higgins, take these three down to the Yard and hold them."

"It's our gold! It's our gold!" she yelled.

"Remove them, Constable," instructed the Inspector.

The constables led them away while they still were protesting their claim to the stolen gold.

"May I take Miss Talberg and her mother out of here now?" queried Mr. Browner.

"Yes, Miss Talberg can go. But I need Miss Johnson to stay. I will need a statement from you later though, Miss Talberg. A constable will come over later to take it."

"I cannot leave without my mother."

"Then perhaps Mr. Browner and his sister will stay with you in the next room. I need to speak to your mother and Inspector Lestrade," interjected Holmes.

The three went to the next room, leaving Miss Johnson, Inspector Lestrade, Holmes and me in the back room.

"I'm not sure about this," said Lestrade. "What's all this about stolen gold?"

"The newspapers covered it back in 1840. It is as Miss Johnson has described. Johan Talberg's maternal grandmother was Michelina Jehan. She and her husband were part of the theft. Her daughter, Mary, married Francis Talberg. Their son, Johan Talberg, married Miss Johnson here, you see.

"But where is Mrs. Talberg?" Lestrade.

"I am she," offered Miss Johnson.

"I changed back to my maiden name after my husband died, trying to avoid any attention or connection to the theft. My father always said to beware of the remaining Gabbarts family."

"I will need to charge you with theft, madam," asserted Inspector Lestrade.

"Now, Inspector. You have yet to state Miss Johnson her rights about stating anything that may be used against her in her Majesty's courts."

"Ah, you're correct, Mr. Holmes. You have the right..."

"Come now, Lestrade. This woman did not steal the gold. And I would venture to say that both the theft and receipt of it have long passed the limitation of applying the law. And lastly, they have been traumatized enough being the subject of kidnapping."

"You have several valid points, Mr. Holmes. All right I shall discuss it with my superiors and at this time I will simply reserve the right to pursue this matter later."

"Thank you. Inspector," said Miss Johnson.

"Mum," mumbled Lestrade.

"One thing, I do not understand Mr. Holmes. How did you know where to find these people?" enquired Lestrade.

"After finding the names of the families at the General Registry Office, I was able to uncover Mrs. Talberg's, maiden name. I then was able to find her address."

"Well done, Holmes!" said I. "Shall we not join the others?"

Lestrade led the way but did not stay to converse more. We reunited Miss Talberg with her mother.

"Come, Helen. Let's get you and your mother to our home," said Mr. Browner.

"I'll get you both a warm cuppa when we get there," offered Jane.

"Holmes, you have done it again. Such a strange story. How a crime from the past could find itself harming people not in existence and unknown at the time it was originally committed, well it's beyond me."

"Watson, the criminal mind is delusional when it comes

to the future. It sees only the present as a reality. Little does it comprehend the consequences of its actions even should they be executed as precisely as they are planned. Nature, life, have a habit of getting in the way."

THE ADVENTURE OF
THE CITY OF LONDON

I had been staying in my new accommodations for just over a few months with this gentleman, introduced to me by Stamford, who had been my dresser at Bart's. While convenient for me from a fiscal perspective, I was beginning to wonder if my quick decision had been a wise one or not. Sherlock Holmes is his name, and he is a most peculiar individual. I had queried myself repeatedly about my hasty decision prompted by my need to find a suitable domicile at a reasonable price in London. Could I endure the odd habits of this man, I began to wonder?

Holmes had begun an experiment of sorts at the beginning of the week. The chemicals he used were yielding profoundly odoriferous results. I found that I was glad to be spending so much time out of our new residence at 221B Baker Street. Not interfering with his work by direct inquiry, I concluded by the smell of the compound used, or perhaps being produced, that it must have a sulphur component. The acrid odour would at times overwhelm me. I had to leave rather than complain to my new roommate. I had also discovered there were times when his mood was as foul as his concoctions. I wished to avoid beginning a quarrel that might lead to each of us being on our own again, at least in the near future.

Complaining to him was always an option I had, but I was not ready yet to do so, for the likely repercussions of such a confrontation would not be a good, I concluded. To be fair, he had warned me of such possibilities, and I had chosen to decline to object when I had the opportunity. I suppose my imagination of what he had meant when he described his propensity for 'conducting experiments' was much less creative than his scientific curiosity. But now, I did know. My only solutions for dealing with his annoying research were to endure these experiments, make myself scarce whilst he conducted them, or choose to terminate our just formed relationship.

I chose the middle option for now, which led me to find ways to occupy my time out of our abode when Holmes was busy at his bench.

But I had now a good reason to be away, as I had been seeking some monetary backing in order to acquire a surgery from which I could attend patients. It was a promise I had made to myself after my return from my duty to Queen and country. As I delved further into attempting to secure such backing, it became more obvious that this direct method, while seemingly most pragmatic from my point of view, was far less convincing to the various bankers with whom I discussed my situation.

In each case, the questions were the same. Where had I gotten my degree? How long had I been a practicing M.D.? How long was I in the military? When did I leave the service? How many patients had I? Had I ever operated a surgery before? It was relentless and left me quite discouraged. A certain amount of melancholy would overtake me from time to time, but I knew I must persevere, lest I end up doing nothing fruitful in what remaining time I was destined to live.

The last banker I had spoken to was actually rather helpful in the end. Rather than quickly assessing that I was too great a risk, as had all the prior ones with whom I had spoken, he actually spoke with me in a manner that was quite civil and devoid of the rudeness I had felt displayed by the others towards me. He was an older gentleman who was near the end of his banking career, or so I surmised. I believe he could easily see my frustration and disappointment. But rather than making me feel as though I was wasting his time, as the others had done, he changed the course of the conversations into one of teaching me why I was getting the responses I had gotten up until then.

He explained that, from the perspective of a banker, he

was taking too much of a risk on a person, even a medical doctor, who had not much practical experience with patients who had to pay for their appointments. He pointed out that whilst I was an Army doctor, the fees were not a part of the service I provided. I had to agree that was true. He advised me to consider finding another doctor who perhaps was soon to close his own surgery for good, and who might consider bringing me on to help him ease out of his practice. I could then gain the experience of running a surgery, not just practicing medicine, which he pointed out were two entirely different things.

I had not thought about it that way before. While he did not lend me any money, he did plant a seed in my mind that perhaps this was a more realistic solution to my problem than my original plan could have produced.

I returned from that encounter and found that Holmes had abandoned his experiment and was entertaining an official of some sort.

"Ah, Watson, glad you have returned. May I please introduce you to Commander Nigel Williams, from the City of London's Police. Commander Williams, this is Dr. John Watson, late of Her Majesty's Berkshires and my roommate."

"Nice to meet you, sir," said I.

"Doctor," said he curtly, with a most restrained look upon his face.

"Watson, Commander Williams was just telling me a most fascinating tale and I am glad you have returned to hear of it."

"I'm sorry, Mr. Holmes. I would prefer we keep our conversation private. No offence to you, Doctor, but this is an official police matter, and I would prefer my conversation remain confidential with Mr. Holmes."

"That is not a problem, Commander. I certainly understand. I shall retire to my room and leave you gentlemen to your discussion," said I.

"Commander, I think we can count on Dr. Watson's discretion in this matter."

"Mr. Holmes, I am uncomfortable discussing this even with you, so I must insist that we keep this between ourselves."

"Holmes, it is all right. It is nice to have made your

acquaintance, sir," said I. I walked away to my room and closed the door.

In any event, I decided that I needed time to think about what that last banker had said to me. I had no particular interest in what Holmes and the Commander were discussing. I felt I would be interfering, and the Commander had made his thoughts on the subject quite clear. After sequestering myself in my room, I began to write in my journal different ideas that came to my mind regarding what the banker had said to me and what actions I must likely take to follow up on. I took his suggestion as a wise one.

It was perhaps one-half hour later that my efforts were arrested by Holmes knocking on my door.

"Watson, you should come out now. The Commander has left," said he.

I finished my last thought and entered it into my journal. I emerged to find Holmes in the state of some excitement.

"Watson, I have another case!" exclaimed Holmes.

"What's that you say, Holmes?"

"The Commander is in need of my help."

"I am happy for you, Holmes. Does this mean you will forego your experiment at least for the time being?" queried I, expressing some hope for a positive answer in my tone of voice.

"I'm afraid sadly, I must. The experiment is one that I can pursue at a later date. The case, though, is a fascinating tale and it is quite a challenge he has presented to me. Let me explain it to you."

"But Holmes, he specifically requested that I not be privy to it. Didn't he?"

"He is embarrassed, Watson. He has a problem that he cannot solve on his own."

"I somehow doubt that, Holmes. Does he not have all the resources of Scotland Yard at his disposal?"

"Watson, you are not thinking correctly, or perhaps you did not hear me clearly when I introduced him to you. Commander Williams is with the City of London Police, not Scotland Yard."

"I'm sorry, I do not follow you."

"I suppose it is to be expected since you are not originally from London. The Square Mile is not under the jurisdiction of Scotland Yard. The whole of London is, but not the City of London. The City has been its own bailiwick from the days of its founding. It has retained its own police and there is a large amount of pride about this fact felt by those on that force. The City of London Police have their own ways and they consider the men of Scotland Yard to be outsiders. While they could ask for the Yard's help, I believe what we are seeing here is a desire to not do so, so he can avoid embarrassment. His case is baffling him and he cannot solve it. I do give him credit for realizing his limitations. His solution at present is to seek help from me, Sherlock Holmes, the world's first consulting detective! Is that not grand!?"

"Well, I knew it was its own little town, so to speak, but I was unaware that it had its own police force. But I do recollect, Holmes, reading something a while back. It was not something that much mattered to me at the time, but I do remember about some commission or other, a few years ago, trying to eliminate the difference between the Square Mile and the rest of London. Is that what you mean?"

"Exactly, Watson."

"Seems a bit of a waste. I mean, why have the same services for a mere square mile? Does not seem very efficient to me."

"You are correct, Doctor, but sometime tradition overcomes efficiency and even logic. It is the way of the Square Mile and so we accept it as the basis for our next little problem."

"Holmes, I understand, but as concerns my helping you, since he has requested that I not be made privy to his problem, why are you willing to share his tale with me?"

"His problem is in regards to a death, which I believe will be determined to be a murder and I believe your medical background will be of great use to me in my effort to solve it. I would much appreciate it if you would assist me in my little adventure here. What say you?"

"I'm not sure what to say. I suppose I could, if you believe I can be of some help."

"Excellent. I believe there is to be an autopsy tomorrow. Shall you join me in witnessing it?"

"Yes. But what if the Commander is present?"

"Leave that to me. As far as I am concerned, and as he shall soon learn, you are my *dresser* in this case. If he wishes me to help him, he must allow me your presence. I doubt most sincerely he will object since his only other choice is to ask for the Yard's help, which he will not do under the circumstances."

"All right, Holmes, but I am still a bit concerned I will not be welcomed."

"Watson, all will be fine. Just follow me."

I did not think this was wise of Holmes to go against the wishes of his client, but I decided to let this play move on to the next act and see what came of it. It was getting near dinner time and Holmes suggested we go to Kettner's over in Soho. I was up for a change of pace and decided on the spot to accompany him there. But, after I agreed, again my mind began questioning even this decision.

It had been over twenty years since the cholera outbreaks had devastated the people living in Soho. I had heard about the epidemic as a youth and we later studied its history while in medical school. While now the area was more known for its reputation as a part of London where one can satisfy one's less than virtuous desires, I felt that somehow that pestilence might still be lingering about and wondered why I had said 'yes' so quickly. He was, though, so alive in his reaction to this new case. I found that I was sharing in his excitement. My melancholy seemed to have faded just listening to him. I admit that his need to have me help him was like a healthy tonic to me.

Our enthusiasm for going to the establishment was both diminished and at the same time encouraged when we arrived, as we found it was so crowded, we were required to wait a good one-half hour before being able to be seated and order our meal. I must say it was worth it, and I was happy that Holmes had invited me. It would seem that my rescue from his experiments that is to say, his acquiring a case, had its advantages since it was obvious his mood was much improved with this challenge before him. We enjoyed the atmosphere, but before we had finished, I realized that his mind had already begun drifting from the revelry of the other patrons to focus his intellect on the problem confronting him. I later saw this ability of his frequently and learned of his uncanny ability to block out what ever distractions that surrounded him when on a case.

"Holmes, shall we go?" asked I, shouting at him as the din of the place made a normal volume impossible to hear.

"Perhaps, we should. I find I have already two or three theories about my little problem that would be better served if I could ponder them while smoking my pipe, which I have forgotten to bring with me. The meal has served its purpose. Let us retire to Baker Street and along the way I shall tell you what I know about it all so far."

We exited Kettner's and hailed a cab. He began his tale which would once again draw me into the world of crime and his detection and fight against it. I had only assisted him on one previous adventure, but I had not yet decided from that experience if I possessed the character demanded of the role, in which he had cast me, to continue. I decided that night I would again keep in my journal some notes of this new adventure, as I had done before.

I thought and hoped right then that someday I would have the opportunity to present this case to the public, in order to further explain this amazing man's intellect. I likely shall have been long deceased, since this case is of such a discreet subject at this time, that I am sworn to its secrets for now. Having assisted him only once before, as I have described to you, my dear readers, in the *Study In Scarlet*, I find it cathartic to memorialize his adventures. I believe it allows me to make sense of what I experience when I am helping him.

It is not all together that different from my medical practice. The notes I make concerning my patients were a habit I had developed from my time at Bart's. I felt I could better be of help to Holmes if I could recall details later. It was not long before I realized that, while I was dependent on my note taking to bolster up my memory of facts and information, Holmes needed no such crutch. When engaged in a case, it would seem, his mind was superior to mine in its ability to remember the minutest detail and not only retrieve it when needed, but make connections between such details that would never have occurred to me.

"You see, Watson, the problem that confronts the Commander is that the crime occurred at the domicile of the Commissioner of the City of London. A most delicate situation indeed!"

"Holmes, if it is of such a nature, do you not believe the utmost discretion is called for?" asserted I.

"Yes, Watson, you are correct. We must pursue this case with the confidentiality maintained by a priest who has heard a confession."

"Then, again, I must question the soundness of involving me and making me privy to the issues."

"Watson, your help in my last case was without a doubt a contributing force in its resolution. I have to admit, relaying to you my thoughts on that case was, I found, extremely helpful.

"While I do not believe the notes you take are completely necessary, I admit to you, your notes and comments have a value to me."

"Are you saying that my notes, helped you solve the case?"

"Yes, but not perhaps in the way you are implying. No, your notes and suggestions I found were quite worthless in solving the case, except that you did chronicle the events which were unimportant."

I was insulted at these words from his mouth.

"If they are so useless," said I, "why do you wish for my assistance in this case?"

"Your notes helped me to eliminate the possible, yet improbable points of the case. I find that by eliminating the improbable, I was able to more quickly find a resolution and that is invaluable. It is much like an experiment that does not work. A true scientist must admit that failed experiments can yield results in that it eliminates the possibilities that he attempts to prove valid.

"In this case we have a corpse of a young woman who was in attendance at a dinner party at the Commissioner's residence. She arrived as the guest of a young officer. I do not believe they were engaged, if I accept what the Commander conveyed to me as being correct.

"He stated they, along with two other young couples, were invited to dinner by the Commissioner and his wife. Each of the other officers also are on the force at the City of London Police. It seems that this is an annual event. The Commissioner and his wife invite two or three young men of promise to have a dinner with them. Williams said that the Commissioner has several rules with regards to this dinner. He only invites unmarried men, who are required to bring a lady guest, and they are only invited once."

"That seems like a rather odd rule, don't you agree, Holmes?" said I.

"Yes, it struck me so as well. In any event, these eight people found themselves together just two nights ago. As I understand it, the evening started out quite normally. The guests arrived and introductions were made. I am to go to the Commander's office after the autopsy tomorrow and obtain the list of guests. I plan on meeting with each separately as soon as is practicable afterwards."

"So, I take it by the fact of there being an autopsy, that the cause of death is unclear?"

"Yes, the only data I have so far is that the young woman had perhaps consumed a bit more sherry and later wine than was perhaps good for her. She was, by some attendees' description, 'inebriated'. After dinner had been served and consumed by all there, she then, it is reported, started feeling ill.

"It was not until after dinner when the group had separated, that she later complained about some pain in her back and then eventually collapsed never to regain consciousness again.

"The Commissioner and his young charges had gone into his study for a smoke and the young women had stayed with the Commissioner's wife in the parlour. Once she collapsed, the Commissioner's wife called for help and they tried making her comfortable. A doctor was called but it was too late. Shortly after he arrived, she died.

"That is the extent of the data I have so far. I am anxious to speak to each of the guests myself. I am certain important data has been lost in this retelling of the tale. I will think much better of my chances at solving this, once I have queried all seven of these people. I will of course need to question the servants as well. There are but two of them, though, according to the Commander."

We retired and had agreed upon an early start so as not to be late for the early morning proceedings.

The next morning found us at the City of London morgue. I worried about my appearance and acceptance of my attendance, but Holmes seemed to have no concern whatsoever. I kept looking for the Commander, but saw not a sign of him. There were several young medical students in attendance anxiously waiting for the procedure to begin. One appeared to have said something humorous as another student tried most desperately to suppress a laugh. This resulted in the presiding physician in charge turning quite quickly towards them. He displayed a scowl that told whomever had caused such a disturbance in his presence that they'd best not do it again.

"You are, I presume, Mr. Sherlock Holmes?" said this physician, looking at Holmes and ignoring me as I stood behind Holmes. "Commander Williams told me of his request for your presence. I am Dr. Witherspoon. Please stand over there and do not interfere in any way." Turning to me, he enquired as to who I was and the reason for my presence.

I introduced myself to him. It took me a moment, but I remembered that there had been a Witherspoon at Barts, while I was in attendance. I enquired and found out that indeed this Dr. Witherspoon had a son who also had attended when I did and thus there was a relationship of sorts that quickly allowed for the acceptance of my presence, at least by Dr. Witherspoon.

He invited me to observe next to the table, which I readily accepted and to which Holmes showed the most pleasant approval. I was handed a white apron to put on by one of the students nearby. We were about to begin and luckily there was yet no sign of Commander Williams.

"I shan't wait any longer," said Dr. Witherspoon. "I imagine something of greater importance has delayed Williams, but I have my own appointments for the day. Let us begin."

It was a normal procedure from the few autopsies I have done and others I have observed. It was, though, quite obvious once we had cut through enough of the *hypodermis* that the woman had suffered from internal bleeding. The exact cause of this was unclear for now.

After further examination, it was clear that the haemorrhaging had primarily come from the liver. A painful death without a doubt.

"Internal bleeding from unknown causes I would say," said he as he looked over to the court documentarian. That should do it, don't you agree Dr. Watson?" Dr. Witherspoon was beginning to untie his apron, when suddenly there was a voice from the back of the room.

"Turn her over."

"Who said that!?" replied Dr. Witherspoon, his eyes darting around trying their best to identify the speaker. The students cringed and avoided eye contact with their instructor. I, though, had recognized Holmes' voice, but I remained silent.

"I did," responded Holmes.

"And who gave you permission to speak, sir, for I did not?"

"The dead woman cries out for justice," replied Holmes.

"What's that you say?"

"If you weren't such a fool, you would look at her back."

"How dare you speak to me in that manner, sir? I shan't be spoken to that way. I don't care if you are Commander Williams' guest or not. Now get out!"

"Not before you turn her over."

"I shall do no such thing."

"You must be afraid of what you'll find, then."

"I will not stand by and be insulted like this. You," he said pointing to one of the students, "go and ask that the constable of the day be sent here immediately to throw this man out of here."

"You, sir, have attended your last autopsy in my presence, I assure you."

"That may well be, but will you not turn her over?"

"I will not."

"Then I shall do it for you," said Holmes as he approached the table and motioned for me to assist him.

"Holmes, this is most unorthodox. I do not think we should be doing this" said I, in a whisper.

"It will be all right, Doctor," said Holmes.

We had the body turned over and while Witherspoon was in shock at what had taken place, Holmes was searching the woman's back with a magnifying glass.

"Ah ha! Here, you see it, don't you, Watson? Take a look."

I took the lens from Holmes' hand and focused on the area where he had placed his left middle figure.

Then I saw it. A small dark red dot that looked to be quite similar to those that sometimes are left behind by a hypodermic needle after giving an injection.

I nodded my head in agreement and then Dr. Witherspoon approached the table. I leaned over to him and spoke quite softly.

"Sir, no disrespect at all, but I believe Mr. Holmes is correct. This entry wound, if we may call it that, may be the cause of this lady's haemorrhaging. I think you may want to examine it in more detail."

He grabbed the magnifying glass from my hand and observed the puncture wound for himself. He then asked that the body be turned over again and I and a student accommodated this request.

He then removed several organs and then the liver. As he turned it over one could see where some thin sharp object had indeed penetrated into the liver and had in all likelihood begun the poor woman's long painful death.

"What you have proposed to me Dr. Watson, appears to be correct." He turned to the documentarian and told him to make an additional note in his record.

"I am done here!" said he emphatically, and without another word he left the room, not looking at anyone, especially not at Holmes.

By this time the constable of the day had arrived. With Dr. Witherspoon gone, there was nothing for him to do. He turned around and left also.

"Well Watson, what do you think?" queried Holmes as we left the theatre.

"Holmes, I think you acted most ungentlemanly in there. We were guests and you completely humiliated that man."

"Watson, that man was a fool. He should have started with her back since she is said to have complained about it hurting."

"Holmes, there are many things which cause back pain. There was no reason to believe it was some external force behind all this."

"But you agree, now that we at least have data which supports that it was something external which likely caused her death. This is what I must find out. I appreciate your help today, Doctor. I daresay without your help I'd have not got him to turn her over and find that puncture wound. You are a very helpful associate, Watson. We'll make a fine team working together!"

I could not believe what had transpired. I had never seen someone behave in such a manner. My medical training had ingrained in me a certain unquestioning respect for those ahead of me in the medical field. I had never seen someone be quite as disrespectful to a colleague, especially one as senior as Dr. Witherspoon. The confidence Holmes exhibited and his forthright attitude was, I felt, beyond arrogance. I was embarrassed and did not know quite how I handle his exuberance.

"Holmes, I can agree that it was important that we discovered the wound, but I must say your behaviour was not that of a gentleman. You have embarrassed me in front of a man I hold in respect."

"Come now, Watson. As I said, the man is a fool. We are in the pursuit of a killer. I will not have such a person deter me from solving this case."

"Holmes, I am not likely to proffer my further assistance if you insist on behaving this way. Do you understand me?" queried I.

"There, there, my good man. I can see by the blushing of your face you are sincere in your statement. If you are in need of an apology, I shall give you one, but I see no reason for it, or that one is truly necessary. I pursued the logic and found the clue we needed. But as we are getting to know each other, I shall try to keep in mind that you seem to be a sensitive soul. I cannot, however, promise it shall not happen again. I have found that the decorum of our civilization leads to many errors and mistakes. I push through these niceties when I am on a case, because not doing so frequently causes there to be no movement forward to solving the mystery before me. I will not let such social proprieties get in the way of obtaining the truth. For that, I make no apology. If we are to work together, I think you shall have to get used to my methods or our association will indeed be in jeopardy."

His rebuttal and defence of his actions took me aback. I realized I had but once encountered such a person before. The closest thing to it I had experienced was in the Berkshires when a senior officer would seemingly blindly refuse to admit to the error of an order that had been given. Such occasions frustrated me then and I discovered Holmes had resurrected a similar feeling in me, by this rationalization of his behaviour. I suppose the only difference was that at least Holmes appeared to have thought out his behaviour, while that of the officers I had encountered were merely refusing to acknowledge a poor decision. I had to admit that Holmes at least had a sound reason for his actions and had achieved the desired result, despite my objections to his method of obtaining the answer he sought. It was still quite unsettling to me. While I was proud of my time in the service, his behaviour had reminded me of the less than pleasant experiences that I had thought were behind me. But alas, I was again confronted with a dominating personality and was presently at a loss on how to deal with him.

I thought again, that perhaps my decision was a poor one, but the thought of trying to find a new abode while I was on my quest for a surgery did not appeal to me at all. I decided to end the quarrel that seemingly sprang up in this instant. I thought it best to simply leave the morgue to avoid saying something I might regret later. My ability to be confrontational was lacking. A doctor is not trained to be so. We are trained to heal, and confrontation is rarely called for when dealing with a patient. With my decision made, I spoke to Holmes in as calm voice as I could muster.

"Holmes, I disagree with your method in this instance. I agree you have discovered an important clue. I wish, however, to avoid further misunderstanding about this. I see no further need to continue this discussion at present. Perhaps later we can engage in it with less emotion. I am going to get some lunch. You may do what you like."

"Doctor, I sense some anger in your tone?"

I said nothing and I left.

Holmes did not come with me and I was glad he chose not to join me. My thoughts were in a tumble. I decided the best thing for me would be to return to our domicile and write in my journal. I found some comfort at this thought and plan of action which helped settle my nerves.

It was later that day that Holmes returned. I had decided not to speak to him but rather wait to see what it was he had to say. Would he apologise as a more normal gentleman would or, as I was expecting from the few months of being around him, ignore what had happened?

It was the latter and I waited for him to finally speak.

"Watson, I have arranged to speak to the guests from the dinner party. I would be greatly appreciative of your presence and especially your note taking. I do value your assistance, don't you know?"

"Holmes, do you know that I am still upset with you about what happened today at the morgue?"

"Are you?"

"Yes."

"Well, then, that will not do. I find your lack of detachment from emotion, a bit concerning Doctor. I would have thought your training and experience would have better prepared you for the methods with which I conduct my business."

"Your business seems to include insulting people and offending your friends."

"You put me at a disadvantage, sir. I was not aware that our sharing this apartment had actually elevated our relationship to that of friendship. I am honoured."

"What's that you say?"

"Watson, I am quite aware my methods and style is usually prone to putting people off. But you must know by now I cannot suffer those of lesser abilities. It is the bane of my existence! I'm am surrounded by fools and incompetents at every turn. It has only been you, Doctor, who has seen clear to accept my methods and shown me some appreciation for the talents I have shown. Your reporting of my last adventure was that of someone who understands what I am about. I have never met the likes of you, save my brother. But he, I believe, resents my chosen line of work since he cannot have the leeway my methods allow me. There is an envy in him."

"You have a brother?"

"Yes, but that is for another time."

"Holmes, I find you a fascinating and most remarkable man, but there are times…"

"Watson, let us not quarrel. I have grown fond of you, as you seem to have of me. I know I am a difficult person to be around, especially when I have no puzzle to solve. This, my friend, is what makes you such a reliable person to me. That you can put up with my eccentricities is truly quite admirable. I was concerned on several occasions before now that you were going to call it quits and I would have to find another roommate quickly or give up these fine accommodations. Having met you, I realize my study of human behaviour is not yet complete.

"I promise you I will do my best, to not embarrass you any more than may happen in the pursuit of the clues in one of my cases, whatever it may be. But know, if I do, it is not to cause harm, my good fellow. It is all in the quest for the truth of the matter. It is only sometimes I get too impatient and my sense of civility is overridden by my need to solve the problem.

"I take it an apology is in order. I hope that no more will be said of it. Scold me when you must, but I believe you do help me stay balanced and hope you will choose to remain. Of course, the choice is yours."

"Holmes, I don't know what to say."

"Then say nothing more. Simply stay. That will speak for itself."

Again, I was taken aback. Holmes had never spoken to me like this ever before. He said the things I suppose I had wished for him to feel, but I did not expect him to speak of them or act on them. Was I ever to understand this man?

"When is your first appointment to speak to the guests?" queried I.

A smile arose on his face. "Tonight, Watson, tonight!"

"Then shall we get some dinner first. I want to understand your thoughts and what specifically you want me to do when we interview them."

"Ah, Watson! You are a gentleman for certain."

We found a small restaurant for dinner and Holmes explained while we ate that our first interview was with the young sergeant who had invited the deceased woman to the dinner party. He had arranged for the young man to visit us at Baker Street at eight o'clock. We were back in time and were on our way up to our rooms when we heard a knock at Mrs. Hudson's front door down below. We stopped at the landing, and she politely, but in a raised voice told us of our visitor's presence. Holmes waved him to come up the stairs and we greeted him there on the landing.

"Sergeant Reede, isn't it?" queried Holmes.

"Yes, sir."

Holmes invited him into our rooms. "Please come in. Let me take your coat. Watson, a little help here?"

"Let me introduce my associate, Doctor Watson."

"Please to meet you, Sergeant," said I.

"Brandy, or perhaps a cigar?" offered Holmes.

"No, thank you, sir."

"Please make yourself comfortable here on the couch."

"Thank you, sir."

"Sgt. Reede, what can you tell us about the other evening when Miss Townshend took ill and died?"

"I was shocked. The honour of being invited to dine with the Commissioner was what each of us at the department wished for each year. This is my fourth year on the force. I was beginning to think I was never to be chosen. But this year I was. Perhaps you know, one of the rules the Commissioner and his wife have is that those invited must be unmarried. I am not, of course. In fact, I had only met Miss Townshend once before. I would say that we were acquaintances at best. I was in need of a female companion for the dinner party and thought of her. I asked her, could she please accompany me to the dinner. She responded that she would be delighted."

"Where had you met her?"

"It had been about six months ago. A mutual friend had given a New Years' Eve party. We met there. I remember that night distinctly, as a friend of the host arrived late, just after the stroke of midnight. He being a ginger and first through the threshold, well, everyone got a bit down, saying that now we'd all have bad luck for the year."

I ignored his apparent belief in the old myth.

"You took a liking to her?" interjected I.

"Well, sir, I don't know how to properly answer your question. I would not so much say I took a liking to her. She is, I mean was, a rather handsome woman. But she had a way about her that was not altogether appealing to me."

"Then why did you invite her?"

"To be honest, I almost didn't. You see I had been engaged, but that engagement was broken off by my fiancée about two months ago. I was rather melancholy after that and I had made a point of concentrating on my work. I've not had much luck with the ladies since then and I decided to just not put myself into another situation like that again, not for a while anyway. Then the invitation came and I was in quandary. I had always hoped for the invitation as I said. Now that it had come, I needed a guest to accompany me. While I was not particularly fond of Miss Townshend, I thought she might be a good choice. She is known, I mean was known, for being quite active socially. I know this all sounds a bit uncivil and uncouth of me, but I thought it might be to my advantage to have a person who was so comfortable in social settings accompany me, especially on such short notice. I felt that she would contribute to a positive atmosphere. And she did, at least, that is, before she took ill. She was quite an entertaining individual. Always had a story to tell and was comfortable telling them. I believe she rather enjoyed being the centre of attention. This, again, suited my need as I had heard from previous attendees that the Commissioner had always paid perhaps a bit more attention to the young ladies who came to the dinner than to the men of the force. That seemed to be the case the other night as well, but I have no real knowledge that he is always that way. I can, though, attest that he seemed quite amused by Miss Townshend and her tales."

"That night, did she seem concerned at all for her safety?" asked Holmes.

"No. Why do you ask? She was taken ill, wasn't she?

"Yes, of course, pray continue."

"She seemed quite happy. I believe she was an individual who thrived on such things as parties and social affairs. These things seemed to provide her with much excitement. She seemed eager to attend."

"What else can you tell us about the evening?"

"It was all rather normal in my mind. We arrived and were all seated in the parlour for a while. Everyone was exchanging pleasantries. I knew both Corporal Jenson and Constable Sandercock but I knew neither of their lady friends. Before long, we entered the dining room and were seated and served. After the meal, the ladies retired to freshen up and then I was told they went back to the parlour. The men retired to the Commissioner's study where he offered us all some Scotch and a cigar. We all accepted and were sharing some stories about things that had happened in the recent weeks in the Mile. Nothing of any consequence, I assure you. But the little stories seemed to entertain the Commissioner. Each of us found ourselves trying to tell a more interesting tale than the other. But really, they were quite trivial.

"A short time later, the Commissioner's wife came to

the door and said to him that it appeared Miss Townshend had been taken ill. She was inquiring what he thought she should do.

"We all went to the parlour and found Miss Townshend prostrate on the lounge. She looked most uncomfortable and seemed to be in much pain, complaining about her back hurting and feeling very weak.

"The Commissioner ordered his manservant to have a doctor gotten there immediately. Various things were done to try to make her more comfortable, but none truly succeeded. The doctor finally arrived and by then she was worse. He ordered everyone out of the room. I said I would prefer to stay since she was my responsibility. He allowed me to do so. He ordered that she be gotten to hospital as soon as possible, but she seemed to fall asleep. He then worked rapidly to awaken her, but it was too late. She passed right there on the Commissioner's lounge."

"Did the doctor administer her anything that you happened to notice?"

"No. I do not believe so, except perhaps for some *'sal volatile'* which I believe he used to try to revive her."

"Is there anything else you can remember?"

"No, I think that is it."

"We had been told that perhaps, Miss Townshend had, shall we say, imbibed a fair amount that evening. Can you confirm that?" queried Holmes.

"I'd not like to speak ill of the dead, sir. I would say that she had perhaps more than I would have expected a young lady to consume. I had begun to fear she would drink too much, but I did remember when I met her, she'd also seemed to have consumed rather a large amount, but was not, *tipsy*, as they say."

"Thank you, Sgt. Reede. I think Dr. Watson and I have enough of a picture with which to work now. If you think of anything else, please let us know."

The young Sergeant exited, and Holmes and I began discussing the what the Sergeant had told us.

"Holmes, what did you think of Sgt. Reede's story?"

"It was about what I expected. I am anxious to talk to

the others as soon as I can. People's memories fade, Watson. I want to gain as much information as I can before it is lost. Tomorrow we must talk to the rest of the guests, including the Commissioner and his wife."

The next day came quickly. Holmes had requested that Commander Williams arrange to meet with the Commissioner and his wife after lunch. While he was successful, his message to Holmes indicated that the Commissioner was most annoyed at the request for the meeting.

"Those in high places and with power rarely like to be questioned by others. They no longer feel in control," Holmes explained to me.

Holmes' methods and attitude were becoming known and the rumour of the events and his behaviour at the autopsy had made their way through the medical circles. I had already been asked more than once about it by an old friend of mine from Bart's, as well as a doctor whom I had just met. There was no doubt in my mind that the Commissioner had heard about it as well.

We arrived and were greeted by the Commissioner's butler. He showed no enthusiasm at meeting either of us. He was no doubt numb to Sherlock's recent celebrity. My conclusion was that a man in his position would have likely received many more distinguished guests over the years than Mr. Sherlock Holmes. Without a word, he took our coats and motioned us into the Commissioner's study. We must have waited a good half an hour. Holmes was growing impatient, when suddenly we were requested to join the Commissioner and his wife in their parlour.

"Good afternoon, Commissioner, I am Sherlock Ho..."

"Let me be quite clear. I am indulging you this opportunity, Mr. Holmes, is it?... to speak to my wife and myself strictly upon Commander Williams' advice. I believe it to be utter nonsense and entirely unnecessary. How one could think that my wife or I had any connection to this poor young woman's demise, I do not understand. To be frank about it, I consider it insulting. Be careful what you ask, Mr. Holmes. I will not tolerate any rudeness or insinuations as to my wife's, or my behaviour regarding that nights' activities!

"Who are you?!" the Commissioner rudely asked me with his eyes peering into mine.

"That is my…"

"I wasn't speaking to you, Mr. Holmes. I was speaking to this man! Well, who are you?!"

"My name is Dr. John Watson."

"What are you doing here? I understood this was to be a meeting with Mr. Holmes. I insist you leave."

"Commissioner, you, sir, are out of line," said Holmes in a tone of voice I'd never heard from him before.

"How dare you speak to my associate, Dr. Watson, in such a manner as that?"

His admonition of the Commissioner, took the Commissioner by surprise.

"I will not offer my services to help you unless you apologise to Dr. Watson at once! I did not approach you and offer my assistance, sir. Commander Williams asked for my help. If you are foolish enough to continue to behave in this manner, then I suggest you contact Scotland Yard and have them solve your little problem. I am sure the entirety of London would love to read in the dailies about a *Murder in the Commissioner's Home*. Come, Watson. Apparently, our help is not needed."

The Commissioner's face was as flush as one can imagine. To be dressed down verbally in such a manner, in front of his wife no less, was too much for him. Guessing from his appearance that he was at least three score in age, I feared this sudden rise in his blood pressure would have a most undesirable visceral effect on him. I would not have been surprised if the man did not have a stroke right then.

Holmes turned on his heel and was met by the butler, who no doubt had heard the loud exchange as he had our coats in hand ready for us. As we put them on, we suddenly heard a female's voice from the parlour cry out, "Wait! Please gentlemen, wait! Won't you please come back?"

Holmes finished adjusting his coat and scarf. I had gotten mine second and had not started yet to put it on.

"What is it, Madam?" said I, as she approached us.

"Gentlemen. My husband is not used to this. Please, he needs your help. Do not abandon him. He is a proud and stubborn man, but he is a good man. Please come speak to him again, won't you?"

"Madam, your courteous pleading demands an amiable answer. I will give this one more attempt at least for your sake. Watson, shall we?" said he, as he unwrapped his scarf, took off his coat and waved me back into the parlour from which we had been expelled a few minutes before.

"My wife insists I owe you gentlemen an apology. I suppose I do. She is usually right about such things. Ever since the other evening, I have not quite been myself. Let us get on with it then."

"Very well, Commissioner," said Holmes.

"What can you tell us about the other night that is of importance?" queried Holmes.

"That just it. There is nothing to tell. Our guests arrived on time, except for one couple. There were no ill words spoken that I recall at any time. The young woman who died, Miss Townshend, I believe, was quite entertaining. I did not even know there was a problem until my wife informed me that the young lady was ill."

"You have heard, I surmise, that the autopsy has revealed an injury, correct?"

"Yes, most disturbing. To have had someone assaulted in one's own home and not even know of it until it is too late…. Well, gentleman, it just does not happen and should not happen to me!"

"We shall continue our inquiries as discretely as possible, Commissioner. We bid you good day, sir."

"Um, yes, well, good day, gentlemen."

As we left, we remained silent but I could not wait to speak to Holmes outside.

"Holmes, not even an apology!"

"Realize Watson, a man such as he is used to, and has, in fact, been trained to be the one asking the questions, not answering them. Overall, he did quite well, though it was easy to tell he was most uncomfortable at my inquiries."

Holmes next suggested we visit Corporal Sandercock.

He was on duty at Wood Street as we had been told he would be. He was a fair looking young man. His appearance impressed me as what a policeman in the Queen's service should look like. When he rose to greet us upon Holmes' introduction, he stood at least six-foot-four, I would say. I estimated he was at least seventeen or eighteen stone. His hair was neatly trimmed and his face clean shaven. He made a striking appearance in his uniform.

"It is nice to meet you, sir." said he to Holmes. "Commander Williams told me you would be coming by today to speak to me."

"This in my associate, Dr. John Watson. Is there somewhere we might speak to you that might afford us a bit more privacy?"

"Certainly, sir. Perhaps we should retire to one of the rooms across the hall," said he as he directed us towards an open door opposite the desk at which he had been sitting.

We sat down and his demeanour changed somewhat after he had closed the door.

"I must say, I have heard of your recent exploit Mr. Holmes. It is you, Doctor, we can thank for telling us about it. It is a pleasure to meet you, too. We here at Wood Street talk about how you so ingeniously solved your last case.

"I was looking forward to meeting you. But I must tell you, the circumstances that have brought us together are most distressing. I, as many of the other young members of the force, have always wished to attend the Commissioner's dinner party. To be invited is considered quite an honour and it has been seen as an opportunity that generally seemed to help one's career. But this tragedy has left us worried. It is seen by many of us as a bad omen now."

"I understand, Corporal. Perhaps you can tell us what you know about the events of that evening?" queried Holmes.

"Yes, sir. My guest, Miss Jennifer Hammonds and I arrived at the appointed time. We were both rather nervous, I guess you might say, it being an important occasion and opportunity, like I said.

"We were introduced as we entered the parlour. Miss Townshend and Sergeant Reede were not there yet."

"What about Constable Jenson? Were he and his guest there yet?"

"Yes, sir."

"How long before Sgt. Reede arrived?"

"Miss Townshend and Sgt. Reede arrived shortly after we did. I would say perhaps five or ten minutes later. I remember since the Commissioner looked at his watch several times before they came. Reede later told me he feared he'd made a blunder of things since they had arrived late. I told him not to worry about it, but I know he still was concerned about it as he seemed to fret and said some awkward things trying to make up for it.

"Then about seven o'clock, before dinner, the Commissioner bade us all to come upstairs. There was a grand view of the Thames from a third story balcony. We all went up and indeed the view was spectacular.

"After about ten or fifteen minutes we returned downstairs and were soon seated for dinner. Miss Townshend was quite entertaining in that she seemed to have been able to catch the Commissioner's attention. I had met her at a few parties in the past. She was one who had a way about her that allowed her to be very comfortable in such settings. She always was good at chatting and telling stories that most people found entertaining."

"It has been suggested that perhaps Miss Townshend had imbibed maybe more than might be polite, is that true?"

"I couldn't really say, sir. As I said, she had a way about her in such social gatherings. I didn't particularly pay attention to how much she consumed. I would not be the one to ask about that. I presumed she just came by her relaxed presence naturally.

"We were all rather dumbfounded by what had occurred. After they removed Miss Townshend's body, the Commissioner said we should all go home. He swore us and our lady guests to secrecy. Said it wouldn't be good for the Constabulary should this get out to the press. I escorted Miss Hammonds home and we bade each other good night. I was exhausted and frustrated. So was she."

"She?"

"Yes. It was not the evening I had expected. And poor Miss Hammonds' hat fell off when we alit from our cab in front of her home at the end of the evening. I did my best to try to catch it, but to no avail and it landed in the wet gutter. She said it was ruined. She actually swore when it happened. Very unlike her. I remember thinking I'd never heard her swear before. I suppose a failure of a woman's accoutrements can cause such reactions. I know they always did for my mother. God rest her soul. So, it was all in all, a very unpleasant evening, sir."

We thanked Corporal Sandercock and went to find his guest, Miss Hammonds.

Miss Hammonds was difficult to track down. It wasn't until we found out she was employed at a hat shop that we were able to catch up with her.

It was obvious that our presence in the shop was noticed immediately by a young woman who was trying on hats. Two men were not the normal customers to enter such a place. We quickly caught the attention of a sales clerk and asked for Miss Hammonds. We were told she was in the back and would be out shortly. Rather than waiting, as I presumed we would, Holmes slowly strode towards an unclosed door and eavesdropped on a barely audible conversation.

"You will have to find that hat, or pay for it, or be dismissed, Miss Hammonds!"

"I assure you. I don't know what happened to it, Madam."

"That is not acceptable. You have until Friday. That is all. Now, return to your work."

At that dismissive command, Holmes withdrew his ear and stood as though we'd not heard a word. Shortly thereafter a young woman came out whom we took to be Miss Hammonds.

She did not smile when Holmes introduced us. He handed her a short note from the Commissioner. It explained our reason for being here and that the reader should cooperate with Holmes. Having finished reading it, she then displayed a face which suggested she'd not wish to speak of the event and certainly not here in front of her employer.

"Perhaps you could allow Dr. Watson and me to invite you to have lunch with us?"

"No, sir. I cannot."

"Then dinner perhaps?"

"I cannot promise, as I must help the proprietor with a new shipment that has arrived today."

"We understand, but it is important that we talk with you. Shall we say eight o'clock then?"

"Alright, since you insist. Where is it that I shall meet you, gentlemen?"

"I would hope Holborn, at eight, would be acceptable?"

"Yes, I know it. I shall be there at eight. Good day, gentlemen," and she quickly returned to her duties under the watchful eyes of the shop keeper.

"Holmes, she seemed rather sullen, but what is it you think you shall gain by talking to her?"

"Watson, I am in need of data. My goal is to speak with each of the attendees. I cannot say our interview with her will be productive, but I wish to hear her story and eliminate her as a possible villain."

"You don't really suspect her, do you?"

"I must keep all possibilities open, Watson. It is part of my method. What the police of today do has led to many unjust arrests and sentences which, had I become involved, would not have taken place. I must keep my mind open, Watson."

We continued our travel back to Baker Street and had a quick meal at the hands of Mrs. Hudson. I spent the rest of the day writing in my journal. First about what we had experienced on the case and then some further thoughts about how I might find an old surgery in need of a new young partner.

We made our way to the Holborn and had to wait just a short while to be seated. Miss Hammonds joined us shortly thereafter. We all ordered and in a short while began our meals. It was after that that Holmes began his questioning.

"Miss Hammonds, can you please tell us how you came to be at the dinner the other night?"

"I was a guest of Corporal Sandercock."

"Have you known Corporal Sandercock a long time?"

"Yes, he and my brother grew up together."

"I see. Then you are merely friends?"

"Yes, Corporal Sandercock is like a brother to me, Mr. Holmes. He was happy to be invited and since he had not a steady young lady as of late, he requested me to accompany him. I know how important it was to him, and so I agreed to be his guest."

"Did you notice anything unusual about the deceased, Miss Townshend?"

"No, not really. I thought perhaps she was behaving a bit out of place."

"What do you mean by that?"

"The dinner is for the constables to get to know the Commissioner better, or I suppose you would say for him to get to know them better. She seemed not to understand that, by the way she dominated so much of the conversation."

"Do you recall her perhaps drinking a bit too much? It has been suggested."

"Yes, I would say perhaps so. But then again, I have seen Miss Townshend at other events and she is, I mean was, a rather gregarious person. Always laughing and talking. Most of the young men were usually taken in by her looks and behaviour. Most events I have attended with her always seemed to end with her being surrounded by many of the young men. I've even heard of a squabble or two resulting from a debate as to which young man was to escort her home."

"You did not approve of Miss Townshend, then?"

"I do not believe in speaking ill of the dead, sir. I think I shall leave the dead to themselves and their God."

"Is there anything else you remember from the evening?"

"No. I am trying to forget it, actually. It was a very unpleasant event."

"Thank you, Miss Hammonds. Please let us know if you remember anything else. Here is my card," said Holmes, handing her a card from his pocket.

"Good evening, gentlemen," said she, with no further concern. We rose, as she did, and she left our presence.

"She seemed a bit aloof, did she not, Watson?"

"Holmes, can you blame her? A young woman like that has not seen much of the world. I cannot imagine she would wish to dwell on anyone's death at her age."

"You are correct, Doctor. I sometimes forget that youth believes they are immortal. It is with age and experience we find ourselves realizing our time here is but brief."

The next day we found ourselves walking along St. Paul's Churchyard next to the Cathedral with young Constable Jenson. He was very tall, like Corporal Sandercock. He stood at least six-foot-six. I'd have guessed twenty stone at least. His face was adorned with a fashionable moustache of the day.

"How can I help you, Mr. Holmes, Dr. Watson?"

"Please tell us about the other evening, if you could."

"Yes, sir. Well, sir, it was a difficult evening. By that I mean, I was so nervous, I almost made a mess of it.

"Sergeant Reede and Miss Townshend were late, you see. The Sergeant told me later that she was not ready to go when he fetched her. All he could do was wait for her. Once they arrived, they were, oh, at least ten minutes late. I could see by the Commissioner's face he was none too pleased about that! I'm afraid he made a very poor impression at first."

"Can you tell us about after they arrived? Was there anything that you remember?"

"No sir, I was quite worried about them being late. Sandercock teased Reede about it. I do remember that."

"And your lady friend, Miss….?"

"Oh, yes, Miss Devercux."

"Well, she seemed distracted during the meal."

"What do you mean by distracted?" enquired Holmes.

"She, barely spoke to anyone. Of course, with Miss Townshend present, it is sometime difficult to get a word in edgewise, as they say."

"So, Miss Townshend was, dominating the conversations, as it were, correct?"

"Well, sir, I guess that would be one way of putting it."

"Did you or Miss Devereux know Miss Townshend well?"

"No, sir. I mean we knew her, sir. She is frequently at the parties of our social group. She has been known to be in the accompaniment of different officers and constables on many occasions."

"So, Miss Devereux knew Miss Townshend?"

"Yes sir, but to what extent I do not know."

"Is there anything else you can remember about the night, Constable Sandercock?"

"I only remember Miss Devereux, saying something like 'I must say something to her'. She whispered it to me. But I was not expecting her to say anything to me and I am not sure what she meant by it or to whom she was referring."

"Thank you, Constable."

"Thank you, sir. And it has been an honour to meet you sir!" said he with some enthusiasm as he realized our interview was over and his ability to converse with the now popular 'consulting detective' was coming to a close.

I proposed we walk the two or so miles back to Baker Street, but Holmes wished to travel back more quickly. We had only but Miss Devereux to interview. Up to now, he had failed to mention that he had arranged for her to come to Baker Street at 2 o'clock. I acquiesced to his point and we soon found ourselves heading west out of the City of London to our abode in a cabbie's hansom.

It was a few minutes past two o'clock by my watch when we had a knock in the door. I received Miss Devereux, introduced myself and asked that she please sit down. She accepted my invitation such as it was. I then informed her that Mr. Holmes would be present in but a moment. No sooner had I said this than Holmes walked in.

"Ah, Miss Devereux, how good of you to come."

"Yes, sir. But I have been sworn to secrecy, you understand. I have come only because Reggie, I mean, Constable Sandercock, said I should."

"And right he is to encourage your help."

"I do not see how I can help?"

"One never knows what the significance of things experienced will tell. What can you share with us about the other night?"

"Oh, sir it was a most horrid evening. I've never seen a dead body before!"

"We have spoken to Constable Sandercock. He stated that you had whispered something to him. Do you remember?"

"I whispered many a thing to him, that evening, and surely those are not in question, sir."

"No, my dear, he mentioned something about…what were his words Watson?"

"My notes say, she said 'I must say something to her'."

"Oh, you mean about Miss Townshend, why yes."

"What did you mean by that and who was the 'she' to whom you were referring?"

"Why, Miss Hammonds, of course."

"Why Miss Hammonds?"

"I don't think she expected Miss Townshend to be there."

"Why not?"

"I'm not sure. But ever since her brother died, she's not spoken to her."

"Miss Devereux, could you explain? Who's brother?"

"Why Miss Hammonds' brother, Gerald. He died about a year ago" she then leaned towards us and whispered, "Suicide, they say."

"What does her brother's death have to do with this?"

"Don't you know? Miss Hammonds' brother was madly in love with Miss Townshend. He'd asked her to marry him; several times, I think. But she's not the marrying type or so I've gathered, if you know what I mean.

"Anyway, poor Gerald couldn't take the rejection. He went into a deep melancholy. He stopped working. Lost his job and then jumped off a church steeple! It was quite a sad time.

"Miss Townshend had seemed to be a bit unmoved by it all. She's said to have said his death proves she was right in not accepting his proposal.

"Anyway, after that, no one really talked about it anymore. Too morbid.

"Maggie, Miss Hammonds, just looked shocked to me when Miss Townshend showed up.

"I was telling Reggie, that I thought I should say something to her to help her not get too upset. They hadn't spoken to each other since the day her brother Gerald died, as far as I know."

"What else can you tell us?"

"I do not believe there is anything else I can remember. When she took ill, everyone became so concerned. Then when she passed, I became quite upset."

"Thank you, Miss Devereux."

I walked her to the door and bid her good day.

"Holmes, I think we have nothing. I don't see any new light on things," exclaimed I in frustration.

"I disagree, Doctor. I see the pieces of this puzzle coming together and quite quickly."

"I see nothing. What do you mean?"

"We have uncovered a motive, dear Doctor."

"I do not follow you. What motive?"

"I wish to make some inquiries before I answer your questions, Doctor. I shall be back late I think," and with that he was out the door grabbing his hat and cane as he left.

A while later I had a note arrive stating that one of my patients had had a relapse. I picked up my bag and headed out to their home after writing a brief note telling Holmes I would likely be late myself.

When I returned, I found Holmes resting comfortably with his eyes closed and smoking his favourite pipe.

"Holmes, have you had any further thoughts about the murder," queried I.

"I have Doctor. It is actually a rather simple crime."

"Oh, how do you know this?"

"I have spent time rummaging through some rubbish bins and have found a most interesting clue," said Holmes.

"Rubbish bins? How can those provide a clue?"

"What does one do with something that has been ruined?"

"I supposed you try to have it fixed or repaired."

"And if that is not possible?"

"One discards it, if it is truly ruined, as you said, one would throw it out."

"Precisely."

"But Holmes, what has all this got to do with our Miss Townshend's murder?"

"Everything, Watson, everything. Please do me the honour of bringing your notebook with you tomorrow. We shall convene a gathering of our suspects and I believe we shall be able to solve our little murder, *post haste*."

Holmes had arranged for all of the dinner guests to arrive at the Commissioner's house at ten o'clock the next morning. We gathered in the parlour where Miss Townshend had taken her last breath. No one wished to sit on the lounge that had cradled her lifeless body, so the constables found themselves sitting in chairs behind it.

Holmes was leaning against the fire place. I stood next to him. "Please do relax everyone," said Holmes. "I am glad you were all able to make it.

"While this has been a challenging task, I believe I have solved this unfortunate crime."

"There is no sound evidence of a crime, Mr. Holmes! Just your theory," interrupted the Commissioner.

"Ah, but there was a crime of murder, Commissioner. And it was committed by someone in this very room."

There were gasps from the ladies present and the constables cleared their throats and shifted uncomfortably from side to side.

"I don't believe it!" cried out the Commissioner. "You are making this up, Mr. Sherlock Holmes. You and your '*consulting detecting*', isn't that what you call it? I have spoken to Dr. Witherspoon. I know all about your little commotion at the morgue. This is just another attempt to gain publicity for yourself. He assures me there was no foul play."

"Witherspoon is a fool. I am not here to play games with you, Commissioner."

The Commissioner was aghast at being rebuked again, this time in front of his men. He fell into silence.

"Miss Hammonds, have you found the hat?"

There was no reply.

"Miss Hammonds, again, I ask you, have you found the hat?"

"I beg your pardon," she replied.

"I said, have you found the hat?"

"I do not know what you mean, Mr. Holmes, I am sure."

"Oh, I think you do. When you stepped out of your cab in

front of your home the night Miss Townshend died, the hat you were wearing fell into the gutter. Is that not correct?"

"Yes, it did, but what has that got to do with anything?"

"What did you do with the hat, Miss Hammonds?"

"I had to throw it out. It was ruined."

"Yes, I agree. It was," said Holmes. He turned around and picked up a brown paper bag. He opened it and removed what had likely been a fashionable woman's hat, but it was now soiled and crumpled.

"This is the hat, correct?"

"No, I don't believe so."

"Yes, it is," ejaculated Corporal Sandercock.

"Perhaps it is. Where did you get it?" she replied.

"I found it in the rubbish bin behind your home Miss Hammonds. Now do you admit to it?"

"I fail to see the importance of this, Mr. Holmes," said she.

"It is very important. This is the hat you wore that night. This is the hat, shall we say, you *borrowed*, from the shop, at which you no longer work, since you have been fired for not *'finding'* or, in fact, returning it, as I suppose you had planned to do."

"Oh, Maggie, you've been sacked?!" said Miss Devereux.

"It's of no matter, Julia. Don't worry, I was planning to serve notice anyway."

"Oh, my dear!"

"Why did it fall off, Miss Hammonds?" queried Holmes.

"What do you mean?" said she rather squeamishly. Her earlier show of confidence appeared to have deserted her.

"Just what I asked. Why did your hat fall off?"

"Just like anything else, I suppose, it came loose and fell. That's all."

"I propose it fell because it was no longer correctly attached. How does one attach a hat such as this to one's head, Miss Hammonds?"

"With a hair pin," she said softly, lowering her head.

"This hair pin, to be precise," said Holmes, as he held a very long discoloured hair pin high in the air.

"If you please, Mr. Holmes," requested the

Commissioner, as he reached out as Holmes handed it to him. He examined it, but seemed unimpressed.

"May I, Commissioner?" said Miss Hammonds, requesting the pin from him.

"What are you saying, Mr. Holmes? Out with it, sir!" queried and demanded the Commissioner.

"I am saying, sir, that Miss Hammonds removed that pin from her hat. At some time during the evening she thrust it into Miss Townshends' back. Whether or not she knew it would kill her, is not for me to decide. But her action resulted in the death of Miss Townshend. And as you know, sir, that is murder."

"Maggie, that can't be true!" Miss Devereux asserted.

Miss Hammonds said nothing but buried her face in her hands and began to sob uncontrollably

"I believe when Miss Hammonds chooses to speak, we will find that the hatred she carried for Miss Townshend had gotten the better of her the other night. I believe she blamed Miss Townshend for causing her brother to, shall we say, pass on, due to Miss Townshends' rejection of his offer of matrimony. Perhaps not expecting Miss Townshend to be at the event, her presence took her by surprise."

As Holmes spoke, Miss Hammonds began slowly nodding her head as if in agreement. Her sobbing stopped.

"She killed him the same as if she herself had stabbed him in the heart! When I saw her carrying on like she always did, I couldn't take it anymore! My poor brother wasted his life over that strumpet!"

"Sergeant, arrest this woman," commanded the Commissioner. "That's enough of a confession for me."

As Sergeant Reede rose from his chair behind the settee where she had been sitting, to take hold of Miss Hammonds, she jumped up and ran to the main hall. Sergeant Reede reached for her, but a settee was in his way. Holmes and I being by the fireplace, could not block her path.

We all chased after her, but she had the advantage of many steps. As we entered the hall, we saw she had not run for the door, but had begun ascending the staircase. I could not imagine where she was going.

"We must catch her, Watson!" Holmes shouted at me.

"Stop, Maggie!" cried Sergeant Reede. "Please stop!" but she heeded no one's calls.

As we got to the third story, I recognized her true intent.

"Maggie, please, don't," I heard Sergeant Reede call out from the doorway that led to the balcony.

Holmes and I reach the doorway ourselves. She was facing us, standing on the stone parapet.

"Miss Hammonds, please do not do this," said Holmes in a somewhat subdued tone.

"Yes, my dear, no good can come from this," added I.

"But you are wrong, Doctor. I am going to join my brother." And with those last words, she thrust the pin into her side, contorted from the pain of it and then simply allowed herself to fall backwards.

"No!" cried the Sergeant. But to no avail. She had fallen.

We ran to the edge and looked down to see the devastating outcome of her fall.

As the others who had tried also to climb the stairs ascended, we could only shake our heads and tell them of the unfortunate event. I went outside with Holmes, and while I had no doubt as to the state of her body, I checked for a sign of life, but there was none.

The Commissioner, now having a second death at his abode, was most unsettled.

"Mr. Holmes, I don't know what to say."

"I recommend now that we have solved this little mystery, that you have your men, remove Miss Hammonds' body. The first murder has been solved and this event has perhaps solved your problem of publicity, which I know is of importance to you. How you wish to handle these two deaths is up to you. I have uncovered the murderer and it would appear that justice has been served. I bid you good day, sir."

I had no choice but to follow Holmes out the door. I bowed to the Commissioner and his wife as best I could muster under the circumstances and found myself walking briskly to try to catch up to Holmes. His long strides were carrying him away quickly down the street.

"Holmes, Holmes, wait up!" I cried out to him.

He either did not hear me or was ignoring my plea. I trotted a few paces and finally caught up to him.

"Sherlock, what is the matter?" queried I.

"I was a fool, Watson. I should have anticipated her response to my confrontation."

"But how could you, man? You aren't a soothsayer. You don't possess a crystal ball."

"Watson, the mind of one who can commit murder is one I intend to master its inner workings. How else can I compete with such beings? I have failed."

"But Holmes, you did solve it, I'm not sure how, but you did!" exclaimed I, trying to make sure his self-admonition did not lead him into some dark place I had witnessed in him before when he failed at something. "I disagree; you have not failed"

"The lady is dead."

"Holmes, yes, she is. But you solved the murder."

"Yes…I suppose you are correct, Doctor."

"How is it that you knew to look for the hat?"

"You remember the day we went to the hat shop and overheard Miss Hammonds' manager tell her to find the hat. I made no mind of it then. But then Sergeant Reede described the hat falling off her head and being ruined. It occurred to me that something had happened in between to perhaps dislodge the proper attachment. Had the hat she was wearing been the one that had been lost? I found the hat as I said. I then went to the shop and described it as one I was in search of for a lady friend. The same manager we saw talking to Miss Hammonds said that, yes, they had had one just like that, but no longer had it. I sensed a bit of consternation in the manager's tone that made me think perhaps this was the hat Miss Hammonds might have borrowed, but then couldn't return it since it had been ruined. I inquired and found that such a hat is typically held in place by one or more rather long 'hat pins' of the kind I found with it. You saw that it is approximately eight inches in length. I concluded, once I heard of the death of her brother, that Miss Hammonds bore a rather lethal attitude towards Miss Townshend. Her unplanned and sudden appearance must have overwhelmed Miss Hammonds. I suspect that with the amount of spirits Miss Townshend was said to have consumed, she perhaps did not completely understand the sharp pain she must have experienced when the pin was thrust into her. Being, the type of person she was, I doubt she would have immediately complained as that would have somehow dampened her ability to keep entertaining of all the guests.

"Whether or not Miss Hammonds intended that the attack should kill Miss Townshend, we will not likely ever know. But causing bodily harming that causes a person's death is murder nonetheless."

"Amazing, Holmes."

"So, Doctor, I would prefer you not publish an account of this most unfortunate affair. And I am sure the Commissioner would appreciate it be forgotten as well."

"I will do as you request, Holmes."

"Thank you, Doctor. I believe I will take a less determined walk home now. I wish to make some mental notes on my errors today. You may join me if you wish, but you will likely find my lack of interest in any further discussion a bit boring."

"It is all right Holmes. I understand. We will return to Baker Street in silence as you suggest."

"Thank you, Doctor."

We continued to Baker Street in an indirect route. Neither of us spoke nor desired to eat when lunch time arrived. The day had been an odd one. Perhaps there will be a day when this story will come to light. Until then, the Adventure of the City of London shall remain secreted away in my tin box.

THE ADVENTURE OF THE BARMAID'S GRIEF

It was just after tea and I wanted to finish reading the afternoon editions. My evening appointments were to arrive shortly and it was important I get to my surgery soon.

There was one last article that had caught my attention.

'New Coin Causes Confusion'

The recently issued 'double florin', containing the silhouette of Her Majesty, is causing problems in shops and pubs about the Kingdom. In their haste to issue it, (in a rash attempt to follow the American colonies' decimal monetary system as opposed to the well-known historic system[7] of our fore-fathers!) the choice was made to use the same image on the obverse side as is found on the crown, which has a value that is one quarter more than the double florin. It is just $1/12^{th}$ of an inch smaller in diameter. Now this slightly smaller double florin is being mistaken for a crown! Shops and pubs are not happy when their clerks and waitresses accept the double florin as a crown, only to find out later it is not one. It has caused much grief in the commercial establishments that come in to contact with it. Will the Exchequer ever learn, one must ask?

I noted to myself that care should be taken when accepting payment. Looking up, the clock on the mantle showed me to be late even if I were to leave immediately. When I came downstairs, I found the front door was open and Mrs. Hudson was sweeping the step.

---

[7] Editor's note: At the time of this article, the British monetary system was based in part on: **1£** = 4 crowns = 20 shillings = 240 pennies = 960 farthings and various other coinage.

"Mum, does Mr. Sherlock Holmez lives here?" a visitor asked Mrs. Hudson. Before she could answer, I stepped out the doorway and replied to the young female who appeared to be about sixteen years of age, "Yes, young miss, he does. What can he do for you?"

Mrs. Hudson, finished her sweeping and re-entered her abode and went on to other of her chores of the day.

"Youz, ur Mr. Sherlock Holmez?!" said she somewhat incredulously.

"No, miss," replied I. "I am Dr. John Watson. I am, though, Mr. Holmes' associate. Mr. Holmes is not here at present. How can I assist you?"

"Wellz, I don't noze if youz can, sir. Ya seez I'z only wants to talk with Mr. Holmez, now. Do youz noze when Mr. Holmez will be back?"

"I am not sure, miss. It might be late tonight or might even be tomorrow."

"Hmm, wellz I cannot wait all nightz for him. Could youz dooz mez a favour, Dr. Wat…"

"Watson"

"Yez, could youz dooz mez a favour, Dr. Watson? Could youz tells him to come seez me at the Ye Old Red Rooster Inn and Pub? Me name's Annie, and I needz to speaks with hem rightz away."

"Where is this Inn, miss?"

"It's right across from the newz Met's Wembley Park station. I'z got to go now or I'llz not make it in time for me shift. Pleaz, sir, pleaz have Mr. Holmez come to seez me!"

And with that last plea, she turned and started running down the street in the direction of the Baker Street Met Station.

This, my dear readers, was not the first time I had encountered Holmes' future clients prior to him meeting them, nor likely was it to be the last. When this did happen, I always wished that I possessed those abilities that Holmes has. That is to say, as it often has seemed to me, he would magically deduce what the client was in need of before they even revealed it expressly to Holmes themselves.

In this case I wondered what on earth this young woman was needing from Holmes. Was she having trouble with her employer? Or maybe it was her beau? Was something or someone missing and needing to be found?

It was a mystery to me, but no doubt Holmes would quickly discern her needs and, in a short while, would solve the little mystery that had overwhelmed her and caused her to seek out the help of the now London-famous *consulting* detective, Mr. Sherlock Holmes.

It was not until shortly before dinner, which I contemplated my having to eat in solitude, that Holmes returned to Baker Street.

"Holmes, how are you, my friend?" queried I.

"I am fine, Watson. How are you, and what do you think of my newest client?"

"Holmes, I have said nothing! How do you know you have a new client? You were not here when she came!"

"Correct, but I know *she* came today seeking my advice."

"I do not know how you do these thing Holmes. I find your abilities most incredible!"

"Settle down, dear Watson. It is not all that incredible. You give me too much credit. It is likely that, having seen my abilities on so many occasions, you make the mistake of jumping to the conclusion that perhaps I am omniscient. The truth is, and I hope I do not disappoint you, I merely asked Mrs. Hudson if I'd had any visitors today. You see, that didn't take much effort, did it? There is nothing magical about it."

"You're correct, Holmes. I am so used to you observing a variety of things and events and making sense out of them when no one else can, I have become accustomed to your superior mental abilities impressing me on a daily basis. I should have realized the simplest solution was it, as you have said before. You simply asked Mrs. Hudson!"

"Ha, there, you see! No magic, just simple logic and common sense. You can't imagine how many people clutter their minds with everything but logic and common sense, especially when solving problems. Mostly, they let their emotions play a role in their decision making, which is certainly a road to disaster.

"Do you think the engineers that are designing the new

Tower Bridge can allow their emotions to get in the way? Of course not! They are bound by the laws of physics. They cannot choose the members used in the bridge to be smaller than they need to be, to appeal to the *look* of the bridge, for nature would punish them in a most hideous fashion, likely with the loss of life. But everyday people make choices not being restrained by the laws of physics. Just take the clothes you wear. I choose my clothes for their practicality, and you choose yours for their looks.

"I cannot allow emotion to happen in my profession. That is why I have such disdain for the emotions, they distract and create false premises. It is rare that the logical conclusion of a problem is wrong. If one accepts false premises as true, then, while the conclusion may be quite logical, it will not be correct in the real world.

"The premises in each case must be analysed and their near certainty be established before we can reliably accept the resulting conclusions. The logic must prevail and so, emotions in my work, have no value."

"I suppose I agree, Holmes, medicine is similar. I frequently must distance myself from my emotions when treating my patients. What I wish for them and what becomes of them is mostly out of my control. If they follow my instructions, they are likely to heal. If they do not, then all I suggest cannot help them if they fail to do so."

"So, who is this young miss? Did she have a message for me?"

"Ah, Holmes, so you aren't omniscient!"

"Mrs. Hudson said a young miss arrived, but that once she commenced speaking to you, she left you to deal with her. Thus, you see, she had no idea what the young miss wanted."

"That is correct, Holmes, Mrs. Hudson was not present for most of the conversation. Her name is 'Annie' and she asked that you call on her at the *Ye Old Red Rooster Inn and Pub*. She said it was right across the lane from the new Met Wembley Park station."

"I see. Then perhaps we should find ourselves there this evening for our dinner, as I see you have not eaten."

"I am up to the invitation Holmes. Let us go at once."

With that we left our rooms. Unfortunately, there was

not a cab to be had. I suggested to Holmes that since our destination was opposite the new station, why not simply take the Met line to it? He reluctantly agreed, and to this day I do not know why he has always preferred cabs to the modernity of the Underground. We thus set off southeast, away from our final destination. Going to the Met station on Baker Street took us in the wrong direction. But there we'd catch the train going in the right direction, just as our new client had done.

It was not long before the train arrived. Soon we were on our way passing each station, first St. John's Wood, six more Marlboro Road, Swiss Cottage, Finchley Road, West Hampstead, Willesden Green, Neasden and finally the new stop on the Met line, Wembley Park.

I could tell Holmes was not impressed with the trip. He seemed uncomfortable. While it got us to our destination in a short time, which he acknowledged by asserting that he believed a carriage would not have been as quick, his staring at his watch the whole time appeared to me to be a distraction for him.

Was his normal unwillingness to make use of the Underground, as people now called it, perhaps the result of a case of what Dr. Bell, just a decade ago, had defined as this '*claustrophobia*'?

It would not be Holmes' style to admit to such a fear as that, I realized. I thought I might find a way later to confirm my suspected diagnosis. At least I had now something new to observe about my colleague. I could practice his methods by observing him for a change.

After ascending to street-level we found ourselves at the wrong end of the exit. By that I mean, we had a choice to come up stairs at one end or the other from the platform. The way we went let us out further away from our destination than had we gone out the other end of the station platform.

We began walking now in the other direction and soon found our destination.

Ye Old Red Rooster Inn and Pub was now directly ahead. Those pavement stones nearest the new station were new, level and made for a comfortable stroll. Once away from where the new construction ended, the old surroundings showed their age having likely been built several hundred years before. These old stones were in an old and dishevelled state. One had to watch one's step. The lighting was poor and the pavement had been lain with stones and, in places, they had gone missing. An uneven walk it was. No doubt quite a few turned ankles resulted from traversing this stretch every day.

The Pub was an old one and announced its long existence proudly in large red lettering on a black shield trimmed with a gold:

Old Red Rooster Inn and Pub
Since 1673

We entered and found ourselves a table near the hearth. A comfortable and welcoming fire was crackling in the old stone fireplace. Soon a waitress came to our table inquiring about our order. It was not the young lady I had met that morning. This lady was much older.

We ordered a pint for each of us and began looking over the board on the wall listing their fare. She left to get our drinks and soon returned with them. She said to wave her over when we had made up our minds.

"Well, Holmes, perhaps we've been invited on a wild goose chase?" said I, disappointed that our newest client did not appear to be here.

"Are you sure, Doctor that this is the correct pub?"

"I am quite sure. She was most emphatic that she should speak only to you and she specifically named this establishment. I know I am not mistaken."

When the waitress returned, I was more assertive in my quest to find the young woman with whom I had spoken earlier that morning.

"Excuse me, mum. Is there a young barmaid here, I think her name is Annie?"

"Whoz would be asking for herz?" said she, somewhat suspiciously and with a face that forebode unpleasantness.

"My name is Dr. Watson. I spoke with her this very morning."

"Well, nowz. Maybe shez here and maybe shez isn't. I don'tz go telling strangers about the whereabout of me girlz."

"Holmes, there she is!" cried I.

"Soz maybe you knowz her, since you can pick her out. "What waz your name again?"

"Dr. Watson, she came to speak to me this morning. I am sure she will remember me."

"Annie!" she suddenly called out across the length of the pub and loudly enough to be barely heard over the din that pervaded the establishment.

The young miss heard her being called and quickly came over to our table.

"Thiz here gentleman, Dr. Watzon, sayz he spoke with you thiz morning. Sez you asked him to come. True?"

"I don't know what hez talking about. I never seen him before in my life," said she tartly, then she turned quickly and ran off.

"But, that's not true!" said I, with as much indignation as I could muster at having just been called a liar in not so many words.

"There, there, Watson. We must have made a mistake. Let's depart and find another place to partake our dinner."

Holmes rose and fetched our hats and coats.

"We must have made a mistake, mum. Sorry, mum."

"I'd say youz did. Don't youz *gentlemen* come 'round here again cauzing trouble with me girlz. I runz a respectable place here!"

"But Holmes!"

"It's all right, Watson. We shall not trouble you any further. Let us take our leave. Good evening, madam."

And with that Holmes grabbed my arm and helped me to my feet. He handed me my coat and hat and ushered me towards the door.

The older woman, satisfied she'd won our little encounter, turned and began talking to other customers.

We dodged tables and chairs on our way out. It was only

as we had left and were outside that we saw a face come close to the multi-paned window. It was Annie. She frowned at us and shook her head slowly as if she were saying all was not right. She then turned abruptly and went back farther into the pub.

It was then that I realized Holmes was correct in having us leave. Something was amiss. Certainly, Annie could not acknowledge she knew me in front of the mistress of the place.

"Holmes, what do you think has happened? queried I.

"No doubt she was fearful of acknowledging that she knew you in front of her mistress. Let us find another place to eat and we shall discuss the possibilities."

We soon found another establishment nearby. After settling in and ordering a simple meal, we discussed what had just happened.

"I can only conclude that her visit to you, or in fact her attempt to contact me, was a risk to her. Something she cannot reveal to the woman. Perhaps she will come to Baker Street again, soon hopefully, and we will be enlightened as to why she has chosen to contact me.

"Since she has sought me out, no doubt having heard of my successes with such odd cases as you have written about, she is in need of some sort of help. I theorize, which as you know, I do not subscribe to doing, but I theorize she cannot go to the police or that would have been the more reasonable thing to do if it involves some sort of illegality. But then again, it may be that she has witnessed or is somehow caught up in something from which she cannot get away.

"The most interesting part to me so far is her willingness to come seek me out, but when I arrive in front of the mistress of the establishment, she cannot acknowledge it. I am intrigued."

"But, Holmes, shall we not go back tonight? Might she be in some sort of danger?"

"I think not, Watson. The quick denial on her part and the other woman's ephemeral attention to the confrontation, makes me think the mistress believes we were only there for disreputable intentions. She has not, it seems, made a connection with whatever it is Annie wishes my help with and Annie. This is a good thing for now. Should we return now, the mistress will certainly question Annie. I fear she may not be able to withstand a severe inquiry as to why we were there asking for her. No, it is best we wait to hear from Annie when she feels safe enough to seek me out again. I predict it shall be a week from today."

"Holmes, have you become a soothsayer? Why a week?"

"She works to a schedule and today was a chance for her to come by Baker Street and still have some time before getting to the pub. Next week should avail her the same opportunity."

"A week? We must wait a week?"

"Calm down, Watson. It gives me time to plan my next experiment. The time shall fly by. You really must learn patience, dear Doctor."

"Holmes, she may be in trouble and I do not like waiting under those circumstances."

"All will be fine, Watson, all will be fine."

As Holmes had predicted, an entire week passed with no word from Annie. However, this time Holmes made sure he was at Baker Street at the hour Annie had made her appearance the week before.

Holmes began the morning quietly. I went into my surgery attending to several patients with whom I had appointments.

I had rescheduled some of my later appointments to allow me to be back at Baker Street when hopefully our new client would seek Holmes' help again.

I arrived early, at about half three o'clock. I noticed Holmes was anxiously anticipating our guest but perhaps was questioning whether or not she would, in fact, arrive. I concluded this because he was playing his violin. I had noticed he frequently played it when he was unsettled. I, myself, chose to read through the papers of the day to help me relax.

Our waiting was rewarded. At about twenty minutes to four o'clock, we were notified by Mrs. Hudson that our young visitor was indeed calling again.

I asked that she send Annie up to us.

I could hear Mrs. Hudson, speaking in low tones and eventually she said loud enough for me to hear.

"I will do so, miss, but I am here to tell you, you have nothing to worry about."

And after that I heard both Mrs. Hudson and Annie climbing up the staircase.

Now at our door, she seemed a bit shy. Mrs, Hudson waved her into our quarters and then stood by the open door. Annie stepped a few feet past Mrs. Hudson and stopped dead still.

"Mr. Holmes, Doctor, this young miss has asked me to stay here while she speaks with you. I told her she has nothing to worry about as both of you are gentlemen and that she would be safe in your presence."

"It is quite all right Mrs. Hudson. Annie, correct? Please come in and sit down. We met last week. I am, of course Dr. Watson. And this gentleman is Mr. Sherlock Holmes, whom you sought out for advice last week."

Annie, made a poor attempt to perform a simple curtsy, and then rather sheepishly stepped a little farther into the somewhat cluttered room.

"Hello, zir," said she directing her greeting to Holmes.

"Mrs. Hudson, perhaps you could accompany Annie to come sit over there on the sofa. There we can be a bit more comfortable and discuss just what problem has prompted Annie to seek my advice," suggested Holmes.

This behaviour of hers did not at all remind me of the confident and energetic young miss I had met the week before when this all started.

"Annie, how is it that you think I can help you? That is, why did you come to see me?"

"Well, zir. I'ze not got much time. I'z must be at the pub by fivez o'clock. If I'm late, I'll be zacked."

"I understand," said Holmes.

"Then, please tell me quickly, what is troubling you?"

"Well, zir. I'z seen some strange goinz onz at the pub. And I don'tz knowz whatz to dooze about it."

"What kind of strange things, Annie?"

"Oh, zir, uhm, ah, I don'tz knowz," said she. She then looked at each of us and a panic look took over her face.

Suddenly, she leapt up and ran towards and out the open doorway before any of us could speak.

"I'mz zorry mumz," yelled she, as she ran past a startled Mrs. Hudson.

She practically flew down the staircase and was out the front door before I reached our doorway.

Holmes had gone to the window and no doubt watched her flee down Baker Street toward the station.

"Oh, Mr. Holmes, I'm so sorry."

"Why, Mrs. Hudson?"

"I don't think I helped make her feel comfortable enough. Such a waste of your time, Mr. Holmes, Doctor. I told her downstairs she could trust you, and she seemed all right when we first came up."

"But you know how these young ones are today. Some of them scared of their own shadow."

"In this case I think we have one that is courageous, but overly cautious. She seeks my help, about something important no doubt, but her fears, this time, seem to have gotten the better of her. I believe her fear may be justified if what she is concerned about is real enough for her to seek my help.

"Hopefully she'll soon find the courage to seek me out again. I think this will be a case requiring much patience."

Nothing related to this case occurred over the next two weeks. Holmes was getting restless as usual without anything to occupy his brilliant mind. It was in this time, dear readers that the *Adventure at Osborne House* took place, which I have chronicled elsewhere. Due to the physicality of that adventure, I believe Holmes had perhaps forgotten Annie and her problem. I know it was not on my mind at all.

Now, more than a month later, again, one late afternoon, we were again called down to the front door by Mrs. Hudson. We arrived and Mrs. Hudson, returned inside. Outside by the curb stood Annie. This time, since the weather had changed, she was wrapped up a bit more warmly.

She seemed shy, but determined. She then suddenly ran up to us and said,

"Thiz iz whatz itz allz aboutz zir." She then looked up and down the street, which was full of the commerce of the day, but I saw no one paying any particular attention to us. Annie then reached into the layers of shawls, sweaters and such that she was wearing and pulled something small out. Again, looking both ways, she motioned for Holmes to open his hand. He did so and she placed it in his hand and took both her hands and closed his hand around the little object.

"Youz takez itz, I don't understandz it, zir. Butz Iz knowz itz notz right!"

With that, she was off again running to catch the underground at the Baker Street Station.

"Holmes, what on earth has that young miss given you?"

"It seems nothing, save a double florin."

"A double florin? But that is likely a months' pay to her. What can be the matter?"

"I don't know, Watson, but her behaviour is quite unique. I become alarmed when normal people behave outside what is normal for them. It is a signal of sorts. Not unlike your noticing an inflammation of the skin that alerts you to some underlying ailment. It is but a symptom. There is an ill-omened presence about all this Watson. I believe she has done all she can, mustering up the courage to do what she has done so far. It is up to us now to figure out what she is trying to tell us."

We returned to our rooms and I went to my papers. Holmes, on the other hand, grabbed a clay pipe and some fresh tobacco from the slipper on the mantle and then reclined on the sofa.

After lighting his pipe, he held the coin in his hand and flipped it over and over. Occasionally, he would stop and look at it closely. I was sure he would soon either ask me to retrieve his magnifying glass or perhaps leap up himself to obtain it. He did neither and continued his silent thoughts on his new clue. As time wore on, he would close his eyes, presumably deep in thought, and then only once in a while, open them as if under water and coming up for air. Then once again, his eyes would close and presumably his deep thinking continuing anew.

He did this through dinner time and I knew no disturbance, question or encouragement from me would dissuade him from his mental journey through the myriad of possible reasons she had given him the coin.

Was it a down payment for services soon to be rendered by him, I speculated? But that did not make sense, with the words she had uttered, '*This is what it's all about…*'.

As I never have achieved the skills of my friend, dear readers, I could not make sense of it. I abandoned my quest to solve what appeared to be a most insoluble riddle. I left Holmes and retired. He remained on the sofa and the dark blue haze of the tobacco smoke continued to fill the room.

When morning came and I arose, I found that Holmes was gone, as was the coin.

It was about twelve o'clock when he returned.

"I have spent the morning at Baldwin's down on Duncannon Street. I must give them credit for finding the blood spots upon the trail, so to speak."

"Who? Are you suggesting we should change our tobacconist, Holmes?"

"What's that you're saying, Watson?"

"I assume you wish to change tobacconist and start procuring our tobacco from this 'Baldwin's' you just mentioned to me."

"I know not how your mind leaps to such conclusions. Were mine so undisciplined, I could not feed myself."

Of course, I took these words to heart. Holmes frequently seemed to enjoy making fun of my reasoning.

"Stick to your medical diagnoses that are clearly prescribed by the text books, Doctor. Deciphering new ailments is not for you."

Insulted as I was at these comments, my pride was not as fragile as sometimes it could be and my curiosity of his morning quest bandaged over the wound to my confidence.

"Then to what are you speaking about, Holmes?"

"Numismatist. Baldwin's are numismatics. They deal in

coins. Collectable coins, to be more precise. Who else would know the intricacies of minted objects? I simply know where the experts are when I need them. Baldwin's are experts. While the details and variations are enough for me to find interest, it is like many other things with which I do not clutter my mind."

"Like the time I chastised you for not remembering the earth goes 'round the sun?"

"Exactly! Should the solution to a case require that knowledge, I would surely take more notice of it. But so far none has presented itself as needing that data. Thus, useless to me. I have had the same attitude regarding coinage, until today."

"So, how did they enlighten you?"

"They specifically pointed out that the coin was too big.

"Too big?"

"Yes, it appears to be the correct weight, but is wider than it should be, but not by very much.

"How queer is that?"

"I agree. They were quite helpful and I do believe have helped me considerably in the quest to understand what this case that Annie has presented to us is all about."

He then proceeded to examine the coin at his desk with the assistance of his glass. I left him to his silent inquiry and returned to my papers. Shortly thereafter he left our lodging only to return just before dinner. After settling in, he spoke to me again.

"You see, Watson, they are most clever. The crown coin is as we know, valued at five shillings. This new double florin that has been issued, with a slightly smaller diameter, we know is valued at four shillings. Due to same profile of our Majesty's on the obverse side of both coins, they are frequently confused by unobservant receivers of such coins in a transaction. Rapid exchanges cause an even greater chance of mistaking one for the other. When one includes the dimly lit atmospheres of pubs and the likely inebriated condition of the patrons of such establishments, it is easy to see their inability to quickly notice the difference.

"Since the coin was introduced just last year, in what I believe is a futile effort to decimalize our currency like that of America, the poor barmaids in England have borne the brunt of this poor introduction of such coinage. They receive such coinage believing it to be worth one-quarter pound when in fact it is only worth the one-fifth pound that is assigned to it. Many have learned the hard way to look at the reverse side which then reveals whether it is a crown or a double florin. I am told the barmaids call it the *barmaid's grief.* Should she not take the time to look or in situations where a patron leaves their payment on a table and walks out, the barmaid is left to make up the difference with her employer.

"This set of thieves, as we must label them, seems to have decided to make their patrons pay for past transgressions."

"I'm sorry, Holmes, I still do not understand?"

"Watson, look here.

"You remember Mr. Edelstein. You chronicled our adventure with him in some tome of yours about '*Hatton Garden*' if I recall."

"Yes, of course I remember. But what has he to do with this case, Holmes?"

"Nothing directly, but I was able to visit him this afternoon and make use of his newest *Palmer.*"

"*Palmer,* I am not familiar with a person of such name?"

"No, Watson, I would think not, as he simply is the Frenchman who was the inventor of an extremely precise and sensitive instrument for measuring small distances.

"Fortunately for me, Edelstein has just acquired one of the '*Morley*' improved, Brown & Sharpe instruments from America, only two months ago."

"Holmes, what has this to do with our case?"

"Watson, I am about to describe some information I have gained from using Edelstein's *Palmer-Morley* instrument. Please read my summary of data carefully and hopefully all will be made clear.

Holmes invited me to our table, and even pulled a chair out for me to sit in. How could I deny such an invitation?

He then placed four coins on the table in front to me
Two were 'face up' and another two were 'face down.'
"Please observe the coins, Watson. They look normal do they not?"

Holmes then handed me a piece of paper upon which he had written the data he had referenced:

	Double Florin	Crown	Annie's
Weight:	0.79 oz	1.01 oz	0.79 oz
Thickness at edge:	0.088″	0.098″	0.071″
Diameter:	1.42″	1.50″	1.49″
Value:	⅕ ₤	¼ ₤	¼ ₤ - ⅕ ₤ ?

obverse

Double Florin

reverse

obverse

Crown

reverse

"I see the data, Holmes, and certainly something is amiss, but what, I cannot precisely say."

"Are you sure?" queried Holmes.

I could only shrug my shoulders.

"Watson, then let me explain," said Holmes as he handed me two coins.

"Without looking at the coins, can you discern a difference in weight?"

"No."

He then took one coin from me and handed me another.

"Now can you tell a difference."

"I think so, the one you just handed me in my right hand seems a slight bit heavier."

"You are correct, Doctor. The one in your right hand is a crown. The one in your left hand is a double florin."

He then took all three coins and stacked them together and handed them to me in my right hand. He instructed me to keep the coins stacked and examine them as if picking up a stack of coins thus only using my fingers along the edges to then explore the coins.

"Again, Doctor, can you tell a difference in the coins?"

"Yes, Holmes, one is not as wide as the others, no doubt the double florin, yes?"

"Correct again, Doctor. Let me remove the double florin from the mix. Please hold the two remaining coins by your fingers along only the edges just like before."

I did so again and felt no difference.

"So, the coins appear to be the same, correct?"

"I feel no difference, Holmes,"

"Now, I am going to lay the two coins flat on the table and touching each other," stated Holmes. When I looked down, I saw two coins, both with Her Majesty's Profile facing upward.

"Please rub your finger across the point where the two coins touch. What do you feel?"

I did as Holmes instructed.

"One seems slightly thicker than the other?" offered I. I suggested this because I was not sure of what I was felt.

"Correct again, Doctor."

"Holmes what is this all about?"

"It is really quite simple, Doctor. Someone at the Pub is passing double florins off as crowns. Rather than depending on drunks and non-observing barmaids and patrons, they are tilting the scales, as it were, in their favour.

"Most people can easily discern the difference in the diameter of the coins when stacked just as you just proved. If one makes a double florin the same diameter as a crown, it is not so easy to pick out. With our Majesty's profile gracing both coins, it adds to the illusion.

"Considering the value exchange, these fraudsters are making a twenty-five percent profit on their little scheme. The obvious point is that it is being done. The modified double florin is proof enough of that. We must now uncover *who* and *how* they are doing it."

Holmes, strode away from the table. I picked up both coins and turned them over. The reverse side of the 'thinner' one showed the marking one would find on a double florin, that is, the *crown shields and sceptres*.

The crown's reverse held the image *St. George slaying the dragon* as I expected.

In both cases, the double florin's features appeared worn and less crisp at the edge of all its details.

"Holmes, how is this possible?" queried I, but I received no answer. "Holmes?"

He had disappeared on me as was his custom when the trail became odorous with the scent of his quarry. I knew something must have triggered in his mind that gave him the reason to leave so abruptly and without notice to me.

With no direction from him, I decided to begin recording the incidents to date, for you my dear readers, of this seemingly simple but fascinating tale about which we were certain to dig down to its roots. I would simply have to be patient until Holmes returned or perhaps sent me a note or letter requesting my help or giving me direction to assist him in this case.

It was late that night that Holmes returned. His less than silent entrance had awoken me from my slumber. Granted I was not in my bed, but stretched out upon our sofa with the evening edition of the *Times* still gripped in my right hand that had fallen toward the floor.

"Watson, wake up!" intoned Holmes.

"Holmes, what is it? Are you all right?"

"Yes, yes, my good man. Come see what I have found!"

Holmes waved me to our table to which he had sat down. He opened the strings to a moderate sized money-bag and emptied it contents upon the table. The contents, perhaps one hundred in all, jingle-jangled as they fought each other for a prominent place in the resulting pile. Once they settled, the last coins out of the bag winning the top spot of the pile, Holmes began sorting them out. All he was concerned with were crowns and double florins.

Once he had those separated, he made sure none were on their obverse side. All showed either the *crown shields and sceptres* or *St. George slaying the dragon.* At this point it appeared he still had thirty or forty coins.

He then sorted those by their imprinted design, crown shields/sceptres versus St. George.

After that he began stacking them. Once that was done, he drew them close to the edge of the table and squatted down eye-level with the table top.

"Yes!" he exclaimed, as he picked up the stack of double florins and again showed a sign of gaiety at his discovery. He then set them back down.

"There Watson, feel for yourself."

He pointed to the stack of about twelve to fifteen or so double florins. I picked them up and felt the unevenness of the various coins.

"They should all be the same, should they not?"

"Yes, they should but some seem less wide."

"Watson, these 'less wide' as you referred to them are the non-modified double florins, I am quite sure of it. The wider ones no doubt should compare even to the crowns."

He then separated out the wider double florins and stacked then atop a stack of crowns. He again waved me to pick up this new stack of coins.

They all felt to be the same width. I couldn't tell them apart.

We then set down each of the wider double florins.

Holmes had now gotten out both his magnifying glass and asked that I uncover his microscope.

He first looked at each coin with his glass and made notes about each one. He placed them in order and then put each of them under his microscope in the same order, adding notes to his previous ones for the specific coin.

I had left Holmes alone during this exercise as my experience with him had taught me that my silence was more valuable to him than any insight that I might have thought was of value. I had learned to accept this and now anxiously awaited word of what he might have uncovered.

I have to admit I fell asleep whilst waiting for Holmes to complete his analysis. It was not until morning that we spoke of the previous night's revelation in this most queer case. It was Holmes who spoke first.

"Watson, are you not in the least interested as to my acquisition of the coins we observed last night?"

"Well, of course Holmes, I concluded you went back to the *Ye Old Red Rooster Inn and Pub,* and spoke with your client whence she gave these to you.

"No, you are wrong Watson. And that is why this is a case which will no doubt be of interest to Mycroft."

"Why, what has he to do with this?"

"The coins we examined last night were not from the *Ye Old Red Rooster Inn and Pub.*"

"There were not? Where then?" queried I.

"Those coins were collected from five different establishments and none of them were the *Ye Old Red Rooster Inn and Pub.*"

"But Holmes, how is that possible?"

"It is unbelievable, is it not?"

"I believe now we are facing not just some pub owner who has sought to turn the tables on his patrons, but a more powerful force trying to implement a plan of economic chaos on our dear country. And you know the one person who would think up a scheme like this and have the means to try to pull it off, don't you Doctor?"

"Professor Moriarty?"

"It likely is, Doctor. He is the evil genius behind these

types of plots to make a farce and disaster of our country's way of life. By wrecking the monetary system, the populace would quickly lose faith in Queen and country. We must act quickly, as the game started without us knowing the game was moving."

With that thought lingering in my head, he then explained he was off to meet with Mycroft and explain to him what we had discovered.

Again, left without direction from Holmes, I decided to take my own advice and divert my attention to some thought I had been pondering for some time with regards to my surgery. Having read of numerous advancements in my field, I thought that perhaps I should collect data on my patients, much in the same way Holmes would in his cases. It seemed to me that perhaps with more data I might be able to foretell, at least with some of my more regular patients, what their physical futures might hold. Should, for example, those that I had used my new pressure machine upon, and whose measurements were high on a regular basis, be prone to certain maladies, and if so, could I contemplate ways to avert such outcomes and prescribe actions or medicines for them to live longer lives? I fell into this work and discovered it to be quite fascinating. I'd come up with several ideas that I wished to start on anew as soon as I was able when I arrived at my surgery.

Unfortunately, my plan would have to wait until the morrow. Holmes had arrived with Mycroft in tow. I expected to be sworn to state secrecy as was always the case when dealing with Mycroft. But to my surprise, he said nothing along those lines. In fact, he simply greeted me and I felt that his greeting was one of acceptance and trust.

I was comfortable with the fact that on each and every occasion that I had assisted Sherlock and him in some adventure that pertained to the security of the kingdom, I had acted properly and with aplomb.

"Glad you are with us, Doctor," said he.

"As always, Mycroft, here for Queen and country," said I.

"Her Majesty's government appreciates the loyalty of her servants such as you, Doctor. Always at the ready."

"It is my honour."

"Sherlock, what is your plan?" enquired Mycroft.

"I believe we can be sure as to the who, as I explained back at the Diogenes Club. And I believe I have a good explanation of the how. It now falls to the *where*?"

"You say you know how?" queried I.

"Yes, I have run experiments in the past which required the knowledge of the melting point of silver which, if I recall is, 1,763 F°. The villain need not achieve the full melting point, in fact, he dares not. Stopping when it turns dark red would do the trick. If he did go beyond that, he would be left with a lump of molten silver. While the silver itself would be of value, it would not retain the value and ease of exchange of the coin.

"Once it is pressed with the correct force it would take its new dimension. No doubt he has a furnace of some importance and likely several presses.

"The dyes in which he would place the coins would have been specially designed to not damage the coin to any extreme, least users think his end product as counterfeit to begin with. It would end up looking worn down I conjure like these specimens do. Also, he would need many dyes. To press these one at a time would not likely be worth the effort. Thus, with this amount of detail required to accomplish these things, I conclude Moriarty is involved.

"So, gentlemen, we are looking for a building where there is a furnace and would have enough room for several presses. I would think an abandoned factory along the Thames would suit his shrewd plan most accommodatingly."

"But, Sherlock, there are hundreds of such buildings like that. How can we search them all?" It could take a year," retorted Mycroft.

"Yes, you are correct, Mycroft. So, I've come up with plan to have Moriarty tell us where his factory is."

"How can you do that, Sherlock?"

"Let me see if my instincts are right and you will figure it out for yourselves."

"I should have our answer within a few days. Mycroft you must be ready to have agents of the treasury available to capture this site, if not Moriarty himself. I doubt he would be there, but one never knows.

"I would think a squad of twenty would be a good number, so please have them at the ready, shall we say forty-eight hours from now? Also, please give orders for firearms, with this being one of Moriarty's gangs, they will likely be carrying weapons and may not give up without a fight."

"Yes, Sherlock, I will arrange for the squad. 'Mum's' the word on all of this. We cannot have the public become alarmed over this *counterfeit* money. I must, go now. Please advise me as soon as you have located his place."

Sherlock simply bowed his head in recognition of his forthcoming duty to inform Mycroft of the raid. I was pondering myself, by this point, how was it that Holmes was to get Moriarty to 'tell us' where his location was. Certainly, he would not simply disclose it. Could Sherlock even capture Moriarty? Would he give it up even upon being tortured?

I was at a loss as how Holmes would accomplish such a trick and have the location told to us.

"The time shall come, Doctor when we shall be joining Mycroft and his squad of agents. Let us be prepared. Can you please clean both our weapons and have them at the ready? Where I am going now, I shall not need it, but when we join the raid, we both best have adequate firepower as I believe it may easily turn into quite a duel. I shall return late, Watson. Do not wait up for me."

And as was his usual behaviour in such cases, he left without further discussing all that was swirling in his head. No doubt he had many preparations to make to ensure contact with Moriarty and his gang within the next two days.

On the second night, I received a telegram from Holmes.

```
Have located them. Mycroft to
pick you up. Along with my
pistol, please also bring a
bottle of ether.
```

It was less than an hour and a police carriage pulled up on the street.

I rushed down the staircase in such a hurry that, Mrs. Hudson, came out to see what the commotion was about.

"Sorry, Mrs. Hudson," yelled I over my shoulder as I was scrambling into the awaiting hansom occupied by Mycroft. I am not sure to this day that she even heard my apology, perhaps it was in vain.

"Where are we going?" queried I of Mycroft.

"It is along the wharf on the west end. My men are arranging to meet us one block away from where Sherlock has told us to come. I do not wish the clip-clopping of twenty horses sounding the alarm to these fellows. We want to catch them red-handed!"

It was but a short ride to where we disembarked. I held Sherlock's pistol in my left hand and the bottle of ether in my right. I was determined to deliver the sleep-inducing liquid to Sherlock intact. I had fitted my service revolver in my waist. I had not much time to prepare the weapons as Sherlock had requested, but I did what I thought was most preparatory for providing ease of action on such a night.

After traveling a block or so, we finally met up with Sherlock. I handed him his firearm and offered the ether.

"Thank you, Doctor. Hold on to the ether, will you? Spare rounds, have you any?"

"Yes, Sherlock, I anticipated you wishing more than the cylinder holds. Here is a full box of cartridges."

"Doctor, you are certainly to be counted upon."

"It is an old habit from my Afghanistan days. Even though my duty was surgery I was taught to always bring along more ammunition than you think you'll need. I thank my RSM[8] for that lesson."

"Excellent advice."

"Sherlock, tell us where they are and what is the ether for?" directed Mycroft with impatience.

"Dear brother, do not be over anxious. They are at their work and do not appear to have anyone on guard but one

---

[8] Editor's note: Regimental Sergeant Major

old gent, who I have observed nods off from time to time. He just reawakened and left his post likely to use the loo. He has now returned to his post, so based on the data I have gathered tonight, he'll nod off again in approximately one-half hour. We shall wait until he does so.

"I plan to encourage the depth of his slumber with this," as he raised the bottle, "perhaps more than he'd wish, so as to have more time to make our entrance without alarm. He does have a gun, so best be prepared.

"I think there are two entry points. This one and the dock doors which are closed.

"Once I have made sure the sentry is asleep for the duration, I intend to see if I can unlock the dock doors. Have some of your men ready there. The second dock door should be easy to breach as it shows signs of fatigue. You and Dr. Watson shall have my back."

It was but twenty minutes to wait after all had been communicated to Mycroft's men. It felt like an hour. The only sounds now were that of the press being used and the clanking of the coins once they had been ejected from the press.

Sherlock headed toward the sentry's post which was a stool at the entrance to the warehouse floor. He hesitated as he looked around the corner to reappraise the condition of his quarry. Turning the corner, we followed behind him.

Apparently, he had again drifted off, abandoning his duty, and with that knowledge, Sherlock turned to me to dispense the ether into his handkerchief. I recapped the bottle quickly to ensure we were not overcome ourselves by its raw power. Sherlock then sidled up to him and administered the ether. He gave little resistance as he was half asleep to start with. His body crumbled down further than it already was. Sherlock helped his body to the ground to avoid any noise whatsoever. He relieved him of his weapon.

He then signalled for us to follow him.

When we entered the large warehouse, the lights were on only where the six or seven men operating the machinery were standing. This caused many dark and shadowy spaces in the large building. There were old crates and what looked like abandoned and likely inoperable machinery all about.

Sherlock crept along the edges staying out of the lighted areas and was able to reach the side of the first dock door without being detected. But now there was no protection. The pathway to the second dock door was clear as it had been used recently, no doubt. Were the workers to look that way, Sherlock would be seen without question.

"We must help him," whispered I.

"What do you suggest, Doctor," replied Mycroft.

"A distraction, perhaps we just hold them at gunpoint? I do not know. But we must do something!"

"Sherlock will have certainly thought this little hurdle out. I wish to see how he plays this, eh?"

I could not believe these words, from his own brother! Here was my dear friend about to risk life and limb in the service of his Queen and country and his own brother was willing to see how things turned out!

"I shall not stand by," responded I, with indignity that I hoped dealt Mycroft a blow to his sense of being a gentleman.

I arose from my position of hiding and quietly approached the operator of the closest machine to me. I raised my pistol to the back of his head, cocked the hammer and spoke.

"Good evening sir!"

The man turned around slowly and saw the barrel of my gun pointing straight between his eyes. For a slight moment, I felt he thought about reaching for his weapon that was laying on a bench next to his machine. But then he thought better of such a rash act and slowly raised each of his hands to either side of his shoulders. The other operators, one by one, noticed their comrade's predicament and turned toward me and my captive.

That was all it took. Sherlock abruptly ran for the dock door and opened it with ease. It was not locked!

In came the officers with guns pointed at the other operators. There was a scuffle or two when then suddenly a loud bang rang out and echoed throughout the building.

"Quick, he's getting away!" shouted Sherlock, as he pointed to a man who appeared to be dressed in the evening attire of a gentleman. He was ascending a cast-iron stair case up to a mezzanine with an office of sorts that overlooked the floor of the warehouse. As he reached the top he turned and shot down at us again.

Several of the officers returned fire, but the angle and height did not make for any easy shot for those who so infrequently shot guns, as these men did, having only been given their firearms for tonight's raid.

"Is it Moriarty?" yelled I at Sherlock.

"We'll only know for sure if we catch him!" he shouted back at me as he raced to the first steps of the old black cast iron and cobb-webbed stairs.

Another shot rang out from above, this time directly at Sherlock. It missed, but it seemed to take Sherlock's breath away as its proximity to him caused him to dive for cover. But from whence it came on the darkened mezzanine, I could not tell for sure. The office walls blocked my view.

"Sherlock, be careful," I cried out.

It was then that Mycroft stood up from his hiding place, aimed and fired.

There was another shot that rang out and this time I saw the flash from above. It did not appear to strike near anyone. The cast-iron balustrade rattled just a bit and then a body came over it and landed unceremoniously nearby.

I ran over and reached to feel the man's carotid artery for a sign of life, but it was to no avail. Whether the shot or the fall had killed him was for the Coroner to decide.

Sherlock quickly converged on the body. He motioned for me to help turn him over that we might more easily see his countenance. Was this finally Moriarty? Had Sherlock scored his final victory? I thought to myself as we struggled with the weight of the dead man.

"No, Doctor. It is not he. This is Mr. Wilford Rexson. He had put in with Moriarty some time ago and I have run across him on occasion. He is but a low-cunning sort only aspiring to become an equal to Moriarty, but his dream would never have come true for he lacked the professor's intelligence. Had he even gotten close to Moriarty in his schemes, the professor would have made sure he met a similar demise as he has met tonight.

"Well, I see you've not lost your aim, brother."

"It is not the first time I've had to save you, nor likely will it be the last," replied Mycroft.

Sherlock ignored his brother's remark.

"It would appear we have stopped his gang this time," said I.

"It is too bad we didn't catch the professor," said Mycroft disappointedly.

"True," replied Sherlock.

"Sherlock, how did you find them here?" queried I.

"Watson, I had a scheme which I thought would cause Moriarty to lead me here, but it was not to be. There are many old abandoned warehouses along various sections of the Thames, too many in fact. I then decided to enlist the aid of the Baker Street Irregulars. I promised a large reward to the one who located them. I told them to look for machines working in a building with no else around. After that, all that was needed was time and patience. When on such a mission, they are like a swarm of bees, visiting every location until they find the nectar."

"You have helped save the currency, Sherlock," said Mycroft. "For that I am most appreciative."

"I have no doubt that as long as Her Majesty's advisors continue to push this scheme of decimalization upon the good people of England, we all will continue to suffer," proffered Sherlock."

"Perhaps you are correct, Sherlock. But these types of decisions are not for the likes of us to be concerned. We have stopped the counterfeiting and that was my goal. We shall have to find and remove these counterfeits as we come across them. But there should be no more new ones now."

Mycroft then turned to the officers and issued orders to collect all the coinage. The gang was hand-cuffed and led away without any more resistance.

"Sherlock, what is there for us to do now?" queried I.

"Watson, first, thank you my friend.'

"For what?"

"I had not seen the inside of the dock doors and hoped

they were more protected from the gang's line of sight. I was conjuring up an improvised plan on the spot, but then you made your move. It was risky, Doctor, and had it gone amiss, I would not have forgiven myself."

"Well, Holmes, your brother is to blame. The man seemed to have no regard for your well-being. I knew you were in trouble and acted as any friend would do. Your brother on the other hand... well I no longer have the respect I once held for him. He seemed delighted in your sudden quandary tonight."

"Pay him no mind, Watson. We have delighted in watching each other battling such puzzlements all our lives. He means no harm by it. He knew it would turn out in my favour. You saw that when it counted, he eliminated the threat of our deceased man here. I hold no grudge against him. It is an old game we play and, in the end, I can count on him and so should you."

"If you say so, Sherlock, if you say so."

"I do say so. We must return to Baker Street now and get some deserved rest, my good friend. I much appreciate your allegiance. It is a most valuable thing to possess."

It was a week later that our *client* came by to see us.

"Wellz, Mr. Holmez, I gotz a mezzage from a young street lad. He toldz me youz wanted to seez me."

"Yes, Annie. I did send such a message. You are quite an observant young lady."

"Oh, Sirz. I'm not what youz callz a real lady. I'z mean I'z is just a poor barmaid, sirz."

"Well, you are a *lady* in my opinion," replied Holmes.

"You did your country and your Queen a great service, did you know that?"

"Oh, no sirz, I'z just did whatz was right, right sir?"

"Right, enough. In any event, I have a present for you."
"Oh, sirz."

Holmes pulled a small money bag from behind him and handed it to Annie.

"Now, I don't want you to squander this on frivolous things. Go ahead, open it."

Annie pulled the mouth of the bag open and a large smile broadened across her face. Her eyes lit up.

"Oh, sirz! Thankz youz, sirz, Thankz youz!"

"You've done a very good job."

"Oh, Sirz! I don'tz know what to say!"

And with that she suddenly reached up and grabbed Holmes' shoulders with both her hands. She pulled his large tall frame downward a bit and gave Sherlock a peck on his cheek. She then quickly turned and ran down the street with the money bag disappearing beneath her outer clothing. I observed Holmes' cheek with slight tinge of red from the blush that had suddenly overwhelmed him.

"Holmes, what did you give her?"

"Umm…Watson, that poor miss did more to help keep our country safe from the likes of Moriarty, than an entire army."

"I do not recall *paying* a client before, but as you said, she does deserve it," said I.

"But could you not have given her a large banknote, perhaps instead of a bag of coins?"

"Ah, but Watson, the bag is full of double florins!"

"Holmes, you didn't do what I think you did."

"Watson, that young lady is a heroine of our country. She deserves to be rewarded.

"I simply helped myself to some of the unconverted double florins from our little adventure the other night. I see no harm in it, as she had the courage to help solve this unique problem. I simply rewarded her with something practicable."

Holmes then retrieved his violin and began a playful tune that reminded me of my childhood, though, I could not place it. With that act, I knew this adventure had finally come to an end.

THE ADVENTURE OF
THE ASHES

"**W**atson, what is all this commotion I am reading about here in the Gazette?"

"I have not yet read today's paper, Holmes. I cannot fathom what is happening from so little data, as you would say. Once you have finished and are willing to share the paper with me, I shall read it and give you my most educated opinion on whatever subject it is to which you are referring."

"I agree. I shall hand you the paper momentarily."

I waited approximately two minutes and then the paper was thrust in front of me. Sherlock's thin index finger, stained with pipe tobacco, was pointing directly to a headline which simply asked a question:

"Ashes to Remain?"

"Please explain this to me, Watson. What have ashes and this upcoming Cricket match have to do with one another? The paper is full of this connection, yet I can make no sense of it whatsoever.

"Did a sports arena burn down? Are the clubs' supporters so saddened that they wish to retrieve some of the ashes? If not, why does it talk about 'retrieving the ashes'? I do not understand."

My dear readers, before I recount my explanation to Holmes, I will be telling him a bit about the history of the sport of Cricket in England. The only sports that I know Holmes to be interested in, are those that deal with the protection of ones' own body. He excels in boxing, fencing and the Asian art of baritsu. To my knowledge, he has had

Daniel J. Darrouzet

no occasion to dive into the intricacies, nuances and pleasures of the sport of Cricket played by adults. I am most certain as a youth, he must have had to play it while in school, but his interest surely waned upon exiting his formal education. So, his ignorance of the more recent history of game of Cricket is understandable.

Having told me once that it was of no importance to him that the solar system is heliocentric, because it was of no value to him in solving his mysteries, I concluded quickly he would need an explanation to understand what he was experiencing. I also knew, that once he grasped the meaning, he would no doubt, expel it from his mind, realizing its worthlessness to his understanding of the criminal world for which he lived to understand.

Those of you who follow the grand sport and are familiar with the forthcoming tale, may read ahead should you so desire. Should, in fact, I get a detail or two incorrect, please excuse my fault. (I beg you, dear readers, please, do not write to me to complain about my making such unintentional errors).

While I enjoy, and am a supporter of the sport as much as the next Englishman, I do not consider myself one of these 'fanatics' (or 'fans' as I believe they are now called), but I do enjoy a good and robust match.

"Holmes, I will endeavour to explain what 'all the commotion' is about, but you must agree to hear me out completely. My fear is you will dismiss me before you have even heard the complete story. If I am to explain it to you, I would appreciate that you not evidence your boredom while I am taking my valuable time to explain it to you. Agreed?"

"Since I began this discussion by asking the question, I shall agree, but I reserve the right to fall asleep should this be as boring as you seem to imply, and therefore I infer, it will be."

"In the spring of '82, a year after we met, Holmes, the English press was dumb-founded by England's loss of a Cricket match, played over in Kennington at the *Oval*, against the Australians. It was not just 'a' Cricket match. It was what was deemed a 'Test-match', meaning only the best players from both countries were allowed on the field. The match takes place over several days, to 'test' the endurance of each club and to see which is worthy of being the champion of the match. Each country's honour is at stake!

"The English press were so upset at the loss, they declared, in a fantasy obituary, that Cricket had 'died' in England. It was thence cremated and the '*Ashes*', placed in an urn, and they were sent back to Australia with the conquering club, forthwith.

"Thereafter, the match between England and Australia has been referred to as playing for 'The Ashes'.

"Back in the '91-'92 season, our boys lost again while touring in Australia. What you are reading about, is the upcoming second test-match to be played again here in England. They played once all ready back in July and England won. This second test is here at the Oval. The English are determined to keep, that is, recover the *Ashes* and have them stay here. The Aussies are determined to keep them and take the *Ashes* back with them to Australia.

"Do you understand, now?"

I had watched his eyes glaze over as I told my tale. While he did not feign snoring or drop his chin to his chest, it was obvious that he was, in fact, bored with these facts and recent history of the game.

"Thank you, Doctor." He then arose and walked into his room. I did not hear from him for the rest of the morning.

That is how he responded, and I felt as if he had honoured his agreement. I could not chastise him, as he claimed no harm, nor did he ridicule me for my comments or my obvious interest in and defence of the glorious sport.

I had been reading about the upcoming match for the last several weeks. Tickets were impossible to get, but even if I were to have had a chance to buy some, their price would have been beyond my budget.

I looked forward to reading the accounts after each day's play. The press was very good at describing what had transpired. I anxiously awaited each edition to keep up with the match.

It was four days before the opening of the match when a

note was delivered to me at my surgery. It was from one of my patients, Sir Henry Holdsworth. His family had all been ill recently and I had helped mend all of them. He had been most appreciative then.

The note read as follows:

My Dear Dr. Watson,

I again wish to thank you for all you did for my family last month.

I remember when last we met, we discussed with excitement the upcoming Test Match. to be played between England and Australia at the Oval. I have managed to acquire a pass to the match which I had planned on attending.

Unfortunately, I am called to Paris next week and cannot attend. My wife and daughter have no interest in sports. I would very much like you to have my pass as a gift from me to you.

This is in thanks for not only the recent treatment of my family but for all the times which I have called upon you for your services to both my family and me, never complaining about the time of night or the most-foul weather in which you travelled to come to our aid.

Enjoy the match and we shall talk all about it when I return.

Sincerely Yours,
Sir Henry Holdsworth

P.S. Not wanting to chance a loss (or worse) by the courier, please stop by and Manfred will see to it that you receive the envelope.

Cheers,
SHH

The smile that came across my face I am sure would have made me appear as a young boy who'd just gotten a much desired and long-awaited new toy for his birthday or for Christmas. I certainly felt like a child again, if even for a moment – a pass to the Test Match!

I arrived back at Baker Street in time for dinner. Holmes suggested we go out as the evening was quite comfortable, but still a bit brisk.

My excitement of receiving the pass carried the day though. Whatever frustration I may have felt about anything in my evening, they were but a minor thing now. I had a pass to the Test Match!

I shared my excitement with Holmes, somehow hoping against hope he would be able to share my excitement, but I should have realised from my explanation, when last the subject came up, that he was not interested and my joy and excitement would not be shared by him, nor highly encouraged.

"I'm not sure you fully understand the luck with which I have been bestowed, Holmes. Do you realise that it is all but impossible to get a pass to the match?"

"Watson, you realise you have all but contradicted yourself. If it were impossible you would not be obtaining it. And, I point out, you do not actually possess it as of yet. Once I see it in your hand, I may be a bit more impressed, but that is not likely."

"Oh, Holmes, I think you are envious."

"Envious, how so? That makes no sense to me."

"You have all your exotic connections throughout the city. You are always calling in favours of one kind or another to solve your cases.

"It is now I who have been able to redeem, from one of my patients, a gift that is most valuable to me."

"I understand what you are saying, Watson, but I do not possess envy for you or your acquiring the pass. In fact, I am happy for you. Yes, I am. You deserve this treat of sorts. I do know how hard you work treating the ill and without much change. I can only conclude you live quite a boring life, seeing the same aches and pains and diseases over and over again. Prescribing the same remedies over and over again. Some of your patients not taking your advice and either getting worse or never recovering.

"I could not do it, Watson. The monotony of it would drive me insane. I must have new and fresh challenges! It is why I now turn down more cases these days than I take. Where is the joy and excitement, just like you have been describing for the game, in solving the same types of cases over and over again? No, I must sail into uncharted waters anymore to find any joy in them.

"So, I say, I am happy for you. You deserve this gift."

While his final words were in fact positive, I have to admit, his soliloquy regarding his feelings about my daily performance of my profession cut me a bit. But I knew Holmes well enough by now, to know he meant no harm. It was just how he saw the world. I said nothing in return, for there would be no changing his mind upon how he saw my work as compared to his.

Soon, after I shook off his attack on my daily duties, my excitement returned, and I suddenly realised again; I had a pass to the Test Match!

Later that day I went 'round to Sir Henry's residence to collect the pass from his manservant, Manfred.

"Please come in, Dr. Watson," said he.

He closed the door behind me and went to a side table in the foyer, picking up an unassuming brown envelope. He turned and handed it to me.

"Here is the pass and the tickets, Doctor.

"Sir Henry expressly directed me to tell you, to enjoy them as he would have, should he have been here."

"Tickets?" said I, not believing what I had just heard.

"Yes, Doctor. Is there a problem?"

"You mean there is more than one pass?"

"No, Doctor. Sir Henry has acquired one pass, but that pass provides two tickets for each day of the match."

You could have knocked me over with a feather, as they say! I could not conceive of such a gift! I had to breathe deeply for a moment or two before replying.

"This is too much, Manfred. One ticket for one day is quite enough. Surely, Sir Henry has others he would wish to provide this gift."

"I do not think so, Doctor. His wife and daughters have no interest in sports of this kind. His brothers have their own passes and tickets, as do most of his close friends.

"I must tell you, Doctor the last time you saw the family and helped them through that lingering illness, Sir Henry went on and on about how much faith he had in you and your medical abilities. 'Dr. Watson is a God-send' were his exact words, as I recall.

"I think, Doctor, and if you do not mind nor think it beyond my place to say so, the family and especially Sir Henry look very fondly upon you and treasure your services to them. Please accept the pass and tickets as a token of their appreciation."

"Manfred, thank you very much. Your words are most kind and appreciated." My shoulders held back and my chest extended, I left feeling a renewed man.

On my journey back to Baker Street and felt as I were carrying a sack of gold with me. I rarely walk about the city with much coin or paper on my person, but now I was carrying something of real value in my chest pocket. Of course, the odds that I would be accosted for the tickets was unlikely as no one saw me place them on my person.

Upon my return to 221B, I showed Holmes the pass and all of the tickets I had received.

"Well, Watson, it would appear you have a benefactor *extraordinaire*. I have read a bit more on my own about this

Test Match of which you have spoken. While I never saw or enjoyed the running back and forth part, I do admit to some joy in hitting the ball with a bat and having someone try to catch the flying object with their bare hands. That always did seem to me to be a bit of a challenge.

"So, you did play in school, I thought so."

"Yes. I admit it. I did not enjoy it as much as fencing though.

I was quite a good bowler in my day. No lollipops from me. When on the pitch, I threw the best leg-cutter on the club. Threw the occasional beamer, too, which I thought made sense to intimidate the opponent, but our coach described it as being not gentlemanly, and not in good form.

"And, I was put out on the occasion I tried hitting the ball with the back of the bat instead of the blade. My thinking at the time was, the curved surface of the back would cause the ball to fly off in a direction the fieldsmen could not easily anticipate."

"So, then Holmes, since you participated, why do you have no interest?"

"Watson, it's the endless running back and forth. If I run, I am intending to get somewhere quickly. I just didn't enjoy what I thought was a boring part of the game.

"Besides, that time I tried to use the back of the bat it was also because the handle had been bent backwards and I knew the bat had not much use left in it. It was an early experiment, you could say."

"Yes, that problem has interfered in many a match."

"Another strike against the game, no pun you understand. You'd think they'd make the bat from one piece of wood, though, by now. The laws of physics control, eh? The splice always being the weak link."

"Well, Holmes, the bats are still made of willow and handle is still made of cane. And the cane handle is still spliced on. But you'll be glad to know a new type splice was recently invented by an engineer here in England,[9] which has made the bat splice much more durable. Now almost all the bats use his design."

---

[9] Editor's note: Watson is referring to Charles Richardson who invented this splicing technique to make a more durable bat in the 1880's.

"I still think a single piece of wood makes more sense, but if you say a better splice has finally been made, by an English engineer no less, to be more durable, then that is a step in the right direction. But I still have no interest in the game these days. You know, Watson, it is meaningless to me in my work."

"I know Holmes, but for once can you not perhaps, let up on your constant need for such mental excitement? Won't you come with me to the matches? I do believe you would enjoy yourself once there, more than you think you would. Other than the final applause at the end of a concert or play you last attended, when have you been in public surrounded by your fellow Londoners sharing in the excitement of what unfolds before you? You need not wait 'til after the performance at these matches to express your reaction to the play on the field. One cheers throughout the whole match if one wishes to do so. I assure you it is not like the games of your school days when there were so few people watching and practically no one cheering you on. No, there will be thousands! The Oval, my dear Holmes, will hold twenty thousand for this Test Match, I am sure. Have you ever been in the same space, watching the same thing as twenty thousand others are doing, at the same time? It is a magnificent experience I tell you! Think of it as one of your experiments, Holmes!"

"Doctor, I commend you. It is rare that your pontifications inspire me to act in the manner and direction in which you prod me.

"You are correct, Watson. I have not been in a space with another twenty thousand people. Two to three thousand at most, and that was on a rare occasion."

"Yes, Holmes! A chance for a unique experience!"

"All right, Watson. Your reasoning has won the day. I shall accompany you. As you say, it shall be an experiment. One which I shall observe with great interest indeed."

My day was complete. To have received a pass and tickets to each days' match should have been enough. And it was, until my dear friend agreed to accompany me to the match! I could not believe it. It was so far beyond anything

I could imagine happening, I had to check again for myself, that I had actually received the pass and tickets and still possessed them.

It was a just few days to go and then we would be at the Oval, watching the Test Match for the *Ashes*!

The first day of the Test Match finally arrived. Holmes and I arose early. We did not need to get to the Oval early like those who held general admission tickets. The seats which the tickets permitted us to observe from, were reserved. No, that was not our concern. The concern was the multitudes of people who would be descending on the Oval all at the same time. From 221B we need not do much else but head due south. The Oval being in Kennington, was three and one-half miles south, south-east of us, as the crow flies. By coach it was a little less than four miles.

We hailed a cab and headed for Vauxhall Bridge. As we got closer to the bridge, we noticed quite a congestion in the streets. After standing still for at least ten minutes, Holmes, exasperated, alit, paid the cabbie and shouted to me. "Come on, Watson, we're in need of some exercise."

And with that we joined the throngs all walking towards the Oval from the north side of the Thames.

With so many people walking on the bridge it groaned under the weight. Even though the MWB had bought the bridge a little more than a decade before, and there were no longer any tolls to pay, their repairs had not envisioned hundreds of people crossing all at once. It was a sight to see and one to hear, as well.

Before long we arrived at the Oval, entered and were shown to our seats. The match was to begin within the half hour and all ready the venue was filled with excitement.

We settled into our seats and I began conversing with the gentlemen around us. All were determined that this match would certainly go England's way. With Hearne and Humphreys Sr. bowling and Gunn, Staddart and Ward batting, they were all convinced victory was all ready accomplished. They discussed the many advantages of the other players and that their record was superlative of late.

No doubt the *Ashes* would remain in England this year, that is, if their over-confident prognostications would only come true.

After the coin toss, the clubs took up their positions and the match commenced. Holmes seemed interested in the match, but I soon found him watching the spectators more than the match itself.

"Holmes, is the match boring you all ready?"

"No, Watson. But I am intrigued by the behaviour of the crowd here. You were correct. I've not been in the presence of so many people all at the same time and in the same place. There is a uniqueness in their ability to respond practically in unison to the activities on the field. While similar to a startling change in the plot in a theatrical production, this is more robust and constant. I congratulate you on your persuading me to attend, as I am indeed experiencing a new phenomenon."

"Holmes, thank you."

It was all I could say. I turned my head back to the action on the field and felt a smile come upon my countenance. A compliment from Holmes was a rare and welcomed event.

I was soon to be disappointed, in that, after about an hour of play, Holmes decided to take stroll. His excuse was that he wished to experience other aspects of the event unfolding before us. When I asked what he meant, he simply said he had noticed a few folks he'd come into contact with in his past investigations and some whom he had gained acquaintance of when in disguise on the streets of London. When I pressed further as to his meaning, he simply replied, "Pickpockets."

My challenge was should I turn my attention to Holmes' adventures about the Oval or let go of my friend's attention and allow him to wander the Oval in search of such people, and enjoy the match on my own?

I decided that it mattered not much to Holmes which I did and I had so looked forward to the matches, that I released my hold on him and wished him good luck. I suggested that we should meet up again at the main gate before returning to Baker Street and he agreed.

To my surprise, in about half an hour, Holmes returned to our seats. He informed me he'd run into Inspector Gregson. Scotland Yard and the London constabulary had anticipated this being a pickpockets' dream come true.

"They have posted men at every entrance who have good knowledge of those culprits convicted in the past for their silent and secret crime. No doubt their entrance to the venue was made possible by lifting tickets off unsuspecting spectators in that mob we encountered on our way over Vauxhall Bridge. We are lucky ourselves, that we were not subjected to their light-fingered skills."

"Good God, Holmes! What dastardly villains that lot is. I am glad I took your advice and only brought tickets for today's match with us."

It was just then we heard a commotion above and behind us.

"Doctor! Is there a Doctor here?! We need help!"

I turned and rose and exited my way towards an aisle of sorts. I raised my hand and waved to show I was, and I was coming to their aide. I climbed up several steps and soon saw a gentleman who was lying on the floor between the rows of seats. Someone had already loosened his collar and was waving a pamphlet over him.

My first instinct was that this gentleman had perhaps fainted. The air was quite still where we were seated which increased the temperature with so many bodies so close together. I was soon crouched down and reached to take the man's pulse. But there was none!

"What has happened here?" queried I. "This man is dead!"

Holmes stood right behind me. "I shall call for Gregson at once. Make sure nothing is disturbed Watson. The rest of you, do not leave your seats," Holmes directed.

At this there was grumbling and questions of who was this man to give them orders such as that. These were of course peers of Sir Holdsworth and these men did not take kindly to being ordered about by an obviously common man, which of course was based solely on Holmes' attire as it contrasted with the more fashionable dress of such wealthy gentlemen.

Holmes then went to the top of where our section was

and instructed a page to find Inspector Gregson and return with him as quickly as possible. He then returned to me and began his own inspection of the body.

"Mr. Sherlock Holmes, is it not?" came a voice from a few rows away.

"Yes," said Holmes as he looked up to see who had addressed him. "Lord Backwater, if I am correct?"

"Yes, it is I," said Lord Backwater.

"Please, gentlemen," directed Lord Backwater. "Listen to what this man asked you to do. You may have heard of Mr. Sherlock Holmes in the newspapers and read of his adventures, well this is he. I can attest he has helped me personally. You may trust him. He shall treat you with respect but 'woe' to you if you are responsible for, our friend, Judge Gilmores' demise."

This short speech from Lord Backwater quelled the more vocal objections to Holmes taking command of the situation. There were still whispers, but the majority committed themselves to silence until Inspector Gregson arrived.

The cheers and moans of the spectators in the rest of the arena continued, all oblivious to the tragedy that had occurred in our section. Our group either distracted themselves from the death by turning their attention to the match, while those closest to the dead man whispered their theories on what caused his death while seeming to forget the match was even being played.

"What have we here, Mr. Holmes?" queried Inspector Gregson, upon his arrival with several constables in tow.

"A death for certain, likely murder," said Holmes without consequence of the effect his pronouncement had upon those around us.

"What?" said several of those close by.

"Doctor, what say you?"

"Assuredly the man is deceased, there is no doubt about that. As to the cause…"

"Watson, please observe the white foam on his lips and about his mouth. If you will but smell it, you will no doubt detect the smell of bitter almonds, a sure indicator of…"

"Cyanide poisoning," finished Gregson.

"Exactly," confirmed Holmes.

"But how could that be, I wonder? We will have to inquire about his recent activities, of course. Would you mind assisting me, Mr. Holmes?" queried Gregson.

"If you think I can help, I would be most happy to do so," his voice suddenly shouting above the sudden roar of the crowd.

"I believe there must be some rooms unoccupied currently that offer no view of the field. Perhaps if we inquire with the Cricket Club authorities, we shall gain their permission to move the deceased there and set up a room to question those close around where the incident took place," shouted I against the sustained roar of the crowd, perhaps due to an unfavourable call on the field, I could only imagine.

"Yes, Doctor, I agree. We certainly cannot leave the deceased's remains out here in the open while the match continues. This is much too public. I will inquire and return momentarily. Constable, see that no one disturbs the body," said Gregson.

It seemed but a few short minutes and the Inspector returned. Accompanying him were two constables with a stretcher and blanket.

The row of seats made it difficult for them to handle the body. The judge being of a somewhat portly physique, required a third constable to help position his body onto the stretcher to enable the constables to ferry him away.

As we left the stands and began descending into the rooms of the club, those we encountered were shocked at the sight of a body being carried about. Men removed their hats, hung their heads and stood still while we passed. The few ladies that we encountered, gasped at the sight of the stretcher covered by a blanket, with the obvious shape of a body hidden beneath it. A dead man at the match!

It was a strange event. The contrast of the excitement of the match to that of the required solemnity out of respect for the dead was difficult for those who witnessed both to understand.

Fortunately, for our small delegation, the press in attendance were only concerned with sports. They were all watching the match. It was not until later that they heard about the death in the stands.

We were shown to a meeting room of sorts, one in which the Surrey County Cricket Club dignitaries met and made their decisions concerning the activities of the club.

The body was placed off in one corner. Gregson had sent for the Coroner, but it was likely to take him at least an hour to be notified and then make his way here. Gregson, wanting a bit more immediate information, requested that Dr. Watson examine the body as best he could to determine if perhaps this apparent cyanide poisoning was the only assault on the body.

"Unless the body is disrobed, I will not be able to give you much more information, Inspector."

"I understand, but please look for other signs on his hands, arms and neck?"

"I shall."

"Gregson, it is most likely the Judge has ingested poison. Shall we not query those who accompanied him here and understand what he has eaten today?" suggested Holmes.

"Yes, Mr. Holmes, that makes good sense."

By this time, several constables had, per Gregson's directions, required those individuals who had been sitting in close proximity to the Judge, to wait outside the room.

Several of these men were of distinction and were not pleased at all that they were being considered as suspects in the Judge's death. Even more intolerable, though, was their being denied the right to watch the match, all because someone dropped dead and they happened to have been nearby when it happened! They all insisted on being interviewed first, so as to quickly return to the match.

While I worked on examining the body, I could not help but hear the inquiries put forth by Inspector Gregson. I found no marks or puncture wounds on the hands, arms or neck. No, a full autopsy would have to be performed to validate the cause of death. I knew, though, from the few times Holmes and I had encountered the use of cyanide in the past, the pattern was repeated here as well; the smell and the white foaming of the mouth. As an occasional betting man, myself, I would surely bet this cyanide poison was the cause of death. Officially, though, we'd have to wait for the Coroner's report.

The answers to Gregson's queries were filled with indignation by these 'gentlemen' who obviously cared more about missing the match than that a man, had died today right in front of them. But their answers were to be expected. They had had no interaction with the Judge except to have been seated close to him.

It wasn't until those that personally knew the Judge and had been in his party upon arrival were questioned that there were finally some answers that helped reveal his actions before he died.

There had been three gentlemen that accompanied the Judge to the Oval that morning. Lord Backwater, Sir Philip Tenaford, and Sir George Labradenth.

Gregson first spoke with Sir Philip Tenaford.

"How is it that you know the deceased?"

"Judge Gilmores has been a good friend of mine for over forty years. We met at Cambridge. I am a barrister and we both belong to the Athenæum. Is there anything else you wish to know, constable?"

"It's Inspector, Inspector Gregson. And that is all for now. Please be seated over there, in case I have further questions I wish to ask you."

The look given Gregson by Sir Philip was unmistakable. The battle of the powerful and the law had begun. Sir George was next.

"Inspector, I am at your service," declared Labradenth.

"How do you know the deceased?"

"As my friend, Philip over there, has said, I too met the Judge while at Cambridge. I too am a member of the Athenæum club and have had the pleasure of his friendship these last forty years or so."

"Can you tell me about this morning? When did you meet with the Judge?"

"Ah, yes, well, I met the others here at our seats. I had an early appointment this morning that I could not reschedule. It mattered not that we came together, except as you might have noticed, the crowds made travel here quite a challenge. I did not see the Judge until I met him in the stands."

"Thank you, Sir George. Please give your address to the constable at the door and you are excused."

"Why thank, you Inspector! Should you have any further question, I am at your service."

"Thank you, sir," replied Gregson.

I observed Labradenth's face as he looked at Tenaford. There was an ever-so-small smirk which practically set Tenaford into a muffled rage. It was a game between old friends and Labradenth had won this round. Having seen Tenaford's failure to exercise his position to no avail, Labradenth's tactic had freed him quickly to return to the match, much to Tenaford's chagrin.

"Lord Backwater, may I speak with you now?" queried Gregson with an air of respect a bit more that that he given to the two previous knighted gentlemen.

"Inspector, please ask what you will. If Mr. Holmes believes this was murder, I am at your service. I will do all I can to bring justice upon this horrible event."

"How do you know the deceased?"

"As my friends that you have all ready spoken to have said, we all met at Cambridge."

"Are you aware of any events this morning that could have resulted in the Judge's death?"

"I am not of the calibre of Mr. Holmes here when it comes to observations and deduction, which I have witnessed first-hand.[10] That said, I was with the Judge this morning when he visited both teams in their locker rooms. He had spent ten years in Australia out of Cambridge. While there, he learned to more fully enjoy the sport. He had a soft spot for the Australia team having learned to love the game while there. He frequently explained to us who knew him well, that his loyalty was, of course, to the English team, but that he did secretly wish the Aussies good luck and, when not playing against England, he always rooted for them."

"You say he visited both clubs?" Holmes interjected suddenly, having been silent until now.

"Yes, Mr. Holmes. He had that privilege being one of

---

[10] Lord Backwater is referring to Holmes solving the mystery of the disappearance of a horse from Lord Backwater's Mapleton stables which was a plot to fix a race that would have led to his Lordship's potential ruin. I previously chronicled that adventure in *Silver Blaze* - *JHW*

the Surrey County Cricket Club board members. He'd been the president two years back. So naturally he had that honour along with other board members."

"Can you remember what occurred during these visits?"

"Yes, he gave a short speech regarding good sportsmanship and wished good luck to each team. At the end, he and the other board members offered a small toast to each team's performance. Of course, the players were not allowed by their managers to partake, and none did."

"Gregson, quick, we must try to retrieve the glasses!"

"Constable Perkins, take two men and search each locker room for champagne glasses. If you find them, do not touch them with your bare hands. Handle them with your handkerchiefs. Bring them to me undamaged," said Gregson.

"Gregson, you've read Galton as well," said Holmes.

"Yes, Mr. Holmes. I think he is on the right trail. I've read his papers on the subject."

"Have you read of Sir Herschel's success in India?"

"Yes, and I think this is the future for us."

"Well done, Gregson. I am most proud of your progress."

"Your Lordship, what else can you tell us about the visits to the locker rooms?"

"I don't think there is anything else to tell. We were only allowed but about five minutes. We entered. The President of the club spoke first. The Judge handed a bottle to a team assistant who opened and poured it out into several glasses. While he continued his speech, the champagne was being dispensed to the club board members. I believe then the Judge offered a toast to a gentlemanly match and may the best team prevail. Once this was done, we repeated this in the other club's locker room."

"Which did you visit first?" queried Holmes.

"What?"

"Which team, did you visit first?" clarified Gregson.

"Why the English club, of course."

"The Judge claimed no ill effects after the first toast?"

"Not that I recall."

"And after the toast in the Australians' locker room?"

"None that I am aware of."

"Had the Judge anything else to eat or drink after toasting?"

"No, we all returned here to our seats. I have no recollection of the Judge leaving or eating anything else."

"Thank you, Lord Backwater. That will be all for now. Your information will be quite useful, I am sure."

Inspector Gregson released Lord Backwater, and after he had left turned to Sir Philip and released him as well.

"The drinks are high on my list of introducing the cyanide into his body. What do you think, Mr. Holmes?"

"Yes, Inspector. Most likely…"

"Inspector, sorry to interrupt. We could find no glasses in either locker room."

"Thank you, constable. That is most unfortunate. You were saying, Mr. Holmes…?"

"Yes, that the glasses were not found, was to be expected. Whoever perpetrated this crime knew what they were doing. It would have been quite lucky for us had they been left behind. In any event, how would we be able to take prints of all that could have been in or near the locker room? Perhaps someday it will be more useful and a regular act with which to investigate crimes.

"If the villain was present, it is a list of who was in each room that we need. That would narrow our search considerably.

"Cyanide in large doses causes immediate death. The fact that the cyanide did not cause immediate death, means that it could have been administered in either locker room."

"I see, that does sound reasonable," replied Gregson.

Just then the Coroner arrived and took charge of the body. I introduced myself and explained what little information I could give as to my initial observations. He thanked me and then ordered that the body be taken away to the city morgue.

Gregson shook our hands and departed. Holmes and I returned to our seats. The match had gone on without any knowledge of what had transpired. The Australians having won the toss to begin the match, had elected to bat first. They had piled up quite a lead whilst we were dealing with the death of Judge Gilmores. I must admit, my dear readers, my enthusiasm for the game diminished having to deal so suddenly with the tragedy. As you might also conclude, those of you who are familiar with my tomes regarding Sherlock Holmes and his habits, Holmes was quite intrigued by the whole affair.

I returned for the next day to seek out what enjoyment I could. Australia had finished up with quite a score. But once England got their chance, they score more and won the match. It was now obvious where the Ashes were to be located, once this Test Match ended, England having won the first two matches. There was to be one more Test Match in Manchester in a fortnight, but winning the first two sealed the fate of the location of the Ashes for now.

Not much progress in solving the case was made in the next few days by either Gregson or Holmes. The Coroner's report did validate Holmes' original assessment "death by poisoning (i.e. cyanide), by person or persons unknown" read his report. The Coroner also dismissed suicide upon finding a rather large amount of half-digested prime tenderloin beef in the Judges' stomach. Interviewing his immediate family as well, as to his thinking and state of mind, he readily concluded the Judge was not in any way dissatisfied with his life. Murder it was.

What I did notice over the next several days was Holmes' relentless visits to Scotland Yard. I had decided that should he wish to explain his visits to me certainly he would.

It was the fifth day after the death that I awoke to the smell of some chemical concoction, which Holmes had chosen to allow to fill our rooms.

When I exited my room, the odour was more pungent and I found him with a large basket of peaches. He was cutting open the peaches and tossing the meat into a pail. It was the pits that he was accumulating on his desk.

"Holmes. What are you doing?"

"Doctor. An experiment."

"Why throw away the meat?"

"It is the contents of the pits I am after."

"But why, Holmes?"

"Doctor. You as well as I know it is illegal and virtually

impossible to obtain cyanide from an apothecary or chemical plant. I am trying to re-enact what our killer must have done to obtain enough to kill a man."

"Holmes, yes there are small amounts of cyanide in a peach pit, actually in the seed in the pit, but not enough to kill a person."

"But how many seeds does it take to kill a man?"

"It'd likely vary. I doubt the cyanide from the seeds is very concentrated. For a small person, fewer and a larger person, like the Judge, quite a few I would imagine. I could check my books, but from memory I'd say roughly one hundred seeds would do it. But people don't typically eat the pits or the seeds and certainly not one hundred."

"Agreed, but what if the seeds were removed and the cyanide extracted from the seeds?"

"Well, now you are telling a different story. Should the person know how to perform such extraction the resulting concentrated cyanide could be quite lethal."

"I am determined to find out, Watson. Please don't mind me and I do apologise for the unpleasant odour."

"I do not mind Holmes, pray continue. Let me know if you need help."

It was several hours later when Holmes shouted over to me as I read the afternoon paper. He held out a crown and eventually tossed it my way.

"Three more baskets of peaches, Watson. Would you be so kind? I can see the results of this first basket and think the answer lies somewhere between eighty-five and one hundred and eight. But I want to be accurate. Luckily they are in season or we'd have a real difficulty."

"Certainly, Holmes. I shall return with the treasure forthwith. How much do you have so far?"

"Just over an ounce or about thirty grams if using the *French* system. I believe for a man of the Judge's size one hundred grams would have done the trick."

It was a strange journey to be sent upon. Buying fruit which is consumed to give life, only to obtain the evil inside of it. I had never thought in these terms before. I returned with the three baskets Holmes had requested. I had run across Wiggins and his troupe at the market. They assisted in the delivery and each earned a shilling for their effort.

After providing them to Holmes, I returned to my paper. It was right before dinner time that I heard the final "yes" from Holmes.

"Watson, ninety-seven."

"So, I was spot on, yes? That's quite a few, Holmes."

"If not obtained by theft, then whoever is behind this certainly knows how to make it. Of course, it may not have been peaches, the seeds of various fruits contain cyanide, so it could have been any of them."

"What now, Holmes. I do not mean to diminish your efforts here, but how does this lead us to the villain?"

"You ask a fair question, Watson. Perhaps I have spent too much time confirming how the cyanide was made. At this point the 'how' may not be as important as the 'why'. If not suicide, which I agree with the Coroner it is not, who has done this to the Judge? He sits on cases in the law that deal with business transactions, civil law. Perhaps someone was not happy with one of his rulings? I have been searching records and have found nothing so far.

"This case is confounding me right now. But it is as I wished for. The same type of monotonous cases would be no challenge. I am delighted this is not so easy. I shall ponder it anew, Watson."

And with that he grabbed a clay pipe from the mantel, filled it with tobacco from the slipper and lay prone on the couch. His silence spoke volumes to me and I returned to my paper whilst he used that cerebral tool of his, no doubt to its maximum. I wondered if I would ever know how his mind worked at times like these.

For the next few days it was if Holmes no longer resided at 221B Baker Street. When I would arrive from my surgery, Mrs. Hudson would simply shake her head upon seeing me come in the door. Our rooms saw no trace of him. I began to think he had left London altogether.

After the fourth day, I began to be a bit concerned. His habits, being what they were when he was not challenged, were actually not my concern now. Being drawn to the substances which altered his mind when there was no challenge was the more dangerous, of course. But usually, when on a case, the allure of those substances would never supplant the thrill of the chase. During our adventures, I would hear from him. Mostly when he would require my assistance, perhaps even that of me and my service revolver on occasion.

Late that evening I received a telegram. It read:

COME TO MANCHESTER
BY THURSDAY 8 AM
ROOM RESERVED AT FOX & HOUND

I quickly researched Bradshaw's. There was no one train that would get me straight-away to Manchester.[11] I had less than forty-eight hours to travel over three hundred miles, with no direct carriage!

The earliest leg of my journey left at six the next morning from Kings Cross on the Great Northern Railway. I spent the night preparing to travel. Since Holmes made no mention of how long or whether or not to bring my revolver, I decided my travel kit would be enough but that I would bring my armament, just in case.

Being one of the first trains in the morning, we left on time. When we arrived in Lincolnshire, I was then to transfer to the MS&LR for the final leg into Manchester.

All in all, the journey took most of the day. The train from Lincolnshire was delayed as the designated engine's boiler sprung a leak. Another engine had to be sent from Manchester to stand in its stead and then bring us all the way back to Manchester from whence it came.

The telegram from Holmes had not stated any other information, so his whereabouts were unknown to me. I

---

[11] I write this tale many years after the event, The Great Central Railway had yet to construct its "London Extension" and there was no direct train to Manchester at that time. Had the GCR's Marylebone station been open then, I would have simply left Baker Street walked west on Melcombe and been at the station in just a few minutes - *JHW*

found the Fox & Hound without much ado. Luckily, he had made the reservations for me, as the last Test Match was but two days away, right here in Manchester.

The inn was not filled, but those with more money and time had all ready arrived to witness the final Test Match. As I was checking in, Holmes arrived and dodged his way through the crowded lobby on his way up to the front desk.

"Watson, I see you have made it on time."

"Yes, Holmes, what is going on?"

"All will be made clear soon enough. We are to meet with Gregson for dinner. We must hurry as they will not hold our table for long with all these willing and hungry visitors here."

"Gregson too!" exclaimed I.

"Yes. It will all make sense before too long."

I dropped off my kit in my room and we soon found our way to the restaurant at the Castle Hotel. Gregson was there waiting. As soon as we entered, we sat down, ordered and settled in for the evening.

"What has happened, Holmes?" inquired I.

"Yes, Mr. Holmes, why have you brought us both here?" asked Gregson.

"To catch our killer, of course."

"So, you know who it is?"

"I believe I do. It will take a few more questions and confirmations before I know for sure. I am certain, though, that should I ask these questions and our villain is clever enough to evade them, we may have to give chase. But I suspect, while he provides evidence so far of having a superlative mind when it comes to knowledge of such things as chemistry, he, I believe, lacks the wisdom to not react to our inquiries when face-to-face. But tomorrow shall tell."

That is all he would say. Gregson and I would have to wait until the morning to discover what Holmes knew about the murderer of Judge Gilmores.

We awakened early and headed to Old Trafford where the final Test Match was to be played. It was one day before the match was to begin and the club was scheduled for some practice and exercise before the start of the match on Friday.

Gregson gained us entry and we soon found ourselves outside the Australians' locker room. Holmes stopped us before we entered.

"Inspector, we will be interviewing the one person who I believe had a motive to kill the Judge. Please follow my lead but prepare yourself should my assessment be correct and he attempts to escape once I have challenged him."

"All right Mr. Holmes. What is this man's name?"

"His name is Richard Godwin. He is bright, but I think he has acted out of emotion and not used the logic he possesses when he is dealing with the elements of nature."

We entered the locker room and the club was changing from the street clothes that they had worn while coming to the field. Some were in various stages of undress and some all ready dressed in their practice clothes.

Gregson took charge and found the manager in an adjacent room. The manager came back in and pointed out our suspect.

"That is Richard Godwin, he's our club trainer," said he.

Gregson quickly went over to the man who appeared to be a score and ten in age. He was not changing. As the club trainer, he was responsible for the uniforms and bats and other equipment of the club.

"Mr. Godwin, I am Inspector Gregson of Scotland Yard. We, these gentlemen and I, would like a word with you."

"Can't you see I'm a bit busy right now, mate?"

"Yes, but this is very important."

"Oll right, give me a coupla of minutes."

Gregson chose not to push him too hard. As a measure of caution, Holmes had the door out to the field covered and I stood close to the door from which we entered. After a few minutes passed, the players began leaving for the field. We all kept our eyes on Godwin. He made no attempt to leave. In fact, he seemed quite calm. Had Holmes somehow made a mistake about him, I wondered?

Before long, it was only the four of us.

"How can I help oll you, mates?" queried Godwin.

"We would like to ask you a few questions. This is Mr. Sherlock Holmes and Dr. Watson. They are assisting the Yard's inquiries in the death of Judge Gilmores that occurred at the Oval a fortnight ago. Do you remember that?"

"Of course, I do. But what's 'at got uh do with me? Anyways, what do oll you, wants ta know?"

"Mr. Godwin, you seem to lack the true accent of a native-born Australian. Would that be because you spent most of your youth on the streets of London?" queried Holmes.

"What kind of question is 'at, mate?" responded he with a voice that quivered just a bit.

"You were born here in England, yes?" asserted Holmes.

"Oi, and what if I was? Ain't no crime in 'at."

"True, but now that you bring up crime. Were you ever in prison?" asked Holmes.

The question did seem to catch our new friend off guard.

"Hey now! What is this oll about?" responded he.

"Mr. Godwin, I propose to you, that you are the Richard Godwin that was caught and sentenced for various offences numerous times here in London as a youth and was, due to having no living relations here, eventually sent to the adolescent prison at Point Puer in Australia due to your continued encounters with the law when you were but fourteen years of age," declared Holmes.

"Might be, might not."

"After escaping more than once, you were transferred to Port Arthur prison when you turned sixteen. It was there you began working in the prison apothecary where you likely learned about various medicines, including poisons, such as cyanide, and from whence it can be manufactured from the fruits of nature."

At this, there was no response.

"I take your silence as affirmation that my data upon this subject is correct."

"I's seen no reason uh agree or disagree."

Gregson then pulled Holmes aside.

"Holmes, even if all your data is true, we'll need more than that to make a charge of murder stick. If we'd only have found those glasses back at the Oval!"

"I agree. He'll likely not run as that would indicate guilt. Shall we not adjourn and pursue again later?"

"Thank you for your time, Mr. Godwin," said Gregson.

With that we left the locker room.

"Holmes, he could be our man, but what motive?"

"If you recall Lord Backwater's comments, Gilmores had gone to Australia after graduation for ten years. I have confirmed with Australian authorities via several telegrams over the past few days, that it was Gilmores that participated in Godwin's transfer to Port Arthur prison. All the others involved, save the warden, have also died mysteriously over the past decade. I am convinced Godwin is wreaking his revenge on those who kept him incarcerated."

"So, you are saying, if I follow you, that Godwin must have introduced the cyanide into Gilmores' glass just prior to the toast. Lord Backwater said *someone* filled the glasses and provided them to the club officials."

"Yes, you are quick, Gregson."

"But Mr. Holmes, how do we prove it?" queried Gregson.

"Yes, that is the question," mumbled Holmes.

"Holmes, in your experiment, did not the resulting cyanide take the form of a liquid?" queried I.

"Watson, you are showing great promise. Of course!"

"Pray tell, Mr. Holmes?"

"Gregson, the Doctor is ahead of you. If the cyanide were a liquid, would he not need a vial to convey it?"

"I suppose he would. But it could also be in crystalline form. Where does that lead us?"

"In either event, he'll likely have a vial with some cyanide secreted somewhere," proposed Gregson.

"His murderous game may still be alive. I leap to conclusion here, which violates my principles, but dare I say it must be the warden who retired and returned to England when Port Arthur closed, that has to be Godwin's last prey. We must find where he is."

"Yes, agreed. I will have the Yard find out where he retired. We must alert him forthwith!"

"Shall we not search Godwin's kit immediately?" queried I.

"Yes, of course!" answered Holmes.

We marched back into the locker room.

"We would like to search your kit, Mr. Godwin. You

Daniel J. Darrouzet

don't mind, do you? Of course, we could get a warrant, but the outcome would be the same."

"Well, I do mind, but 'elp yourself."

Holmes grabbed the kit and took it over to a table and emptied it contents. There was no vial.

Holmes had me write down the contents as follows:

1 Wallet, containing 3 £5 notes
1 Pocket watch
£2 5s in loose coin
1 One-way ticket to Liverpool
1 pair of undergarments
2 small keys on a ring
1 note pad with various notes about different players
1 small hand-drawn map labelled 'Birkenhead'
2 pencils
1 cap with the club's emblem upon it

"Thank you, Mr. Godwin," said Gregson somewhat disappointed at not having discovered the vial. We left the room and began walking around the field discussing various aspects of our morning's endeavours.

"It's as if we are playing our own Test Match," said I, trying to lighten the melancholia that beset us. Gregson and Holmes seemed to ignore my comment.

Gregson and Holmes agreed we should remain in Manchester for the Test Match. Due to Gregson's inquiries, we were able to watch some portion of the play. Holmes did not partake, he instead spent much of his time at the telegraph office sending and receiving messages, too many to relay here.

By the last day we'd gained no further significant ground on our prey. He made no unusual moves, nor did he act suspiciously under the circumstances.

"Tomorrow they depart, correct?" queried Holmes.

"Yes, but not yet back to Australia. They have a match in Dublin, I am told. Our opportunity to nab this one is quickly evading us," said Gregson.

"Have you found the Warden yet?"

"Yes, His name is Smythe, He lives in Birkenhead.

"Am I jumping to conclusions again?"

"What's that, Mr. Holmes?"

"Is not Birkenhead across the Mersey from Liverpool?"

"Why yes, but it only makes sense they'd travel to Liverpool to catch the ferry to Dublin."

But was there not a map of Birkenhead in Godwin's kit?!

"Yes! We must get to Liverpool first. Then on to Birkenhead. I do fear for Warden Smythe's life. If I am mistaken, then 'Amen', but otherwise we should err on the side of caution."

Holmes' plan was for Gregson and I to travel to Liverpool, then to Birkenhead to find and warn the Warden of his perilous situation. Holmes would stay behind and watch our prey, lest he decided to abandon his plan and escape.

Gregson and I arrived in Liverpool after a short ride. We then took the Mersey Railway tunnel to the west shore and soon found ourselves in Birkenhead. After several inquiries we found the cottage and explained our presence to the Warden. Not being the first time, he'd been made aware of threats upon his person by former inmates, the fact that we were quite certain Judge Gilmores had died at Godwin's hand, did make an impression upon him.

It was the following day we received a telegram from Holmes, c/o the Warden, stating the club had packed up and were at the station awaiting their train to Liverpool. He would be there within the next few hours if there were no delays.

The hours passed quickly. After discussing with Warden Smythe, we all agreed to secret ourselves should Godwin arrive unannounced. Were the same cyanide poisoning to be the method of attack, he would have to somehow introduce it into the Warden's food or drink.

The next hour was quite frustrating. Our emotions were split between wanting no attack to be forthcoming and yet our one chance to catch the villain without relying on mere circumstantial evidence was to catch him red-handed in the act.

Suddenly there was a knock on the door.

Warden Smythe answered it. It was Godwin.

"Do you remember me?" asked Godwin.

Daniel J. Darrouzet

"I am sorry sir, you have the better of me, to whom am I speaking?" replied the Warden.

"I am Richard Godwin. I was an inmate back on Port Arthur when you were Warden. Now do you remember?"

"I am sorry, there were so many inmates. You cannot expect me to remember all of them. What is it that you want?"

"Well sir, I wanted you to know I am out now. I have a fine job with one of the cricket clubs back in Australia. We are here to return with the *Ashes*, as they say."

"But why are you here at my doorstep?"

"Oh sir, I wanted to stop by and thank you for all you did for me. You assigned me to the apothecary and I learned so much there."

"Well, I am happy for you, but I don't think it is a good idea for us to celebrate your…"

At his rebuff, Godwin suddenly pushed passed the threshold.

Upon this act of assault, Gregson revealed himself and got hold of Godwin, but he continued to struggle vigorously against Gregson's clutches. Holmes came through the open doorway just then and helped subdue Godwin. They found some rope and bound him.

Holmes then picked up the bag that Godwin had brought in with him. It looked very much like my medical case that I take when visiting a patient at their residence.

"I believe we searched the wrong bag the other day," asserted Holmes.

"If you would do the honours, Inspector."

Gregson opened the bag and dispensed it contents on the Warden's dining room table. At first, nothing appeared out of the ordinary. It was when a set of three vials were separated out that Holmes eyes lit up.

"I dare say, these vials would appear to be misidentified, would you not agree Mr. Godwin?"

"I don't know wha' you're 'alking about."

"Defiant to the end, are we?"

Silence followed.

The first was labelled '*Liniment*'. The second 'S*al Volatile*', the third was unlabelled.

"Mr. Godwin, what perchance is this?" asked Holmes.

"It is medicinal caffeine. I sometime give the players as a pick me up."

"Then you wouldn't mind sampling it yourself right now, would you?"

"I'm not in need of a pick me up."

"Warden, would you please be so kind as to put on a kettle?"

The room was silent for a few minutes. Soon the Warden entered with a tray for tea. Holmes poured out a cuppa and then deposited some of the white power from the unlabelled vial and stirred it into the cup.

"Here, Mr. Godwin. Perhaps you will partake of your 'pick me up'?"

"No! Get that away from me!" he yelled out.

"I think we have our man, Gregson."

"Richard Godwin, I am arresting you on the charge of murder of one Judge Gilmores and the attempted murder of Warden Smythe."

"Just keep that away from me!" he cried out.

Gregson arranged for the local constabulary to take charge of Godwin. The Warden was most thankful for the help we all had given him. He thanked Mr. Holmes and the Inspector, profusely. Without Holmes' persistence at the Yard concerning the connections to Australia, it is doubtful Scotland Yard would ever have solved the case.

Holmes and I said our goodbyes to Gregson and Warden Smythe. We then made our way back home to Baker Street. Once there, Holmes retrieved his violin and began a sombre piece I'd not heard him play before. With the excitement of the case at an end, it appeared he had become melancholy again. He, as well as I, awaited the next opportunity that would challenge his incredible mind.

THE ADVENTURE OF
THE DAMAGED TANGS

"I do not know where to begin, Mr. Holmes," said our new guest.

"Begin anywhere you choose, Mister…?"

"Sorry…, I am Gerald Ashburn."

"Mr. Ashburn, I see you are a barber."

"Why, yes! How did you…?"

"It is my profession to know. How might I help you?"

"Umm, well one of my customers suggested I seek your counsel. It is about my razor."

"Perhaps if it is not performing well, it may be due to your unsteady hands?"

"No, sir. I do not think so."

"How, then, do you explain your failure, while you are doing your utmost, to hold them steady?"

"Sir, you are correct. Here, in your presence, I admit, I am most nervous. I am afraid you will think my problem is not a serious one. But I assure you, I am quite concerned. Please do not think me a Klondike!"

"Rarely are my clients mad, sir. What is it about your razor we are to be concerned about, Mr. Ashburn?" said Holmes in a calming tone, to try to get this possible new client of his, to steady himself.

"The tang, sir."

"How is a tang of a razor affecting you so severely? I would think you would be most comfortable with it, seeing as how your livelihood depends on your coming in contact with it every day?"

"Well, sir, it is bent!"

"All tangs are curved. I believe they are designed that way. A tang helps one open a razor without having to touch the blade, and once opened, your finger grips the tang for better control, does it not?"

"Why yes, of course, but …"

"So, what happens to be the problem?"

"I am sorry. I am not making myself clear."

"Perhaps, then, you should start at the beginning. Watson, a brandy please, for our guest?"

After our guest had begun slowly sipping his drink, his anxiousness began to subside somewhat and he began his tale over again from the start.

"Thank you. That does seem to have calmed me a bit. I normally avoid the fruit of the vine. It doesn't give one's customers much confidence to have their barber smelling of alcohol. I am sure you would agree?"

"I do indeed."

"You see, I have a small, but growing shop on Fleet Street. I have been there for four years now. My clientele have been most appreciative of my services. They are all successful men. They are helpful and have encouraged their friends to visit my shop. This has allowed me to grow even more. As the number of my clientele has increased, I have had to add two assistants. That was two years ago. I may, in fact, need to add a third because the number of my clientele has continued to grow. I believe this is due to the satisfaction of the services I offer.

"Business has progressed smoothly and in fact I can count several members of the House of Lords as my clients."

"What has this to do with the 'tang' of your razor?" asked I.

"Watson, let us be patient," said Holmes, rebuking me.

"Last Friday all was as it should be. My normal clients were on time. We did, though, close up a little later than normal since I had a new client that arrived just before closing. He said Lord Addington had recommended that he come to my shop.

"He had introduced himself as Sir Brathwaite and I had not the desire to turn him away. I told my two assistants that they could retire for the evening and that I would take care of him myself.

"I always take care of new clients the first time they come to the shop. That way I can get to know their likes and dislikes. Once I get to know their preferences, I usually will see if they are willing to have one of my assistants help them, especially if I am occupied with another client upon their next visit.

"My two assistants are very good. I have been able to depend on them. Honestly, though, I do fear that someday they will leave and open their own shops, taking some of my clients with them. But such are the risks when one owns one's own establishment."

"I see," said Holmes. "but what has that to do with your bent tang?" queried Holmes, as now even he was showing signs of impatience.

"Right, well, Mr. Holmes, when I opened shop on Saturday morning, and I was starting to work on my first customer, I found that the tang on my most trusted razor felt awkward in my hand. I stopped and looked at it. To my surprise, the tang was bent! It was bent such that it did not line up with the blade. It was bent perpendicular to the blade! I was baffled."

"If I may suggest," said I, "perhaps it has been dropped?"

"No, it is rare that one drops one's razor and does not realize it. I assure you I did not drop the razor."

"What else can you tell me, then? I especially want to know anything that stuck out in your mind as unusual, anything at all."

"Hmm, I should only say that the only queer thing that happened was that Saturday morning as I was preparing for my first client to arrive, I was in my back room with my assistants, when I heard the bell on the door jingle. I sent Harold, one of my assistants, out to see who had come in, but he returned saying there was no one there."

Was this after or before you discovered your razor?"

"Before. I did not notice it being bent until I started working on my first client who came in about ten minutes later."

"Anything else that you remember, Mr. Ashburn?"

"No, but…"

"Come on, man. Out with it," urged Sherlock somewhat aggressively, but I knew him enough to know it was impatience and not anger of any kind.

"Well, sir," stuttering a bit in reaction to Holmes' demanding tone, "the only thing that comes to mind was actually the night before. Sir Brathwaite had paid me with a sovereign when I was finished. I don't keep change for such an amount in the front of the store, so I went to the back of the shop to retrieve his change. But when I returned, he was gone."

"Perhaps he had given you the wrong amount accidentally? I know I have done so on occasion," said I.

"I suppose you could be right, sir."

"Thank you, Mr. Ashburn. Is there anything else you remember or wish to tell me?"

"No, sir. No, I do not think so."

"I suggest then, we call our meeting here to an end and I shall ponder upon it. But please understand, Mr. Ashburn, you have provided so little data, it may be difficult to reach a reasonable conclusion. So far, all my thoughts will be based on mere speculation. And, as my dear friend here, Dr. Watson, will attest to you, I loathe speculation.

"I will come visit your shop, as there may be some datum point overlooked by you which, when I find it, shall, in all likelihood, shed more light upon the matter.

"Good day to you, sir," said Holmes, as he turned away from both of us, with less of an air of dismissiveness I have seen from him before, but nonetheless, the message to me anyway was clear, the meeting was now over. He had reached for one of his clay pipes resting on the mantle and began filling it somewhat vigorously with tobacco from the slipper.

"Alright, Mr. Holmes. I will open tomorrow morning again, bright and early at 6 o'clock."

Holmes did not reply.

"Ah, Mr. Ashburn," interjected I, "Mr. Holmes will be by your shop in the morning, I can assure you. He does have other pressing matters and I believe he is already preparing, in his own mind, for his next appointment."

While speaking these words, trying my best to avoid our new client from feeling abandoned by Holmes' apparent lack of any further interest in his problem, I reached for his hat and coat and helped him with them.

"Thank you, Doctor. Goodbye Mr. Holmes," he spoke quite loudly.

There was no reply from Holmes. Mr. Ashburn's face told me he was confused and perhaps felt like he had said something wrong to cause Holmes to ignore him.

"We will see you tomorrow, Mr. Ashburn, goodbye," said I.

I barely got him out the door without there being some sort of collie shangles about it all.

"Watson?" Holmes practically yelled at me, as he arose from the couch.

"Holmes?"

"Why did you tell that man I had another appointment? You know very well I do not. In fact, I have no case right this moment, which is the only reason I have allowed him to waste so much of my time!"

"I told him that to ease his feelings. You nearly ran him off! Holmes, I have told you in the past, just because you are thinking ahead, you must not leave your clients in your wake. They need your assurances that you are going to solve their problem. When you dismiss them, especially in this manner, as you are prone to do often, they feel abandoned."

"Trifles. These 'clients' come to me with the most ludicrous problems. A *bent tang*, Watson! What kind of a problem is that?

"If I treated my patients how you treat your clients, I would be out of business in a few months at most. The client is coming to you for help, not to be your amusement."

"Have I sunk so far as to be willing to find out why a fellow has a bent tang in his shop? A bent tang!" he repeated, "My word, Watson."

"Holmes, it is, as you say, on the surface a ludicrous problem. But I believe other of your cases have started out seemingly just as ludicrous and yet blossomed into excitement that neither of us could have predicted."

"Ah, you are correct, Watson. Forgive me, but I do not think this one is of that calibre. But I shall take your advice, my dear fellow, and not prejudge this case. I will try to be patient as you have advised, though, for how long I may sustain a calm façade, I cannot tell you."

This time Holmes sank into his favourite chair and closed his eyes. Despite his protestations of this being a 'ludicrous' case, I knew he was already mulling about in his mind what could account for such a strange occurrence if one dismissed the likelihood that the razor had simply been dropped.

I left him to his thoughts and I entertained myself reading the afternoon papers.

Next morning, we grabbed a cab and after a short journey alighted in front of Mr. Ashburn's barber shop.

"Good morning, Mr. Holmes, Dr. Watson," said Ashburn. I am so happy you have come so early.

"Harold, please help the gentlemen with their coats."

The assistant quickly relieved us of our outerwear and quite sharply hung them up.

"Would either of you wish a shave this morning? There will be no charge."

Oh, that is quite generous of you, Mr. Ashburn. I do not require one. Holmes?

"Hmm?"

"Holmes, would you like a shave this morning?"

"No, but, where is this razor of yours Mr. Ashburn? I wish to see it."

Ashburn turned to his other assistant and commanded him to retrieve it from the back room.

"Geoffrey, get Mr. Holmes my *poli glace* razor."

Geoffrey nodded and quickly retired to the back. In but a few moments he returned with a small wooden box. The lid was not completely closed. Holmes took the box and noticed that the lid would not lay flat as it should. Something was stopping it from complete closure. Finally, Holmes opened it. Inside was a superb looking instrument that had obviously been well used but also seemed to have been well kept. The blade was shiny but worn down. The ivory handle was finely carved, but I saw no crack in it at all.

"May I?" queried Holmes.

"Yes. Of course, Mr. Holmes."

No matter which way one placed the razor in the box, either the tang itself or the entire razor not sitting right was preventing the lid from closing.

"Perhaps, you would like to use my stand to inspect it?

"Yes, yes."

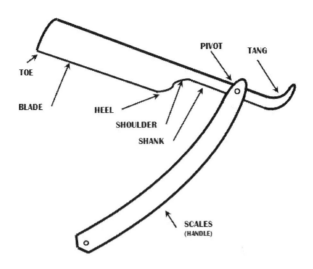

STRAIGHT RAZOR
(a.k.a. *Cut-throat Razor*)

The light over Ashburn's stand was bright. I am sure it aided Holmes in his observation of the razor with his glass that he had retrieved from his pocket.

After a somewhat lengthy review of the item, he looked up and spoke.

"I see what you mean, Mr. Ashburn. The tang is definitely bent perpendicular to its major axis. I agree that even had you dropped the razor and it hit the floor even at the most critical of angles, this tang, as thick as it is, would not likely have bent as much as it is."

"Yes, yes, I thought you would agree, Mr. Holmes."

"There is something quite queer about this. Your problem intrigues me, Mr. Ashburn. May I spend some more time looking about your establishment?"

I was delighted to hear Holmes' statement. He was now very much caught by this unusual problem and I could now count on him to see it through.

I followed Holmes around as he inspected the entire

shop. Behind the main salon, where Ashburn and his assistants performed their services, the back portion of the shop had various closets, rooms and two hallways that got me confused as to exactly where I was quite quickly, as the hallways twisted and turned for no apparent reason.

Holmes, seemed more at ease with the layout of the back rooms. I took a few notes, as he mumbled to himself on various things that he found interesting enough about which he intentionally, or perhaps more correctly – unintentionally, commented upon aloud.

We found ourselves in what appeared to be Ashburn's office. There was a small desk and atop it was a small safe. Next to it was a single flame range with a teapot atop it. Holmes looked at the safe closely and had a ponderous look on his face after viewing it with his glass.

"Did you note, Watson, that there are no marks upon Ashburn's safe that one would attribute to it be assaulted by an object such as his razor's tang?

"Also, as a precaution, you must have noted that when we were in the salon, I found no marks on the floor about his station or barber chair. But having found no marks is not conclusive, in itself, that he has told us the truth with regards to not having dropped the razor. But, then again, if he had dropped it, why come and ask for my help. Why not just buy a new razor, correct? This case is odd, that is for certain. You have all this written down?"

"Yes, Holmes, I have so noted those points."

"I wish next to look outside to see if that shall bring anything more to light."

We strode outside and Holmes took time to note the various shops across the street from Ashburn's establishment. Directly opposite was a small butcher shop – "Perry's Butcher Shoppe". To the right of the butcher shop was a – "Leather Shoppe". To the left of the butcher shop was an empty shop with a sign in the window 'FOR LET'. Holmes crossed the street and gazed upon our client's shop.

To the right of Ashburn's was a salon for ladies – "Fashion & Hat Shoppe". To the left was a photography shop "Samuel L. Edward – Photographer".

After saying our good-byes to Ashburn, we went around the back of his shop onto Pleydell Street. We found the shops behind Ashburn's and made note of them.

Directly behind Ashburn's was a carriage shop. It took up the space behind Ashburn's and the ladies salon. The other shop, behind the photography shop, was a bakery.

After this journey, I could not help but be reminded of our adventure together, in my earlier tale (that my faithful readers remembered as being chronicled in, *The Red-Headed League*).

But from our exploration of the surrounding neighbourhood, there was no bank in sight as had been in our previous adventure. It made sense to me that Holmes would follow this line of investigation. But this time, it was not reasonable to come to the conclusion of a pending bank robbery. There was simply no bank within a reasonable distance from Ashburn's shop.

And, unlike with Mr. Wilson, neither of Ashburn's assistants were new employees, both having been there for at least two years. There was no ruse being used to get Ashburn away from his shop either.

So, while this brought to my mind a similar feeling of a strange occurrence at a proprietor's place of business, the similarities were simply that – similar, but not the same.

As the weather was cold, but pleasant, we decided to walk. Holmes was silent all the way back to Baker Street. As was the case in the past, I kept quiet and tried to use Holmes' methods to see if I, by myself, could possibly solve this case with the few facts to which I had been exposed, the same as Holmes. I had seen his method up close and I was determined to endeavour to make good use of it.

My efforts though seemed in vain as, after at least a full one-half hour, I found myself no closer to a solution than when I'd started. I comforted myself with the *observation*, that neither had Holmes resolved the problem. While my skills were certainly not equal to his, I did conclude this was now a more challenging problem than either of us had given it credit for when first we heard of it.

We arrived back at 221B and I again quickly took up

the afternoon paper to see if there was anything newsworthy. I had become quite interested in a story that had recently grabbed the attention of many inhabitants of the Empire. The Morning Post had begun reporting a series of stories of an exciting tale about a former British lieutenant who had turned journalist and was reporting on the Boer War from South Africa. He had been captured by the Boers, thinking he was part of the army. The latest report was that he had escaped his captors and was returning to England.

The stories reminded me of my days in Afghanistan. While the exciting story about the escape of this particular young man (he is only one score and five) - and his return - interested me, it also brought back some painful memories of friends lost in battle. I was thrilled and a bit melancholy all at once.

"Remembering the war, Watson?"

"Yes, Holmes. You are correct. But this time, I know how you did it! I have noticed on occasion, that when the painful memories of the war return to me, my right foot tends to twitch ever so slightly, as I was just doing while reading this amazing story in the Post of this young fellow named Churchill.

"Doctor, Correct! You have discovered one of your *tells*.

"When you have discovered all of them, you will know more about yourself. You know, I only use them to deduce your mood."

"I know, Holmes. You do know, Holmes, I have used your own methods and can now recognize some of your '*tells*' to deduce your moods?"

"I would hope so after our long time spent together." replied he, with a bit of annoyance in his voice.

"Have you solved our little mystery yet, hmm, Watson?"

"No, I have not. Have you, Holmes?"

"No, neither have I. We've not enough data."

"What do you propose to do, then?"

"I plan on retuning to Ashburn's shop tomorrow. I want to look around again."

With that he slunk down on our couch, closed his eyes

and closed himself off from me for the rest of the evening. This was more than a 'tell'. It was open, albeit silent, communication from Sherlock Holmes that he wished not to be disturbed.

It was sometime after we'd breakfasted the next morning, but before we left for Ashburn's, our attention was called to the sound of rapid footsteps up the stairs followed by incessant knocking on our door.

As I was closest to the door, I rose and opened it. It was Ashburn, nearly out of breath.

"Dr. Watson," said he, as he brushed past me and in three giant leaps was in front of Holmes. "Look! It's happened again, Mr. Holmes! You must help me!"

"This is my second blade. It is one of my *Thiers-Issard's*! I cannot afford this! I will be out of business in no time!"

"Please, Mr. Ashburn, please, calm yourself. I cannot help you if you fall into hysteria."

"I only have one good blade left sir! I must know why this is happening. Who is doing this?"

"I would wish to return to your shop at once," announced Holmes with a tone of urgency I had not expected.

"As we go, I want you to tell me everything you remember about yesterday. Who were your clients? When did you open? When did you close? Do you understand me? Everything!"

We assembled outside and hailed a Growler, needing more room than that which a hansom normally gave Holmes and I alone. It took some extra time to flag one down.

Once we were all settled and the address had been given to the coachman, Holmes immediately again asked Ashburn to tell him all the new facts.

"Well, sir, I attended to my usual Thursday clients."

"Can you name them all?"

"Yes, of course.

"First was Mr. Terrance Letteer, a barrister, as I understand. Then I served Mr. James Jenkins, who is an accountant and works for the Exchequer. Then I attended to Sir Christopher Wells, I believe is an undersecretary to the Colonial Secretary."

While Mr. Ashburn continued his litany of clients, Holmes, as well as I, were caught a bit tongue-tied as we heard the various names that were so well connected with the current Government. It was not as though he was counting *The Marquess of Salisbury*, himself, among his clientele, but certainly those who assisted most of the Government were included.

"And lastly, Sir Brathwaite, who again overpaid me and left before I could retrieve his change," explained Ashburn, as we stepped down out of the Growler.

I must admit, my dear readers, that several of the names were obscured to me by the noise of the carriage from which it gets its well-deserved nickname. But as we shall see later in this tale, the few names missed by me were inconsequential in the resolution of this case.

Upon entering the shop, Holmes squinted up his face to an odoriferous assault to which I too instantly reacted.

"No doubt the photographer next door to you is developing his photographs?"

"Ah, yes. I have complained to him on several occasions that he must stop this practice since he moved in several months ago. The landlord is of no help. As you can readily deduce, Mr. Holmes, my clients object to having to put up with it.

"I thought we had reached an acceptable compromise. He had agreed to work on his photographs in the evenings and has been doing do for a few months now. It seemed to be working out. This is the first time he has broken his pledge not to release the foul smell during the day."

"It is no concern now, but it does get one's attention," stated Holmes. "I did not notice it outside, though."

"Unfortunately, we have a common wall and share a ventilation shaft. That appears to be the source. I have closed it off in the past to avoid the lingering odours, but on certain days when the weather is particularly unpleasant, I have to open it up again, or my clients complain of the stuffiness of the shop."

"I understand," said I. For myself, I was remembering all the various noxious fumes I have had to endure being exposed to by my roommate's experiments over the years.

While I have worried on occasion as to their effects on both Holmes' and my health, I must confess, that to date, I do not believe either of us has been in any way permanently affected by them. Holmes ignored Ashburn's remark, as well as my short comment.

"Hello! What have we here?" said Holmes.

I walked over to where he was standing. By then, Holmes was already on his knees with his glass in hand peering through it at a slight dusting of white powder on the floor just below the screen of the ventilation opening in the wall. The screen was approximately three feet wide and two feet tall. It was positioned, I guessed, six inches or so, off the floor.

"Watson, would you be so kind as to take one step to your right, for you are blocking the light.? There's a good fellow."

"So sorry, Holmes, of course."

I stepped away as he requested and the white powder came a bit brighter once my shadow escaped it.

"Watson, can you see the slight outline of a footprint? Right here, do you see it?

"Yes, Holmes."

"Please also make a note this powder and the footprint are but a foot from the screen of the ventilation shaft."

Holmes quickly led his glass to the edge of the screen.

"Here, Watson, see for yourself. There are several fresh scratches on the edge, and notice how the screen appears to have been forced back or at least some leverage appears to have been applied to try to remove it.

"Mr. Ashburn, have your removed or handled this screen in any way recently?"

"No, I have not."

"When you said you blocked it, by what means did you accomplish this?"

"I have tried a few different things, but the method that seems to have worked best was that I found an old artist canvas that was in a blocked frame in the back. I draped several towels over that. I then placed that against the screen. Then I placed a crate that comes with our supplies up against the canvas to hold it in place."

"Can you tell me, Mr. Ashburn, what this powder is?"

"Well, sir, the only powder we have like that is the talcum powder we sprinkle on our clients at the end of our services."

"No, I do not think it is that," responded Holmes. "There is no perfume in this, as best as I can tell. Of course, being exposed to your neighbour's chemicals perhaps has temporarily dulled my senses. Perhaps it is just that. Would you mind if I collected this sample?"

"No, that is fine. Do you need a sample of the talc?"

"Yes, and I would also like to take a sample of the plaster from your wall, perhaps in one of the rooms in the back, preferably one that is along the wall here with your photographic neighbour?"

"Yes, of course. Help yourself, Mr. Holmes."

We took a hansom back to Baker Street and I was able to converse with Holmes intelligibly without the racket made by the Growler.

"Holmes, what do you hope to find with the powder?"

"I strongly suspect it is more of the same, plaster. But with Ashburn's talc all about the place I want to be sure. Once I know it is plaster, then I think we will be able to reasonably deduce that someone is tampering with the screen of the ventilation shaft. But, should it not be plaster, then perhaps it is simply the talcum. I will compare the substances shortly.

"Like clearing one's palate between courses in a meal, I wished to retire from his shop to assess the samples in a less contaminated place."

It did not take long for Holmes to confirm the residue from the floor matched the plaster sample from the wall.

"I think it likely, Watson, that someone is attempting to gain access to the photographer's shop next door via Mr. Ashburn's establishment.

"As to why, it is not clear, but several possibilities present themselves without too much thinking involved."

"No doubt, evidence of some kind. Perhaps our photographer is involved in some sort of blackmail?" asked I.

"Perhaps, but you know what I think about speculation in cases, Watson."

Holmes sent a note to Ashburn, requesting that we be allowed to stay in his shop over the next several nights, alone.

Holmes explained his reasoning that perhaps his shop was being used to gain entry to Edward's photography shop. At first, Ashburn was a bit hesitant, but quickly relented once Holmes told him, that if he and I were not able do so, that Holmes' doubted there would be a satisfactory solution forthcoming.

The next few nights we had taken our torches and arrived at the shop just before closing. Each night, there was always at least one client being attended to by either Ashburn himself or one of his assistants. Our luck was not with us for the first two nights.

On the third night, Ashburn was attending to what appeared to be his last client.

Before long, Ashburn joined us.

"Sir Brathwaite, again. I have told him he need not pay me again as he has over paid me already. But he insists it is of no concern to him. I *insisted* back to him that I must give him his change, but no doubt he'll leave before I return," and before he finished his sentence, we heard the jingle of the doorbell announcing Sir Brathwaite's departure.

"Well, there he goes again," said Ashburn, replacing Sir Brathwaite's change into his drawer.

Ashburn asked if he should remain, but Holmes was against this.

"I do not see it as necessary. Our experience in matters such as these has taught us that, while there may be nothing of any consequence that will happen tonight, should there be any confrontation or violence, I would prefer you, my client, to be out of harm's way."

Ashburn, reluctantly accepted this answer from Holmes. He grabbed his three razors, the two with the damaged tangs, and his last good *Thiers-Issard* and nodded to us.

"Good night, gentlemen."

"Good night, sir," I responded for both of us.

After we heard the jingle of the bell and the slight metallic sound of Ashburn locking the door, all was silent.

Holmes and I then again retreated silently to a small closet close to, but not directly next to the screen as we had done on previous nights. Holmes closed the door except leaving it just enough ajar that we could see out through the remaining slit. We could see the closet across the hall where he'd found the plaster footprint. Our eyes adjusted to the darkness after some time, and we were finally able to see reasonably well. Then, we waited again as we had done the nights before.

It was perhaps 2 o'clock in the morning, when suddenly, we heard an ever so slight creak of a door.

"Holmes!" I whispered. Holmes grabbed my arm and placed the index of his other hand to his lips.

We saw a figure step out of the closet and make its way toward the screen.

"Let us get him now!" I again whispered to Holmes. His only response was to grip my arm harder and shake his head with a look of ferocity I had seldom seen directed at me.

There were sounds of rummaging and objects being moved about. Finally, there was a crash of sorts. Some more dull sounds and then silence.

At the silence, Holmes pushed me out of the closet and passed by me to stand next to the opening in the wall where once the screen had been attached. There was broken plaster about. The screen was lying to the side of the opening. It had suffered some damage when removed. Next to it on the floor was a crow bar that was at least three feet long.

We heard thrashing and other various sounds difficult to describe except for the muffled sounds of a frustrated voice coming from the burglar next door. There was a faint light coming from the opening, but when we peered through it, we could make out nothing of consequence. The opening did not provide a clear view of exactly where our night prowling visitor was next door. Unless we had decided to crawl through ourselves, we would just have to wait.

"Holmes, should we not go through to catch him red-handed?" whispered I.

"I think not, Watson. He is most likely to retrace his steps. We must remain patient and our quarry will come to us," he whispered back.

It was quite a long time, at least an hour according to my time piece. Our patience was rewarded when suddenly we heard footsteps coming towards the opening. The light from the opening became brighter.

The slight sound of a breath of someone crouching down. Next an arm holding a lantern came through the opening and was placed off to one side. Our presence was quickly illuminated and would have been known to our prowler had he anticipated such a possibility. Then we heard a slight grunting of our prowler as he presumably got down on his knees preparing to crawl through the wall.

With the light from the lantern right next to him his features were now more visible, at least on my side. A hand crept through onto the floor with a small envelope in it. Then the back of a man's head facing downward came through the opening and another hand of the man crawling on the floor.

Holmes stepped on the first hand and the crawling man screamed in pain. Holmes bent down and quickly grabbed the envelope.

"No, give that back to me," screamed the thief.

"I think not, Sir Brathwaite, or whatever your real name is," announced Holmes.

"Please, I must have it!"

"You will likely never see it again until you identify yourself and explain your actions."

"I have nothing to say," our thief said as he turned and sat upright on the floor. He stared at Holmes.

Holmes stood above him holding one end of our thief's crowbar in one hand and resting the other end on his shoulder. While not directly threatening our guest, it was held in such a manner as to silently communicate that he had best cooperate and not pursue violence against either of us least Holmes have to enforce his superior position in the matter.

"Watson, would you be so kind as to retrieve *Sir Brathwaite's* lantern, please?"

I knelt down and retrieved the lantern.

"Holmes, what is in the envelope?" queried I.

"Here, Watson. You do the honours," said Holmes as he handed me the envelope all the while keeping our guest under observation. I handed Holmes my lantern and then opened the envelope.

"They are negatives, Holmes."

"Negatives of what?"

I held up them up to the bright light of the lantern and viewed one of the negatives.

"It would appear our photographer, Mr. Samuels, has as his clients, some females of the younger generation, who seem to be enthralled with simulating poses that we only see today in a museum of Greek marble statues, and so, *sans vêtements*."

"That does not surprise me. Your girl?" queried Holmes.

"No, ah, they are of my ...my...sister," said our young thief as he hung his head in shame.

"Shall we not sit down and discuss this, young man?" suggested Holmes.

"I suppose, but who are you? Are you the police?"

"No, we are not the police."

"Then what right have you to detain me?"

"At the minimum, young sir, you are trespassing and have caused damage to, and theft of, property not your own. Should you prefer, I will be happy to step outside and call for the nearest constable."

"No, no wait, please, don't do that, it won't be necessary."

"Then, please tell us what this little 'scavenger hunt' of yours is all about, although I believe I can already discern your motive. Your sister's indiscreet photos about to bring shame to you family, no doubt?"

"Yes. My name is ... is Albert Bellingham.

"My sister, Emma, is about to be married. She's not like most young girls. Mamma says, she's quite a filly on the dance floor. Papa says, she's been trouble 'since the day she was born' I don't think so, no, not to me, mind you, but ... I think more that, well, she's just a bit *bricky*.

"So, about a month ago she pulls me aside. We're twins, you see, and she's shared stories of most of her adventures with me. I've never had her get herself in real trouble before. Always just standing next to a parapet, never on it.

"Anyway, she tells me that she and Hattie, that's her

best friend, decided to get their photos taken a few years ago. "Just for fun," she said. So, I asked what was wrong with that? She said that, they both, Hattie and she, were posed *au naturel*. I knew she was always pushing the edge, but this was a bit much, even for me.

"She'd just gotten a letter from someone saying they were aware of the photos. They said for £500 they would not send them to one of those 'society journals.' She said that she thought it was a joke at first. Then she heard that a girl, who knew another girl, …well anyway, some girl's fiancée had found out his girl had had similar pictures made. He called off the marriage since the story made it into one of those journals.

"A week later she got another letter. Only this time it included a picture of her. It was one of the poses for which she and Hattie had done, just for fun, she said crying.

"She's frightened that the same could happen to her. Of course, Mamma and Papa know nothing about it. She begged me to help her. Neither of us have £500. There is no chance of asking either Mamma or Papa.

"I went to the photographer and enquired as discreetly as possible about perhaps buying such pictures, not mentioning who I was or that I was trying to get the photograph of my sister. At first, he denied having such pictures. But after continuing our conversation, he more than implied he could 'perhaps acquire some' should I be willing to pay handsomely. He said I should return in two weeks."

"What was I then to do? That would be too late!

"While in there, I heard some laughter coming from the barber shop next door. It seemed to come from the screen in the photographer's shop. I couldn't force him to say he had the pictures, so I decided I'd have to come see for myself.

"I left and went next door to the barber shop. I saw a similar screen in the barber shop and decided to see if there was some method by which I could gain entrance into the photographer's shop through it. I was in need of a shave and haircut, so I introduced myself as '*Sir Brathwaite*'. Lord Addington is a friend of my father's and so, I wasn't exactly lying."

"While being attended to, I kept pondering the screen. I had no plan, but suddenly an idea occurred to me. If I could stay behind in the barber's shop, perhaps I could gain entrance to the photographer's shop without anyone knowing.

"If I did so at night, I might have enough time to find my sister's photos. But how could I gain entrance at night to this shop without breaking in as a common thief? I thought all I needed do is secret myself somewhere in his barber shop and wait until Mr. Ashburn had left. Then I'd get through the screen and search.

"I decided that I must follow through on this plan at once. As I look back now, that was a mistake.

"When payment was due, I gave Mr. Ashburn a sovereign. When he went to get my change, I went through the other doorway and found myself a storage closet in which to secret myself.

"Waiting at least an hour after the shop closed, I came out and went to the screen. At first, I tried to simple wiggle it loose. But I had no success. I then started looking for some implement with which I could pry off the frame of the screen. But there was nothing that I could find that was small enough to wedge between the frame of the screen and the wall. My goal at this first attempt was to try to leave no trace of my attempt to remove the screen and enter the other shop.

"I started rummaging around with some frustration when I finally came upon a razor. I saw the tang sticking out and decided I would give it a try. But the tang bent.

"It fit nicely and it started to work, but then I heard a noise coming from the other side. It was the photographer, or at least someone in his shop and so I had to abandon my quest at least for a time.

"I settled down to wait for him to leave, but he stayed and stayed. I remember looking at my watch and seeing it showed 2 a.m. I did not realize so much time had gone by. I did not think it wise to leave then as there was a constable who was frequently passing by the shop at irregular intervals. I was trapped. I returned to the storage closet to plan how I would escape.

"After the sun arose and Mr. Ashburn opened up his shop, I set the door ajar, listened and waited until he might not be in the salon itself. I eventually heard him call to his assistants to help him with a crate that had just been delivered in the back. It was risky, but it was my only chance. I quickly ran to the door and exited. I forgot that the bell would jingle, but I was able to escape without being seen or so I concluded, since there was no one chasing after me and when I next returned to the shop, no mention was made of me being seen leaving."

"So, your first attempt was a failure?" stated Holmes.

"Yes. I thought about how I might reperform my little task for the next week since it would not make sense to come for another haircut in so short a time."

"My next attempt was to be just as unsatisfactory. I had decided the same approach would work, I just needed to have enough time when Mr. Samuel would not be in his shop.

"I came again late in the day and refused to be served by an assistant. Ashburn sent them home as he had done the first time I had come and I was again alone with just him. I again paid Mr. Ashburn with a sovereign and hid as soon as he had left to retrieve my change.

"Once he had left, I found the nearest razor and began my assault on the screen. I thought certainly this would be the night for a successful retrieval of the pictures.

"I was able to remove the screen on this side, but it took a long time. I did notice in doing so, I had bent the tang. My earlier attempt had also bent the tang, but no one mentioned it to me. Why would they?

"I was able to access the shop that second try, but I could not find my sister's photographs. It may sound strange, but since a gentleman does not normally see a woman without her clothes on, it was awkward at best, at least for me. It took longer than I thought. When in public, one focuses on a person's face mostly. Having to look only at faces and ignore the rest was, well, gentleman, it was difficult to say the least."

"Tonight, I see you came prepared," said Holmes, as he wiggled the crow bar he held in his right hand.

"Yes, and it worked well. Using the tang had taken me nearly an hour to dislodge the screen as I said. It took me only five minutes with the crow bar. I was determined to get in quick and finish the job. You see my sister's wedding is planned for next week. This was my last chance."

"I take it you took off your outercoat yourself when you entered the shop?" queried Holmes.

"Yes, but how did you know?"

"A simple deduction, young Albert. There can be no doubt you hid your crow bar in your outer coat. To be seen walking on the street of London as a well-dressed young man openly carrying such a tool would certainly have aroused the suspicions of most of our fellow Londoners, as well as even our most challenged constables.

"When Mr. Ashburn's assistants offered to take your coat, you could not afford to let them hold it as the additional weight would have certainly caught their attention."

"Yes, you are correct."

"I also take it, that should you have not found your sister's negatives, you were prepared for perhaps more drastic measures…perhaps a touch of arson?"

"I considered it as a last resort. The bond between us is strong, sir. A twin is a special sibling. So, yes, the thought crossed my mind, I admit it. I was prepared to do almost anything to protect my sister. Even if it meant destroying the man's entire collection of such lewd photos. But since I finally found hers, I quickly dismissed that solution, although part of me did wish to save all those young girls from such a foolish choice."

"So, what say you, Watson? Shall we call the constable down the street?"

"No, please!" pleaded Albert.

"Holmes, I believe the young man's intentions are honourable. It would not seem to benefit anyone but our disreputable photographer, Mr. Edward, to turn Mr. Bellingham over to the police."

"It would, yes, be to Mr. Edward's advantage, but then on the other hand, his photography might become a concern under the laws regarding morality. I do not think he would be willing to have his clandestine business become known to the public, as it may find itself shut down either by law or vigilante. Our Majesty would be aghast at such *goings on*."

"What say we destroy these negatives of his sister and let this little adventure come to its natural conclusion?" suggested Holmes.

"I would agree, Holmes."

With that, Holmes took a small box of matches from his outercoat and as if lighting a cigarette, struck a match. He quickly placed the negatives close to the match. They burst into flames instantly. He dropped the conflagration to the floor and I quickly stamped out the ashes left behind. I retrieved a dust bin and broom and swept them into it.

Bellingham dropped his shoulders in relief and nodded to us. A smile of thanks came upon his face.

We then explained why we were here and that the bent tangs had caused Mr. Ashburn much anxiety.

"Here then," said Bellingham, "please make sure Mr. Ashburn receives this, gentlemen."

He then handed Holmes ten sovereigns, more than enough to purchase two brand-new *Thiers-Issards.*

Now we only had the problem of how to get Albert to exit the shop without being detected. Holmes suggested that we all three stay the remainder of the night.

In the morning Ashburn arrived with Geoffrey and immediately queried us about what had transpired the night before. Bellingham remained hidden in the closet that had secreted him on each of his night-time adventures.

I requested of Ashburn that perhaps we might have a cuppa since our night's work was long. He agreed and wished to hear all about what had happened.

Ashburn, Geoffrey, Holmes and I retreated to his office and he put on the kettle. We explained that we had waited all the night, but that nothing of importance had happened.

"Nothing? That is so disappointing."

"We, do though, believe you will have no more damaged tangs."

"How can you be sure, gentlemen?"

"We have discovered the reason for them being bent."

"Why, what is the solution?"

"We have bound ourselves to secrecy, though. The reason shall remain with us, but the perpetrator of this adventure wishes to make amends for his damage to your property."

Holmes handed him all ten sovereigns. Just then the doorbell jingled.

"Harold, is that you? We are in the office," shouted Ashburn. There was no reply.

"Geoffrey, go see who that is, please, if it is not Harold. If it is one of my clients please inform them, I will be right out to serve them. I don't know what to say! That is more than enough to buy new razors."

"Then we have solved your problem of the damaged tangs, Mr. Ashburn, correct?"

"Yes, you have. But I am bewildered by the outcome!"

"Geoffrey, who is it," he interjected.

"No one, sir!"

"No one?"

"No one, sir, just like the other times."

Ashburn looked to me and then to Holmes.

"Gentlemen?"

There was not a recognizable grin on Holmes' face. But with my history of adventures with London's finest consulting detective, I knew at this moment, what was going through Holmes' mind.

"Our work is done here, Mr. Ashburn. Good day to you, sir."

"Well, …. I uh… thank you, Mr. Holmes, Dr. Watson. I was told you could solve my problem and you did. Please be sure to come by should you require my services. What do I owe you?"

I knew Holmes would likely say nothing so, I spoke up. "Perhaps, when you receive your new *Thiers-Issards*, you would be willing to part with one of your damaged razors, to Mr. Holmes? I believe he would value such a souvenir from this adventure. Otherwise, the pleasure was ours."

"Of course, certainly. Thank you, gentlemen, Thank you. When my new razors arrive, I shall deliver one personally. And should you ever be in need of my services, know that you will always be welcome, and at no charge."

"That is most generous of you, Mr. Ashburn."

"It is my pleasure, Dr. Watson, Mr. Holmes," said he as he bowed his head towards us. Just then two gentlemen came in the shop.

"Ah, Sir Wells, welcome, sir. The usual I presume?"

With that, we left with the doorbell jingling behind us as we closed the door on our way out.

We again decided to walk back to 221B. I had not queried him before but could not help myself but had to ask Holmes how he came to his solution.

"The solution presents itself to those who follow the facts.

"Over the years, in a profession like mine, one is bound to run across charlatans by deceit, or in this case a desperate person who by necessity, and in some cases a person, I believe, simply for the joy of it, that they pretend to be someone who they are not.

"Any good actor or actress will attest to this desire and the satisfaction of becoming this persona even if for just a few hours on the stage.

"So, as you know, Watson, I have, especially when dealing with cases involving the upper class, always taken the time to validate the stated position of the gentleman or lady with whom we find ourselves coming into contact. Burke's Peerage is always a trusted source.

"You see, there is no Sir Brathwaite. He is fictional nobility. The known facts of overpayment, the doorbell jingling as if a ghost were there, all pointed in the same direction. Once I knew that we had an actor, of sorts, lining up with overpayment and mysterious doorbells, it became obvious that the person was secreting themselves in the shop only to come out at night and leave the next morning. But why, was the question.

"The bell at the door jingling each morning after 'Sir Brathwaite' had been there the night before also intrigued me. I knew there had to be a connection.

"Had we any indication that our photographer was indulging in the type of *art* from which we have since discovered he was profiting, then the motive would have been more obvious. But we discovered in the end his secreted work. The disaster of the engagement was averted and our client was repaid. Is there anything else to be done?"

"I think not, Holmes."

"Then, thank you, Watson."

"Thank me?"

"I found the case refreshing, even if somewhat simple. I obtained an excellent blade, by your intervention, even though it has a bent tang. Again, thank you my friend."

"You are quite welcome, Holmes," said I. It was an odd moment to have Holmes respond this way. I decided to leave it as it was. No further discussion was needed and I did not wish to spoil the moment.

But Holmes again surprised me.

"I suggest you return to your little addiction, Doctor."

"My little addiction?"

"Certainly. I have prevented you from your reading the 'truth' and 'gossip' of our fair city. I believe you are as drawn to them as much as I am sometimes drawn to the drugs you caution me about."

"Ah, but Holmes, my 'little addiction' as you call it, is a healthy one. It harms me not and I increase my knowledge," said I.

Holmes rebutted, "But was it not that American writer, he has an unusual last name, Mark… Mark…"

"Do you mean Mark Twain," responded I.

"Yes, you are correct! A newspaper man himself if I am not mistaken. I think, he is said to have written: 'If you do not read the newspapers, you are uninformed; if you do read the papers you are misinformed.'"

"Hmm…I do believe I read that some time ago, myself. And perhaps you are correct. The newspapers are sometimes erroneous but they entertain as well. How else does one obtain knowledge of what it happening around him, eh? I argue my 'little addiction' is a safe one. Yours, as I have told you many times, will likely kill you. I will take mine over yours every time."

"Touché, Doctor, Touché.

Holmes, though, was correct. I had gotten behind in my reading of the local newspapers which I enjoy perhaps more than I should. My desire to keep up with the latest news of fair London has always been a delight to me. But I had not thought of it in the way Holmes had described it to me.

In any event, I began to read again, and in several days, had caught up to the present days' offerings.

Then I found an interesting article one morning which read:

*P*all *Mall Gazette*, 20 November, 1892

FIRE ON FLEET STREET!

Last night a fire engulfed a photographer's shop on Fleet Street. The shop of "Samuel L. Edward – Photographer" was entirely destroyed.

"It is a complete loss," stated Lt. G. C. Penefort, fire squad leader in change at the scene.

Local fire officials, indicated the presence of the new 'celluloid' film and required photography chemicals stored there, were the likely cause. Celluloid - it being highly volatile - and the flammable chemicals used to process it, are easily ignitable.

Lt. Penefort stated further, "This new substance, 'celluloid' that these photographers are now using, does not appear to be very stable. We have witnessed these 'spontaneous combustion' fires before and will no doubt see more of them in the future."

THE ADVENTURE OF
THE BLUE-GREEN MUROID

"**M**r. Holmes? Mr. Holmes? Are you there, Mr. Holmes?" That was the voice I heard whilst accompanied by a rapid pounding on our door. I was quite sure that the voice was that of Wiggins, the leader of Holmes' Baker Street Irregulars. I'd become familiar with the pitch and cadence of the eldest of the street urchins Holmes had befriended, and to some degree, had trained over the past few years on different points of how to collect data for him.

I opened the door and confirmed my initial conclusion that the voice was indeed that of Wiggins.

"Wiggins, my lad, what is it that you want to speak to Mr. Holmes about with such vigour so early this morning?"

"Well, sir, it's me cousin's pet I needs his help with."

"His pet? Why in the world would you come here and practically wake up the dead with your yelling and pounding on our door as you did?"

"I told the lad not to come up, Doctor," yelled up Mrs. Hudson from below. "He just ran right past me!"

"It's all right, Mrs. Hudson. I will handle this intrusion," replied I. I heard her mumble something but, could not discern her exact words. Her tone, though, conveyed her dismay at what had just occurred.

"You know, Wiggins, Mr. Holmes does not arise early unless he is on a case. Now you go downstairs and apologise to Mrs. Hudson and return at a more reasonable hour, say, after noon."

"But sir, Jonesy's pet may die!"

"Wiggins, Mr. Holmes is not a veterinarian…"

"What's a veter… ter…?"

"A doctor for animals."

"Oh, yes, but you're a doctor. Ain't you, Dr. Watson?"

"Of course, I am, you foolish boy," said I, with perhaps too much indignation at this young man whose only education was that which he had learned upon the streets of London. It is likely he'd never seen the inside of a proper school room.

"Then can *you* look at Jonesy's pet?"

"Did I not just instruct you to come back at a better time?"

"Yes, sir, but he might die! Please, sir, please?"

"If it will stop your pleading, yes. But first you must go down and apologise."

"Yes, sir. Mrs. Hudson!" he yelled out as he flew down the staircase with alacrity.

Again, I heard mumbling between Wiggins and Mrs. Hudson. Her tone was more compassionate now, like a mother correcting her own mischievous child. In a moment, he was again at our doorway.

"Mr. Holmes is quite fatigued from the last few weeks, I will do as you ask. But mind you, I am not a veterinarian."

"Oh, that's fine, Dr. Watson. I don't think Jonesy's pet will know the difference."

"Tell him to bring his dog over and I'll have a look at him. Is it his paw?"

"Dog? Paw? What do you mean, Doctor?"

"His pet is a dog, isn't it?"

"Why no sir, ha, ha, it's no dog! No, sir, it's a *rat*, sir."

"A rat!" said I, with more than a bit of astonishment.

"Yes sir, and a pretty smart one he is. Why Jonesy's got him trained to do tricks and all."

"Rats carry diseases, young man. I am not sure I can agree to handle this creature."

"But sir, we think he'll die if it doesn't get help. Please, sir, you promised!"

"I do not recall promising, Wiggins, but bring him to me and I shall take a look at it."

"Oh, thank you, sir, I'll go get Petey right away."

"Who's Petey? I though you said it was Jonesy's rat?"

"Oh, sir, Petey's the rat, sir."

"I see," is all I could respond.

In a short while both Wiggins and Jonesy had returned with a small basket in hand.

"Am I to come in, sir?" whispered Jonesy, standing at the threshold holding a wicker basket.

"Yes, why wouldn't you?"

"Wells as I remember, Mr. Holmes said only Wiggins was to report to him. I don't want no trouble."

"I believe in this case you are permitted to enter. You are the patient's guardian so to speak."

"Guard…, sir?"

"Never mind. Jonesy, Wiggins tells me your *Petey* is a bit under the weather, eh? Let's have a look at him, shall we?"

Jonesy, with quite a concerned look on his face, opened the basket lid and gently reached in and recovered Petey from his wicker carriage.

The poor little creature was a mess. His fur seemed to be stained with a mixture of blue and greenish colour of some sort. He was as lethargic a creature as ever I have seen. His breathing was laboured and his eyes were droopy.

"When has he last eaten," queried I.

"It's been two days, sir," answered Jonesy. "He ain't gonna dies, is he, sir?"

"I do not know, young man," said I.

"Over there are a few bits of toast from my breakfast. Bring them over here and let's see if he'll eat."

I motioned for Jonesy to offer him some of the crust of the toast. I must tell you, my dear readers, I was still a bit unsure of handling this creature despite the obvious lack of his species' natural and normal effervescent behaviour. He was laying there on his side in a most unusual stupor-like way. I was used to seeing rats scurry, not lay still.

The history of its species conveying devastation on our species was foremost in my mind having studied at Bart's the terrible illnesses conveyed to mankind buy such creatures. The results on my fellow humans throughout the ages have been devastating.

Jonesy picked up a small piece of crust and held it in front of Petey's nose and mouth. His pinkish nose quivered as he sniffed and his tiny whiskers fluttered all about. His mouth opened slightly and we could see his interest to try eat, promised new hope. His tongue slipped out to taste the crumb and I then noticed it was likewise stained as we had observed on his fur.

"What has he been into?" queried I.

"I don't know, sir" replied Jonesy.

"Well, whatever it is, it certainly has almost killed him."

"Where did you find this creature? Petey, that's his name?"

"Over by the train station, sir."

"Watson, what have we here? Wiggins, what are you doing here? I have not sent for you?" interrupted Holmes.

"Oh, sir. I came over to speak to you about Jonesy's pet, but Dr. Watson, said we ain't suppose' to disturb you."

"That is correct, Holmes. I told the lads you were in need of rest. I offered my assistance rather than they try to get a veterinarian to help them. I am not quite sure what this little creature has gotten itself into, but it certainly has experienced some harm. It seems to have come in contact with some sort of dye and possible some solvent of some type."

"I see. Well, lads, you're in good hands. Dr. Watson is a good physician."

"But, Mr. Holmes, Doctor Watson only treats people, not animals, like a verter… vert…."

"Veterinarian, Wiggins. Yes, I know, but I doubt you could afford such a visit. I doubt a veterinarian would agree to treat such a creature. Dr. Watson is a good second choice for a case like this."

My initial sense of pride at Holmes' first comment about my competency was, of course, quickly dashed as a wet dinner plate is when it slips and suddenly is on the floor in a hundred pieces, when hearing I was only a good *second* choice.

I suppose Holmes meant no real harm. I am not a veterinarian, so his comment was correct, but it stung just the same.

"I think Wiggins," said I, "if he starts to eat again, it is likely he shall survive. I think his nibbling is a good sign. Give him fresh water and make sure he eats nothing but these scraps of toast for the next day or so and I believe he shall recover."

"Oh, thank you, Doctor," said Jonesy. "I knew you could fix him up for me."

"Young man, I did noth…"

But before I could finish my sentence, Jonesy had placed Petey back in the basket and grabbed the few crusts of toast and run out the door.

Wiggins was a few steps behind him, but being older and having been trained a bit more by his relationship with Holmes, he hesitated just a moment. He tipped his cap to me and said, "Thank you, Dr. Watson. I'll be sure he follows your instructions."

"Be sure Mrs. Hudson doesn't see that creature. If she knows you have it, she will not let you back in again!" said I.

"Yes, sir. I mean no, sir. We'll not let her see him, sir. Goodbye, sir. Goodbye, Mr. Holmes."

And with the door closing behind him, the morning's excitement was over.

"Watson, your good deed for the day has been done."

"I suppose, Holmes, but I didn't really do anything."

"Ah, but you gave them hope. I believe that can be a most important medicine when people are ill, or in this case, attending to the ill."

"Yes, you are right, I have seen the effect before. I guess I didn't think about that this time. I mean the patient was a rat! The creatures are to me a natural enemy of humankind. I must admit they disgust me."

"Yes, and I too. But those boys have so little that even such a disgusting creature provides some amount of joy in their lives."

"I guess you are correct, Holmes. Wiggins told me that Jonesy has actually taught that little thing some tricks. Perhaps when it fully recovered, we'll get to see it ride a miniature bicycle or some such thing, eh?" said I, in jest.

Holmes' refusal to even acknowledge my attempt at humour told me his focus had already changed to some other subject of which he had not yet confided in me.

I picked up the early edition of the Times and was surprised by the headlines:

'Banker Murdered!'

Mr. Albert Kirkland was found dead last night in his office at the Newcastle Bank and Trust in London. Kirkland, being the President of the Bank, was reported as working late. His assistant. Mr. David Marold, reported that Mr. Kirkland was preparing for an appointment which was to take place today on the premises of the bank.

The sale of several thousand Pounds worth of bonds were to be sold to a client, who at this time, Scotland Yard wishes that his identity remain anonymous.

Inspector Gregson of the Yard is investigating this deadly crime. More information is to follow.

I chose not to mention this to Holmes as his need for rest exceeded his need for more stimulation, in my opinion, as his physician. I continued to read other articles in the paper and soon had forgotten the headline.

Holmes had called out to Mrs. Hudson and requested that she provide him with some tea. He sat pensively in his chair and awaited its arrival. I believe Mrs. Hudson had all ready anticipated Holmes request, since she was rather quick with its presentation.

"Well, Mr. Holmes, how are you feeling this morning?" queried Mrs. Hudson.

"I am well, and you?"

"Very well myself, sir. Enjoy your cuppa."

Holmes sipped his tea and thereafter remained silent. I returned to my scouring the Times for the news of the day.

I was pleased that Holmes was relaxing as I had been concerned over the last few days. We'd had a quite intense adventure over the past several weeks. Holmes had exerted himself far beyond what a normal man would have. This, in itself was not unusual, but the endless exertion without rest was catching up with him.

He, for once, it seemed, was actually following my advice and was resting. My thought of finally getting through to him on this issue gave to me a certain sense of success.

We spent most of the morning in a quiet, yet refreshing atmosphere. His normal agitation at having no problem to solve, was missing. I observed no languid attitude in his behaviour so I concluded he had not indulged himself in his occasional descent into his poorly chosen and addictive habits.

It was quite a pleasant morning.

After a brief walk and lunch which were both in silence, I decided to query him as to how he was.

"How did you sleep, Holmes?"

"I slept well, Doctor. And yourself?"

"I believe I woke once or twice. But all in all, I shan't be one to complain."

"So, you are feeling refreshed this morning?"

"Doctor, I would hope by now, you could discern for yourself, with all that I have taught you these past years."

"Well, I'd say you appear, umm, shall I say, umm, satisfied. Yes, that's it. I believe you are satisfied."

"Satisfied?"

"Yes. You do not appear frustrated. You seem satisfied...content."

"I am not sure I agree with you, Doctor. But I do believe I am feeling something I rarely do feel. I am not anxious, nor am I tired. I believe the more correct word would be *relaxed*."

"I observed, though, that this, relaxation, as you describe it is not artificial. Am I not correct?"

"You are, Doctor. For some reason, I cannot understand at the moment, I am relaxed without help."

"Ah, you see, Holmes! I am excited for you!"

"What is it that I am supposed to see, Doctor?"

"You have done it. You have relaxed without the aid of that vile substance you inject into your veins!"

"Correctly observed, Doctor."

I took this as a success. I knew there would be no more praise heaped upon me. I was now the one who was satisfied.

I took a deep breath and pondered the moment as one does when epiphany strikes. What a glorious day it was!

By now we had returned to Baker Street and had but a block or so left to go to reach the door of our abode when I looked ahead and saw them. There, parked in front of 221B, was a carriage from the Yard.

I suppose it is the part of life, that the moments one encounters, when all seems to be in its proper place, in fact, cannot remain so for long.

There was Inspector Gregson awaiting our return.

"Good day to you, Mr. Holmes, Dr. Watson," said he, as he respectfully tipped his hat to both of us.

"Good day, Inspector. What brings you to Baker Street this fine day?"

"Well, Mr. Holmes, it would appear we at the Yard are in need of your assistance."

"And just what is this little problem you cannot solve on your own, may I ask?"

"I am certain, sir, you have heard of the murder at the Newcastle Bank and Trust?"

"Mr. Holmes has been recuperating these last few days per my direction and he has not been reading the news. I have forbidden it."

"I see, well, sir, we've quite a case here and we certainly could use your help, that is, if you would care to oblige us."

"I think, Gregson, I have spent enough time, dawdling about these past few days. So, I would be delighted to lend you a hand."

"But Holmes, you've just today begun to regain your energy. I must advise against it," insisted I.

"Doctor, I know you have done your best, but it is all I can take of this relaxation. I believe my mind is once again yearning for a challenge. Come upstairs, Gregson, and tell me all about it," said he, with a rising excitement in his tone.

With that, my victory seemed quashed. Once again, the allure of the game was upon him. I could do nothing to recall or prevent its seduction of him.

We settled in and Holmes sat listening intently as Gregson described the scene and facts as he knew them.

"We were called late last night. A Mr. Marold, who

worked with a Mr. Kirkland, the deceased, said he had gone to his employer's office to inform him that he, Marold, was retiring for the day. He knocked briefly as was his habit. But rather than hearing the normal 'enter' with which Mr. Kirkland would normally grant access, there was no reply. He knocked again louder and finally called out to him. Receiving no response, he decided to enter and then found Kirkland slumped over his desk with a knife stuck in his back. The window behind Kirkland was open, he claims."

Gregson continued, "Marold immediately called for the police, who then called us."

"When we arrived, Marold was quite helpful. Then Marold, who was quite in control of himself up until then, suddenly said, 'The rest of the bonds, where are the rest of the bonds? Five are missing!'"

"We all looked around, but found nothing. The appointment and sale were scheduled for this morning."

"Gregson, did not the buyer show up on time for his appointment?" queried Holmes.

"I don't know. Between the murder and now the missing bonds, I didn't think to ask."

"It might be best to go to the bank and talk to this Marold again. We should ascertain if the buyer was in fact real, or perhaps an imaginary ruse. What do you say, Inspector?"

"I agree. Shall we go to the bank now? He is sure to still be there. The death of Mr. Kirkland has caused the board of directors to call an emergency meeting."

"Let us go. Watson, shall you come along or are you still prescribing relaxation for yourself?"

"Holmes, I shall come."

We hopped in Gregson's carriage and were soon at the bank. We were escorted to the third floor and found ourselves waiting outside a boardroom as their meeting had begun an hour before.

"What do you make of it so far, Mr. Holmes?"

"There are several obvious possibilities, but more inquiry and data are needed. I foremost wish to question this Mr. Marold, if I may."

It was at least another half hour by the clock in the waiting area outside the boardroom, before the doors opened. The board members all had a most sombre demeanour and exited in silence.

"Mr. Marold, may we speak to you for a moment as we have a few questions?" enquired Gregson.

"Yes, of course, Inspector. Have you caught him yet?"

"Caught whom?" queried Holmes.

"Why the murderer and thief, of course."

"Mr. Marold, please excuse me. I would like to introduce you to Mr. Sherlock Holmes. And this is his associate, Dr. Watson."

"Yes, I've heard of you, Mr. Holmes. But why are you here?"

"I have asked for Mr. Holmes' help in this case, Mr. Marold. I hope you don't mind?"

"If you insist Inspector. I suppose I have no objection."

"May we retire to Mr. Kirkland's office? I believe Mr. Holmes would like to inspect it."

"Yes, of course. Right this way gentlemen."

We walked down the heavily ornamented, walnut-panelled hallway with polished marble floors and soon found ourselves in the President's chambers. It was elegantly adorned with the most exquisitely detailed bookshelves and cabinetry that one would expect to find in such an establishment.

The dark oak desk was finely carved and its mass conveyed the sturdiness and confidence that any client would expect to see when engaging in business with a bank and trust.

Holmes' first move was to go to the rather immense window. The arch which framed it was at least forty feet in diameter. The ceilings were more than twenty feet tall. It was a magnificent room in which to do business with the bank and trust's clients.

I followed him there and looked down on the street. There were latches but no locks on the windows. The ledge outside was quite wide as the stone edifice was of neo-classical design. Plenty of room for a villain to walk or crawl along to gain access.

"There, Watson, do you see it?"

"What is it Holmes?"

"I think I must have a sample."

Before I knew it, Holmes had opened the window and stepped out on the ledge.

"Holmes, good God man! What are you doing out there? It's three stories up!"

Holmes had gotten down on his knees and was crawling along the narrow stone window ledge towards a brownish spot. He took out his pocket knife and scraped a bit of it.

"Quick, Doctor, an envelope please."

I turned to the desk and riffled through its sturdy drawers and found one. I reached out and handed it to Holmes as he reached behind himself as if waiting for the baton to be passed to him during a relay race.

He slowly crawled backwards all the while trying to avoid the pigeon droppings that adorned the ledge. Going out he had missed most of them, but crawling backwards he was not so successful.

"What is it, Holmes?"

"Mr. Marold, may I have a bit of that rug?" said Holmes, ignoring my query.

"Mr. Marold, I would suggest you allow Mr. Holmes permission," said Gregson.

"Must you? I mean that is a Persian. Why do you need it?"

"I would like to compare the spot of blood which is obviously on it right beneath where Mr. Kinkaid was sitting, with this one I have retrieved from the ledge."

"Well, yes then, but can you please take very little?"

"Of course."

Holmes found a pair of shears in the desk and snipped off barely an eighth of an inch of the closely woven rug where the now clotted blood had landed.

"Now please tell me about these bonds and the client. Have you determined if he did or did not show up for his appointment?" requested Holmes.

"The bonds were being sold by the Royal Bank of Scotland. We were simply an agent in the transaction. There were seven bonds, each with a face value of £5,000. The client was a Mr. Pottman."

Marold handed one of the two remaining bonds to Holmes after Sherlock gestured his request to see one. Holmes spent several minutes examining the bond in a detailed manned that only Holmes would do.

"Had you ever done business with his Mr. Pottman before this most recent transaction?"

"No, never. But he had come in a week ago, and deposited half the amount of purchase price of the bonds. That was approximately £7,000. He stated he was awaiting the remainder and would have it by today. He was to bring it at the closing of the transaction."

"Did he ever show up?"

"No, I have checked. I found no record of his arrival today."

"So, his money is still here?"

"I believe so, why would it not be?"

"Mr. Marold, I recommend you verify his account is still active and his money is still here."

"Well…, yes…, I believe I should. Just one moment."

Marold left hurriedly and then Gregson began to question Holmes about his thoughts on the case.

"What do you think, Mr. Holmes?"

"While the more obvious answer is that perhaps our Mr. Marold is not telling us all he knows, but I do believe he is likely telling the truth.

"I believe these blood samples will match. If they do, that will tell me that our assailant likely did exit from the window and upon his exit, deposited a few drops of our victim's blood on that ledge. Mr. Marold does not seem the type to have risked life and limb out there at night."

"Mr. Holmes! Inspector! It is gone!" exclaimed Marold as he entered the office.

"What's that you say?" queried Gregson.

"Mr. Pottman, he withdrew all his money yesterday afternoon, just before the bank closed!"

"What does Mr. Pottman look like?" queried Gregson.

"Oh, well, he's about average height, maybe twelve or thirteen stone. He had brown hair and moustache. Oh, my, this is a real problem. I've got to tell the board about this right away. They shall be none too happy about this!"

"I'd like to speak to the teller who helped this Mr. Pottman with his withdrawal," directed Holmes.

"Certainly," responded Marold.

We all went down to the ground floor and Marold took us to the teller. His name was Mills. Mills' description of Pottman matched that of Marold's. He confirmed and his records showed that Mr. Pottman had retrieved his entire account at 2.58pm just prior to the bank closing.

"I remember telling him that he would not earn any interest on his deposit since he was withdrawing it prior to month's end. He said nothing, but I noticed what I took to be a slight grin upon his face. I queried him again to be sure he wished to make the withdrawal. I've had customers change their minds, you know, and then not wish to make their withdrawals when they find out they'll lose their interest. But he finally spoke and said, 'Just give me my money'. At that point, he became most aggressive in his demeanour and I was happy to finish the transaction. With it being such a large amount, I needed my manager's approval. I received it and presented him with his funds. Then he left abruptly. He did not even say 'thank you'. Most of my customers say 'thank you' when I make dispersals to them. He was quite rude."

"Thank you, Mr. Mills. That is all I need to know.

"Mr. Marold, Inspector Gregson or I will be in touch soon. Good day to you, sir," said Holmes.

We returned to Baker Street where Holmes immediately went to work analysing the blood samples he had acquired. He first, of course, made sure they were blood by making use of the method he'd invented and I became aware of on the first day I met him back in '81 when Holdsworth had introduced us.

I had no doubt that it is was blood on the rug, but that which he found on the ledge, well, it might have been blood, but more likely from a pigeon for all I knew. I told Holmes as much.

He set down his samples and went out our door. It took but a brief moment for me to realize he had gone upstairs and not down. The only place up, was our roof top. It was some time until he returned. I could not fathom why he had ascended there.

Without speaking he began his analysis. Then after a while he exclaimed aloud.

"Yes! Watson, they are both human blood!" shouted he with conviction and a joy that one would expect to be exuded after sports victory.

"How have you confirmed that?" queried I.

"I took the liberty of extracting some blood, as you have suggested, from a pigeon on our roof. My ability to convince it, and its reluctance to donate to the cause took longer to reach an agreement than I anticipated.

"You were correct that the odds of it being non-human, and likely avian, had cast some doubt on my presumption. To know for certain, I needed to compare with the most likely source of avian blood.

"Not having contemplated it before, I find it interesting that avian and human blood appear different under the microscope. Human blood appears round, whilst this pigeon blood is oval. Quite interesting and no doubt of value for future reference in investigations, I should think.

"The blood from the bank, in both cases, is round, shall I say almost donut shaped, which corresponds exactly with my previous experiments and which you no doubt observed and were taught about in your studies. Look and see for yourself."

I arose and peered through the lens. After taking a moment to adjust my eye and turn the fine focus knob, I saw quite clearly what Holmes had seen and described to me. The avian blood sample on his slide was distinctly oval, unlike all the human blood I had ever seen.

"But Holmes, all we know now is that what you found on the ledge is human. We don't know if it is Kinkaid's or the villain," said I.

"Correct, Doctor, but it *is* very likely one of those two persons, don't you agree? I argue that it is not Kinkaid's blood as it is not likely he would be climbing outside on the ledge. If he did so, why? If it is not Kinkaid's, it is most probably our murderer's. He would have a motive for being out there, that is to escape from the room undetected. I only wish we could find a way to identify each person's blood separately.[12] That would improve our art of detection greatly. But for now, just to know that our suspect likely left via the ledge is clue enough.

"I think now I must make inquiries with regards to the sale of those bonds. Certainly, there will soon be a transaction somewhere. I intend to contact several banks and other institutions to be on the lookout for them. With any luck, we shall have our Mr. Pottman soon enough."

Holmes left and I found myself alone contemplating this newest adventure into which he'd gotten himself, and me, so thoroughly entangled.

It was obvious that Pottman would soon try to cash in the bonds and this action would trigger an alarm of sorts, ultimately causing his capture. I was so confident of this, that I had concluded the affair was all but over. We both soon discovered this was not to be the case.

In fact, several weeks passed and there was no word or hint of the sale of the bonds. Holmes, I could tell, was becoming a bit agitated by this lack of development.

"Watson, I have missed something," said he.

"Pottman, who seems to have disappeared into thin air has not yet cashed the bonds!"

"Well, perhaps he intends to hold them for a longer while, making a more 'long term' investment, ha, ha!" jested I.

"They are of no great value to him until he sells them. He can't very well receive their dividends unless he presents the coupons, which would expose him and so he'd have to sell them, perhaps to an individual and not a bank," asserted I.

"Yes, but the new buyer would wish to cash in the redeemable coupons, though, and that should trigger an alarm, would it not?"

"Give it more time, Holmes. I know you've done all you can on this case so far."

---

[12] Note: This adventure took place before 1900 and prior to her Majesty's death on January 22, 1901. As I write this, it was not until just a few years ago, later in 1901, when Karl Landsteiner, an Austrian biologist and physician, developed a system of blood grouping, "ABO," that I have begun using in my practice today. This has allowed medical science, to distinguish differences in human blood types. Prior to this, we physicians considered all blood to be the same. Many of my associates, and I myself, consider Landsteiner to be the *Father of Transfusion* for all his pioneering work on this important biological and medical matter. - *JHW*

"I disagree, Doctor. There is something I have missed, but I have not figured it out yet. I pray you will allow me some solitude. I intend a long pipe on this problem and will re-think the whole affair."

As he spoke, he had retrieved his new churchwarden I had given him this past Christmas, filled it and lit it within a few short seconds. He nearly leapt onto the sofa, closed his eyes and was deep in thought. I knew no more conversation would be forthcoming. It had not taken me long in my early years with Holmes, to know that once he had fled into his mind, I might as well be a bookcase or a chair. My presence now mattered not to him, so I gathered up my newspapers and began reading what news there was of the day.

To that end, my attention was quickly focused on several stories in each paper regarding the opening of the 'London Extension' of the newly formed 'Great Central Railway'.

'GCR Passenger Service, Begins 15 March'

The Manchester, Sheffield and Lincolnshire Railway, henceforth the Great Central Railway, will offer passenger service beginning 15 March of this year from Nottinghamshire to London via its new "London Extension" which will connect to the existing Metropolitan Railway at Quainton Road.

Parliament approved the extension in 1893. After several delays, the GCR (formerly the MS&LR) has finally been able to complete the line and thus provide a final link to our northern most towns and counties, directly from London.

The grand opening of the extension is scheduled for the afternoon of 14 March, at which time it is anticipated that the line will be officially deemed opened by Her Majesty at a ribbon cutting ceremony to mark the event.

"Finally!" shouted I. I admit to thinking this was long overdue. The unnecessary burden to the modern-day traveller bordered on the absurd! With as much progress as we have already achieved, to have to switch trains, stations and lose time just because there was no direct connection was quite an embarrassment to a country as sophisticated as that of Great Britain!

Holmes, of course, ignored my outburst. I quickly regained my decorum and continued my perusal of the many varied articles that were presented to me. The only other article that stirred my interest was that of a short article which noted the release from prison of one of Holmes' previous adversaries.

'Conk-Singleton Forger Released'

John Jones, the convicted forger, was released from Fleet having served his complete sentence which began five years ago. Jones, originally from Gellilyfdy, Wales, was convicted of forgery in the case known as the Conk-Singleton affair. His mastery of the British Twenty Pound note had allowed him to duplicate it with such accuracy, that it was nearly impossible to tell the difference between his forgeries and that of the official note.

Thanks to the efforts of Inspector Lestrade of Scotland Yard, Jones was finally discovered and put in gaol for the last five years.

It was thought at the time, that Jones had had accomplices but that was never proven.

"Poppycock and bollocks!" again, I lost all decorum. Had one witnessed my outburst, no doubt such an observer would have seen my face flushed with anger!

"What's troubling you, Watson?" queried Holmes with a tone that told me he was not happy that my outburst had disturbed his thinking. It must have certainly been loud, since normally Holmes could ignore almost anything I had said or done in past occasions when he was deep in thought.

"That Jones forger you caught in the Conk-Singleton affair was just let out of prison and the paper claims Lestrade captured him!"

It will be no surprise to my readers that this was a falsehood if ever there was one! Lestrade had done virtually nothing to solve that case. Holmes had done it all. My frustration at Holmes' unwillingness to take, or demand - as he rightfully should, credit for his solutions had again arisen in my mind.

How he could allow the likes of Lestrade and the others to take credit, when it was Holmes who had solved their cases? It sometimes just overwhelmed me.

"You don't say. Well, hopefully now he will put his talents to more acceptable goals, but it is not likely."

"It is not fair!"

"Watson, I prescribe a walk for you. You need to evacuate this visceral reaction you are having."

I had read enough of this gibberish and Holmes' suggestion of a stroll appealed to me. I asked if he wished to join me, and said he was welcome to do so.

I expected no answer and got none. I left and made my way to the Gardens. I hoped a good walk would help relieve me of my agitation. Having made several rounds, I found myself more relaxed and headed back.

As I headed down Baker Street, I found Gregson being deposited at 221B by a jarvey and not one run by the Yard.

"I say, Gregson, the Yard not providing you with coaches these days?"

"They were all out with others, Doctor. So, I hailed this one outside the Yard to get here as quick as I could. The bonds have been sold!"

"Have they, now?!" exclaimed I.

We both quickly climbed the stairs and found Holmes still in his nicotine-induced state of semi-consciousness, or so it seemed.

"Ah, the bonds have sold," said Holmes before either of us could say a word.

"How did you know?"

"Gentlemen, please. The event we have all been waiting for has occurred and you burst in here with expressions of excitement like young school boys. What else could it be? Really, you must learn to anticipate better."

"You are correct, Mr. Holmes, the bonds have turned up, but only two of them," stated Gregson.

"Only two, you say, hmm?"

"They were sold in Lincolnshire to a Mr. Langsdale. He is a wealthy landowner in the area. We were alerted when he went to redeem the 1st coupon for both bonds. Had no idea there was any problem with them. He is most distraught at having received stolen property and is even more anxious to find the man who sold them to him.

"He claims he bought them for only a quarter of their face value. He should have known something was not quite right. I've no sympathy for him. But seeing that he's at least four score, I rather doubt he's our villain. Claims to know nothing more. Claims the gent who sold them to him was emphatic that he not redeem the coupons until after 15 March. He agreed, but later thought he shouldn't have to wait."

"Only two," muttered Holmes, almost inaudible.

"Holmes, does that surprise you?"

"Were I our thief, I would dispose all of them at once. Less chance of problems. The question now is, does he know, we know, he's actively selling the bonds? Did this Mr. Langsdale describe the man from whom he bought them?"

"Yes, but it was not any help. His description matched that which we obtained from the bank and the teller. That is not much to go on, though. Our Mr. Pottman, if that is his real name, seems fairly average. Nothing distinguishing about him."

"I disagree, Gregson. We have all manner of new clues."

"I do not see how we know anything new. We certainly don't have any more information!"

"Gregson, I am worried about you. If it were Lestrade here, I would expect as much. But I have seen promise in you. It would seem, though, that perhaps this case has gotten the better of you."

"I do not understand, Mr. Holmes. We have gotten knowledge that Potter has been in Lincolnshire and has disposed of two bonds!"

"Agreed, but what can you deduce from that?"

"Well, sir, he still has three bonds."

"Yes, but no, no, no! Must I spell it out for you?"

"Our Mr. Potter has sold only two bonds. He is in need of more money. I say more, since he already possessed half the amount necessary to purchase the bonds in the first place. I believe Marold stated the purchase price was about £2,500 each, £17,500 for the lot and that he had deposited £7,000 as a show of good faith. So, he already had over £7,000. If his goal was theft for pure cash, he'd not have sold just two and certainly not at half price? No, he needs more cash. But why is that the case?

"Secondly, he is only concerned that the coupons not be redeemed before 15 March. Something in his plans must occur before then. If he allowed Mr. Langsdale to freely cash them in before that date, then his plans would likely be compromised. The date is important to him. In fact, he cares not that we would discover he had sold the bonds to Langsdale as long as we were not made aware of it until after 15 March."

"I see what you mean, Mr. Holmes. But what good does knowing such a date if we don't know his plan?"

"That is for us to find out. It is our villain's first misstep."

Just then, there was a sound of stomping feet coming from the stair well. Then a rapid knock on the door accompanied by a shout, "Dr. Watson! Dr. Watson!" It sounded like the young voice of Jonesy, the owner of my newest four-legged patient.

I opened to door to stop all the commotion. "Young man, we are in conference. This is no time to be …"

"But Dr. Watson, it's Petey. He's ill again!" yelled he.

"Did you not hear me?"

"I know sir, but he's worse than the last time, look."

He'd opened his wicker basket and there lay a blue and green coloured rat. There was not a natural grey hair to be found on the poor animal.

"Jonesy, Mr. Holmes and I have a visitor. We cannot be disturbed right now with this creature. It will have to wait."

"But please, sir!"

"No. Now, if you will please wait outside. I will attend to Petey when we are through. Run along, now."

With his face exuding dejection, Jonesy hung his head and slinked out the door.

"Sorry for the intrusion, Holmes, Inspector," said I, deferring to their conversation

"What shall we do to move this case forward?"

"I cannot dismiss this newest clue. That the event takes place on or prior to 15 March is too important to throw away as having no significance," said Holmes.

"I must continue to ponder this newest clue. I suggest, Inspector that the Yard consider events that may be between now and 15 March. I would, though, suggest looking at those events closer to 15 March rather than those significantly before it. Good day, Inspector."

With that, Holmes reclined again on our sofa, tapped the ashes from his pipe into an ashtray and re-lit it, as it had gone out whilst we discussed the newest information.

Inspector Gregson, having started to become a little more accustomed to Holmes' curt dismissals, showed much less distress at being dismissed by Holmes this time than my memory serves me of their initial meeting.

If I remember correctly, when Gregson had met Holmes for the first time, not ten minutes later Holmes had abruptly dismissed him. Gregson then had pulled me aside. He said that he had felt as if he'd been dressed down by the head of Scotland Yard, himself. Was this the normal behaviour of this man, whom he'd just met, and in whose hands, he was placing his career, based on Lestrade's recommendation?

I remember telling him to have faith in Mr. Sherlock Holmes. There was not a man, on this side of the law, that was his equal. Gregson took his time coming around to Holmes' ways, but he did so only after he realized Holmes' genius.

I bid Gregson farewell and returned to my room.

There was a rap on the door and it is then I remembered my commitment to Jonesy. I headed to the door and opened it looking down to where I expected to meet Jonesy's eyes, he being but a youth of about four feet tall.

But to my surprise I found myself looking at the waistline of two official looking gentlemen.

"Mr. Sherlock Holmes?" queried one of them.

"No, I am not. And whom might you two gentlemen be?" asked I.

"We need to speak to Mr. Holmes, is he in? We do have the correct address, do we not?"

"Yes. He lives here. Again, gentlemen, I ask, who are you?"

"We represent Her Majesty and wish to speak to Mr. Sherlock Holmes."

"One moment, gentlemen."

I walked back to the sofa and informed Holmes that he had guests. He ignored my first try, but my persistence eventually got through to him.

"Please show them in, Doctor."

I returned to the door and asked them to please come in.

"Gentlemen, Mr. Sherlock Holmes" said I, as I waved my arm in Holmes' direction.

The look they gave each other was actually quite amusing to me. They no doubt were expecting someone in more formal apparel than the way Holmes was currently attired and perhaps with a more professional appearance.

As Holmes sat up from the sofa, he addressed his visitors, "Gentlemen, how is that I can help the Criminal Investigation Department?"

"How did you know…?"

"It is my job to know. I am now presently working on a murder case. Have you something of more interest or something that is of some higher priority? If not, I would ask that you return, shall we say at the beginning of a fortnight from today? I believe I shall have solved this little murder by then."

"Sir, we are here to deliver an invitation to you."

"An invitation?"

"Yes, Her Majesty has heard of your exploits. She wishes to seek your counsel. Please prepare to meet with her Majesty tomorrow at 2.00 pm at the Palace."

"I gather I may bring my associate with me as well?"

"Sir, the invitation mentions no one else."

"I see. I shall be there tomorrow as commanded."

And with a curt '*thank you*' our two visitors left.

"Holmes! How exciting! The Queen, the Queen Herself has sought your advice!"

"Watson, I shall contact Mycroft and find out what this is about. I doubt it is of much significance. Our dear lady has probably got hold and read some of your senseless babble and exaggerations of my exploits. Perhaps, she merely wishes to hear them from my own mouth."

With that he scribbled a quick note and arranged for its delivery to Mycroft.

It was but a short time later I went to the door again expecting Mycroft or at least his reply. It was neither. It was Jonesy.

I took the boy and his pet into the other room and proceeded to inspect it again. The same symptoms as before were present. The animal was lethargic and again multi-coloured in its appearance.

I asked if they had watched it closely.

"Yes, sir, and he was getting better. But he got away two days ago. He came back and was as you see him now."

"Where did he go?" queried I.

"I don't know, sir."

We then offered the poor animal some food in which he barely was interested.

"Jonesy, I don't know what to tell you but you must keep an eye on him. If he gets better, then next time he leaves, you must follow him to see what he is getting into."

"Yes, sir. I wilz sir. Youz can count on me, sir." And with such adamant assurances, Jonesy left.

It was just after dinner that the knock on the door came. Holmes was the closest and began his greeting before he turned the handle.

"Thanks for coming, Mycroft."

"What have you done this time Sherlock that needs my help?"

"It is my help you are seeking I believe."

"Mine?"

"The Queen has summoned me. I concluded you would know why, but instead you feign to have no knowledge of it. Interesting!"

"I do not know of what you speak, dear brother."

"Well, then you are of no use to me. I dismiss you."

"Sherlock, please explain yourself!"

"I have been invited by the Queen for a meeting tomorrow, and you know nothing of it?"

"While I am privy to most things the Prime Minister considers worthy of my time, I do not have intimate knowledge of every thought that comes into Her Majesty's head. She perhaps has read too many of our dear Doctor's stories and merely wishes to meet you, for all I know."

"We think alike, as I just a moment ago commented the same when Watson celebrated the invitation."

"So, dear brother, do you wish me to inquire about the invitation or not?"

"Facts always help. If you have time, why not?"

"I will inquire and let you know. And you, Doctor, please make sure he does not embarrass me when in Her Majesty's presence."

"I am confident he will show his utmost respect for Her."

"Good day, Sherlock, Dr. Watson."

With that, he turned and left the room. Holmes had already re-filled his pipe, had lit it again and had expelled a voluminous amount of blue smoke into the room. He sat down with his eyes closed. I said nothing, as I was all ready aware that he was thinking about the dialogue that had just taken place. I expected silence, but then suddenly…

"What do you make of it, John?"

I was taken aback by both his speaking to me after he had assumed his normal position for diving into his mind and contemplating the facts before him, but mostly that he called me by my first name. Rarely had he done so. I concluded quickly that the immediacy of his encounter with his brother had somehow triggered a more familial attitude which cascaded over into how he addressed me. I was brought back to our normal type of discourse when he repeated his question.

"Watson, did you not hear me? I asked, what do you think of it?"

"Holmes, I think it odd. It would appear your brother

has not been made privy to Her Majesty's request, which I do find difficult to believe."

"Or?"

"Or, what?" responded I.

"Or....?"

"What else could there be?" said I.

"Watson, you disappoint me. Of course, my brother knows what this is about."

"But Holmes, he denied it to our faces."

"Of course, he would. You expect too much from him. He was outraged that I was being brought in without him knowing or managing it. You know the language of my body by now to some extent. You know my grimaces and smiles, do you not…"

"Which hardly are expressed at all…"

"Exactly, but you have become aware of some of them. Having a whole life to learn my brother's quirks and tells, I assure you he is quite unsettled at the invitation."

"Then this is mere envy?" queried I.

"No, I sensed a bit more of fear in him than anger. I believe he is worried that whatever information he is aware of has somehow gotten out by this invitation to me. He interprets that as danger. I believe he will process the data and find he needs to change his plans. He will likely return or message me to discuss this further. We must be patient."

Holmes' vision of what was to come was not far off. The next day we received an invitation from Mycroft to join him at the Diogenes Club for lunch.

When we arrived, we were escorted into a separate dining room. Mycroft was already seated there awaiting us with a face that matched that I'd seen on Sherlock's when I knew he was anxious to begin a discussion. The familial duplicity was obvious to the experienced observer.

"Please take a chair," said Mycroft to both of us. We reached the backs of the finely carve mahogany chairs pulled them out and sat down to a table set with the finest silver settings now available in London. Mycroft then turned and dismissed our waiter, "I will ring for you when need be."

The waiter bowed respectfully and left the room. My

distraction of the setting was abruptly disturbed by the first words out of Mycroft's mouth after the waiter had departed were addressed to me and not Sherlock.

"I first wish to bind you Doctor, on your word as an English gentleman and a faithful servant of Her Majesty, that nothing that is spoken of here will be repeated to anyone. Do I have your word?"

"Yes, of course," responded I.

"I do this since Sherlock has made it clear to me on several occasions, that he will not participate in such discussions without you. When we first met, this annoyed me to no end.

"I have, however, learned in the years that I have known you, that you are true to your word, Doctor, and I count on you remaining loyal to Her Majesty."

"I am honoured that I have earned your confidence."

"Can we not get on with it, Mycroft, to the real reason you brought us here?" said Sherlock.

"In time brother."

"I am on a murder case, or didn't you know that?"

"I am aware of that. But this matter of which I will speak to both of you is of vital interest to the Empire."

Sherlock leaned back in his chair, closed his eyes and set his posture in a mode of listening.

"We are concerned about a threat on the life of the Queen. There are murmurings which indicate a plot of some kind is afoot. We have not, though, much more than that. We do not know which group is attempting it, where or when it is planned to take place. As Her Majesty's life has been in jeopardy before, it is not a surprise, but since we have such little data, all have become concerned.

"I advised the CID that if they could not produce more data that we might wish to engage additional help. And that is you, dear brother. And, yes, I am suggesting that perhaps you will observe something they have missed.

"I did, though, expect that they would contact me, to contact you, but alas, they chose to approach you directly. We frequently have these little internal squabbles between my department and theirs, you see."

"You know, Mycroft, of my dedication to Her Majesty. Of course, I will help. Do you have the data with you or must I come to your office?"

"I will get it to you this evening. As is my habit, I decline to bring work of this sort here to the club, as we have even discovered over the years a member or two who have had less than faithful patriotic intentions."

With that, the discussion of the task at hand was concluded for the time being.

Mycroft called for the waiter and we were served. We sat in silence for the remainder of a short meal.

When we had finished, we bid Mycroft adieu and returned to Baker Street.

"Holmes, what do you think of this threat?" queried I.

"It is most intriguing, there have been several attempts over the years on Her Majesty's life and this will likely not be the last. But this one appears different. The known antagonists are nowhere to be found. They are typically clumsy in their methods and end up circulating their plans as if they were a London daily. This seems much different in that regard it would seem."

After that I could no longer get Holmes to speak as he secluded himself, no doubt pondering what he might do to help protect Her Majesty.

It was but a short time later that there arrived at 221B a courier. Holmes answered the door and signed for the package. I tipped the boy and shut the door.

Holmes had retreated to his desk and was carefully opening the package with his silver letter opener. He pulled out a large amount of paper and then...

"We've been duped, Watson!" there is nothing here but blank pages!"

"What's that you say, Holmes?"

"Look for yourself, man! There is nothing here!"

Just as I turned to approach him and see for myself, there was a light tap at our door.

I looked at Holmes with a query on my face. He opened his drawer, retrieved his revolver and nodded for me to answer the door.

I turned the handle quickly and flung the door open whilst moving out of the line of fire should Holmes discern the uninvited guest appeared to be ready to do either of us harm.

Having done so, I was not facing the doorway but looking back at where Sherlock was standing. His frustrated face and the lowering of his revolver told me there was no threat about which we should be concerned."

"I suppose you have received my package?" queried Mycroft.

"Mycroft?!," ejaculated I.

"Yes, it's Mycroft, Watson. Why these games, Mycroft? I almost killed you!"

"Now, Sherlock, you know that wouldn't do. I wanted to be sure that if you were being watched that the perpetrators behind this plot would first attack the courier. I would never have sent the document that way. Too much risk."

"I thus conclude you have it with you?"

"Quite right, Sherlock. And here it is."

"This is it? One piece of paper?"

"Yes, I told you we've not much data. I will remain here as long as you wish to review it. Commit it to memory, if you must, but I shall not leave it with you."

Sherlock appeared as perturbed as I believe I had ever seen him. But he took the paper and read it. He held it to the light for watermarks. He noted the thickness and the quality of the paper. After, what I interpreted as his checking his memory of what it said, he handed it back to Mycroft.

"Thank you, Mycroft, I will get back in touch as soon as I have anything for you."

With that he promptly escorted Mycroft to the door and ushered him, quite unceremoniously, out the door. He closed it and locked it.

"I'll be back, Sherlock!" we heard Mycroft shout, somewhat dryly, through the door.

Holmes quickly ran to his desk and began writing what could only be described as a quick note. I dared not disturb him and waited for him to speak.

"There!" said he.

"Holmes, why such a hurry?"

"Watson, Mycroft and I have played games like this since we were children. He always wishes help but does not hesitate to challenge me more than is necessary.

"I chose to spend what little time I had taking in the physical qualities and characteristics of the paper while I possessed it. The verbiage upon it I committed to memory without attempting to de-cypher its meaning, as that could be done later.

"So, I wrote down what Mycroft denied me from retaining that was on the original document. Now, there is more time to deal with it properly."

"May I see it?" queried I.

"Certainly, but there's not much to go on."

Holmes handed me the paper. It read:

Continue with plan for VR

"Holmes, that could mean anything!"

"Agreed, Doctor. But since both CID and Mycroft believe it to forebode some sinister plot against Her Majesty, I must conclude we cannot dismiss it out of hand.

"I also took note that it appeared to be a woman's hand writing. It was of an elegant cursive style not associated with writing typically produced by a male. I attempted to repeat it as best as my mind photograph would allow me. Mycroft would not have been too excited should I have traced it."

"I observed, Holmes, as you have so often criticized my lack of doing so, that you spent much time with the paper. I must ask, why?"

"Watson, the paper caught my attention right away. It was not ordinary paper at all. It was of a heavier bond than normal writing paper. It…, and I know this seems queer, …it felt *familiar* to the touch, is the only way I know how to explain my reaction to it."

"What shall we do now, Holmes?"

"I have several ideas on the matter which I wish to ponder about."

I knew this was my cue to leave Holmes to himself. He

quickly recovered one of his clay pipes and planted in its bowl some of the fresh tobacco that we had procured just the day before.

Leaving him to his ways, I retreated to my own room to ponder the events of the day and make notes with which I am using this very instant, my dear readers, to re-tell this tale to you. I am in hope that I shall leave nothing outstanding and provide a complete and true account of this amazing adventure.

It was later that night, that there was a knock at our door. Surely, it was not Mrs. Hudson at this late hour. I arose and found Holmes reaching for the handle. He opened it and said aloud before I could even see who was our late-night visitor, "What is the matter?"

Mycroft and Inspector Gregson entered without a reply. Mycroft removed his hat and coat. He walked to the hearth and rubbed his hands to warm them.

"We have found him," said Gregson, dryly.

"Found whom?" queried I.

"No doubt our bond thief, Pottman" replied Sherlock.

"Yes, but…" started Mycroft.

"He is dead," finished Sherlock.

"Quite correct, brother."

"You are sure of his identity?"

"Yes, Gregson took both Marold and Mills to the morgue and they both identified him as Pottman."

"Doesn't this end our tale," proffered I.

"No, Watson, it merely makes this whole affair more sinister with each passing moment.

"Where and how was he found?" asked Sherlock.

"Not too far from here as a matter of fact. Just across the way at Marylebone Station."

"You don't say? Isn't that convenient?" queried Sherlock.

"Sherlock?" queried Mycroft.

"No doubt the remaining bonds where not amongst his affects?" said Sherlock.

"Correct" answered Gregson.

"The method of his demise?"

"It would appear to have been a gunshot to the head. But witnesses say they heard no sound."

"What else did the witnesses say?"

"He was seen talking to a man when it happened. But all the witnesses say the other man was perhaps six feet away from him as they talked. They said they saw no weapon in this other man's hand and in fact he seemed to be in a cape of some type. They never saw his arms or hands. Then suddenly the victim fell to the ground. The other man walked away. Then a woman walked by the fallen body and screamed. That's when everyone took full notice. There was blood all over the platform."

"Ah, then we must assume the worst, Mycroft."

"There have been one or two other such attacks of which I am aware and I fear the deathly hand of our mortal enemy is behind this."

"Moriarty?" asked I.

"Who else, Doctor?" replied he.

"I would like to see the crime scene, Gregson," asserted Holmes with much command in his voice.

"Of course, shall we not walk? It is so close."

"That is fine. Watson, join us if you please. Mycroft?"

"Certainly, Holmes," replied I.

"Not for me, I'm afraid, I must return to the ministry. Sherlock, let me know anything you discover, please" said Mycroft. Mycroft left and it was just the three of us left.

We walked over to Marylebone Station and Gregson took us to the platform. The caretakers had almost finished cleaning where the body had lain. Their efforts were somewhat inconclusive in removing the blood stain, that is to say, an unknowing passenger would likely not have perceived it as anything of consequence, but to our knowing eyes it was the spot where death had claimed someone's life.

"Out in the open, here on the platform? Sends a message doesn't it?" stated Holmes.

"What do you mean, Mr. Holmes?" queried Gregson.

"Gregson, if you want anyone else involved in this to know that deviations from the plan will not be tolerated, this is how you send that message. You are not safe even in public. You can be killed even in public."

"I see. Quite a message."

Just then we were surrounded by Wiggins and his tribe of young irregulars.

"Hello, Dr. Watson!" cried Jonesy.

"Hello, Mr. Holmes!" Wiggins said.

"Wiggins, we are here on important business. Please take the lads away. Why are you here, anyway?"

"We come here often and, ah, ah, ...*pick up* loose coins, you know what I mean, don't ya, sir." said he sheepishly.

"We finds um on the ground, honest!" said one of the other boys.

"We saw you and Dr. Watson and well, we just wanted to tell Dr. Watson we found out where Petey was gettin' into trouble," said Jonesy.

"Not now, Jonesy," said I, sternly. "We are here on important police business. This is Inspector Gregson of Scotland Yard, you see."

Wiggins eyes widened a bit and he quickly said, "Com'on lads, they've got work to do. We'd best be going. Let's stay out of these gentlemen's way."

The band of boys retreated quickly. They turned away and mumbled amongst themselves. Suddenly, one pulled the ear of another and then took off running. The assaulted boy ran after him yelling at the assailant while the others laughed at both of them. Then they all ran off sprinting to see what would come of the spontaneous altercation.

"Who were those young ruffians?" queried Gregson.

"Never mind Inspector, they are young acquaintances of mine. They go where no policeman can go and are invaluable in retrieving data in some of my cases. Should they ever come in your bailiwick for having done something that they shouldn't have, please let me know and I shall deal with them myself. They're a good lot, just need some discipline and something decent to eat now and again."

"Hmm, as you say, Mr. Holmes."

"It is too bad I could not have seen the body before it was moved."

"I'd have ordered to stay for your inspection, Mr. Holmes, but the Railway insisted otherwise and it was causing quite a stir amongst their passengers. The Yard agreed and they ordered it away on the double."

"Do you recall its position? And the wound, which side of the head was it on?"

"As I rightly remember Mr. Holmes, the body was lying somewhat perpendicular to the tracks with his head towards the station. The bullet had entered the right side of his head."

"So, we could conclude he was looking back towards the station. That would fit with what the witnesses stated.

"And you said they stated the man with whom he was talking was in front of him, correct?"

"Yes."

"So, it would likely be impossible for the man to whom he was speaking to be our killer, for how could he have shot him in the right temple, unless at that very moment he'd have turned his head?"

"Yes, I see your point."

"So, either he turned his head, or as I think is more probable, the man he was talking to was likely just a decoy of sorts. I think his purpose was to get Mr. Pottman to stand still long enough to be an easier target.

"If I am correct, then we stand where he stood and then look to our right."

Holmes went to the edge of the blood stain. He laid down a moment and then got back up.

"You see how the platform slopes towards the tracks. The blood had to follow to slope towards the tracks. Thus our Mr. Pottman's head must have fallen here.

"Doctor, in war time you have witnessed a standing man being unfortunately struck in the head by a bullet, yes?"

"And I wish never again to witness such a tragedy."

"Explain how they fall."

"Holmes?"

"How do they fall, man?!"

"Well, not always the same, but I'd say they crumble."

"Yes, exactly, and so we can say, if his head landed here, he likely stood here!" Holmes bent his knees saying

"Pottman was about a foot shorter than I."

"Now we turn our head to the right, and well, well, well…!" as Holmes raised his head ever so slightly.

"What is it, Mr. Holmes?" said Gregson.

"Come see for yourself, Inspector and you too Watson."

"Very interesting," said Gregson.

I took up the position and found myself looking through a cobweb of cast iron of the supporting structure of the depot and there at the end was a window in the distance. It was the only window in a building next to the station. There was, a clear path from the window to where we stood.

"I think a quick visit is in order to the adjacent building, gentlemen?" suggested Holmes.

We left the station and went around to the warehouse that we had observed.

Gregson introduced himself and we were allowed to enter. We found ourselves in some darkness as we stumbled along trying to find the window which I was sure was on the second floor.

We finally found it and Holmes cautioned us to not get too close as he wished to study the trails of footprints leading to and from the window.

We borrowed a torch and it was obvious that there had recently been some activity in this secluded portion of the large warehouse.

"I believe we have found our assassin's perch. Observe the toe and knee mark of his right leg, where he knelt on his knee to make his shot," stated Holmes.

"And if I am not mistaken, we shall find no bullet casing as this would appear to be the work of Moriarty's henchman, Colonel Sebastian Moran and his 'air gun'. I have seen its devastating affects before, and now again. Someday I hope to have my hands on it and get to inspect Von Herder's master craftsmanship."

There was nothing more to see than that this was indeed a perfect stand from which to take down one's prey. We returned to Baker Street and Gregson went on to the Yard.

"Holmes, why would Pottman be killed? I do not understand this at all."

"His purpose was likely no longer needed and while I am averse to guessing, without more data, I can only imagine that perhaps his sale of the two bonds was not in the scheme as set out by our friend Moriarty."

Our further inspection produced no new data. We thus bid Gregson goodbye and returned to Baker Street.

As we approach our abode we found, Wiggins and his tribe waiting for us.

"Oh, hello Mr. Holmes and Dr. Watson."

"Wiggins, have I called for you?" responded Holmes.

"No sir, Mr. Holmes, but we're not here to see you sir, no disrespect, sir. We would like to talk to Dr. Watson, sir."

"Help yourselves," said Holmes with some relief as he retrieved his pipe from his pocket and began to start it. I could see that Holmes was already pondering what we had learned from Pottman's death as he leaned against the door jamb of our abode. His eyes were closed, deep in thought.

"What is it now lads, Mr. Holmes and I have quite a bit going on at this moment." I wanted to get the boys off so that Holmes and I could discuss the case without more interference. "Is this about Petey?"

"Yes, sir. We found out what he's bin getting into."

"And just what would that be?" queried I.

"Well, we tied a very long string to Petey's back leg so we's have a better chance at following him," Wiggins said, as he elbowed Jonesy with a grin indicating it had been Wiggins' clever idea to do so.

"We let him go over by the station and he scampered into a drain pipe on one of the building near there. We didn't see him but we saw the string disappear up the drain. We's figure he has to go to the roof since its one of those drains on the outside of the building, ya know the ones that the rain water comes down. So, we get up there and sure enough he's right there. So, we keep watching and the next thing we know he slithering under some sort of hatch on the roof. We finds our way inside ourselves, and there's a man in there. He's hunched over a table and has a bright light on above him.

"We's know we shouldn't be there, so I motion for the

others to stay behind and not come any farther. I crept along a bunch of boxes and I see Petey eating at a sandwich the man's got next to him on a crate. I was so close I could'a grabbed the sandwich meself.

"But the man, he don't seez me or Petey. He's so busy working at his table he doesn't seez anything. And he's got these strange glasses on. He's writing, I guess, 'cuz he keeps dipping his pen in the ink bottles on the table.

"Well, all of a sudden the man sits up straight, pushes those funny glasses up onto his forehead. I can see he's got blue or green ink stains on his hand and he wipes 'em off. He squints and rubs his eye and reaches over to grab his food. But, wow! He touches Petey instead and does he start a hooping and a hollerin'!

"He got so excited, he knocked over one of the ink bottles and then started cursing to high heaven. He jumped off his chair and started chasing Petey. Petey scampered across the man's table and then the man went berserk. 'A whole weeks' work! I'll kill you! You damn rat! I'll kill you!'

"He picked up a knife and starting swinging wildly at Petey. Well, by this time I figured, this wasn't just a funny game anymore. He seemed to catch sight of me, but it was if he was blind or something. 'Whose there? Colonel?' said he. It was if he knew sort of where I was, but it was as if he could only barely see me. He kept squinting. I just don't know how to explain it Doctor.

"Just then another man showed up and called out 'Jones, are you finished?'

"The man raged at him and shouted

"'No, damn it! That damn rat! He ruined it! I'm going to kill that rat!'

"'What are you talking about,' said the other one.

"'That damn rat ruined it, it cost me a week's work!'"

"'You'd better start over at once. You know the professor will not be pleased.' or something like that. Anyways, we's got outta there as soon as we's could."

"A bit later Petey shows up and he has the same old blue and green colour on him again. See, here he is, but not so ill this time."

I looked down and Jonesy opened his basket. The

creature was there none the worse but this time looked like he'd taken a bath in that ink.

Suddenly, Holmes opened his eyes and looked over at Wiggins intently.

"Wiggins, say that again. The man who showed up, what was the name he used to call to the man with the ink?"

"Jones, Mr. Holmes."

"And what name did this Mr. Jones call out when he wanted to know who was there, when he first noticed you?'

"I think it was, 'colonel', sir."

"That's what I recall you said. I wanted to be certain."

"That is quite an interesting tale, young Mr. Wiggins. Now that you know what Petey's getting into, you need to keep him away. I recommend you all stay away from that man. It being none of your business, and besides he's got every right to be upset if Petey destroyed his weeks' work."

"We must go now. You boys must run along. Here's a bob for ya." said Holmes, as he flipped it into Wiggins hand.

"Gee thanks Mr. Holmes! Goodbye Dr. Watson, and thank you again, sir," he nodded to Holmes as he tossed the coin up and caught it.

"Yes, goodbye, sir" said the two youngest in unison, having not said a word the whole time Wiggins told his tale.

"Why so interested in their story all of the sudden, Holmes?" queried I.

"I will explain later, Watson, but must get ready now. My appointment is in two hours and I do not wish to be late. I asked Mycroft to have you invited also, but he decided against it. There are times when one must request favours, but he felt you were likely not to be offended that he declined to do so on this occasion. Please come with me, though, and we shall see how far you may make it into the inner sanctum."

We freshened up and caught a cabbie to the Palace. At first, he thought we were putting him on. Once he realized it was Holmes, he became more serious and there was an air of pride about him as if he were letting all the other cabbies along the way know he was taking his fare to the Palace.

We arrived a good hour early and Holmes showed his

invitation to the guards. He was allowed in, but, alas, that was as far as I was allowed to go.

I decided to make a go around St. James Park and find a quiet place along the way, knowing I had at least another hour or two before Holmes' return.

I watched the various people strolling along, mostly visitors to London, I observed using the methods I had learned from Holmes over the years. Clothing out of style, a Scottish plaid or an Irishman's cap gave them away in an instant. I imagined why they were here on this day, at this place. But at once my mind imagined too much and I found myself daydreaming and completely forgetting why I was there.

"Watson, come, we have work to do."

"Holmes, you are through?"

"What was she like?" queried I.

"No time for that now, Watson. It is nearly four o'clock and we've not much time. Today is the fourteenth and the game is afoot."

I quickly stood up and ran a few yards to catch up with Holmes. He had hailed a cabbie which we got into. We soon were back to Baker Street.

As we sat in the cab, Holmes retrieved an envelope from his breast pocket. He opened it and pulled out two ornamented pieces of paper.

"Watson, do you notice anything special or unique about these 'passes' that I was given for us to gain admittance to the ceremony at the station?" Holmes handed it to me for my examination."

"No, but they are rather exquisitely drawn up. Perhaps we shall be allowed to keep them? We could frame them and place them on the wall as another trophy or souvenir of sorts, eh? That's what I shall do with mine, if I can."

"I believe it is the key to this whole affair and to the death of our Banker and Mr. Pottman as well.

"What's that you say, Holmes? How is that possible?"

But Holmes did not answer me and it was not until we arrived back at Baker Street that he spoke to me again.

I disembarked, but Holmes remained in the cab and closed the door behind me.

"Watson, please find my binoculars and both our revolvers. We must be ready. I shall return shortly."

"Holmes what is this all about? Won't you tell me about your meeting and the invitation? I do not understand," queried and protested I against his silence towards me upon the subject.

"No, Watson. There will be time to explain all later," and with that he tapped the cabbie and shouted to him, "the Savoy, quick as you can!"

This I did not understand. Why was Holmes headed to the theatre at a time like this? I have on occasion accompanied Holmes to a concert in the middle of a case, but why was he going to a play and without me? I could not, even with all my previous daydreaming, come up with a reason for such an extraordinary behaviour on his part. I would have to wait.

It was not until later that night that I again saw Holmes. He was as excited as ever I think I had seen him in the past.

"Holmes, will you not now tell me what is going on?"

"Watson, it is perhaps best if you do not know all the details at this moment. We have an important engagement tomorrow and we cannot be late. We will have to be vigilant. I am prescribing a solid night's sleep tonight as tomorrow will no doubt be quite taxing. If I tell you tonight the play that is to be performed before us tomorrow, I doubt you would sleep a wink.

"Good night, Watson."

He stepped into his room and shut his door. There would be no more discussion tonight. I was completely overwhelmed by what Holmes had said. Did he not know that I would not be able to sleep, even with what little information he had disclosed to me?

I decided to not fight over it and do my best to accommodate his request. I even considered, my dear readers, of administering to myself a slight sedative to help me sleep. But I quickly dismissed the thought and realized just then, how easy it would have been to justify taking such chemicals. Thankfully, I saw that such a choice could then turn into a habit that perhaps I would not be able to shake. I forced myself to relax and was able to calm myself down. I then poured myself a brandy, drank it and went to bed.

It was now 15 March and I found myself, anxious. After dressing and a quick breakfast of sorts, I gathered my revolver and Holmes' binoculars. We went downstairs and were soon climbing into a hansom.

"Metropolitan Station at Quainton Road," announced Holmes to the cabbie.

"Holmes why are we going there?"

"There's to be a grand opening today, Watson. Do you not want to experience the festivities? They are opening a new line there today."

"But do we not have a more pressing matter? Are we not in need of doing Her Majesty's bidding? And what about our dead banker? Has that case been cast aside as well?'

"Watson, all fair and valid questions. I am hopeful we shall have answers to all of them today."

We arrived and found ourselves in a large gathering. There was a military band, railway officials, spectators, hawkers of all kinds mingling in the crowd selling their wares.

We got out and went into the station. We approached the stage area and Holmes produced our two papers. We left the public behind and I soon found we were behind the makeshift stage at which the opening ceremonies were to be conducted. The stage was set up such that when the curtain was drawn, the crowd would be presented with the front of a freshly painted and sparkling clean steam engine.

Holmes stepped away from me and towards several neatly dressed, but not uniformed, men. He spoke with them for a short while and then returned to me.

"I think all is ready. We must now be very vigilant."

"What, Holmes, are we being so vigilant for?" asked I, in what I must admit was a somewhat perturbed tone of voice.

"You have yet to tell me what is going on!"

"Watson, we are up against our old nemesis and his most notorious henchmen.'

"Moriarty? Moran?"

"Exactly, there is likely to be an attempt on the Queen's life today. I have been asked to help prevent it."

"If they know it is to be here, then why is she coming?"

"I recommended that she not, when she disclosed to me that her security officials thought such an event was the likely venue. With all that we have discovered over the last few days, this is the obvious event.

"She refused to cancel her appearance. She said it would cause fear in the people of the nation to know that their monarch is not safe and was not strong enough to face such cowards in public. She would not have her mind changed. The public must see her at the opening."

"What shall I do, Holmes?" asked I.

"Be ready at a moment's notice. I believe our assassin is among us and we try to catch him before he strikes."

Not very long later, the royal carriage arrived. Shortly after stopping, Her Majesty disembarked and was quickly ushered into the station. There were guards everywhere.

Holmes went over to where she had been sequestered and soon came back with a worried face.

"What is going on, Holmes?"

"Watson, I made my last attempt to convince Her Majesty that she should not attend, but it was to no avail. She insisted on cutting the ribbon. The only thing I was able to do was to convince her to stay out of sight until the last moment and to please make her ribbon cutting appearance as quick as possible."

I could see that Holmes was concerned. By now, the station was filled with the public. Our villain could be anywhere around us.

"My binoculars, Watson. You did bring them as I had asked, did you not?"

"Of course, Holmes. I have my revolver as well. Here is yours," said I, handed him his as discreetly as possible.

I then gave the binoculars to Holmes and he began scouring all the buildings across the street and closest to the station. It seemed useless to me. There were so many windows within sight.

Not taking his eyes away from the eyepiece, he spoke to me. "I am quite sure we will have another attempt with the Colonel's airgun if I am not mistaken, and that could be to our advantage. While it produces very little sound compared to a gun-powdered rifle, which is its main advantage, its main *disadvantage* is that the power of its launching mechanism is greatly reduced compared to that of gun powdered rifle. Thus, its range is limited. I doubt it is accurate to within a foot in diameter at more than fifty feet. The projectile it launches, or bullet should we refer to it as such, will fall rapidly downward after that distance, if my calculations are correct."

"So, we need not look too far away to find where our assassin has positioned himself?"

"Correct, and thus to be close enough would require a written pass like ours to get this close."

"Have you spotted anything yet, Holmes?" queried I.

"No, Watson, but I must keep looking."

Just then the band struck up and started playing *Little Annie Rooney* followed by other popular tunes. We moved closer to the stage and before long, the president of the Great Central had taken to the podium.

"Ladies and Gentlemen, it is a great honour to have all of you here today to witness the opening of the line…"

I had heard such speeches before. Trying to keep up with Holmes as he moved about the station distracted me enough that I soon no longer focused on the orator's words.

The Queen was not on the stage yet, but as the event unfolded it was only a matter of time before she was introduced. At least she was adhering to Holmes' suggestion to keep her actual exposure to a minimum.

"… and it is with my greatest pleasure and honour to present to you, Her Majesty!"

From the left side of the stage the woman, whose image the whole world knew, walked on to the stage. She wore her traditional widow's veil and due to the cold weather had on an additional scarf to help protect her from the winds that were buffeting all the loose scenery erected for the event.

She moved slowly towards the ribbon and was handed a pair of shears. She spoke a few words, but I was too far away to hear her clearly. Her voice was soft as would be expected from a woman her age. With fanfare, and on cue no doubt, the band began to play and the curtain behind her was quickly drawn open revealing the large and brightly decorated steam engine! The crowd clapped and cheered with excitement. The deed was done and she turned to return from whence she came, not doubt again in keeping with Holmes' suggestion.

It was then that she collapsed.

A collective cry and gasp of great concern emanated from the crowd.

Her guards at once collected her up and hurried her into the offices of the station.

"There, Watson! Do you see him?" Holmes yelled at me and pointed to a figure in the distance.

We both tried to follow him but the crowd was moving towards us like a rip tide and we were caught in its pull. As much as we tried, we could not gain ground on the man. Holmes tried his best to alert the guards in the area, but it was to no avail. The crowd was nearly riotous and there is no doubt the guards did not hear Holmes. I could but just make out that he was shouting, but I was trying to listen for his instructions and the guards were not, and I was but six or eight feet from him. Holmes gave up on catching the man. He turned and moved towards the office. Once at the door he turned and yelled back at me.

"Watson, quickly!" I barely heard him say but I saw him motioning me towards the office door.

"I am coming Holmes!" I shouted back ineffectively against the din of the crowd.

I danced through the crowd as fast as I could, trying desperately to make my way through. The crowd was pressing towards where the Queen had been taken.

"Watson, in here," Holmes grabbed me and pushed me over the threshold of the door. He then closed it behind me with the help of several of the guards as they struggled to keep the pressing crowd out.

The office was that of the station master and it had a small couch which easily accommodated Her Majesty's short frame.

"Your Majesty, I am a doctor. Please let me tend to you."

It was then that I saw to my surprise that the women lying on the couch was not the Queen!

I looked at the woman again. She was bleeding from a wound to her shoulder.

I examined the wound and realized it was not serious but appeared that it was luckily just a graze. While there was a fair amount of blood, no serious injury or permanent damage was likely.

"Holmes, who is this woman? It is certainly not the Queen," protested I.

"Watson, let me introduce you to Dame Elizabeth Isherwood. One of the finest actresses in London today."

"Dame Isherwood, I am Dr. John Watson, a confidant of Mr. Holmes. It is a pleasure to meet you, but I must say we should get you to either my surgery or a nearby hospital to mend this wound."

"I would most appreciate that very much, Doctor Watson, isn't it?"

I applied my handkerchief as compress and found some gummed tape to act as a wrap to hold it in place. Holmes arranged a carriage for Dame Elizabeth. She put on an outer coat and the widow's veil and scarf were removed. She could now exit the station as if she were just another member of the public.

As we exited, I could not but help myself except to ask Holmes the most obvious question.

"Holmes, where is Her Majesty?!!"

"Why at the Palace, Watson, where else?"

"Are you telling me she never came here?"

"Correct, Watson. And I must apologise for keeping this little secret from you, my dear friend. I pleaded for your inclusion, but Her Majesty's guard would not allow it.

"Once I had convinced Her Majesty to avoid this unnecessary exposure, I needed to keep the story intact that she would still attend the ceremony. I have seen Dame Elizabeth perform on many occasions and have seen her imitation of Her Majesty, which she performs quite convincingly. Her performance today was no exception to that conclusion of mine. Do you not agree?"

"Well, yes, of course. I was sure it was the Queen."

"When I went to the Savoy, it was to request that she

consider honouring Her Majesty by placing herself in harm's way, that we might catch this villain. Dame Elizabeth graciously accepted the challenge. She knew her life was in danger.

"It is unfortunate that our Colonel was able to avoid capture. My hope was to spot him before he could shoot. He no doubt is far away by now."

"Holmes, how did you know all this would transpire?"

"Our passes and your new patient, that little blue-green rat held the secret.

"Do you remember when we received the document from Mycroft about 'Continuing the plan for VR'?

"Do you recall that I commented that the paper on which it was written felt familiar?

"It was the bonds. That paper is used for bonds and not much else, except for royal invitations such as this event.

"It was never about the money. Moriarty wanted the paper. The paper used for the bonds and for the invitation is in fact, made by the same manufacturer.

"When Wiggins said that the man called out 'Jones' things started to make sense to me. John Jones of Conk-Singleton fame has recently been released from prison. His ability to replicate an invitation for the event made it clear to me that the plan was all focused on the ceremony.

"Remember, the date before which the bonds were not to be sold? Of course, it was after the opening of the new line. I am quite sure if our Mr. Pottman had kept his end of the bargain and not double-crossed Moriarty, he might still be alive. But then again, Moriarty might not have wanted to leave behind any evidence or witnesses of his scheme."

"Why kill the Queen, Holmes? What had she ever done to Moriarty?"

"Nothing, but to a man like Moriarty, that does not matter. His sole quest is to constantly sow discontent and destruction in our fair England. Death of a monarch alone causes disruption to a nation such as ours. Assassination would cause chaos.

"Our Grand Lady has ruled for over sixty years. Some of Her subjects have been born and died knowing no other. To unnaturally remove Her from Her throne would be devastating to the country. It would please Moriarty as perhaps nothing else would. In the ensuing chaos, he would no doubt execute many of his remaining diabolical schemes upon our land."

We arrived at my surgery and I attended to Dame Elizabeth. She was quite a soldier and did not make a sound as I cleaned her wound now with proper medical accoutrements and put on a fresh dressing.

She thanked me and Holmes escorted her to a cab. They got in and Holmes gave the cabbie an address I had no doubt was the domicile of Dame Elizabeth. He tapped his cane and off they went.

The events of the day had taken their toll on me. Once back at Baker Street, I climbed the stairs to our rooms and, when inside, collapsed into my chair.

The day was an active one, and one I shall never forget.

The papers the next day simply stated:

'Queen trips at Ribbon Cutting'

On 15 March, Her Majesty took a spill, having tripped on the stage, at the ribbon cutting ceremonies for the Great Central Railway. The ceremonies marked the opening of its Nottinghamshire to London line, via its new "London Extension". A full recovery of Her Majesty is expected.

THE ADVENTURE OF
THE SALISBURY SPIRE

Pleasant breezes and sunshine greeted me early that morning. A perfectly blue sky could be seen! The air was cool and clean. The storms from the previous evening had lasted well into the night, but broke after midnight. The hard rain had washed the air and one could take a deep breath without worrying about inhaling the soot that so normally inhabited the atmosphere of our grand city. Half of London had opened their windows knowing the air was being refreshed and rejuvenated.

When I felt the breeze upon me, I determined to spend the day resting. It was a Saturday morning and I had made sure my surgery had no appointments scheduled, as I felt two days of relaxation were in order. I began my self-prescription with the joy of knowing that this day contained no demands upon me.

I heard songbirds in the distance, warblers, I felt sure, but of what type I could not discern with my limited ornithological knowledge. Nearby Regent's Park must have been the domicile of the winged creatures, no doubt.

I languished in bed, not wishing to begin any endeavour which would cause me to plan or to anticipate future events. It was as pleasant a feeling as I had experienced in quite some time. With my roommate's demands on me to assist in his latest adventure and the strenuous recent appointments at my surgery behind me, I was determined to make good on my '*doctor's orders*' to relax for two days. Even if I accomplished one day of relaxation, I would have considered it a successful fulfilment of my prescription.

As I lay there listening to the birds, all was as pleasant and relaxing as I could have wanted had I been able to orchestrate the day's morning myself. I heard no sound of Holmes and had enjoyed the thought of letting the old dog lie. He need not be the one who interrupted my glorious morning!

My mind wandered as I had no one thing or purpose on which to focus it. The multitude of ideas I suddenly fancied myself accomplishing with this free time began to overwhelm me. While my eyes were open, staring at the bland dull and fading white plaster of the ceiling, my mind was picturing all the venues I dreamed to visit. Experience, being the best teacher in many venues of life, began to slowly creep into my thinking. Of the many things I thought to do in these two days, I realised soon enough that I was adding to an endless list. I felt a pressure building and an uncomfortableness that began tearing apart my earlier found pleasure.

I could not accomplish one or two of these ideal scenarios should I chose to act upon them. The practicable habits of my profession rushed in to explain to my fanciful side that to partake in these quests most often took some degree of planning, time and money to indulge them.

Suddenly my relaxing morning took on an air of tension which was, of course, self-induced, and contrary to the prescription that had been ordered.

I quickly closed my eyes, took a deep breath and exhaled slowly. This helped me to relax again, but I struggled to find the drifting sound of the singing warblers.

I finally found it and was able to eject the fanciful items from my thoughts and felt my whole body relax once again.

I decided to concentrate on maintaining this state until at least seven o'clock. I would then face the rest of the day as best I could.

My dear readers, it was not to be. With the windows open it was not long before the warblers' songs were being drowned out by the din of my fellow Londoners, as they began their busy day.

By six and three-quarters, the sound was so much I decided the advantage of the breeze was being outweighed on the scale by the magnitude of the noise and confusion of commerce in the streets outside.

I arose and shut the window. I fell back in bed, but alas,

it was no good. I had awakened to a point where the instincts and needs of my body were in control. The grumbling of my stomach demanding breakfast and the slight ache of my head which demanded the caffeine of my regular morning cup of coffee, overwhelmed my ability to return to my daydreams.

My dressing gown around me, I went to our living area, rang downstairs and then awaited the breakfast I had arranged with Mrs. Hudson the night before.

The papers lay at the doorstep of our residence and I allowed myself to return to one of my daily habits that aligned with my day of relaxation. I started with the *Times* and found a fair amount of pleasure in knowing I could spend all day perusing the paper, should I wish to do so.

We'd opened the windows to Baker Street last night after the storm had passed and they were still as we had left them. Somehow the sounds from there were of no consequence as I found my ear could easily ignore these.

I was always amazed at how our cerebral machine, appearing to be no more than a grey cauliflower-like form could accomplish such a feat. Listen intensely to the slightest pin drop when it counted and then able to conversely block out extraneous sounds of everyday life in a large city as if they did not exist at all.

Before too long, a knock on the door alerted me to my breakfast being delivered. Mrs. Hudson had outdone herself. The meal was enough for two!

It was then that I knew I would not be eating alone, as Holmes' door flew open.

"Ah, Mrs. Hudson, thank you!"

"You are certainly welcome, Mr. Holmes," said she, as she set the tray down, turned and exited, closing our door behind her.

"Shall we not partake?"

"Of course, but Holmes, how is it Mrs. Hudson has seen fit to make extra for you?"

"Watson, you have a loud voice when you speak to our dear Mrs. Hudson, no doubt trying to make sure she hears you. I too have noticed a decline in her ability to catch all of a normal voice lately. I simply asked her, on my way out the other evening, to please include the same meal for me when she prepared yours.

"The rich smoky smell of the frying bacon is what awoke me. I listened to that Reed warbler for a while. Then, when I heard Mrs. Hudson ascending, I knew the feast was soon to be enjoyed. Again, I say, shall we?"

As normal, Holmes' explanation was as simple as could be. I was delighted for his company and he seemed to be in a good mood despite having no puzzle before him. We had but a few days ago finished a little case which I have chronicled in my tale entitled *The Adventure of the Speckled Band.* I was glad to see that the darkness had yet to present itself, which I knew could eventually return to him, should nothing challenge him requiring his unique skills.

His attitude was refreshing and his appetite was ravenous. I was afraid I would be left without a full meal had I not asserted myself.

"Holmes, you have had more than your share of bacon, dear fellow!" I admonished him.

"So sorry, Doctor! You are correct. Somehow, I feel a craving for the saltiness of it. You must explain that to me some day, Doctor. Cravings!"

"Too much of anything is not good for one, Holmes. You should know that by now."

"Well-spoken and true, Doctor. I leave the rest to your palate and stomach.

"What does the *Times* have for us today? Is there news of any interest? Perhaps a suspicious death our dear Lestrade is in charge of but is still '*investigating*'?"

"No, Holmes. Nothing I have come across so far. Relax my friend. We've had quite a time just days ago dodging death by that poisonous viper. Shall we not rest and gain strength before our next adventure calls us into action? No doubt there will be something soon amiss in a city as large as London."

"For now, I agree to your prescription, Doctor. I have had several topics matriculating within me upon which I believe a solid and detailed monograph is in order for the furtherment of my profession. Shall you come across anything of interest, I know I can count on you to bring it to my attention."

And with that the room became silent. I finished my meal and then found myself in my comfortable chair set by the window where there was a bright sun shining in from the east. So bright was it, that I found myself squinting at the light reflecting off the paper. I had to reposition myself so as to avoid being temporarily blinded by the persistent intensity.

After the rearrangement, I settled in and was soon engrossed with the various summaries by the paper's editors on the recent actions of the Parliament and the various military movements, engagements, and skirmishes around the Empire.

Holmes had filled his pipe and was beginning to get paper and pen ready upon his desk no doubt to begin a draft of his monograph of which he had mentioned. I had no inkling of its topic but knew it would be an interesting one. As I have mentioned before in my other tales, I always thought it an honour that Holmes entrusted me with the opportunity to read his monographs before he even sent them to his publisher. I was looking forward to this latest one no matter what the subject might be.

The Times possessed no story that kept my interest and I soon found myself picking up the Gazette. I should have realized if the Times had no story to keep me enthralled, the Gazette was not likely to either. I had come to know in these past few years that once a story of consequence to Holmes and me found itself in one paper, the other would certainly have articles about it as well. These papers constantly tried to better one another. The writers tried to cover any aspect associated with the main story and often went out on tangents, no doubt to satisfy their editors' constant desire for more enticing copy. It was a wonder that the stories were different, since the writers usually had talked to the same people involved. It was only the style and embellishment that made much difference. There were, of course, several writers that I preferred. And it was those that I could rely upon to tell a reasonably good story about what had happened whom I read first. Having written about some of my adventures with Holmes made me more aware of getting details correct. I appreciated when the writers got the facts correct, but more often than not they would give credit to the likes of Lestrade or one of his fellow inspectors and fail to mention Holmes' involvement at all. This of course is why I had begun writing down the tales of our adventures separately, so as to give the real credit to whom it was due, Mr. Sherlock Holmes.

The Gazette was not presenting any more pleasure than the Times, so, I decided to abandon my goal of a lengthy morning of reading hoping to educate myself on the latest of the goings on of the peoples of London.

Holmes was deep in thought and I dared not disturb him. I thus decided to dress and go for a leisurely walk in the Park.

It was as I returned, having been lifted in spirit by a rejuvenating walk and after enjoying feeding some of the waterfowl that inhabited Regents, that I arrived back at 221B Baker Street only to find the noon post being delivered.

There were a few notes to me and a few to Holmes, but it was the letter addressed to Holmes from Salisbury, Wiltshire, that caught my attention. The envelope was of an extraordinary paper. This was a letter to be taken seriously.

I climbed the stairs to our rooms and laid Holmes' letters next to him on his desk making sure that the Salisbury letter lay on top in a most conspicuous manner. I hesitated a moment, hoping he would see it and perhaps immediately share its contents with me. But he did not even acknowledge the delivery. I retired to my chair and began opening my letters.

None were of any great importance. I then decided to wait for a while hoping to see if Holmes would care to join me for lunch.

"You seem anxious, Watson, eh?"

"I don't know what you mean, Holmes."

"Ever since you delivered the letter from Salisbury, you have awaited my opening it.'

"What makes you think that, Holmes? I mean… I did not think you even noticed it." I arose and walked up behind his chair.

"Watson, your body screams to me with your wanting to see what correspondence lays within. I shall open it now, if only to help relieve you of your failing attempts to subdue your feelings on the subject."

Holmes picked up the letter and then his letter opener. With one swift, back-handed like motion, he opened the letter, put down the opener and took out the contents.

Unfolding a cream coloured paper, it consisted of only that one sheet. It took Holmes but a minute to read its contents and then he handed it to me over his shoulder with a certain attitude which relayed to me that, despite its contents and from whence it came, he did not seem all that interested in what it had to say.

I took the paper and stepped over to my chair. I sat down and began to read this intriguing letter hoping it contained a new challenge for my roommate.

The hand written letter read as follows -

April 15, 1883

Mr Sherlock Holmes
221 B Baker Street, W1
London, England

My dear sir,

I have heard of your expertise in matters that either baffle the police or are considered not worthy of their investigations.

My situation is one which I cannot, in good conscience, state is either of these, but being troubled by it, I write to you so as to get your opinion on the matter.

If it would be possible for you to accommodate my invitation to come and speak to me upon it, I would most certainly be in your debt.

I apologise that I cannot come to you for advice, as my duties here in Salisbury prevent my travel.

Hopefully, this letter, when delivered, finds you in good health and with a spirit perhaps ready to assist me with my problem.

If you would be so kind to inform me, should you choose to accept my invitation, of when you shall arrive. I will then

Daniel J. Darrouzet

arrange for your transportation from the rail station to the Cathedral.

Lastly, I shall arrange lodgings for you in the Cathedral Close. Please let me know what payment you charge for services such as you provide,

With all God's blessing upon you,
I remain,

Most Reverend John Wordsworth
Bishop of the Diocese of Salisbury
Wiltshire, England

"I say, Holmes, you've gotten popular even outside London, my good fellow!"

"And for what might a country Bishop need my services, Watson, eh? Perhaps he's looking for some lost sheep from his land? I doubt this invitation will provide much challenge, Doctor. I shan't respond for a fortnight and we shall see if anything else comes along providing more excitement."

"But Holmes, a man of the cloth is asking for your help. Would it not be in good form to assist this bishop? You never know when his help may be of an advantage to you in some other case."

"I dare say, Watson, the likelihood of needing the help of the Bishop of Salisbury is not high. I shall stay with my decision and let us see what arises in the next few weeks. If by then we have nothing, perhaps I shall agree to visit him."

That was the end of the discussion and I knew no further protestation on my part would budge Holmes from his position.

I returned to my newspapers which were very paltry in their offerings and soon was bored. This day of relaxation had turned into one of frustration with Holmes' attitude about the letter.

I decided there was no good advantage to me in my quest for relaxation should I continue with any more interchange with Holmes. I would have to stay to myself and stick to my self-prescribed remedy for relaxation.

I sat in my chair and began to daydream as best I could allow myself.

"Watson, Watson!"

"Wha… What?" replied I, half awake.

"Wake up, man. Wake up! Shall we go out and get dinner?"

"What's that you say?"

"You have slept the day away, my dear friend."

I looked about me and found the day had indeed gone. The sky was dark and as I arose from my chair, I could see the yellow gaslights of the streets being lit one by one.

"Oh my! Have I truly been asleep all afternoon?" queried I.

"Yes, my friend. I had to jostle you a time or two to stop that snoring of yours. You undoubtably sound like Carroll's *Walrus* would have, when he slept."

"Oh, Holmes, tell me I do not snore! You've not mentioned it before in all this time we've shared Baker Street?!" said I pleadingly and much embarrassed.

"Watson, I have heard it many a time before, but the walls separating our rooms spare me the brunt of it. Once I choose to sleep, it bothers me not. But here, in the same room, 'twas even a challenge for me to continue to concentrate this day. I have to admit, I chose to experiment on you, my dear friend."

"You did what?"

"You see, I decided to see what distraction placed upon you in your slumber resulted in the longest time between your snoring fits.

"I started with a feather under your nose. This worked, but only for the least amount of time. I believe your record with this technique was a mere two minutes and forty-nine seconds.

"Next, I tried slamming a book on the table here. But that was not much better. You lasted only three minutes and twenty-six seconds until you started again.

"After that I found that jostling your shoulder produced the best results. I could stop your snoring for more than twenty minutes! On average twenty-four minutes and seventeen seconds, to be exact. The longest being twenty-six minutes and thirty-eight seconds!"

"Holmes, you are in need of a good puzzle, my good friend. Why on earth would you spend time watching me snore and not only watch me, but time the cycles of my snoring?"

"Watson, I find this type of information, to which no one else pays attention, vital in my line of work. These obscurities happen every day and no doubt play a part in mysteries that I must solve. What wakes one up from a deep slumber is of interest to me. When a client comes and reports a theft to me and I ask them were they not awakened, I query that to understand what does and does not awaken one. What does the body do when stimulus is applied during those hours when we spend that part of our life with the cousin of death? Your snoring and response, has given me a whole new idea for a monograph on sleep, my dear fellow!"

What could I say, my dear readers? How could I respond to this man's queries into one of the more bizarre aspects of human existence? In a way, I knew as he spoke, that these items could easily be of use to him. Thus, my rebuttal against his statements, were I to attempt one, and which would likely lead a stranger to question his sanity, would be of no merit. This was the Sherlock Holmes I had come to know so well and I found myself actually intrigued by his statements. What did we do or react to whilst sleeping? Were we able to discern anything in that state? It was Holmes' queries about such occurrences in life that had me questioning half the things I'd taken a lifetime to learn. The man never ceased to amaze me.

"Well, Holmes, I apologise if I kept you from your work. I was not aware that I snored."

"Of course, you didn't, Watson. I enjoyed every minute of it. The most interesting experiment was when I set the kettle to boiling and once it had begun, I brought the kettle over and pointed the steam in your direction. It took several minutes, but before I knew it your hand had reached for your collar and was trying to loosen it."

"Well, now that is fascinating, Holmes! I had a dream I was back in India on my way to the front in Afghanistan. The weather was abominable. The heat and humidity were most unbearable. I loosened my collar and was called down for it by our Regimental SM!"

"That is certainly interesting, Watson! You somehow brought the actual stimulus into your dream. How intriguing! I must sometime spend more time on this unusual activity. How our minds work, eh, Watson?

"Shall we not find dinner, now? I am famished. Let us go to Ship and Turtle's, as I fancy some turtle soup. Hopefully we shall find it still open, as I fear it may have been condemned. The last time I was there it was in need of much repair. If it is open, we shall eat there. If not, we'll find another that boasts of its turtle soup and in either case it shall be my treat."

"Holmes, I accept," said I. Having involuntarily been a subject of Holmes' experiment, and in keeping with my self-prescription, I was delighted to be compensated for my contribution to his work and to end the day without having to plan from whence came my evening meal.

As the air was still fresh, we decided on an open carriage and enjoyed the wanderings of the citizens of London who likewise decided to spend the cool evening out of doors enjoying the cleansed air. The ride to Leadenhall Street was not too long and was uneventful.

While it looked as if it were to collapse whilst we were there, it had an atmosphere not found elsewhere We enjoyed their famous dish and the service. We listened to others' stories who spoke without regard for those around them hearing their tales. The night there ended quite pleasantly and we returned to Baker Street without event.

A fortnight passed. No new puzzle had presented itself to Holmes. I could discern a shift in his attitude. I had hoped Holmes would decide to contact the Bishop, but he had not mentioned him at all.

It was the next morning that the next letter arrived. The same envelope with the same single sheet enclosed.

Holmes refused to open the letter this time, although I was highly suspicious that he delayed opening it just to rustle my feathers!

"Why don't you go ahead and open it, Watson? I am quite sure it is the same request as last time."

"All right, Holmes, I shall."

The Bishop sounded more despondent this time and literally begged Holmes to come to Salisbury.

Daniel J. Darrouzet

April 29, 1883

Mr Sherlock Holmes
221 B Baker Street W1
London, England

My dear sir,
I have not heard from you. I am in desperate need of your help.
Please let me know if you can help me or not. If you cannot, I know not where else to turn next.
Please find it in your soul to help – I find myself not beneath begging you to come to our aide.
Please also inform me of your charges for your services.

With all God's blessing upon you,
I remain,

Most Reverend John Wordsworth
Bishop of the Diocese of Salisbury
Wiltshire, England

"Holmes, how can you ignore this man's pleas? It has been a fortnight and nothing has presented itself to you. I must insist that you at least respond to the Bishop's letter."

"Watson, I shall, and I shall do so this very moment."

That was all he said. What else could I then say? He'd taken the wind out of my sails as he had agreed with my instruction to him. I commenced to remove myself from his immediate presence and watched as he gathered up paper and pen with which I could only conclude he was writing back to the Bishop. I heard no more from him upon the subject for two or three days. It was when a third letter from Salisbury arrived that the subject came up again.

"Watson, are you free to join me?"

"That depends on why you wish for me to join you. Another of Hallé's concerts or some adventure for which I must bring my pistol?" said I, having perhaps released some stored-up anger as to Holmes' reluctance to help the Bishop of Salisbury.

"Now there, Watson. I take it that you are upset with me?"

"Well, to be quite truthful and blunt about it, yes. Yes, I am. I am quite perturbed with you, Holmes! You pout about with no puzzle to satisfy you and there was a perfectly good call to action, by a Bishop no less, and you ignore it as if it was one the Irregulars being accused of stealing sweets. There are times I do not understand you, Holmes!"

"Rest assured, my friend, I do not hold your outburst against you. You are correct, I have quite purposely delayed helping the Bishop. I have not had a great desire to travel right now. But it appears I will have no choice but to go to Salisbury. It was this case on which I was asking if you wished to accompany me. Since I find you unhappy with my decisions so far, I see why you would be critical of my choices. I shall be content to go alone."

"It is not that I do not wish to accompany you, Holmes, I just did not understand your lack of interest in his case."

"He makes not one mention of what it is about, Watson. How is my curiosity to be piqued, if he shan't tell me what the problem is in his letters?"

"Well, you have a point. I agree he is not forthcoming with any 'data' as you would say. Because I know the kind of cases that intrigue you, how about we agree that I visit the Bishop and should it be the type of case that would interest you, I shall inform you immediately? That way we move forward on my desire to help the Bishop and you do not travel unless it is deemed worth your while. What say you?"

"Doctor, you are most kind. That suits me well. I cannot explain to you my desire not to leave London at the moment. I am quite sure it has nothing to do with our most recent adventure, but there is a sense to which I am responding that is telling me that I am to be needed here soon. To be honest, I have never had such feeling before. A premonition perhaps? I find your solution acceptable and I appreciate you offering it under these circumstances."

"Not at all, my good fellow, not at all."

Holmes then showed me the correspondence he had received from the Bishop giving him instruction as where he was to stay. The Bishop's assistant was to meet

Holmes at the station and take him to the lodgings. The plan was for him to return the next morning and bring Holmes (now me) to the rectory at the Cathedral in time to meet with the Bishop for a ten o'clock appointment. Holmes then dashed off a quick telegram apprising the Bishop of my arrival in Holmes' stead.

In the mean time I checked Bradshaw's for the time-table of the LSWR to see when the next train would arrive at Salisbury, Fisherton Street Station.

I believed that my journey would be a short one, so, I merely grabbed my travel kit that I always had prepared for such events. I had three days' worth of my needs covered and I was sure I'd be back by then.

The next train left at three o'clock in the afternoon from Waterloo and I had arranged passage on it. Directly, I soon found myself aboard, traveling steadily towards the Bishop's Cathedral in order to find out what help Holmes could provide him.

Several hours later I reached my destination and was approached by a young prebendary who offered to take my kit. I insisted that he not, as it was of no great burden upon me.

We soon departed the station in his dog-cart and within a short time he had deposited me at a quaint cottage in the Cathedral Close. This provided quarters for visitors of the Bishop, when he had them. It was modest but neat. All was clean and the view from the small sitting area looked out across a tree-lined, velvet, green meadow at the great Cathedral. I felt I was viewing the Cathedral as perhaps Constable had, when he painted his famous rendition.

I settled in and then took a brief walk around the Close to find an establishment for my evening meal. After having satisfied my hunger, and then with the sun setting on this mid-spring evening, I returned to my lodgings. The arrangement was for the prebendary to pick me up tomorrow at half nine o'clock, for my ten o'clock appointment with the Bishop.

Right on time was he with his dog-cart. He spoke little and I had no idea as to what topic should I attempt to engage him in conversation. It would have been in vain, though, as the dog-cart had a loose fitting somewhere in the undercarriage that made conversation all but impossible.

He deposited me at the entrance to the ancient Cloister and it was there that I was greeted by another cleric, a small, gaunt bespectacled man named Father Anthony. He was a precentor, or so I learned whilst we conversed as he accompanied me to the Bishop's office.

"Your trip was without problems?"

"Yes, yes it was."

"I'm glad to hear that. Sometimes it seems our visitors have problems getting from London to Salisbury."

"Here we are," said he, as we entered an ante room just outside what I presumed was the Bishop's office.

"Brother Jillion, this is Dr. Watson. I believe Dr. Watson is on the Bishop's schedule for today, is that not correct?"

"Yes, ten o'clock."

"It was a pleasure to meet you, Dr. Watson. I must return to the Cathedral, now. We have choir practice at ten o'clock and I mustn't be late."

"Thank you," said I to Father Anthony.

"Please have a seat Dr. Watson. The Bishop is finishing a meeting and will soon be available," said Brother Jillion.

I took a seat and began a visual excursion trying to absorb the ornate design of the place. The premises were built in the thirteenth century and thus were of a gothic design. The pointed arches cascading throughout the place lent it a beauty that one rarely sees in the modern architecture of London.

The craftmanship of the stone and wood were of the most superior quality. The perfection of each piece seemed to convey the desire of the craftsman who created it to provide only the best and by doing so, their work became an offering or prayer to their God.

The Cathedral clock had struck ten and I was still seated. It was but a few minutes after ten o'clock that I was led into the Bishop's office.

"Dr. Watson, My Lord," said Jillion.

The Bishop greeted me with much enthusiasm.

"Dr. Watson, I am delighted you have come. I'd hoped

Mr. Holmes would have been able to arrive himself, but I must console myself that at least he felt my request was important enough that he saw the need to send his most trusted associate.

"I have read the tales of your adventures with Mr. Holmes and I dare say they leave me thrilled with excitement! Mr. Holmes' and your ability to solve the most unique puzzles is so fascinating!"

"It is my pleasure to accommodate your invitation, My Lord," replied I to his highly supportive reception of my appearance at the Cathedral.

After being ushered over to a long deep-red-leather chesterfield, the Bishop took his seat in one of the opposing matching chairs. I marvelled at the style, and comfortableness of the sofa.

He, no doubt a man who knew how to manage his time, quickly dove into describing the problem about which he was asking for Holmes' help.

"I've asked for help, Dr. Watson, because I believe we have something or someone, trespassing or even *living* in the tower or perhaps the spire of the Cathedral. I am sure you know of its fame, it being the tallest spire in all of England?

"Yes, of course. It is quite a well-known church," said I, not wishing to let on that I had just learned this fact from his own tongue this very moment!

"Cathedral," corrected the Bishop, showing a slight sign of perturbance at my *faux pas*.

"Yes, Cathedral, my apologies" said I.

"How long has this been going on?"

"We suspected something was amiss after Lent began this year, which was 7 February."

"So, for several months now?"

"Yes."

"You have posted guards of sorts?"

"Yes, but to no avail. When we post them, nothing is seen or is noticed. After a week or so, no one believes that anything is happening and we let down our guard. It is always a few days later a suspicious event occurs and we try to post observers again. This has been going on since February, Dr. Watson."

"What happens, that raise such suspicions?" queried I.

"They are little things, almost nothing really. Several of the monks said they had noticed things, but initially dismissed them. They did not even mention them to anyone thinking they were of no consequence. It was only after the first time the bell rang, that they discussed these between themselves."

"The bell rang? Don't the bells ring normally?"

"Yes, yes, of course. I'm sorry. So, to be clear, the original bells were removed about a century ago from a separate bell tower which was demolished. We have clock bells that ring every hour and at a simple quarter hour and half hour as it should. It was when it rang when it was not supposed to, that got one's attention. And I suppose I should clarify that when I say 'rang,' I don't mean in a normal clear fashion. The sound it made was muted. I'd almost describe it as if one had bumped into the bell. But you see, that does not exactly make sense, because the smallest bell weighs over 500 pounds. It was a mystery to us all. But the couple of times these incidents have happened are what got the whole monastery discussing what could be happening in the tower."

"I see. Is that all?"

"No. We've had other events that sound ridiculous when spoken aloud, but when confronted with them first hand, they seem to get the better of one's thinking."

"After the Easter Vigil, we were exhausted. The ceremony starts at sundown on the Saturday night before Easter Sunday, and finishes when it finishes. The normal service can easily be three hours, but this year it took longer, closer to four, for all sorts of reasons I will not bore you with since they were administrative errors that I should have myself have taken responsibility to do, but I did not do so, having delegated them. Thus, I must take blame.

"In any event, as I said, we were all exhausted from the long service which ended practically at midnight. What with Easter morning services upon us early, we did not catch much sleep between services.

"We headed to our cells back over on this side of the monastery in virtual darkness. We were in the courtyard of the Cloisters and that was what was so strange. We suddenly saw our shadows once we had gotten clear of the Cathedral itself. 'How odd?' we said to one another.

"I turned around to see what it was that was the source of the light causing the shadows. And to my surprise it was coming from one of the windows in the tower that supports the spire. I did not believe what I was seeing. There was no reason for there to be anyone up there at that time and certainly no reason for a light to be on. I sent Father Anthony back to see who was in the tower. I then went on to my cell to catch some sleep before the early Easter morning mass.

"Well there were so many things on my mind when preparing for an Easter service, I'd completely forgotten about the light. It wasn't until later that day that all had settled down a bit and we retired for a quiet dinner in the Cloister dining hall.

"We ate a delicious dinner of smoked ham and spent the rest of the evening in quiet conversations mostly centred on the events of the glorious day. The day we had celebrated our Lord's resurrection!

"I must say it was one of the more pleasant Easters I have spent here at the Cathedral except that our little incident of the night before was about to disturb us further.

"Father Anthony came over to me and said, that he had gone back to see about the light. When he got there the light was out. He had seen it from the outside, so I knew he knew what he was looking for. He had taken a torch from the lower level of the tower and found himself in complete darkness at the top of the tower.

"He said that he thought he heard an occasional board creaking, which was as best he could surmise the sound made on the floorboards of the different levels in the tower leading up into the spire. He went so far as to peer up into the spire but decided, and rightly so, that it was not wise to venture into the spire for many reasons, the primary one being that some of the supporting structure is timber and several centuries old. In fact, no one is allowed in the spire. As it is supported with many cross-bracing wood struts and rises one hundred eighty feet, his torch could not provide enough light to determine if there was anyone actually in the spire.

"Other than the pride of its height, there is no treasure in the spire. It is a dangerous place even in good light, as the wooden bracing is old and the architects that occasionally come to inspect it have warned us to not climb up in it without good reason. And I have no reason to chastise him for not going farther for he was as tired as the rest of us. And besides, why would anyone wish to seclude themselves in the spire? It makes no sense, Dr. Watson."

"I agree with you, Bishop. Could perhaps I go visit the spire, so that I may tell Mr. Holmes what I have learned so far?"

"Of course, of course, but I must warn you, the journey up is not for the faint hearted."

He arose and went to the door through which I had entered and leaned out.

"Brother Jillion, please have that new inquirer, uhm..."

"Mr. Ortraimy, My Lord?"

"Yes, please have him come over and escort Dr. Watson here over to the Cathedral and instruct him to show Dr. Watson the tower and especially the entrance to the spire."

"Yes, My Lord."

"Dr. Watson, I am so glad you came. Do you not think this is the type of problem Mr. Holmes would find interesting? I certainly hope he does.

"I will have to say goodbye now, as I have a meeting shortly for which I must make further preparations. I hope we will be able to count on you and Mr. Holmes to solve our little mystery. Good day to you, sir."

And with that I found myself outside again in the waiting area with Brother Jillion having sent a note to this person who was to escort me to the tower. It took a good twenty minutes between the time he sent his note off and when Mr. Ortraimy arrived.

"Mr. Ortraimy, this is Dr. Watson. The Bishop has requested that you take Dr. Watson to the Cathedral and show him the entrance to the spire. As you are new here, yourself, Mr. Ortraimy, please remember that admittance into the spire is prohibited. Please, I must ask that both of you agree that neither of you will go any farther than the top of the tower itself. Again, entry into the spire is forbidden. Gentlemen?"

"Yes, I understand," replied I.

"Yes, Brother, I agree. Please follow me, Dr. Watson."

This *inquirer* appeared to be about one score in age, a normal age for one seeking entrance into the religious life, one would think. But his hair was thinning a bit and there were the occasional grey strands mixed in with the remainder of his dark brown mane. Perhaps it just resulted from poor fate in his family lineage passed down by some prior generation.

Mr. Ortraimy retrieved the keys for the Tower and we left. I trod along behind him in silence as we wove our way through the various hallways and rooms leading to the courtyard of the monastery. After walking around the courtyard under a gothic arched ambulatory carved of a light-coloured stone, we passed the Chapter House and finally entered the Cathedral proper at the south transept.

I expected to travel to the centre of the Cathedral to enter the tower which rose over the intersection of the two lines of the Latin cross plan. But Mr. Ortraimy continued on to through the nave and we entered the narthex of the Cathedral. He then motioned me over to the corner.

There was a door which he unlocked and we both entered. We then travelled down a short, narrow, stone-walled passage with pointed archways, which ended at a spiral staircase. The space was poorly lit with a subdued light coming from somewhere in the stairwell above. Ortraimy had a torch with him but he chose not to use it.

As we began our climb, I noticed the treads and risers were all hewn from solid pieces of stone. The roof of the stair above us was made of the treads of the next level above. As each stone circled a central point, the rounded end of each piece created a column holding up the centre of the staircase. There was but a yard, I'd say, from the outside wall to this centre column. The ingenuity of the masons who built the Cathedral was apparent in the construction of these vertical passageways. The odour of the stone was omnipresent as every surface was made of it. One could still smell the dankness of it, most of which had not seen the light of day in nearly seven hundred years.

I could see no windows, but after a minute or so, that dim, strange light I'd noticed when we entered, seemed to get brighter as we ascended, Finally, I saw the source. A narrow window, of sorts, not operable mind you, just leaded glass of diamond shapes, built into the stone work. It reminded me of one of those narrow slits from which the archers of medieval times would fire their arrows down upon their enemies.

"Thank God for some light!" said I.

"The *lancet* windows help us for now. We shall use our torches in the attic."

"Almost as in a prison," I shouted upward, but got no response. I found myself climbing more steps than I believed possible. Again, dear readers, the stairs did not have long straight flights like the two flights at Baker Street. Soon, the steps felt to my legs as being endless.

The stone treads had been worn down at the edge no doubt from over the last six to seven hundred years of traverse by the prior clergy responsible for maintaining the Cathedral.

After we had passed the lancet window, the light became dim again. Before long, though, another faint light foretold that another of these lancet windows to the outer world was to present itself to us.

How high one had ascended was difficult to tell. It occurred to me, I know not how, but that here I was, maybe sixty or seventy feet above the ground by now and it was but a few feet of stone that separated me from being in thin air! I must say, that the thought of both being confined in such a narrow space and yet knowing the same stone which entombed me was keeping me safely contained in its grasp while so high, gave me a chill up my spine!

We finally reached the top and exited out into an attic space. The smell of the centuries of accumulated dust was overwhelming. As I took a more normal step forward, I realized the mesmerizing circular climb had taken its toll on my equilibrium.

"May we wait a moment, Mr. Ortraimy? I think perhaps the stairs have gotten the better of me."

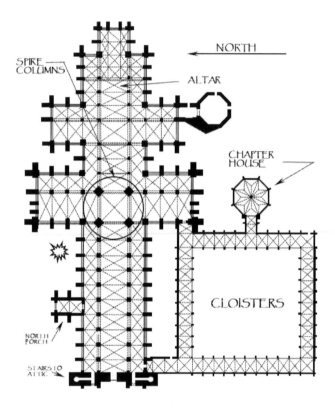

SALISBURY CATHEDRAL

PLAN

NO SCALE

DJD '19

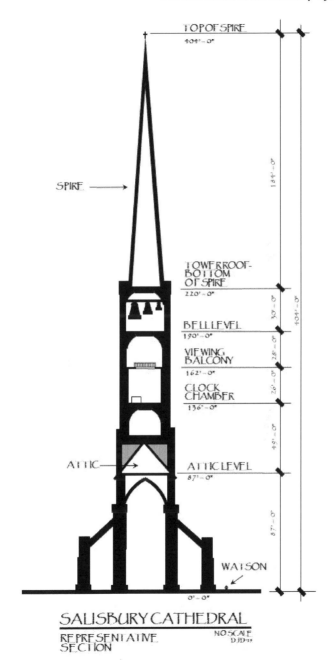

TOP OF SPIRE
404' - 0"

SPIRE →

184' - 0"

TOWER ROOF-
BOTTOM
OF SPIRE
220' - 0"

30' - 0"

BELL LEVEL
190' - 0"

28' - 0"

VIEWING
BALCONY
162' - 0"

26' - 0"

CLOCK
CHAMBER
136' - 0"

404' - 0"

49' - 0"

ATTIC →

ATTIC LEVEL
87' - 0"

87' - 0"

WATSON ←

0' - 0"

SALISBURY CATHEDRAL

REPRESENTATIVE
SECTION

NO SCALE
DJD-19

299

"If you wish, Dr. Watson. As we have arrived at the attic over the nave, we are merely eighty-seven feet up. The top of the tower is two-hundred twenty feet, so we are less than half way. There is another one hundred thirty-three vertical feet to go."

I was not dizzy, but the tightness of the space and the endless climbing and the circular path affected me more than I had expected it to do.

As we were not yet under the tower proper, we experienced mostly darkness and now depended on the torch to see our way as he had alerted me before. The natural walk on a relatively level surface was a welcome change from the arduous circular climbing. As I now relieved the burning feeling in my quadriceps, I started to feel a bit normal except for the darkness of the attic. I was also delighted that I could spread out my arms and not touch anything.

"We should wait," said Ortraimy.

"Yes, I am happy to do so."

"No, I think it would be wise to wait for the hour."

"I'm not following you, Mr. Ortraimy, wait for what?"

Just then the bells began announcing the eleventh hour. We were still in the attic and the bells sounded as if they were on the other side of the door we were about to open. The last bell struck. Ortraimy then opened the door before us.

The lingering sound of the last rung bell was still audible. Its hum slowly died away, though. I was grateful he had paused as the sound surely would have been painful had we been in the tower itself.

"The bells are tolerable and not fatal as some bell towers are, but why endure their auditory assault when it is not absolutely necessary. It would be best if we avoid the bell level when the noon bells ring."

This seemed reasonable and I realized should we be trapped in the bell level of the tower when the mid-day bells would be ringing, it would likely be a very unpleasant experience. I promised myself I needed to move quickly.

Soon, we crossed over to one of the corners of the tower and began another climb in a circular stairway.

"We've another fifty feet or so to go to get to the clock chamber," said Ortraimy to me, as he continued to climb.

After a few minutes more, I was glad to again exit the circular stair and found that we were in an open space that no doubt was in the tower proper. There was sunlight from above which I was ever so glad to see.

I looked up and could see high above me a somewhat empty chamber soaring upwards for what I estimated was nearly sixty feet. There were iron bars crisscrossing to each side of the structure, no doubt in an effort to stabilize it since its original construction. My staring at them caught Ortraimy's attention.

"The larger bars closest to us are the most recent additions," stated Ortraimy quite matter-of-factly. "The smaller thinner ones were put in place in the fourteenth century. I've been told each bishop who presides here wishes to avoid the calamity of Lincolnshire while they are in charge of Salisbury Cathedral."

"Oh, yes, I've heard of the poor Lincoln Cathedral. Fell down or something, right?" said I remembering some long-lost historical data from my school days.

"Yes, from 1311 until 1538, I'm told it was the tallest building in the world, even surpassed the great pyramid in Egypt. But in 1539, their spire collapsed and was never rebuilt. Thenceforth, Salisbury has held the title of tallest spire, at least for churches in England, and does not wish to relinquish it," continued Ortraimy.

"No doubt, no doubt," mumbled I, continuing to observe the architecture of the tower base.

The room had tall gothic arches with solid walls just behind these arches. There were two hexagon-shaped columns along with slender circular columns rising in between. The light in the room was most adequate but came from a level high above as there were no windows on this level.

"Over here is the clock mechanism," said he, pointing. He walked over to a large wooden box with a plethora of gears and levers. I followed him and was amazed at the mechanical apparatus.

"We cannot see the spire from here? queried I.

"No."

"I see. Then we are to go higher?"

"Yes, as I said before, Doctor, we have roughly eighty-five feet more to climb if you wish to see the spire itself. Are you ready, Doctor?"

"Yes, I suppose I'll have to be," said I, as I had felt some relief being in a more open space with the sun shining into it.

"I have come this far, let us continue our journey, young sir," said I with renewed vigour now that my legs had had a chance to reacquaint themselves again with a level surface.

"How do we ascend?" queried I, as I saw no means to do so.

"Over here, sir. There are but more of the same as before."

My enthusiasm shrank from me. Hidden in the corners of the structure, were more circular stairs!

We proceeded to one of the corners and again entered another spiral staircase.

This time the stairs were narrower. Certainly, less than three feet. I went slower and again began to feel some of the same sensations as when in the first spiral staircase, but a bit more intense as the walls were even closer.

After rising about thirty feet we entered into a new space that was not much more than a balcony which looked down into the clock chamber. We again entered an even narrower spiral staircase which had to be less than two feet wide. As a result, there was not much tread upon which to place one's foot. This caused much contortion of my body.

This stair went up clock-wise, as had all the other we had climbed. Thus, it was my left quadricep which bore the brunt of lifting my entire body weight upward in what I guessed were roughly eight-inch intervals. I tried alternating my step by using my right leg, as one would when going up a normal set of stairs, but that caused me to practically cross my legs so as to get my right foot on enough tread to allow me to take a step up. It was not practical and I once again began only making use of my left leg to ascend. I knew before long I would have to give the poor muscle some rest. But Ortraimy was not flagging. I had to keep up as he was out of sight.

There were only two lancet windows to light the way, and then one small triangle shaped window with rounded edges. When I had got to it, there was Ortraimy waiting for me.

"What an odd shaped window?" said I.

"Trefoil."

"What?"

"It's called a trefoil window. It is a common element in gothic architecture. I believe it comes from the Latin, *trifolium*, which means 'three-leaved plant.'"

"I see, yes, *trifolium*."

"Have we much further to go?"

"Next is the bell level. We will be there soon."

We continued our journey and soon reached the bell level.

"We are another fifty-four feet above the clock chamber or one hundred ninety feet above the Cathedral floor. Only thirty more feet to the top of the tower and the bottom of the spire."

In the bell level, there were large windows on each of the four walls that brought light into the chamber. These were of leaded glass. On the eastern side of the tower, one could see the louvers by which the sound of the bells escaped from their domicile to shout out to all those around Salisbury the time of the day.

"Our bells were in a separate tower, but were removed a century ago. All we have now are these bells that are strictly for the clock."

We began our final trek again. The endless circuitous route, the narrow passage, which constantly caused my coat to scrape against the wall, became more than I could handle all at once. After at least ten minutes of climbing, I had to stop. "Shall I wait for you, Doctor?" yelled he down to me.

"Perhaps, that would be helpful," responded I.

After a few moments, Ortraimy began again.

"I believe it would be wise to rest a while longer before we go further. This type of exertion is not something to be done when not prepared for it. While I see myself as reasonably fit for my age, it is not often that I require my body to ascend to such heights, especially with any thought of doing so, so quickly.

"I am quite able to handle a few flights of stairs, as even my current dwellings demand of me each day. But what we are trying now, is to climb twenty-two floors!"

"You are correct, Doctor. And to the top of the spire, could we go there, would be by your reasoning, an additional eighteen."

"My good man, just a quick journey to the top of the tower would kill a man unfit for it. No, we must take our time. While I am interested in helping the good Bishop, I have no desire to cause myself to expire with unnecessary effort whilst climbing stairs, even if it is in a house of God!"

"We shall do as you say then, Doctor. But let us remember the noon bells. How long shall we rest here?"

"I recommend a good five minutes. Then we shall start again. Let us take this in parts. At least one more break should do for me."

"Doctor, while not absolutely necessary, I should be back in time to help the cook prepare the evening meal, as I help in the kitchen."

"I think we shall be back in time," said I.

I checked my watch and found that we had already spent a good hour ascending to this level and travelling to this part of the tower. The five minutes soon passed and we began our upward climb again. I took note of our starting time and determined that our pace would get us to the top of the tower in another ten minutes.

I had mistakenly thought that getting to the top of the tower would not require so much effort. Knowing we could not ascend into the spire itself, I simply imagined a quick trip up and saw myself standing at the foot of the spire looking into it. This journey was not what I anticipated at all.

One suddenly realized that, there was in fact, no way out, except down. To continue up, one would find eventually a different level to escape out on to, but then one would be high above the ground. The only way down being back down this falling, imposing, circular stair which felt like being in a maze which one could not easily get out. The other option, of course, was the ill-advised and unacceptable option of going over the parapet wall at the top of the tower. It began to affect me, as I suddenly realized I could not so easily escape should I wish to do so. It was not the *claustrophobia* that I had thought affected Holmes when we had used the *Tube* on one occasion. It was a different feeling altogether as if one were trapped, but not oppressively as true *claustrophobia* would produce. It was similar to being on a ship on the open ocean, where one simply cannot get off! The sensation was a surprise to me. I was used to being able to walk out of Mrs. Hudson's front door and be on God's solid ground with nothing restraining my movement. These stairways were indeed a unique adventure.

By the time we got to the top of the tower it was nearly noon. My estimate had been wrong, as the higher and longer we climbed, my left quadricep muscle, unused to this singular demand on it, could not go but ten or twelve steps without burning and required resting. The last thirty or forty steps took me a good quarter hour to climb.

Finally arriving at the top of the tower produce a great feeling of relief. We had accomplished our mission!

There was a door in each cardinal position, none of which were well sealed. I had no idea how old these doors were. Sunlight from outside secreted its way around the jambs, headers and thresholds of each of them.

Mr. Ortraimy went to one and opened it. The bright sunshine shone in as he did so. We heard the faint whirring of the gears from far below and then the bells. Being as close as we were, we both covered our ears. The twelve strokes were loud and clear.

After they were done, it took a moment to hear each other. I looked at the countryside and then up the spire. There it was, rising amazingly an additional one hundred eighty-four feet!

I stepped out and looked out over the beautiful countryside from the tower roof. The drudgery of the confining journey was rewarded by the spectacular and magnificent view!

"How beautiful!"

Ortraimy said nothing.

"I dare say, Mr. Ortraimy, whomever is playing games here at the Cathedral must certainly be someone in fine physical shape."

"I suppose you are correct, sir," is all he responded.

We spent a few more minutes breathing in the fresh air and enjoying the view.

"Is there anything else you wish to see, Doctor? Shall we not descend now?"

"One more thing, if you don't mind," said I.

I then went closer to the edge of the parapet and looked straight down. All that was below me was the roof of the Cathedral itself. It was then, my dear readers, that I experienced my first visceral reaction to the height to which we had ascended. I was suddenly overcome with a panic of sorts which, had I not been holding on to the structure itself, I could easily imagine losing my balance and tumbling down from that great height. My stomach, in fact, contracted in some sort of involuntary spasm as my brain tried desperately to deal with the unusual data that was flooding into it and to which it had not been witness to ever before. I have never had acrophobia, which would have prevented my climb in the first place and I dare say it was not vertigo as I know it to be defined. It was some primitive reaction to the imminent danger suddenly being understood by the instincts of my innermost mind and body.

I slowly retreated to the safety of the confines of the room and slowly regained my sense of stability.

"Doctor? Shall we not descend now?" repeated he.

His question helped me overcome this odd feeling triggered by my view over the side. It also brought me back to a reality I had been ignoring. I suddenly felt a heaviness overcome me.

I realized the daunting task that now lay before me. While certainly coming down the stairs, I would benefit from Newton's discovery, my leg muscles would object again, only this time participating in preventing my sudden and therefore likely tragic descent to the bottom. Again, Mr. Ortraimy proceeded me and it was a challenge to keep up with him.

This time the stairs downward were counter-clockwise, and at first, I believed my right quadricep would now relieve my left from its duty. But alas, it was not so! My right leg would step down without effort, and my left had to slowly relax to allow my body downward to prevent a more rapid descent. Thus, it was my left quadricep again that took the brunt of the journey!

When we reached the clock chamber, I begged for a break. I sat for a while and enjoyed one last look up into the magnificent structure. It was while doing so, that I noticed, by chance, a single rope over in one corner. It went upward to a location I could not discern.

"Method ringing in the past?" queried I.

"What's that you say, Doctor?"

"Certainly, the clock mechanism was not available in the 1200's, no doubt they performed full circle ringing in the past, ah, but you said the bells were elsewhere, correct?"

"Yes, perhaps, but I have no knowledge of that."

By the time we had reached the ground, my whole body ached but in particular my poor left quadricep was practically quivering with over-use and therefore almost useless to me. I thought and reassured myself again, that if anyone had been spending time up in the spire, or let alone the tower, it would have to be a young and spry person. While someone older and in exceptional physical condition could also have gained access and made use of it, the odds were definitely in favour of a young fit person.

Mr. Ortraimy, escorted my limping body back to the Bishop's office and then bid me adieu saying he must go help in the kitchen.

Brother Jillion was there, but he was engaged speaking to one of the other clergymen. It was several minutes before he turned his attention back to me.

"Well, Dr. Watson, what say you about our spire?"

"To be quite blunt with you, sir, it is both spectacular and exhausting. I shall take days to recover!"

"Yes, I agree. I have only been up a few times, myself. And that was when I was a younger man. It wears out the older ones of us."

Being aware that I fell into this category of which he spoke, it still annoyed me that the fact of it was so easily attributed to me simply by my appearance and comments, and by a total stranger! But if I was honest, I needed to admit, I was not as fit as I once had been. My time allotted to me in this world had been expiring and this journey was definite proof of that.

"Yes, well, erm, it was quite a spectacular view from atop the tower," said I, hoping to change the subject that had invaded our friendly conversation.

"Is the Bishop, available to speak to me?"

"He is currently occupied. He has requested that I accompany you to lunch, should you have returned in time. We've but a few minutes to make it before they stop serving. If you will follow me, we shall go there right away."

He put down the papers he held in his hand and motioned for me to exit his office first. He then walked beside me and indicated each door or hallway to travel through next, silently, but with a sweeping gesture of his arm or the pointing of his finger.

As we passed the Chapter House he spoke.

"Of course, the Chapter House keeps our copy of the *Magna Carta* for all to see. You have seen it?"

"No, I have not."

"We shall have you visit on our way back. It will be here when we return from lunch, as it has been here since our dear Elias became our Canon and gave us his copy. I'm afraid the lunch service ends abruptly and not even the Bishop can cause them to extend their hours."

After a brief prayer of thanksgiving, my host began his meal without further conversation. It became obvious that talking was discouraged during meals as many tables were occupied, but only the occasional clanging of plates, forks and steins could be heard. I fell in with the protocol and soon finished my meal of warm rye bread, country churned butter, hearty thick pea soup with bits of ham and a pint of dark ale, without asking the many questions that had arisen in my mind. I satisfied myself knowing this meal was providing me with much needed nourishment after my morning's excursion.

After finishing, we retraced our steps and were soon back at the Chapter House. We entered and strode over to a display case. Inside was a very faded copy of the ancient manuscript.

"It was written down in 1215, for King John of England to sign. He was at Runnymede. The barons of his time had had enough of his poor decisions and demands on their property, so they forced him to sign it should he desire to obtain any further taxes.

"Elias of Dereham, our first Canon and the stone mason of the Cathedral, was to have dispersed copies of it about the kingdom, which he did, but making sure one resided here.

"One thinks this was all there was to it and suddenly the kings gave up their 'divine rights' to rule, but such is not the case. No, there were many wars over nearly a century before things settled down to the parliamentary government we now enjoy, or not, depending one's way of thinking, eh?

"But, despite the fact that it was rewritten and changed several times, even annulled by a pope when England was still papist, the concept it contained, survived. And it is that concept that brings us to where we are today. A monarchy to bind us, but a parliament of our peoples to govern us.

"It reminds me that long ago, before the Normans, we English used to elect our own leaders from amongst our fellow tribesmen, at least that is what some of our old manuscripts tells us. And it has taken us all these centuries to return to such a way of ruling our land."

"Quite fascinating," replied I.

I peered at the documents with its old script and pondered the clash of such powerful forces of men who would challenge their king and make him submit to agreeing to such things when that was certainly not the way things were done in that age.

"There are other copies, you say?"

"As far as we know, there is one at Lincolnshire and two others at the British Museum in their Library. It is said that ours is the best preserved of the four. As you can imagine, it is quite a treasure for us here."

"I see, again, I must say, most fascinating."

We returned to Brother Jillion's office outside the Bishop's where I was proffered to wait, which I accepted by taking a seat in one of the chairs.

I waited for an additional hour or so. I was getting a bit bored at this and began feeling restless. Having spent the morning on the strenuous and active climb, this sitting and waiting was wreaking havoc on my body. My desire to take a lie down was increasing with each minute that passed. My body demanded to be horizontal.

It was just after two o'clock that a message seemed to be delivered to Brother Jillion. After he read it, he announced to me the basis of its contents.

"Oh, Doctor, I must apologise. I have just received a note from the Bishop stating he will not be able to join you for the rest of the day. He begs forgiveness and would like to have you return tomorrow morning at ten o'clock. Is that possible, sir?"

"Yes, of course. I shall return to my lodging and be here in the morning. Good day to you, Brother."

And with that I left and returned to the Close. The accommodations I had been provided included a bath tub, which I now began envisioning full of hot water to ease my aching body.

Before long, my vision had become reality. I was soon lying in some comfort, as the hot water began soothing the muscles that I had strained earlier that morning.

I must have dozed off in the tub. I awoke and found the water was but barely warm. I climbed out and got into my dressing gown while checking the time. It was just past eleven o'clock.

I settled in for what I assured myself was a well-deserved night of sleep.

My dreams included a pounding sound. But I could not tell from whence it came. Suddenly I realized, it came not from a dream. I struggled to get myself sufficiently awake and got up and went to the door.

"Doctor Watson, are your there?"

"Yes, yes, I'm coming"

I opened the door to find Brother Jillion at my doorstep.

"What is it, Brother? Is there a fire?" queried I.

"No, no. It is a light in the tower! The Bishop asked that I raise you this instant."

I dressed quickly and accompanied him back to the Cathedral. I could see the faint glow coming from the ill-fitting doors at the top of the tower that, on such a moonless night, stood out against the black sky.

We met the Bishop and Father Anthony in the courtyard near the entrance where Mr. Ortraimy and I had entered earlier that same day.

At about that same time, sleepy bodies began filling the courtyard. Men in nightshirts, yawning, mumbling and generally flustered at their untimely awakening.

"I have ordered an account of all quartered here in the Cloister. I must know if one of our own is involved," said Bishop Wordsworth.

Soon after Brother Jillion had spoken to each assembled group, he reported back to the Bishop.

"All accounted for."

"Brother Jillion, please choose enough men of the Cloister that you trust and have them attend to each exit from the tower. I want to have them identify this person."

"Yes, My Lord."

"Dr. Watson, you see now how this situation creates a type of madness? It in and of itself seems to be harmless, but it is so unnerving at the same time."

"Yes, I understand, My Lord."

"Will you inform Mr. Holmes of this event, witnessed with your own eyes?"

"Yes, I shall. I promise I shall send him a telegram the first thing in the morning."

"Thank you, Doctor. Now, please, get some sleep."

"Thank you, My Lord."

I returned to my lodgings. It took some time with all the excitement of the night, but I was able to fall asleep eventually.

The next morning, I dressed early and went and dispatched the telegram to Holmes as I had promised. I then awaited a reply, but after some time concluded perhaps Holmes was not at Baker Street to receive it, as no reply came.

My left leg was still in a bit of misery, but I felt the best medicine for it was to exercise it lightly, simply by walking on level ground.

I strode about the Close and visited various shops. I occasionally found my way back to see if a reply had come, but alas, each time, there was nothing.

I returned to my lodgings and found a note inviting me to partake dinner with the Bishop at five O'clock. I rested for the remainder of the day, except to take another short walk in the afternoon to exercise my legs.

When I arrived for the meal, the Bishop inquired, of course, as to Holmes' reply. I was embarrassed to relate to him that I had not yet received a response, but assured him there would be one soon. Sherlock Holmes was not a man to abandon his clients and certainly not His Lordship.

After dinner was over, I decided on again exercising my leg whilst smoking my pipe. Once having consumed its contents and making one last unsuccessful inquiry at the telegraph office before it closed for the evening, I returned to my quarters.

I entered and was surprised to find a visitor waiting for me sitting on my bed.

"Holmes! What are you doing here?!" cried I.

"No time for that now, Watson. You must do two things. Get everyone out of the Cathedral at once to the south lawn of the Cloister. There will be an attempt to bring down the spire. Have someone retrieve the Magna Carta from its case immediately. Can you do this"

"Yes, but, Holmes!"

"Now, Watson!!"

"Yes, yes, all right."

I carried myself to the Bishop's office as fast as my tortured muscles could move me. I arrived a bit short of breath.

"Brother Jillion, I must speak to the Bishop at once."

"But, Dr. Watson, he is prepared for retiring for the evening. I am afraid…"

I did not hesitate. Passing Brother Jillion, I reached the door and entered the Bishop's office. The door that then went to his private quarters was still open. I found that he had yet to disrobe.

"Dr. Watson, I must protest your behaviour, sir," said he, raising his voice.

"Excuse me, My Lord, gentlemen. This is an emergency. I must insist you leave the premises at once."

"Doctor, this intrusion is most unacceptable. How is it that you dare to enter my private quarters without my permission? Jillion, what is the meaning of this?"

"I do not know, My Lord."

"Please, I insist you heed my warning. There is, at this very moment, an attempt to destroy the spire. If it is successful, it is likely that the entire Cathedral and Cloister will suffer destruction beyond belief.

"Mr. Holmes has requested that we evacuate as quickly as possible to the south lawn and we must retrieve the Magna Carta immediately. It is in danger as well."

"I see. Jillion, is this true?"

"I do not know, My Lord."

"Doctor, how am I to respond to this unprecedented request of yours?"

"My Lord, you requested Mr. Holmes' help, correct?"

"Yes, yes of course I did, but the man never has shown his face to me. You, sir, have come in his stead. How am I to believe and respond to the directions given by a man who I've never met and who seems too busy to respond to me?"

"Bishop, with all due respect, I have worked with Mr. Holmes on many cases. He is not one to falsely claim an emergency. He has assisted even Her Majesty on occasion. It is his way, to sometimes work unseen so as to gain advantage on those he must eventually confront."

"And so, it is your opinion, Doctor, that we then heed these warnings at this very moment?"

"Yes, My Lord. As I cannot force, you or anyone here, to do as Mr. Holmes has directed, I can only relay his message. Knowing Mr. Holmes as I do, there is no doubt in mind that he is currently doing everything he can to thwart the assault on the spire which is in progress.

"I will take my leave now. It is, of course, your decision to comply or not with his directive, My Lord. Should he fail to avert this pending tragedy and you have failed to respond, with all due respect, my Lord, it shall be on your shoulders having been given fair warning. I encourage you to follow Mr. Holmes' advice immediately, My Lord."

At this I turned and quickly left the Bishop's quarters as no further discussion would likely result in swaying the Bishop's mind.

"Jillion, this all seems quite absurd to me, but it was we who called upon this Mr. Holmes for advice. He has now responded in a most peculiar way, but we seem to have no other good choice. Sound the alarm and have everyone assemble south of the Cloister."

As I heard the sound of a strange high pitched bell, I realized the Bishop had agreed to accept Holmes' directions to have everyone leave the Cloister. I heard several of the priests and other clergy shouting loudly, "Go to the south lawn. Assemble on the south lawn. Quickly now!"

I determined that these folks would know the best route to take to accomplish the directions. I got in line with them and followed them out to the south lawn of the Cathedral. As they did not stand still, I was not able to achieve an accurate count, but once most were assembled there seemed to be at least one hundred people.

Small groups began to form and a low murmur began. It grew louder and louder until the lawn was filled with persons talking most loudly in an effort to be heard over the those around them.

The Bishop again inquired as to whether or not all the inhabitants were accounted for. Brother Jillion soon returned from this quest. All here, Jillion?"

"Yes, My Lord, except…"

"Who is missing?"

"Mr. Ortraimy, My Lord."

"I see. Might he not be able to hear the alarm? Perhaps in the wine cellar?"

"That is possible. I can send someone to look, but that may put them in danger. I shall go myself."

"Do so right away. But be quick and be careful, Jillion. I shan't want the entire Cathedral collapsing on top of you!"

Brother Jillion headed off in the direction of the kitchen, which held the entrance to the wine cellar.

Suddenly without warning there was a gigantic boom! It reminded me instantly of the artillery shelling I had seen, heard and occasionally felt, in Afghanistan. The dark night sky was illuminated on the other side of the Cathedral from where we stood. For an instant, and no more, the Cathedral was outlined by an enormous flash of light. The talking stopped immediately.

Most of the crowd ran to the left to see what had happened on the northwest side of the Cathedral.

I stayed with the Bishop who walked at a pace equal to mine. We soon had turned the corner to see what had happened.

Those before us had gathered about a large hole in the lawn very near the north side of the nave between the north porch and the north transept. There was a lingering smoke rising from it. Shortly thereafter, many of those gathered started pointing to the stained glass of the Cathedral itself. The windows were shattered.

The blast, having blown up outside of Cathedral and the glass flying into the nave, left hardly any debris in the lawn. Someone yelled to look inside and several ran through the north porch entrance. A few came back and reported that yes, the stained glass had been blown inward and was to be found scattered amongst the pews.

"Bishop, a complete disaster has been averted, I believe." said I.

"Dr. Watson, I agree. But how has this all happened? Who has done this and why?"

"I know Mr. Holmes is present here, as it was he who gave me the warning to convey to you. He shall arrive before long, if I am any judge of his normal behaviour.

"Have you or your staff secured the Magna Carta, Bishop?" queried I. I had forgotten that part of Holmes' instruction with all the excitement of the blast around us. It suddenly occurred to me to make sure it was safe.

"I believe that we will find it to be tied to tonight's events, otherwise Mr. Holmes would not have demanded its rescue."

"I had instructed Fr. Anthony to take care of that. Let us seek him out and make sure."

We started walking over to each of the small groups of clergy, who were in various states of disbelief at the events of the evening.

At last we found Fr. Anthony. He held a large case of sorts under his arm.

"Anthony, you have it?"

"Yes, Bishop. It is secure."

"Thank the Almighty for that. Let us retire to my office. Bring it along, Anthony."

We went to the Bishop's office and when we opened his door, we found Holmes sitting on the chesterfield. He had lit his favourite churchwarden and I smelt the familiar aroma of our tobacco wafting through the room.

"Who the devil, are you?!" shouted out the Bishop, surprised to see a stranger in his office.

"My name is Sherlock Holmes. You are no doubt, Bishop Wordsworth, I conclude."

"What is going on here?" asked the Bishop, turning to me as if to ask, 'is this the man he says he is?'.

"My Lord, may I introduce you to Mr. Sherlock Holmes of London. He is the man to whom you sent your letters requesting his assistance. We likely have here tonight, witnessed his saving the spire from certain destruction."

"You, sir, have a very strange way of behaving. Is it your habit to enter, uninvited, the private offices of those you have not met? And take the liberty of smoking without their permission? Doctor, certainly this is not the Mr. Holmes, of whom you have told me so much about and upon whose advice you say I can rely, is it?"

"My Lord, it is one and the same. While Mr. Holmes has his own peculiar ways of handling his cases, he focuses on the outcome, all else are mere inconveniences."

"Enough, Watson. I am guilty as charged, 'My Lord' is it not? I will trouble you no further. Good evening gentlemen."

Holmes arose and headed towards us to exit the office.

He passed by all without a further word, until he'd reached the outer entrance of Brother Jillion's office.

He turned back and said, "You may want to collect the body. I doubt you would want to leave it in its current location."

"What's that?" said the Bishop.

"What is he talking about?" said the Bishop looking squarely at me.

I chased after Holmes as fast as my poor aching quadriceps could carry me.

"Holmes! Holmes! Wait up!"

He paused and I caught up to him.

"Holmes, what body? And certainly, you have dealt with more demanding clients than this one. Please come back and explain yourself."

"I save the man's Cathedral and he objects to my waiting for his return to tell him the good news. You did protect the MC, did you not?

"Yes, yes. But Holmes it has been a trying night. They have no idea what you have been doing and I dare say, they are in a state of shock at tonight's events.

"I implore you to return and explain tonight's happenings. If not for them at least for me. I came here and was to alert you to the problem and I believe at least I am owed an explanation."

"I suppose you are correct, Watson. I did ask you to get involved. Let us return and I will explain it all."

We returned to the Bishop's office only this time the Bishop was rightfully in his chair behind his desk. His demeanour was now much more confident than when he first walked in upon the intruding Mr. Holmes. Those there were discussing the events of the night and what they must now do to mitigate the damages to the stained glass caused by the explosion.

I knocked on the door, stepped in and began to speak to all inside…

"Gentlemen, My Lord, we have all experienced an unusual occurrence tonight. I think perhaps emotions are a bit high. But I should like to point out, that due to the actions of Mr. Holmes, a great tragedy has been averted.

"I would like to suggest, that we allow Mr. Holmes, who

has agreed to apologise, to explain all that has happened tonight to more fully understand what we have witnessed."

My dear readers will note that I had not gotten Holmes' agreement that he should apologise, but I thought it best to place him in this somewhat awkward position to get him to behave towards his client in a manner more fitting to someone who is claiming to be a professional. As you know, I have had this discussion with him on more than one occasion and I had a sense that he would respond appropriately once I had him cornered, so to speak.

The glare I received from Holmes, was one I knew which I would later receive vehement chastisement for having gone down this path. It was, though, in the end, the right decision on my part, as he soon entered behind me and we heard his tale about this adventure.

"Bishop Wordsworth, my apologies for intruding into your office without your permission. It was of course the logical place for you to return after the events of tonight. I merely concluded you would come here, which you did, and that we could wrap up this little puzzle for which you had requested my help."

"Apology accepted," said the Bishop, but with still a tone of reservation about his sincerity. I did, though, sense he knew that this strange man, that a few minutes before, who he had practically thrown out of his office, had more than likely saved his future from being overwhelmed by an event that would forever be a stain and overcome any of his other achievements of his life's work.

"Perhaps, Mr. Holmes, we should start over. Please come in and sit down. Please tell us what you know about tonight's extraordinary events. And should you wish to smoke, please do so."

"Thank you, My Lord. It is most kind of you."

Both parties refrained from words that would rekindle their earlier dynamic encounter. Their continued use of diplomatic language began to settle down the earlier confrontational engagement.

"Yes, gentlemen. I arrived a day ago after receiving a telegram from my associate here, Dr. Watson. His accounts of his data gathering, as I refer to it, triggered me into why such activities should be happening here of all places? What is it about Salisbury, that would cause this commotion?

"I researched and found that Salisbury is a unique place indeed. But amongst its many alluring characteristics is that it has the tallest spire in all of England.

"The attempt tonight was aimed at depriving you of this most precious treasure."

"But who would want to do that? Why would they want to do that? Someone envious from Lincolnshire-way, perhaps?" queried Holmes.

"Certainly, they would not do that! There is no good that could come from such destruction?" stated the Bishop.

"You are correct. There is no good to come from it, but there is diversion."

"Diversion? What is all this about? Whom is behind all this, you must tell me!"

"I believe the answer to that, Bishop Wordsworth, is a simple one. Professor Moriarty and in order to steal your other treasure," said Holmes.

"Moriarty? Who is this Moriarty? For he is much mistaken, as we've no treasure here. We can barely make ends meet and are constantly exploring ways to support our Cloister financially."

"No, Bishop. He is one of the most ingenious criminals in all of England, nay, in all of Europe, today. He wanted to steal your copy of the Magna Carta."

"The plan was a simple one but ingenious. Destroy the spire. The collapse of which would certainly destroy if not severely damage the Cathedral. In the ensuing chaos, the Magna Carta would be forgotten about and it could be secreted away while everyone here would be running in circles about what to do concerning the collapse."

"Once I was able to conclude what was the target, I was able to watch and observe how they would go about it.

"Not only would they get the best preserved and perhaps best-known copy of the Magna Carta but they would demoralize the Empire by depriving it of one of its gems of architecture.

"But then it became a more intriguing problem in execution in that they needed to be sure the spire fell away from the direction of the Chapter House, where the MC is housed, since they did not desire to destroy it in the process.

"This logic allowed me to look for the explosives in a location where it would be able to cause the spire to fall to the northward, the opposite direction from the Chapter House.

"I was able to find my way into the tower as is normal and with the many concealed spaces available was able to stay hidden so as to further observe their activities."

"But the entrances have locks!" objected Jillion.

"Yes, I know, but to a determined foe, or, in my case, a proficient locksmith of sorts, they are not the deterrent you believe they are.

"While our Professor Moriarty was not himself here, he rarely places himself at the scene of any of his criminal acts, he had an accomplice who was doing his bidding.

"I believe he calls himself Mr. Ortraimy."

"Jillion, call Mr. Ortraimy in here at once!" directed Bishop Wordsworth.

"That will be unnecessary, and in fact, impossible," responded Holmes.

"What?"

"You will find that his body remains on the floor of the clock chamber."

"How's that?" queried Jillion.

"Mr. Ortraimy is your acting villain in all this. It was he who I observed placing the explosive. I had secreted myself away from him, as I believed it was best to catch him in the act. I was above in the bracing of the spire when he set the charge.

"I wanted to dispose of it after he had left. Which is what I did. I quickly climbed down from my perch in the darkness of the spire and on the way grabbed the device. I thought I could easily dismantle it before it went off. He no doubt needed time to get out, so I would have at least the time it took him to get down to the ground floor.

"His descent was faster than I had anticipated. Rather than transiting down by the stone stairs, he attempted to use the *abseiling method* to lower himself quickly to the clock chamber floor.

"Ah, that was what the rope was for!" said I, when I remembered how Ortraimy had ignored my mention of it.

"That meant the timer was to go off sooner than I anticipated. Fearing I would not be able to disarm it quickly enough, and it proved to be of a design of which I was unfamiliar, I opted to get it out of the tower quickly.

"I knew the plan would mean not having the spire fall towards the Chapter House and that is why I instructed Dr. Watson to tell all to go to the south side.

"I grabbed the device and got out on the roof of the tower. The next problem was that in all directions directly below the tower there is more roof of the Cathedral! I needed to find the place where there was as little roof below me as possible. I gauged I could possibly throw the device and miss the roof, but I knew it would not end up far from the side of the Cathedral.

"Having made my way around the parapet, I concluded the shortest distance was northwest.

"I found a small length of rope in the tower area next to the windlasses. I tied it to the device and went outside. I whirled it above my head and let it fly.

"I should point out that it was not without a moment to spare. No sooner had the device landed on the lawn than it exploded. Whether it was intended to explode then or not I do not know. I doubt Ortraimy would have made it out by then, but it exploded when it did, and outside the Cathedral.

"I began my journey downward, and while I have had some experience abseiling up in the Lake District myself, I freely admit I am no expert. The wisdom of my decision to not descend that way was also validated when I finally saw Ortraimy's body at the clock chamber level.

"I do not know for certain but perhaps my actions caused the device to trigger earlier than he expected distracted him enough that he lost control of his descent and plummeted to the clock chamber floor.

"Well, gentlemen, My Lord, that is the tale."

"Mr. Holmes, we cannot thank you enough. I must

apologise to you, sir. While I reacted strongly to your entrance here at the Cloister, I am afraid it is we that are eternally in your debt for the services you have rendered tonight," stated the Bishop in the sincerest tone I could image one using. His years of oratory on the subject of man's relationship to his maker and advising his flock on the power of humility and forgiveness came to bear on the speech and the thanks he gave to Sherlock Holmes.

"What is it that we owe you Mr. Holmes? What you have done for us tonight is beyond any amount we could pay you. How are we to compensate you?"

"Ah, My Lord, I ask nothing. The adventure has been its own reward. Knowing that I have thwarted Professor Moriarty's cunning plan is enough for me."

"But you say, this Professor Moriarty was behind all of this, how is it that you know this?" queried the Bishop.

"It is true I have no definitive proof it was him. But the plot and the execution of it are in line with similar exploits of his that I have encountered in the past.

"It is as an acquaintance of mine, a Miss Anna Gramm, has told me many times: 'One must look at what you see from all sides to understand what you are actually observing.' I am quite confident that Professor Moriarty was certainly directing and was above your Mr. Ortraimy in this adventure. He thus was just an agent of the Professor and his evil plot.

"Watson, our work is done here. Shall we not return to Baker Street? Perhaps when we arrive, a new letter shall await us and a new adventure shall come of it?"

We bid *adieu* to all present and returned to my accommodations in the Close for the remainder of the night.

By early evening the next day, we were back at Mrs. Hudson's. There, at 221B Baker Street, several letters addressed to "Mr. Sherlock Holmes, Consulting Detective" awaited his attention.

About the Author

Daniel James Darrouzet set his sights early in life. By age five he had already decided he wanted to be an architect.

In high school, like Sir Arthur Conan Doyle, Daniel was schooled by the Jesuits during his formative years. Drawn to graphic and mathematical solutions to life's challenges, rather than literature, he did not enjoy reading until halfway through college.

He had, of course, read "*The Red Headed League*" in grade school as is common of grade school literature classes. The tunnelling in the story fascinated him, but again, reading was not his cup of tea.

Later, while studying in the School of Architecture at the University of Texas in Austin, his cousin, Robert Emmett Leahy, who also attended the University there, took him to many Sherlock Holmes movies, usually starring Basil Rathbone. Being a visual story, the movies planted a seed.

It was later, while he was home from college during a Christmas holiday, that he obtained a copy of the complete Canon from his younger brother, Michael. Taking them back to college with him, he began reading the short stories, one each night. Thus, it was the character of Sherlock Holmes which finally sparked an interest in reading.

While finishing his architectural studies, he was identified by the faculty and invited to obtain a second simultaneous degree in engineering. He then graduated with degrees in both architecture and engineering. By age 28 he became both a Registered Architect and Registered Professional Engineer. He furthered his education obtaining an MBA and recently has been working towards a PhD in Civil Engineering.

After a long career in the world of architectural and engineering design, procurement and construction, he was inspired (but he knows not how or why) to produce these stories for your enjoyment.

If it were not for the well-known fact that Sir Arthur Conan Doyle became quite bothered and disenchanted with his most popular fictional character, it would almost seem as if SACD himself were whispering them into the author's ear. It is not unusual for the plot or pertinent points of the stories to reveal themselves to the author through his dreams.

Perhaps SACD has changed his mind and is a willing participant in their production? As long as the stories keep revealing themselves to him, he will honour and oblige the unconfirmed source by relaying them to you.

When not transcribing the stories, he spends time travelling with his wife of over forty years, Ingrid.

Born in Dallas, Texas, he still lives in the North Dallas-Preston Hollow area of the city where he grew up. He is the father of four grown children and presently the grandfather to nine of theirs.